FORSAKEN

A UNIT 51 NOVEL

MICHAEL McBRIDE

PINNACLE BOOKS
Kensington Publishing Corp.
www.kensingtonbooks.com

PINNACLE BOOKS are published by

Kensington Publishing Corp.
119 West 40th Street
New York, NY 10018

All Kensington titles, imprints, and distributed lines are available at special quantity discounts for bulk purchases for sales promotions, premiums, fund-raising, educational, or institutional use. Special book excerpts or customized printings can also be created to fit specific needs. For details, write or phone the office of the Kensington sales manager: Kensington Publishing Corp., 119 West 40th Street, New York, NY 10018, attn: Sales Department; phone 1-800-221-2647.

ISBN-13: 978-0-7860-4160-2
ISBN-10: 0-7860-4160-9

First printing: May 2018

10 9 8 7 6 5 4 3 2 1

Printed in the United States of America

First electronic edition: May 2018

ISBN-13: 978-0-7860-4161-9
ISBN-10: 0-7860-4161-7

For Jane Gauthier

ACKNOWLEDGMENTS

Special thanks to Gary Goldstein, Steven Zacharius, Elizabeth May, Lou Malcangi, Arthur Maisel, Lauren Vassallo, and the entire team at Kensington Books; Alex Slater and Tara Carberry at Trident Media Group; Chris Fortunato; Andi Rawson and Kim Yerina; Jeff Strand; my amazing family; and all of my loyal friends and readers, without whom this book would not exist.

PROLOGUE

There are some secrets which do not permit themselves to be told.
—EDGAR ALLAN POE

*Antarctic Research, Experimentation
& Analysis Station 51,
Queen Maud Land, Antarctica, six months ago*

The Sikorsky UH-60 Black Hawk streaked across the ice cap and came in low over the mounds of snow at the edge of the cliff. The ferocious gusts from its rotors filled the air with the accumulation and revealed the red arctic vehicles buried underneath. It battled the brutal gales screaming through the Drygalski Mountains until it was steady enough for the men inside to open the sliding side door. Several lengths of rope slithered down into the blizzard. Four shadows disgorged from the chopper and rappelled blindly through the whiteout. The moment they hit the ground, they unclipped and staggered away from the chopper through the knee-deep snow.

Special Agent Rand Morgan signaled to the pilot and the Black Hawk banked away, buffeting the men with one final gust before thundering back across the frozen plains. He unslung his custom SCAR 17 semiautomatic assault rifle and tromped toward the arctic research station, its massive garage doors rimed with ice. His men were nearly invisible in their snow-camouflage GEN III ECWCS fatigues as they advanced.

He knelt and brushed away the upper layers of the accumulation until he found what he knew would be there: an amoeboid pattern of pink ice, which crumbled with gentle pressure. He rubbed a piece between his gloved fingers and sniffed it through the holes in his neoprene balaclava. Stood and wiped it on his pants, leaving a faint reddish smear on the fabric.

Morgan nodded to his men, who fanned out in search of any sign as to where their quarry might have gone. Less than half an hour had passed. It couldn't have made it very far, not with as much blood as it was losing.

The door between the garage bays stood wide open and nearly concealed behind a drift of snow, which extended halfway into the building.

He paused, lowered his thermal vision goggles over his eyes, and switched on his laser sight. The narrow beam cut through the darkness, which revealed itself in shades of gray. His beam reflected from the frozen concrete inside. The droplets of blood were spattered and congealed to the consistency of paint. They retained just enough heat to stand apart from the ice.

"I picked up its trail," he whispered into his com-link.

Morgan entered the garage with his assault rifle seated against his shoulder and swept his laser sight from one side of the building to the other, absorbing everything he saw as quickly as possible. He created a mental overlay of the garage over the blueprints he'd committed to memory.

His rubber soles squeaked when he stepped from the ice onto the bare concrete.

He stopped and waited for any response to the sound. His breath formed a cloud around his head and toyed with his thermal optics. The delicate skin of his lips and the mucous membranes inside his nostrils were already starting to freeze.

Another laser passed over him from behind and traced the workbench against the back wall, beside which lay an overturned tool cabinet, its contents scattered across the floor.

The trail of blood led straight toward it.

Morgan stepped sideways, one foot over the other, to get a better view of the area behind the toppled cabinet. The access hatch to the sublevel was flush with the ground beside the hole in the floor, the rim of which glowed faintly with the residual warmth of the transferred blood.

"It's gone underground," he whispered. "Pair off. Allen. Fitz. You two head down the opposite side. Ryan, you're with me. If it's still down there, it'll be trapped between us."

"And if it's not?"

The reply was tentative, nervous. Morgan had neither the time nor the inclination to coddle these men. They were supposed to be professionals. The problem was they'd seen the live feed from the security cameras inside the station and knew what this thing was capable of doing to them.

"Then we'll have our work cut out for us, won't we?"

Morgan leaned out over the access hatch. An iron ladder materialized from the darkness. The rungs were smudged with blood and the wall behind it dotted with expiratory spatter, which meant that their prey's lungs were filling with blood. A pool of it stood apart from the cold floor at the bottom of the ladder like a beacon.

Hinges squealed from across the room as his men removed the lid from the hatch on the other side.

"In position," Allen's voice whispered through Morgan's earpiece.

"On my mark." He straddled the orifice and aimed his weapon down between his feet. "Go."

Morgan slung his rifle over his shoulder, gripped the side rails with his hands and the arches of his feet, and slid straight down into the depths. Braked ten feet above the bottom to make sure there was nothing underneath him. Let go and dropped into the darkness. Landed in a crouch and shouldered his rifle.

The quarters were tight and limited his movements, but he was able to maneuver his weapon so that it was aimed back underneath the garage. The ground was smeared with blood and patterned with distinct handprints, which led to an industrial fan with a broken blade, behind which was a discrete source of heat—

His laser reflected from a pair of eyes.

A frenzy of movement and they were gone.

"It's coming your way," Morgan whispered into his transceiver.

A blurred heat signature scrabbled through the tunnel in the distance.

Screams erupted from his earpiece. He instinctively ducked out of the tunnel as the man at the far end shot his rifle straight at him. Another scream nearly deafened him. He yanked out his earpiece and shouted up at the man descending the ladder above him.

"Move! We can't let it get out the other side!"

Morgan slung his rifle over his shoulder and clanged up the ladder. He broke the surface on Ryan's heels and propelled himself into a sprint toward the other side of the garage.

By the time he reached it, the floor surrounding the access chute positively glowed with the heat from the blood all over the concrete. Footprints led back into the corner, where the glass bridge to the main complex had broken off. They reminded him of those of a bear, only the toes tapered in length from medial to lateral.

He glanced down the ladder. Allen and Fitzpatrick were heaped on top of each other in a rapidly expanding pool of warmth.

"Jesus," Ryan whispered.

"Stay sharp," Morgan said.

He advanced into the ruined corner of the garage in a shooter's stance, his laser probing the dark gaps between the toppled shelves, fallen cabinets, and the crumbled sections of the walls and ceiling.

"We've got it cornered."

"A cornered animal is infinitely more dangerous."

The footprints led to a narrow gap beneath where a cabinet leaned against what almost looked like a makeshift gurney. Blood covered the floor inside as far as he could see.

Ryan crouched and used his laser sight to explore the rubble.

Plip.

Morgan stepped backward and surveyed the scene.

Something was wrong.

He could feel it.

"Should we go in after it or try to flush it out?" Ryan asked.

A white blur streaked through Morgan's peripheral vision and struck the floor.

Plip.

He retreated another step and readjusted his grip on his rifle. He was only going to get one shot at this.

"Just stay where you are," he whispered.

Ryan must have heard something in his voice. His posture stiffened and he quickly stood—

A white streak struck him on the shoulder.

Plat.

He looked straight up toward the source—

The creature fell from the ceiling. Struck him squarely on his head and shoulders. Drove him to the ground.

Ryan screamed, which only served to expose his throat to the creature. It buried its face into his neck. Shook its head back and forth. Released an arterial spray that turned its entire face and chest white in Morgan's thermal night vision.

He targeted his laser on its exposed ribcage, beneath its left arm.

It rounded on him and bared its teeth. Its elongated head appeared too heavy for its thin neck. It swayed when it leaned forward onto its spindly arms and tensed to attack.

The tranquilizer dart his man had fired from the helicopter during the extraction of the scientists was still embedded in the meat between its neck and shoulder and issued a steady stream of blood. They'd used enough etorphine to drop a charging rhino. There was no way it should have still been conscious, let alone functional enough to take out three of his men. Surely it wouldn't be able to withstand another dose from his retrofitted assault rifle, which had been modified to replace the carbine with a pressurized gas accelerant and the twenty-round magazine with a clip that held eight ballistic syringes.

It hissed and sprung at him.

Morgan fired.

The dart struck it squarely at center mass. Its legs went out from underneath it. The impact knocked it backward into the puddle of Ryan's blood.

Morgan cautiously approached and stood over it. He couldn't be entirely sure what it was, let alone if it was still breathing.

BOOK I: Modern Day

Only those who will risk going too far
can possibly find out how far one can go.
—T. S. Eliot

1
BARNETT

Subterranean ice caverns,
Forward Operating Base Atlantis,
Queen Maud Land, Antarctica, March 24

"This way, sir."

Director Cameron Barnett fell into stride beside Special Agent Rick Donovan. The earthen walls of the tunnel were smoothed by eons of running water, which had taken a serious feat of engineering to divert so they could drain these passageways. Residual puddles splashed underfoot and echoed ahead of them beyond the range of sight. LED lights were mounted to the ceiling and spaced so far apart that they had to walk through walls of darkness between the glowing auras, but they were already taxing the limits of their ability to produce enough electricity, especially with the increased demand provided by the discovery of new tunnels seemingly on a daily basis.

"What do we know about it?" Barnett asked.

"Nothing at this point."

The two men veered to the left and into a narrow corridor. The outlet was so small they were forced to crawl more than a dozen feet, which was made even more awkward by the full-body isolation suits. The Plexiglas shields covered the better part of their faces and upper chests, revealing only a hint of their black fatigues.

Barnett stood and checked the seals around his wrists and hood. Such precautions might have seemed like overkill, but with everything he'd seen in the years since cofounding Unit 51, he'd learned to never leave anything to chance.

"How much farther?"

"Maybe a hundred feet through that tunnel to the left."

Barnett didn't wait for his escort, who carried a SCAR 17 semiautomatic assault rifle slung over the shoulder of his yellow suit, and headed directly toward the passage. He hadn't been this deep into the warrens before, but he made it his business to commit every new inch of the map to memory as they discovered it. As with each new cavern they explored, they'd placed a small black mousetrap in an inconspicuous place, just in case they got lucky and finally caught the escaped rodent belonging to his former microbiologist, Dr. Max Friden. Assuming it wasn't dead already, which he sincerely hoped. It had been infected with the same alien microorganisms as the creature responsible for the deaths of their earlier scientific team, but they hadn't seen any sign of it since first penetrating the research complex, following the extraction of the survivors.

The sloped ceiling was spiked with stalactites that grew longer and longer until they became columns where they reached the ground at the back of the chamber, leaving barely enough room between them for the men to squeeze into the rugged hole at the base of the rear wall. The light on the far end shimmered from standing water so cold that Barnett's entire body clenched when he slid down into it.

He cleared his mind so as not to form any preconceptions. If there was one thing he'd learned on this job, it was that an open mind was critical when it came to rationalizing the inexplicable.

The tunnel terminated at the base of a crevice so narrow he could barely force his shoulders through. He emerged into a frozen cavern the size of a two-car garage and paused long enough to gather his bearings. He was roughly a quarter-mile southeast of the main entrance beneath the pyramid and seventy feet below the bed of the drained lake.

Donovan sloshed from the orifice behind him.

"Through that crevice over there," he said

The walls were coated with a layer of ice so thick it appeared almost blue and refracted the brilliant glare of the lighting array in such a way as to grant it the opacity of diamond. The nature of the running water and the pressure at this depth combined to keep this cavern relatively dry and just warm enough to cause the ice to grow incrementally thicker with each passing year. His team hadn't even been able to enter the passageways concealed behind it until their third day of going at it with flamethrowers. Even now, the ice created an illusion reminiscent of a hall of mirrors, which made it appear as though there were no way through, until he found himself standing in the mouth of a tunnel so tight he had to turn sideways.

He was barely five feet in when the muscles in his lower back tightened and goosebumps rippled up the backs of his arms. He stopped and scrutinized his surroundings. His primal instincts had been honed to a razor's edge during his years as an Army Ranger and an intelligence operative with the NSA, and served as an early-warning system he trusted with his life.

"Sir? It's—"

Barnett raised his hand to silence Donovan.

Something wasn't right.

The sound of dripping water echoed from ahead of him with a metronomic *plink ... plink ... plink*. He could feel the heat from the adjoining cavern even through his isolation suit.

"Who's in there?" he whispered.

"Berkeley and Jonas."

Every one of his men had been selected as much for their mental prowess and discretion as their physical abilities, which was the reason they'd been brought to his attention in the first place. Not only were they all highly trained intelligence officers, they were battle-tested under conditions that would have broken lesser men. Berkeley had survived in the Koh-i-Baba Mountains outside of Kabul for more than a month after his platoon was ambushed and Jonas had single-handedly kept a half-dozen wounded soldiers alive under a collapsed building in Fallujah for three days while he tunneled through the rubble to freedom.

Barnett had memorized the dossier of every man in his unit for this precise reason, so that when placed in a situation of complete uncertainty his actions would be appropriately measured. And he knew, based on his observations, that both men were already dead.

"Give me your rifle," he whispered.

"Sir?"

"Now."

Barnett reached behind him, without taking his eyes off the sliver of light at the end of the crevice, until Donovan thrust the rifle into his hand. He braced it across his chest and sighted over his shoulder as he inched sideways, one silent step at a time.

The isolation hood dulled his senses. He couldn't smell anything and worried it masked the sounds at the lower range of hearing, but the last thing he wanted was to end up like Dr. Dale Rubley, or his former partner, Hollis Richards, whose remains they had yet to find despite six months of exhaustive searching.

Plink . . . plink . . .

The view into the cavern widened with every step. There was no sign of movement, at least not from what he could see, although an inestimable amount of the cavern remained hidden from sight. His position was too compromised to risk a direct confrontation, so he hastened his advance.

The ice abruptly gave way to a cavern smaller than the last, although it was hard to accurately gauge its size since the ice had effectively sealed off the back half. His men had widened the existing passages through it with their flamethrowers and essentially cleared out enough space for the body strewn across the ground. Its isolation suit was torn and the flesh underneath it rent by such deep lacerations that Jonas's face was nearly unrecognizable behind his cracked, crimson-spattered visor. There was so much blood that the pool underneath him had yet to freeze all the way through.

Two rifles lay beside him. Neither appeared to have been fired.

"What in the name of God . . . ?" Donovan said.

"Call for backup."

Barnett tuned out Donovan's voice as he spoke into the transceiver and focused on the carnage.

At a guess, his man couldn't have been dead for more than twenty minutes. He knelt and examined the remains. Jonas's wounds looked like they'd been inflicted by a wild animal, although he could think of no species capable of overcoming two highly trained soldiers without them being able to fire a single shot in their defense.

Indistinct tracks led deeper into the cavern. Most were smeared by what he assumed to be Berkeley's dragged body.

Barnett stood and seated the rifle against his shoulder.

Whatever animal did this might still be in there with them.

He followed the passage deeper into the ice until it became too narrow for him to pass.

The bloody tracks on the ground were sloppy, smudged, and already frosted white. Those ascending the sheer wall of ice were even less distinct, although the punctures and gouges from what appeared to be claws were readily apparent. As was the hole leading up into the frozen ceiling, through which he could see only darkness.

2

EVANS

Teotihuacan, 25 miles northeast of Mexico City

Dr. Cade Evans squirmed through the earthen tunnel, which was barely tall enough for him to raise his head. He was beginning to feel as though he lived underground. Six months ago, researchers at Teotihuacan had only known about two of these subterranean tunnels. It seemed like every day now they discovered a new branch in this warren they had taken to calling Mictlan, the Aztec name for the underworld, although it reminded Evans more of a primitive subway system. How anyone could have conceived of such an ambitious project so long ago, let alone convinced other human beings to excavate these tiny, suffocating tunnels, was beyond him.

He had to turn his head sideways to squeeze into the southwest cavity. There were four main chambers, much like a giant heart, buried at the precise center of the sprawling primitive complex known as Teotihuacan, the name given to the once formidable Mesoamerican metropolis by the Nahuatl-speaking Aztec warriors who discovered the ruins hundreds of years after their desertion. It meant "birthplace of the gods," although to this day no one knew who built it or where they went, only that something terrible must have happened during its final days for more than a hundred thousand men, women, and children to abandon it seemingly overnight.

The lights mounted throughout the network of tunnels were fueled by a solar generator on the surface. While it might have been green-friendly and less costly to fuel, it barely powered the LED bulbs, which cast a bronze glare across the bare earth.

Evans's sweat poured through his brows and stung his eyes. He smeared it away with the back of his wrist, leaving a muddy smudge across his forehead and the bridge of his nose.

"If it were any more humid down here, I'd have to wear a wetsuit," he said.

Dr. Juan Carlos Villarreal glanced up from where he had painstakingly cleared the dirt from a mural featuring a stylized rendition of the feathered serpent god Quetzalcoatl. It appeared to have been painted onto a chunk of plastered adobe, but as far as Evans knew, they had yet to encounter anything resembling a wall down here.

"That might not be a bad idea, anyway," he said. "At least not where you are going."

"What's that supposed to mean?"

Villarreal merely smirked in response and resumed his task.

The main corridor between chambers was tall enough for Evans to rise to his full height. He stretched his back as he walked between the four chambers, where various other researchers and graduate students excavated the gridded floor, sifted through the dirt, and catalogued their findings. Like the main road above him, colloquially termed the Avenue of the Dead, the tunnel was arrow-straight and aligned precisely fifteen degrees east of true north. They speculated it ran from the main gates of Teotihuacan all the way to the Pyramid of the Moon. Together with the Pyramid of the Sun to the east and the Temple of the Feathered Serpent to the south, the three structures were arranged in the exact same pattern as the stars in Orion's Belt, a fact Evans believed was of no small significance.

On September 20th of the previous year, an earthquake had struck this area with enough force to cause sections of the road and the surrounding structures to collapse and reveal these hidden tunnels. And yet, strangely, the event went undetected at monitoring stations in Mexico City, a mere twenty-five miles away. Coincidentally, similar seismic events had been reported in Egypt and England, where the Pyramids of Giza and the Thornborough Henges of North Yorkshire, respectively, had been built in this exact same configuration. These seemingly unrelated events all occurred within minutes of the activation of the pyramid under Antarctic Research, Experimentation, and Analysis Station 51, which Evans did everything in his power not to think about.

Of course, the presence of Dr. Anya Fleming served as a constant reminder. She poked her head out of the circular hole in the ground ahead of him. He had to shield his eyes from the light on her hard hat.

"I was beginning to think you weren't coming," she said.

Anya was one of the sweetest people on the planet,

but she reminded him of the Energizer Bunny after a six-pack of Red Bull, which at times could be a little overwhelming. He envied her the exuberance of her youth, just not at six o'clock in the morning.

"What did you find?"

She grinned and ducked back into the hole.

Evans walked to the edge of the pit and watched her headlamp flash across the bare walls as she descended the aluminum ladder. The hole had been concealed beneath several feet of stone and dirt. They had only recently finished clearing the rubble at the bottom to reveal the passages fifteen feet straight down.

The ladder shook as he descended, his clanging footsteps echoing from the depths. By the time he reached the bottom, Anya was already flat on her belly and slithering into the arched orifice. Her light silhouetted her prone form, which was considerably smaller than his, and even then she barely fit inside the tunnel. She spoke over her shoulder as she crawled.

"All of the rain we've had during the last few days softened the ground enough that we were able to break through the end of the tunnel without nearly as much effort as we expected. And what we thought was just rubble was actually stones mortared together and sealed behind a wall of lime plaster."

"Have you been down here all night?"

"Is it morning already?"

In its heyday, every building in the entire city had been plastered with lime and painted bright red. In fact, they'd required so much lime to keep the buildings looking new that they'd consumed the entire surrounding forest, burning it day and night, to fuel the fires required to make the plaster, effectively altering the landscape.

The mysterious rulers of this advanced civilization even commissioned murals of their gods and sacred events to be painted on the walls inside every home, in what researchers believed were the first overt examples of statist propaganda.

"The seal. Is that what I saw Juan Carlos working on up there?"

"Did it have a really pissed off-looking Quetzalcoatl?"

"Yeah."

"That's the one."

Evans's helmet scraped the dirt overhead. His heart leaped into his throat as clumps of dirt and rock rained down on his extended arms. The ground was disproportionately muddy. He glanced up and realized that Anya was positively soaked. Her jeans were so wet they were almost black. He recalled what Villarreal had said and shuddered at the prospect of encountering standing water in such tight confines. The San Juan River cut straight across the Avenue of the Dead. If they accidentally broke through and tapped into it, they could flood the entire subterranean labyrinth. That is, if it didn't collapse on them first.

Anya's light dimmed as it diffused into a much larger space, from the depths of which he heard the sound of dripping water. The temperature steadily dropped, causing his skin to prickle with goosebumps. It smelled damp and musty, like a cave, which was exactly what it was.

A splashing sound from ahead of him.

He wriggled from the tunnel and found himself staring out across a circular pool. Anya bobbed several feet out, her head barely breaching the surface.

"Careful," she said. "It's deeper than it looks."

Evans twisted his torso and slid his legs down into the cold water. His feet sank into the sediment, all the way past his ankles. The mud released bubbles that burst around him and produced the vile stench of rotten eggs.

"Sweet Jesus. What's in God's name is that awful smell?"

"Decomposition," she said. "Watch out for all of the bones around your feet."

"Oh, is that all? I was worried it might be something gross."

Their lights reflected from the brown water, creating golden sparkles on the stalactites above them. Stone heads protruded from the rounded walls like the numbers on a clock. They had the same faces as those adorning the Temple of the Feathered Serpent, only somehow more realistic and unnerving. Each featured the head of a dragon jutting from what looked like a giant daisy. Quetzalcoatl, the feathered serpent god, who throughout history had been worshiped by such disparate Mesoamerican cultures as the Teotihuacan, Maya, Aztec, and Inca.

"Juan Carlos said the Teotihuacano believed that man was born from the dark waters beneath a mountain," Anya said. "He thinks this chamber was designed to replicate their creation myth and that they conducted sacred rituals in here."

"The kind of sacred rituals that require human sacrifices?"

"Is there any other kind?"

"I was hoping you'd found the burial chamber of one of their kings."

Archeologists had found graves throughout the ruins, and yet based on the relative dearth of grave goods in a city that prospered from the trade of obsidian, they'd yet to find the remains of any high priests or rulers.

"This just might be even better," she said with a smirk.

Evans tripped over a long bone and barely managed to keep his chin above the water. He was in no hurry to find out how it tasted.

The dripping sound originated from the far side of the pool, where water dribbled from the mouth of one of the Quetzalcoatl heads and onto a stone platform. Anya climbed onto it and shined her light into a recess in the wall that had been so well concealed by the shadows that Evans hadn't initially seen it.

He pulled himself out behind her and ducked his head under the stone creature's mouth. Cold water trickled through his hair and down his neck as he crawled into a hollow barely large enough to accommodate both of them and the sheer quantity of discolored bones congealed in an amber crust of adipocere.

Evans traced the skeletal remains with his light. There were twelve distinct individuals, all of them with their ankles bound, their arms tied behind their backs, and their jaws hanging open as though they'd died screaming.

"What in the name of God happened here?" he whispered.

3
ROCHE

The rising sun turned the frost on the onion field blood red. The plants were barely eight inches tall, but that was more than high enough to show the clear delineation between the upright and flattened sections, even this long after the event. The affected leaves were brown and wilted, the hard ground underneath them frozen and beaded with microscopic grains of silicon dioxide.

Due to the diminishing profitability of independent family farms, an increasing number of farmers were forced to grow both summer and winter crops in the same soil. By late May, these onions would make way for barley, assuming enough survived to harvest and the crop circle hadn't damaged the soil, which was why the landowner had been more than happy to lease his back acreage, for an exorbitant price, to Martin Roche, who considered it a sound investment, because if his theory was correct, this parcel of land was special.

Mapping the locations of all the known crop circles in England had been the key. Nearly seventy percent fell along an ancient route known as the Icknield Way, a trail that had been in use for more than four thousand years and at one point connected the English Channel with the North Sea by way of Stonehenge. Its course was dictated by the topography and defined by a distinct demarcation between chalk cliffs and greensand, a type of sandstone that got its name from the high concentration of iron-potassium silicate that gave it its telltale color and had the unique ability to absorb ten times as much moisture as ordinary soil. The combination of the two strata created the perfect conditions for agriculture. Rain fell upon the chalk Downs and the greensand soaked it up like a giant sponge, allowing the excess to pass through the porous sediment and accumulate on top of the underlying layer of impermeable clay, forming a giant aquifer that ran diagonally across the entire country, a veritable river beneath their feet. Further comparison against hydrogeological maps offered the first real breakthrough: ninety-five percent of all known crop circles had formed in areas with significant groundwater.

This particular acreage was special because it was adjacent to a plot of land that had been an active stone quarry a hundred years ago. The War Department had commandeered it during World War I and converted it into a storage depot for ammunition and TNT. The Royal Air Force assumed control of it during World War II and crammed more than thirty thousand tons of explosives into the manmade caverns. All that remained now was a rusted hatch in the middle of a field gone to seed, overgrown by bramble and the signs of disuse. And the twelve acres of tunnels that passed directly underneath Roche's leased land.

It was really Kelly Nolan who had put the whole thing together during the countless hours they'd spent brainstorming via Skype. At first he'd been reluctant to share any details about his work. While he firmly believed in the importance of what he was doing, especially after what happened in Antarctica, he knew that people still thought of the study of crop circles as a joke. The marines and the NSA had taught him to trust no one, so opening up to anyone, especially the younger woman with the red and green streaks in her hair, was one of the hardest things he'd ever done.

She'd rewarded him not just with her support and friendship, but with a plausible explanation that had the potential to blow the roof off the mystery surrounding the creation of crop circles. And if everything went as planned, within a matter of hours they'd know if she was right.

Kelly was sitting in the center of the design when Roche reached it, her head buried in the hood of her jacket and her frozen breath trailing over her shoulder. She glanced up and plucked her earbuds from her ears. He raised the thermos in one hand and the bag of croissants in the other.

"Did you remember the marmalade?"

Roche transferred the bag to his other hand and fished the jar of fresh bergamot jam from his jacket pocket.

She clapped her gloved hands and squealed in delight.

The fruit was too bitter for him, but it made him feel good that such a simple thing could give someone else so much pleasure. He wondered what she was going to do when the citrus fruit was no longer in season, although if everything went as planned today, it was only a matter of time before she returned to the States anyway.

The mere thought of her departure brought with it an intense sadness, which totally caught him off guard. She was a full eight years younger than he was and came from a world he could hardly believe existed anymore. He'd spent so many years sifting through the depths of mankind's darkness that it seemed impossible that there was any light left.

Kelly loaded the thermos and rolls into her backpack, shouldered it, and struck off toward the adjacent field. The barbed-wire fence was broken in places and snarled with tumbleweeds in others. Roche held down the upper wire so she could climb over, then stepped across himself. He glanced back at the design and shivered. There was something about it that made him uncomfortable on a primal level.

"Are you coming or what?" Kelly called.

"Yeah," he said, and turned away from what almost looked like a map from where he stood.

The briars left burrs in his socks and jeans, no matter how hard he tried to avoid them. Most of the weeds were as tall as Kelly, and were it not for the dead oak tree that marked the entrance to the mine, they might never have found it. The majority of the other entrances had been sealed off by order of the Ministry of Defense, who missed what must have been a late addition by the RAF that wasn't on the original blueprints.

The hatch was a rusted sheet of iron with hinges that squealed so loud the sound echoed clear across the plains. The ladder inside was little more than iron rungs bolted to the bare limestone for the first twenty vertical feet, after which Roche and Kelly were forced to use their flashlights and an extreme amount of caution to pick their way down a steep talus slope lined with chunks of nearly petrified wood that could only loosely be considered stairs. The walls were resplendent with artwork, from designs with a strange, haunting beauty to graffiti featuring the kind of language that could make a sailor blush.

Roche and Kelly were a hundred feet down by the time the ground leveled off and tunnels took form. They were smooth and solid, a feat accomplished by early quarrymen who took an inordinate amount of pride in their work, or at least that was what the librarian who first told him about this place had said.

It was frighteningly easy to lose their bearings in the darkness, but they'd been down here so many times during the last week that they'd learned their route by rote. Left, right, left, left, right. Kelly had once said that the echo of their footsteps sounded like the ghosts of the people who'd worked down here a century ago. The image was somehow comforting and became how he chose to think of the scuffing sounds that terminated in the dead end ahead of them, where the cases filled with Kelly's equipment were stacked under a tarp.

They'd used ground-penetrating radar to detect the hollow space underneath the crop circle and had spent endless, grueling hours hammering through eight solid feet of stone with pickaxes. They first broke through last night, but had decided to wait until this morning to finish the job and explore what they believed to be a cavern of decent size. The idea had been that they could do so with clear heads after a good night's sleep, yet Roche was certain Kelly hadn't been able to close her eyes any longer than he had.

"Would you care to do the honors?" she asked.

"You trying to get out of working?"

"I figure this is your moment."

"You're going to wait until I get all the way through and then you're going to run in there ahead of me, aren't you?"

She smiled, unscrewed the lid of the marmalade, and dipped her finger into the fruit. Slurped the bergamot from the tip of a fingernail with yellow and pink polish.

"You know me too well."

When she lowered her hand, her fingers unconsciously tapped against her thumb. It was a nervous tic of sorts, which, now that he really thought about it, she'd hardly exhibited at all over the last few days.

He hefted the pickaxe and drove it into the wall. Cracks radiated away from the small hole they'd made last night. He struck it over and over until the broken rock was shin-deep and he'd created a passage easily large enough to crawl through.

True to her word, Kelly was already halfway through by the time he set aside the tool and flung the sweat from his brow. He might even have said something snarky had he been able to think clearly. As it was, he felt as though he were watching himself enter the cavern from a great distance, somehow a witness to the moment rather than a participant.

Kelly stood at the bottom of the slick stone slope, silhouetted by the beam of her flashlight, which reflected from something metallic. He heard what almost sounded like whispering, but by the time he grabbed his own light and followed her into the darkness, he recognized the sound for what it truly was.

Running water.

The aquifer was barely visible through a manmade hole in the cavern floor, above which someone had installed a waterwheel carved from a single piece of stone. The subterranean river was so far down that his light barely reflected from its smooth surface. It would have to rise a good ten feet to be able to spin the paddles of the waterwheel, which was connected to a series of cogs that rotated a massive lodestone ring around an iron post that terminated against the stalactite-riddled ceiling. The copper wire wrapped around it was bluish-green with oxidation.

"It's just like the machine inside the pyramid in Antarctica," Kelly said.

Roche studied the ancient contraption. In many ways it seemed even more sophisticated than the power source that activated the gene-altering chamber. The height of the waterwheel suggested it would only spin under specific environmental conditions that caused an absurd rise in the groundwater, rotating the lodestone ring around the iron post and inducing an electrical current in the copper wire. Flowstone had accreted over the toroid at the top, absorbing it into the roof of the cavern. In fact, the layers of minerals were so thick that he could barely see the copper design radiating outward from the giant silver ring.

"The electricity passes from the copper wire to the toroid," Roche said, "which distributes it across the design wired into the ceiling."

"That charge is then conducted to the surface by the silicon dioxide in the greensand and the sheer volume of water retained in the limestone, producing a ton of heat and essentially steaming the crops directly above us."

"You're saying that someone built this down here thousands of years ago with the sole intention of producing an image on the surface that could only be seen when the aquifer was running at the exact right height."

"Of course it sounds silly when you say it like that."

"It sounds ridiculous no matter how you say it."

"More ridiculous than using these designs to activate an ancient pyramid buried under the Antarctic ice cap?"

She smirked and spun the waterwheel to make the lodestone ring turn. A faint current crackled in the copper wire.

"Do that again," Roche said.

She spun the waterwheel, faster this time. Bluish bolts of energy rippled through the ceiling.

"Keep going," he said, and sprinted back toward the entrance.

The walls blew past in the darkness as he nearly outraced his light. Right, left, right, right, left.

Up the slope and the ladder.

Out the chute.

The briars raked at his face as he sprinted toward the onion field. Hurdled the fence. Hit the ground running.

The heat from the electricity coursing through the greensand formed a carpet of fog, through which he watched the exact same design re-form in the crops before his very eyes.

This time there was no doubt.

It was definitely a map.

4
JADE

Benue River Delta, 15 miles south of Musari, Nigeria

Dr. Jade Liang slogged through waist-deep water that reeked of sulfur and rot. She kept her emerald-green eyes on the banks and the overhanging palm and fern branches for venomous snakes. The Benue River Delta was positively alive with them, and the nearest treatment facility was in Kaltungo, so far away she'd be long dead before arrival. The jungle was so dense she would never have been able to pick her way through it, even if it meant sparing her the scourge of the mosquitoes humming around her head. Much as she loathed them, she vastly preferred them to the black flies that had been the bane of her existence for the last week. They didn't sting, but after crawling all over the corpses, their little feet transferred all sorts of vile germs and the products of decomposition onto everything they touched.

Upon returning from Antarctica, she'd taken a sabbatical from her teaching position at the University of Colorado Medical School, sold her townhouse, and volunteered her services on a full-time basis to the United Nations' International Criminal Court and its investigation into crimes of genocide by Boko Haram, the de facto western branch of the Islamic State. She justified the decision to herself as doing her part to combat evil and injustice, but when it came right down to it, whether under the auspices of the U.N. Criminal Court or not, she'd still be wading through this swamp in search of answers to the questions that had plagued her for the last six months.

When she was first dispatched to Musari, Nigeria, she'd arrived with a full contingent of U.N. peacekeepers to find the village still burning and its inhabitants piled in a mass grave. Among them she'd discovered the body of a young woman with a strangely elongated cranium, which she'd written off as a product of artificial cranial deformation of the kind practiced by many primitive societies, until she encountered the same mutation on a living specimen in Antarctica, caused by what she now believed to be the spontaneous evolution of mankind. The activation of the machine inside the pyramid submerged beneath the ice had triggered a process by which their chief engineer, Dr. Dale Rubley, had undergone a frightening physical transformation when microscopic organisms of extraterrestrial origin infiltrated his isolation suit, altered his DNA, and subsumed his physical form. The resultant creature would have killed them all were it not for the intervention of a quasi-military group called Unit 51, about which she still knew next to nothing.

Several weeks had passed before she was able to compartmentalize the events that transpired in Antarctic Research, Analysis, and Experimentation Station 51—AREA 51—and she realized what should have been painfully obvious the entire time. For the girl she'd found in the mass grave to have exhibited the same characteristics as Dale Rubley, she either needed to have undergone the same physical metamorphosis or have descended from others who had, which meant that somewhere out here in this infernal jungle there was potentially an alien species capable of unlocking the secrets of human evolution.

It was while investigating the murder of sixteen missionaries outside of Lafia that she first heard the rumors. The victims had been "necklaced"—a horrific means of execution by which the victim's hands were tied behind his back and a tire filled with gasoline was hung around his neck and set ablaze. It sometimes took as long as twenty minutes for the poor souls to die as the flames ate through layer after layer of flesh, which must have felt like an eternity to the lone survivor, who battled through unendurable pain to tell investigators about the nineteen women who'd been abducted with him and the abuses to which they'd been continually subjected. When pressed on where they'd been taken, he could remember only that his captors had referred to their camp as "near the bobbies," but he'd died before he could clarify what that meant.

It took peacekeepers forty-eight hours to find the abandoned camp, along with the remains of thirteen of the girls, in a clearing near the Ankwe River. While examining the victims and documenting their horrific wounds, which suggested that their last twenty-four hours on this earth had been a living hell, she'd overheard her U.N. escorts discussing which way the caravan of perpetrators might have gone while studying the most recent satellite imaging. Several of the aerial views had shown stone mounds nearly concealed beneath the thick canopy that she might have dismissed were she not able to extrapolate their contours into perfect circles. It wasn't until that precise moment that she understood what the dead missionary had meant by "bobbies." Most Nigerians spoke a kind of pidgin English not unlike the Creoles in Louisiana. The term was slang for a woman's breasts.

Local authorities in Yola had tracked the movements of the Boko Haram contingent into the Mandara Mountains, which suggested they were either holing up in the volcanic range or trying to outrun their pursuit into Cameroon. The peacekeepers had been dispatched that very evening, but she'd elected to stay behind in hopes of getting a better look at these so-called bobbies.

Jade was beginning to think she'd either misread the map or misinterpreted what she thought she'd seen. She'd been navigating this maze of channels for more than four hours now and was starting to wonder if she'd somehow lost her way. For the structures to have been visible through the canopy, they had to have been at least fifty feet—

A crackling sound from the underbrush lining the bank to her right.

She drew her hijab across her face with one hand and thrust the other into her jacket. Closed her fist around the grip of the Ruger LC9 handgun in the sling under her armpit. The semi-automatic pistol was almost comically small, but fit her tiny hand, barely bucked when she fired it, and could punch a hole in an attacker large enough to toss a softball through.

A crocodile slid from the bushes and vanished into the murky water. It reappeared several seconds later,

maybe twenty-five feet ahead of her. She held perfectly still and watched it drift away from her on the
weak current until it rounded the bend.

She realized she wasn't breathing and gasped for
air.

What was she doing out here? There were any number of things just waiting to kill her and there wasn't a
single person on the planet who knew where she was.
And why *hadn't* she told anyone? Because no one
would have believed her. She was starting to wonder if
she believed herself.

Jade nearly had herself convinced to turn around
when she saw it through the trees. At first it looked like
little more than an outcropping scoured in places to the
bare granite by the wind, but she was able to push
through a stand of tree ferns and onto dry ground to get
a better look. It was easy to see why they were called
the bobbies. There appeared to be six of them in all, although only two of them clearly stood apart from the
jungle, which had grown over them in such a way as to
conceal all but their shape. Each was built from concentric rings of stacked stones that grew smaller and
smaller until they reached a peak reminiscent of a nip-
ple. The levels had eroded through the years and now
formed what could have been mistaken for oddly terraced piles of rock had she not known exactly what she
was looking at.

They were pyramids.

She was only peripherally aware of the Nsude Pyramids, built by the Igbo people far to the southwest.
Many archeologists speculated they were even older
than those in Egypt, but that definitely wasn't her field
of expertise. All she knew was that she was a hard

day's walk from where she'd found the remains of the girl with the elongated cranium, standing at the base of a pyramid hidden in the jungle, and didn't believe in coincidences.

Jade skirted the bask of crocodiles sunning themselves on the bank and rounded the far side of the pyramid. It was only when she noticed the crunching sounds of her footsteps on the detritus that she recognized the complete and utter lack of birdsong.

She looked up into branches so still it seemed as though even the wind held its breath. There were no lizards staring down at her or monkeys chittering from their enclaves. No warblers or sunbirds flitting through the canopy. Not even a viper camouflaged among the dangling leaves.

A faint buzzing sound beckoned from somewhere ahead of her. She knew exactly what it was.

Jade ducked underneath a fallen tree and fought through saplings and vines all vying for the same light gap. Her pulse thumped so hard in her temples that she could barely hear the flies.

The muddy ground became choppy with what looked like footprints, and a path of sorts formed where there had been none before. The vegetation grew so thick she had to crawl, and for the first time she caught a whiff of the awful stench lurking beneath the intermingling scents of blossoms, moss, and stagnant water. The puddles in the muddy tracks were brick red and roiling with mosquito larvae.

The path led to a twisted tree trunk that angled up the slope of the concealed pyramid. Some sort of animal had excavated a burrow underneath the trunk and tunneled beneath the crumbled granite.

Jade removed the Maglite Mini LED flashlight from her jacket pocket and shined it into the hole. The beam reflected from standing water that terminated against a rock abutment nearly a dozen feet in. The smell emanating from inside was more than she could bear, even with the hijab covering her mouth and nose.

She took a deep breath before she could change her mind and squirmed into the burrow. The water was startlingly cold and filled with organisms flagellating beneath the surface. In her mind, they were all snakes preparing to strike her, but she could only move so fast while keeping her light and gun above the surface. The tunnel ended at the base of a vertical chute maybe five feet tall, above which was a space reminiscent of the inside of an igloo. Spiderwebs covered the domed ceiling, although not so completely that she couldn't see the intricate pattern of stars carved into the granite. She contorted her upper body and managed to get her legs underneath her. Cautiously stood and shined her light into the inner sanctum.

The flies took flight from the remains on the ground and cast amoeboid shadows across the walls. The body was still articulated and undeniably human, unlike the majority of the bones heaped against the walls, which were so jumbled it was impossible to tell where one ended and the next began, let alone to which species they'd once belonged. Judging by the pelvis, the body was female, and likely one of the missionaries left behind at the abandoned camp mere miles away. It had been stripped of muscle and flesh to the connective tissue and knots of tendons at the joints.

The engorged flies ignored her and returned to their meal.

"We . . . know . . . you," a deep, disembodied voice said from directly behind her.

Jade screamed and spun around. Her flashlight reflected from a pair of eyes before they retreated into a dark recess.

She was breathing so hard she feared she might hyperventilate.

A shuffling sound to the left of where she'd last seen the eyes.

The clicking of nails on stone.

"We . . . still . . . live."

The words seemed to originate from all around her at once, the hollow intonation as much a sensation as a sound.

"Show yourself," Jade said, but the tremor in her voice gave lie to her bravado.

Scratching, from even farther to her left.

It was circling around her.

Jade swung her beam toward the sound and caught a glimpse of bare, grayish skin as it scurried into a narrow tunnel. She crawled toward it and shined her light inside just in time to see a blur of movement at the farthest reaches of the light.

"Find . . . us."

The voice echoed from out of sight.

A scraping sound preceded the sudden influx of light.

She realized with a start just how vulnerable she was and how easily she could be sealed inside the pyramid. An animalistic panic took hold of her. She threw herself into the hole and crawled toward the light. She hit her head and scraped her knees and elbows. The sound of her breathing was too loud in her own ears, as though she were in a coffin. She twisted and turned until she crawled through a gap where one of the structural stones had been pushed away from the pyramid and into the undergrowth, through which she could barely see the brown stream.

Movement through the maze of trunks. Something scurrying away from her, low and near the ground.

"Stop right there!" she shouted, and aimed her pistol through the trees.

The pale, skeletal form vanished into the thicket.

Jade dropped her flashlight and ran after it. Branches swatted her face, forcing her to shield it with her forearms. She burst from the jungle and onto the bank of the river where the crocodiles had been basking when she arrived.

The creature crouched naked at the water's edge. It looked up at her from beneath the ridged brow of its elongated head through wide, alien eyes.

"Release . . . us."

It rose to its full height, turned, and waded into the murky water.

The crocodiles attacked with unbridled savagery, and, in a flurry of snapping jaws and thrashing tails, dragged it down into the depths.

Blood rose to the surface and diffused into the current.

5
BARNETT

Subterranean Ice Caverns, FOB Atlantis,
Queen Maud Land, Antarctica

Barnett scrolled through the map of the honeycomb-like passageways on his iPad while he walked. The sonar scans left considerable gaps in the digitally reconstructed data, but there was more than enough to demonstrate that whatever took out his men could be positively anywhere by now. He passed the tablet back to Morgan and quickened his pace toward his destination. His men had widened the stone corridors and cleared all the ice from the chamber preceding the one where his men had been ambushed. The ice cavern itself had been chiseled in such a fashion that his team was able to reach the hole in the roof, while leaving the evidence largely undamaged. Only Jonas's body had been removed and his blood scrubbed from the floor, pending formal analysis by Unit 51's scientific wing, operating under the auspices of the United States Research Institute for Infectious Diseases. So far, they had discovered nothing out of the ordinary, but like the archaea that had subsumed the body of Dr. Dale Rubley, it was always possible that the life cycles of any potentially pathogenic microorganisms were highly dependent upon environmental factors and weren't readily apparent under normal conditions.

Of course, they had more urgent concerns than the possible risk of infection. At this very moment, something capable of slaughtering two elite soldiers was down here in the tunnels with them.

"Did she tell you what this is about?" Barnett asked.

"No, sir," Morgan said.

They'd installed thermal imaging cameras in the main junctions of the tunnels, but there were so many smaller passageways and side corridors that there was no way they could possibly cover them all. Most of them were too small for his men to search anyway, even with the sonar and LiDar scanners at their disposal, both of which were capable of imaging enclosed spaces they couldn't physically explore by mapping points of data using rebounding sonar waves and laser beams. While both technologies formed three-dimensional representations of the tunnels and caverns, the only way either could detect the presence of something living was if it moved while they were actively scanning.

The halogen bulbs had been replaced by black lights and every surface sprayed with a fine layer of Luminol, a chemical that reacted with the hemoglobin in the victims' blood to produce a bluish glow that stood apart from the ice like fluorescent paint.

"Tell me you've found something remotely useful," Barnett said.

"And good morning to you too, Director," Dr. Moira Murphy said. Her bulky isolation suit was like a hot-air balloon over her diminutive form. Barnett had plucked her from the grasp of DARPA—the Defense Advanced Research Projects Agency—not just because of her skill in forensic investigations, but because of her expertise in a wide variety of fields ranging from computer programming and biotechnology to mechanical and genetic engineering, a consequence of being raised by nomadic academics who regarded the pursuit of happiness as secondary to the quest for intellectual enlightenment.

"I'm in no mood, Dr. Murphy."

"Then I suppose it depends upon how you define 'useful.'"

"What do you have?"

"Thanks to the Luminol, we've been able to isolate a few distinct tracks, and, utilizing a program of my own design, have been able to digitally reconstruct what we believe to be a fingerprint."

She removed her tablet from its protective thermal casing, turned it on, and handed it to Barnett. The screen showed an oblong blue design set against a black background. It had the same general shape as a fingerprint, but instead of the familiar whorl pattern, it featured curved horizontal bands that reminded him of ripples and a triangular tip he assumed was a claw.

"So there's no doubt we're dealing with some kind of animal," Barnett said. While he'd suspected as much based on the nature of the wounds it inflicted and its ability to squeeze into such a small space, he'd privately held out hope that at long last they'd discovered where Hollis Richards had been hiding.

"Not just 'some sort of animal.' We're dealing with a species that was able to survive being frozen in solid ice for millennia. A higher order of animal specifically adapted for an extended period of cryobiosis, one capable of essentially slowing its heart rate and metabolism to such an extent that it barely qualified as living."

"Nothing could have survived down here for that long."

"And yet we're surrounded by evidence to the contrary. Let me show you something."

Moira led Barnett to the other side of the cavern, where his men had first breached the ice.

"Look at this right here."

Barnett stared at the solid ice, and through it, at the ancient bones crammed into a recess in the stone wall.

"Are they human?"

It almost looked like a man had been folded into a ball with his knees to his forehead, his arms pinned between his ribcage and his thighs, and wedged into the hole.

"Undeniably, but that's not why I called you down here. Try running your fingers across the ice. Right there in the cavity where his abdominal contents were."

Barnett looked at her curiously for a moment before doing as she asked. There were distinct ridges in the ice he hadn't been able to visually appreciate. They almost matched the contours of the internal margin of the ribcage.

"So what is it?"

"What we believe to be the physical outline of this miraculous species. The majority was melted by the flamethrowers, but we were able to create a plaster mold from that section you just felt." She looked around the room. "Desmond? Can you grab the mold for me?"

Dr. Desmond Bly was their resident speleologist. He was barely five feet tall and skeletally thin, which had helped him map some of the largest and most dangerous cave systems on the planet. As one would expect from someone who spent the majority of his time alone in the darkness, however, he lacked certain social graces. Fortunately, Barnett hadn't recruited him for his personality.

Bly sighed and made a grand show of how put out he was to have to set aside his laptop and the digital maps he painstakingly pieced together, and removed the white mold from the insulated case he'd been using as a stool. He tossed it to Morgan, who was marginally closer than Barnett, and plopped back down with his computer.

Morgan passed the cast to Barnett, who turned it over in his hands. The bottom was coarse and uneven, while the top was relatively smooth, save for the same distinct ridges he'd felt in the ice.

"It looks like an armadillo's shell."

"Carapace, technically," Moira said. "Although if we were to use the distance between the armor-like bands and the degree of curvature to extrapolate its size, we'd be dealing with an armadillo that was roughly three feet long from its nose to the tip of its tail."

"Armadillos can't take down full-grown men."

"Nor are they able to climb straight up vertical sheets of ice, which brings us back to the fingerprints. Those horizontal flanges are called lamellae, and, if I'm correct, function like those on a gecko's toes, which are covered with microscopic structures called setae. Each of these microscopic bristles further splits into nano-sized tips called spatulae that create van der Waals interactions with surface molecules strong enough to support a disproportional amount of weight."

"But none of that tells us how it killed my men."

"I was saving the best for last." She looked at Bly, who rolled his eyes and once again set aside his work. He opened the thermoprene case and removed another plaster mold. "Based on my analysis of SA Jonas's wounds, I concluded that they were inflicted by teeth. The subject's jaws are dorsolaterally flattened in such a way as to create a rostral shelf, and the teeth are interdigitating in orientation."

"In English, doctor."

Morgan retrieved the mold from Bly before he could toss it. When he turned around, his expression told Barnett everything he needed to know.

"This animal—for lack of a better term—has an elongated snout with interlocking teeth designed for gripping and tearing."

Barnett took the mold from Morgan. There were only six teeth, two on one side and four on the other, but their configuration was unmistakable.

"The fourth tooth from the front, as you can clearly see, is longer than the others and designed to inflict the most damage," Moira said. "I've studied similar wounds, although not in person, caused by—"

"Crocodiles," Barnett finished for her. He handed

the mold to her and headed back toward the tunnel to the main complex. "Good work, Dr. Murphy."

"I wish I could tell you exactly what we were dealing with."

"So do I, Doctor, but I think I just might know someone who can."

6
TESS

The Cage, FOB Atlantis

It had taken Dr. Theresa Clarke several months to acclimate to working in the faint glow of the red bulbs, which were so dim she might as well have been trying to function in total darkness. She'd had no choice in the matter, though, not that anyone around here cared much about her opinion anyway. She'd basically utilized her skills in satellite archeology to leverage her position in Unit 51, despite not being entirely certain what it actually was. All she knew was that reality was even better than her dreams and she couldn't wait to get down here every morning when the motion sensors triggered the alarm by her bed and the cameras started recording.

They'd originally mounted overhead lights in the adjacent chamber, but the occupant shattered them every single time, even after they covered them with those metal cage thingies. The night vision cameras had fared little better. It wasn't until they installed the thermal imaging that they'd been able to actually tell what it was doing in there, which was where she came in.

The wall that divided the tunnel from the cavern on the other side was composed of a foot of reinforced concrete to either side of a solid steel core and sunken eight feet into the surrounding limestone. The inset window was the sole point of vulnerability, although it would basically take a nuclear detonation to so much as crack the lead-lined glass. The lone egress was hermetically sealed, utilized the kind of door they used for the vault at Fort Knox, and featured a mazelike chute that allowed them to feed the creature on the other side.

Tess leaned across her console and spoke into the microphone.

"Are you hungry?"

Her voice echoed back at her from the speakers inside the cavern. She watched the heat signature of the subject stiffen on the monitor and turn toward the window, through which she could see only darkness. The thermal imaging didn't provide the sharpest images, especially since she'd narrowed the temperature gradient window level so that everything below seventy-eight degrees appeared black and everything above one hundred degrees appeared white. The twenty-two degrees in between were represented by a spectrum from blue and purple at the lower end to pink and red in the mid-range to orange and yellow at the upper limit, which meant that other than the pinkish clouds of radiant heat emanating from the electrical warmers in the ceiling, the entirety of the cavern served as a black backdrop limned with just enough blue to create texture and depth.

The creature stood apart from it like a blazing beacon. Its outline was formed of a purplish pink that brightened from red to orange to the golden auras that defined its face and chest. Its elongated head cocked first one way, then the other, like a predatory bird. As irrational as the thought was, Tess couldn't shake the feeling that it could see her through the monitor.

The creature had been formally classified as Subject Z—represented by the sixth letter of the Greek alphabet, Zeta—as an allusion to the 1965 newspaper report describing the abduction of Betty and Barney Hill by aliens that would later be described as Grays, the stereotypical physical expression of which looked identical to the mutated form of Dr. Dale Rubley. The article printed a drawing by Mrs. Hill, detailing the route the spaceship had used during her abduction, which an amateur astronomer recognized as the Zeta Reticuli star system, leading to the quasi-official designation of the species as Zeta Reticulans.

Tess had heard the being speak on the audio files recorded inside the research station last year, when it had been responsible for the deaths of nearly the entire staff, but it hadn't uttered so much as a single syllable since being caged down here. It was her job to establish communication with it, and the powers that be were running out of patience.

"Would you like to eat?"

Subject Z stared at her through the camera for several seconds before making a sound she could barely hear. She would have to play it back and enhance the track, but she could have sworn it almost sounded like it said, "Yes."

"Oh, my God," she said, and clapped her hands over her mouth. She turned to face the armed agent guarding the door to the cage. He wore black fatigues and stood so still that she often forgot he was there. "You heard that, didn't you?"

His only reply was a slight shrug of his shoulders, upon which he wore the red insignia of Unit 51: an upside-down triangle offset on top of another upside-down triangle, both of which were enclosed inside of a third. At the very center were the Roman numerals LI.

"Well? What are you waiting for?"

The guard—whose name was Carson, although she didn't know if that was his first name or last—spoke into his transceiver. A horrible squeal erupted from the depths of the earthen tunnel behind her.

She hated this part more than anything in the world.

A silhouette pushed a cart toward them through the unlit corridor. Its wheels squeaked, and the cage on top of it rattled. The squeals became frantic, turning into screams that sounded almost human. The man pushing the cart looked just like all of the others, which she figured was why medieval executioners wore hoods. His name was Les Dutton, and everyone claimed he was the best cook to ever enter the service, but Tess couldn't even look at him without hearing those awful screams.

He lifted the cage from the cart, hooked it to the slot in the door, and pressed a series of buttons on the wall panel. The cage and the seal in the door simultaneously opened with a hiss of pressurized air.

The pig stood frozen in the cage, its cries echoing off into the silence.

"Go on," Carson said, and nudged the cage with the toe of his boot.

It scurried forward and Dutton resealed the opening behind it. He set the empty cage onto the cart and pushed it back down the hallway without a word.

The feeding chute utilized a series of baffles to guide the pig through the maze. They closed behind it, one by one, until it made the final turn, which caused the inner seal to disengage.

It emerged from the left side of Tess's screen as a vaguely piggish shape of pink and orange. She hadn't so much as heard the creature move or noticed its thermal signature disappear, presumably behind one of the flowstone columns.

The pig squealed and issued an orange stream that quickly faded into a blue puddle around its hooves. It took several tentative steps into the cavern and raised its snout. She could hear it sniffing the air through her console. Its ears pricked and it held perfectly still.

Tess looked away, but not before catching a blur of color from the monitor to her right as the creature emerged from an entirely different hiding spot than she'd expected. She closed her eyes and tried not to hear the pig's screams, which, fortunately, didn't last long. When she opened her eyes again, the cavern walls were decorated with golden arcs that darkened from orange to red as they trickled down the granite.

A voice crackled from Carson's transceiver. He made a curt reply and holstered his communication device.

The savage crunching and tearing sounds from the other side of the wall abruptly ceased and the creature turned toward the window. It dropped the squirming carcass to the ground and slowly approached the glass, its facial features clearly delineated by the sheer quantity of warm blood on its face.

"The director's on his way down," Carson said.

"What does he want?" Tess asked.

"You'll have to ask him yourself."

He'd barely uttered the words when the sound of footsteps materialized from the darkness behind her.

The creature crossed the cavern and pressed its bloody palms against the window, almost like it knew.

"Give us the room," Barnett said before he even entered what Tess liked to think of as her office.

"Yes, sir," Carson said, and headed back into the dark corridor.

"I know it's taken longer than any of us thought," Tess said, "but not five minutes ago I was finally able to get it to speak—"

"I need to talk to it," Barnett interrupted.

The creature appeared to smile on the thermal monitor. They couldn't even see its outline through the reinforced glass. The expression was the only thing even remotely human about it. The physical transformation had continued unabated, each passing day distorting more and more of the characteristics of Dr. Dale Rubley and forming something new, something entirely alien.

Tess climbed from her chair and gestured for Barnett to take a seat. He slid behind her console and studied first the monitors and then the window, which offered little more than an uninterrupted view of darkness.

"Jesus," he said. "You can't even see it standing less than two feet away."

The dying pig kicked at the ground with the clacking of hooves, which did little more than push it in a half-circle through its own blood.

"Just push the button there," Tess said, "and speak into the microphone. I have to warn you, though . . ."

don't talk for any length of time or it will be able to isolate the speakers and tear them out. Like everything else."

"Duly noted," Barnett said and pressed the button. A clicking sound echoed throughout the inner cavern. "Can you hear me?"

"You have to release the button if you want to hear the microphones inside," Tess said.

She reached for it, but he swatted her hand away. She'd never seen Barnett like this before. He was ordinarily so collected and almost charming, albeit in a rigid kind of way. Right now he was wound so tightly she could see the vein throbbing in his temple, even in the dim red glare.

"Tell me what else is down here," he said, and released the button.

The creature looked almost contemplative for a moment before the blood on its face cooled to such a degree that its expression once more faded into a vague mass of colors. For the briefest of moments, she almost thought she'd seen a spark of recognition.

"I need to know what else could have survived down here, frozen inside these infernal tunnels."

He released the button and Tess heard a sound from inside that could have been heavy breathing or perhaps throaty laughter as the creature retreated from the window and returned to its meal.

"You know, don't you?"

The creature crouched, gripped the struggling pig in both hands, and buried its face in the poor animal's neck. A sharp crack and a spurt of gold highlighted its elongated skull. The pig stopped moving.

"Two of my men are dead, and we don't have the slightest idea what we're up against."

Tess opened her mouth to say something, but Barnett silenced her with a glare that made his face appear positively demonic in the red light.

"If we die down here, you die down here, too. You understand that, don't you? You'll be trapped in this cage until you starve to death. Or maybe until whatever's out there finds a way to get in there with you."

The creature rose from its meal, its features once more glistening with the fresh application of blood, and approached the window. It wiped the blood from its gaunt cheeks and bony chest and smeared it onto the glass.

Tess thought it was trying to paint over the window so they couldn't see it until a pattern started to form. It traced over the lines until an intricate design took shape.

She glanced at Barnett in time to see comprehension dawn on his face. As quickly as the expression appeared, it was gone.

He stood so fast he nearly knocked over her chair.

"Not a word of this to anyone," he said. "Do you hear me?"

He hurried down the corridor before she could respond, leaving her alone with the echo of his footsteps, the sound of chewing from inside the cavern, and the knowledge that something so terrifying it could scare even Barnett was lurking in the darkness with her.

7
ANYA

Teotihuacan

Anya had been initially disappointed when the concealed remains proved to be ordinary *Homo sapiens*. The way the subterranean tunnels had essentially revealed themselves when they activated the pyramid under the Antarctic ice cap had seemed like a perfect stroke of serendipity. That was the whole reason she'd volunteered to join Evans on this dig in the first place. She'd expected to find coneheaded skeletons everywhere she looked, bodies from which she'd be able to construct an evolutionary timeline so she could finally make some sense of what she'd seen at the bottom of the world. Instead, she'd stumbled upon another mystery, although one of a more mundane variety, but maybe that was what she needed for her own piece of mind, a distraction from the memories that still awakened her screaming at night.

They'd photographed the tomb from every conceivable angle and run a 3D LiDar scan—which preserved the scene as a precise digital model that could be rotated 360 degrees on any axis for increased scrutiny—

before commencing with the arduous task of removing the bones. Earlier archeologists had discovered other mass graves throughout the primitive complex, and while this one was similar, there were enough distinct differences that it qualified as unique.

The other victims had been similarly bound and buried alive, although they'd been surrounded by all kinds of grave goods, from obsidian and greenstone figurines to blades, mirrors, and shells. They'd been highly decorated warriors, judging by the number of human jaws they wore on lanyards around their necks, wrenched from the fallen bodies of their enemies. For men so powerful to be sacrificed in such a manner, they had to have done so willingly, offering their services to the gods in the afterlife.

Unlike the other burial sites, however, there were no grave goods with these sacrifices, or the remains of any revered animals like hawks or jaguars. These victims hadn't been buried; they'd been entombed, which in many ways was reminiscent of how the alien remains had been discovered in Egypt and Antarctica. While they'd been immobilized with their ankles tied and their hands bound behind their backs, there had been no earth packed around them to limit their movements or deplete the finite quantity of air in their lungs. They could have sat back-to-back and untied each other's wrists, then freed their own ankles and made their escape. So why hadn't they? Why had these people acquiesced to their fates when freedom had been within their grasp?

Those were the riddles she contemplated as Villarreal's graduate students in Mesoamerican Archeology—Alexandra, a petite Latina with tattoos covering her arms, and Emil, a hulking local in a Hawaiian shirt whose thick glasses were always opaque with dust—painstakingly removed the bones and placed them in boxes labeled SW-1 through SW-12, corresponding to their relative position, from left to right, within what they were calling the Sacrificial Well. Their final resting places would be on shelves with the rest of the disinterred remains at the cultural center, where future researchers could check them out like books from some macabre library.

There was something about this burial, though . . . something she couldn't quite put her finger on.

"What can you tell me about these victims?" Villarreal asked.

"Hmm?" Anya said. She'd been so lost in thought that she hadn't at first realized he was talking to her.

"The victims. What can you tell me about their physical condition?"

"They weren't warriors like the others. Their skeletal structure doesn't reflect the same advanced musculature. In fact, judging by the pelvic outlet, the width of the sciatic notch, and the angle of the pubic arch, four of them are undeniably female."

"The Teotihuacano did not sacrifice women."

"All evidence to the contrary aside," Evans said from where he waded in a circle around the pool, studying each of the feathered serpent heads as he passed.

"Many of their gods were female, including the Great Goddess," Villarreal said. "You must also remember that this society was built upon commerce. Women wove textiles and carved figurines. Their value to the economy of the state went beyond their role as breeding stock."

"I can only tell you what I see," Anya said. "I leave the interpretation to you guys."

"The fact that there are twelve heads out here and twelve victims in there can't be coincidental," Evans said. "And if you look at each of these feathered serpents closely, you'll see that no two of them are exactly the same."

"They were carved by hand," Villarreal said. "Of course they are not identical."

"What I mean is look at their relative size compared to that of the bodies. I think they were carved after the victims were chosen, not before."

"You are suggesting that this well was under construction while these people were dying mere feet away?"

"That's one interpretation."

"And they just sat there, waiting to die? I do not believe that."

"They didn't just sit there," Anya said and scooted past Alexandra so she could get a better look at the next skeleton in line for removal. She shined her flashlight first onto its chin, then its neck, before looking straight up at the earthen ceiling. "Somebody get me a ladder."

"Where do you propose we get a—?" Emil started.

"That crate will work," Anya interrupted, and dragged over the crate labeled SW-9.

"What are you doing?" Evans asked. There was barely enough room for him to crawl inside with them.

"Look at how the body is lying. Specifically, look at its chin. See how it's broken on the very tip? A com-

minuted fracture of that nature is extraordinarily un-
common. It results from direct impact to the mentum."

"What is the significance?" Villarreal asked.

"The mandible's designed in such a way that it distributes the force of any blunt trauma. That's why most
of the time it breaks on both sides at once, even when
the force impacts only one side, like with a punch to
the face. In this case, the impact was squarely to the tip
of the chin and the force was distributed through the
thicker body and rami, causing the head to be driven so
far backward that it broke the neck at the second cervical vertebra."

"A hangman's fracture?" Evans said.

"Exactly, but in this case internal decapitation would
be a better description." She swept her beam across the
smooth limestone roof, and then onto the partially articulated cervical spine. "And if you look really closely,
you'll see there's a small amount of callus formation
along the fracture lines, which means the injury occurred some amount of time before death."

"I might not be the smartest person in any room,"
Alexandra said, "but even I know you don't survive
decapitation."

"The fracture of the odontoid process of the axis essentially caused what's known as an atlanto-occipital
dislocation. The spine separates from the skull, which
in turn compresses the spinal cord. It's only fatal seventy percent of the time, which is why a lot of people
who are hanged survive long enough to asphyxiate.
Without the noose, the victim can potentially survive,
although the damage to the spinal cord causes some
measure of—if not complete—paralysis."

"So you think someone hit this guy in the face hard enough to break his neck and just left him to suffer?" Emil said.

"No," Anya said. "I think—"

"The injury was caused by a fall from some height," Evans finished for her.

"Bingo."

"So you think these victims were bound and suspended above the ground while they were still alive," Villarreal said.

Anya shined her light across the roof one last time before hopping down from the crate and crouching over the remains.

"But only one of them fell while he was still alive. The others demonstrate fractures consistent with falling, but there's no sign of remodeling or healing."

"So how were they suspended?"

"I don't know."

"There are no hooks or rings. The ceiling is as smooth as the floor."

"Smoother, actually," Anya said, and passed her flashlight to Emil. "Hold this for me, would you?"

She scrutinized the limestone under the sacrificial victim's right hand for several seconds before using a chisel to scrape away the crust of adipocere.

"What did you find?" Evans asked.

"I'm not sure." Anya wiped away the debris, pulled her sleeve over her hand, and used the cloth to clear the limestone. She took her flashlight from Emil and shined it at the disarticulated phalanges. The tip of the index finger had been filed down past the inguinal tuft. The pain must have been excruciating, yet still the man used it to carve a message into the bare stone, while he lay on his side, neck broken and arms bound behind his back. "Can you read this?"

"The symbol is not very clear," Villarreal said.

"Use your imagination," Evans said.

"What he means to say is that if anyone can read it," Anya said, "it's you."

She glared at Evans, while Villarreal noticeably swelled with the compliment.

"It appears to be a combination of two different glyphs," he said. "Or maybe an attempt to carve one on top of the other."

"It's not like he would have been able to see it very clearly," Evans said. "You know, him being in the dark and all."

"It looks like a sea anemone with an eye in the middle of its stalk," Anya said.

"I do not think that is an eye," Villarreal said. "If you turn the glyph upside down—"

"It's a feathered serpent," Evans said. "But what are all of those squiggly lines?"

"Roots," Villarreal said. He became suddenly animated. "It is the tree of life."

"So what does it mean?" Evans asked.

Anya tried to imagine what message could have been of such great importance to a man who knew he was going to die that he was willing to spend his final hours in unendurable agony in order to deliver it.

She wasn't sure she wanted to find out.

8
BARNETT

The Pyramid of Transformation, FOB Atlantis

Barnett ascended the ladder from the subterranean warrens and climbed out of the well into the lowest level of the pyramid, where he was surrounded by the machinations that made it run. The ancient gears had been carefully extracted, cleaned to the bare lodestone, and replaced around the base of the iron column. The copper windings had been scoured of oxidation and polished to the color of burnished brass. His chief engineer estimated that the machine could now produce roughly thirty percent more energy, which undoubtedly would have been enough to instantly kill Dale Rubley, although in conjunction with the genetic alterations caused by the alien microbes, there was no way of accurately predicting what might happen if they attempted the experiment again.

He couldn't help but wonder if it hadn't been the diminished power of a machine designed to produce significantly more that had caused the creature's slowed transformation and frightening levels of aggression, or if giving it more power would have only made it exponentially worse.

He crouched and scurried up the ascending corridor. The walls had been purged of algae and the concealed hieroglyphics renovated to what could have passed for new, at least in a historical perspective. Their staff lexicologist believed they were a combination of Egyptian and Sumerian styles, only undeniably distinct from either. While the pictures conveyed snippets of stories, the actual writing that tied them together was far more complex than any cuneiform tablet or cartouche she'd ever seen. Barnett understood that cracking such complex codes wasn't easy, but with every so-called specialist demanding more and more time, he was nearly out of patience.

The main corridor was considerably larger and brighter and always crowded with people coming and going from the upper levels. In addition to the Grand Gallery with its elaborate statuary of animal-faced gods, they'd discovered more than a dozen different passages that had been clogged with debris for millennia. They ranged in size from large enough for a man on all fours to explore to so small they had to custom-build a camera drone the size of his hand.

Morgan met him at the entrance and together they descended the switchbacking stairs to the boardwalk they'd built to connect the various buildings. Far too many people had sprained ankles on the loose stones of what for eons had been a lake bed.

Barnett didn't speak a word on the way to the base. He didn't have to. He'd been working with Morgan for so long now that his second-in-command had become adept at anticipating not only his needs, but his moods, which Barnett had to admit were more erratic than he would have liked. A consequence of going months on end without seeing the sun, he figured, but he also wasn't handling the strain nearly as well as he had in the past. He couldn't shake the feeling that the speed with which they were making these strange discoveries wasn't coincidental. Something big was coming, and it was up to him to make sure they were ready for it. After all, very few people knew about his unit and what it did, and ever fewer believed in the credibility of the threat he could positively feel building against the horizon.

Forward Operating Base Atlantis was an aggregate of futuristic prefabricated buildings erected in a wagon-wheel formation. Each of the twelve buildings forming the outer ring were connected to each other and the mess hall in the center by hermetically sealed corridors. Like everything else, they were composed of multiple thin layers of steel, wood, foam, graphite, silicone, and aluminum, which combined to form a lightweight product with remarkable insulating properties. The base was fireproof, waterproof, and could withstand every conceivable threat Mother Nature could throw its way, shy of dropping two vertical miles of ice directly on top of it, anyway.

When Morgan finally spoke, it was in little more than a whisper.

"We just received a coded message from The Hanger." It was the code name for Unit 51's base of operations, which was located in a formerly abandoned underground bunker in a remote corner of Joint Base Langley-Eustis, near Washington D.C. "Intel intercepted another encrypted communication from south of the Mexican border."

"Where specifically?"

"Impossible to tell. They bounced the signal off of nearly every satellite up there."

"Have we broken the encryption?"

"Partially?"

"And?"

"Another reference to 'the sleeping god.'"

Barnett froze with the handle of the front door in his hand. He looked Morgan squarely in the eyes.

"You're certain?"

Morgan nodded.

It was the third such message their cryptanalysts back in the States had plucked from the ether using those particular words, for which there was no direct historical or cultural correlation. Unfortunately, gods had apparently become Unit 51's domain, especially considering the first two references to this sleeping god had come in the days following the activation of the Antarctic pyramid and in the vicinity of sites of strategic importance.

Barnett already had more than he could handle right now. He would have to deal with this development later, when he had a few free seconds to consider the implications of there being a second faction hovering around the periphery of his team's investigations.

The facility was quiet this time of day. The third shift was still asleep in the barracks, and the second shift was gathered in the daylight room, where they were subjected to a barrage of ultraviolet radiation designed to replicate the sun's rays. Those who had the day off generally spent their time in the mess or the rec room, where there was a pool table, several big-screen TVs, and every video game console known to man.

Barnett's chambers were separate from all the others. The front half served as a command center, while the rear, which he rarely saw, functioned as his private quarters. He walked around his desk and plopped into the swiveling chair, in which he'd spent more nights than the bed mere feet away on the other side of the wall.

Morgan closed and locked the door behind him. He took a seat in his customary chair opposite Barnett.

"You saw the design on the security camera, didn't you?" Barnett said. "The one Zeta painted in blood on the window."

Morgan nodded.

"It's a match, isn't it?"

"Right down to the smallest detail," Morgan said.

"You know what you need to do."

"It isn't going to be easy."

"Trust me. It'll be easier than you think."

Morgan shrugged.

"I hope you're right," he said.

"When was the last time I wasn't?" Barnett asked.

"I'll take Stevens," Morgan said. "When do we leave?"

"You're still here?"

Morgan smiled and rose from his chair.

"Get some sleep, chief. You look like crap."

"I'll take that as a compliment since I feel a whole lot worse than that."

"You keep biting people's heads off and you'll have a mutiny on your hands."

"If anything like what happened to Berkeley and Jonas happens to anyone else, that's a forgone conclusion."

"Give these people more credit than that. They know what they signed on for."

"We need to figure out what's down here before we put that to the test."

"Everything's under control," Morgan said, and headed for the door.

"Be safe," Barnett said.

Morgan froze and held perfectly still for several seconds. He offered a quick glance back over his shoulder before exiting and leaving Barnett alone with his thoughts. He knew how it sounded, but something bad was coming.

He could feel it in his bones.

9
JADE

Teotihuacan, March 25

It had taken Jade several hours and countless phone calls to track his current location, but once she'd done so, making the necessary arrangements had been easy enough. The drive from Musari to Mallam Aminu Kano International Airport had only taken a couple of hours, and the flight to Mexico City had been surprisingly short, all things considered. Now here she was, speeding across the Mexican countryside less than twenty-four hours after watching what she believed to be an alien drone commit suicide by crocodile, rushing to meet a man who had no idea she was coming and likely had no desire to see her, anyway.

She hadn't so much as spoken to Cade Evans since she'd boarded a plane in Argentina six months ago, bound for anyplace warm and far from the nightmare in Antarctica, but she was certain he was the only one who would be able to help her make sense of her situation. While she had always been fiercely independent and went out of her way to prove it, there was a part of her that was tired of trying to do this on her own.

No one could possibly understand what she was going through, especially if she couldn't. Before she'd allowed herself to be manipulated into going to AREA 51 in the first place, everything in her life had been orderly and compartmentalized. She'd not only been at peace with her place in the universe, she'd genuinely believed herself to be the master of her own destiny. Nothing made sense now, and the process of trying to fit the pieces of her shattered worldview back together was driving her inexorably out of her mind. What troubled her most wasn't that she had tracked an alien being into the darkest depths of the African jungle, but the implications of having done so, which scared her nearly as much as the idea that she had somehow left herself vulnerable to the emotion of fear.

The green-and-white Volkswagen Beetle taxi dropped her off at the visitors' center, where she paid for admission and joined the tourists working their way through the claustrophobic stalls of the souvenir vendors, who shouted over each other in an attempt to sell what appeared to be variations of the same wares. She felt foolish rolling her travel suitcase behind her, but she hadn't really taken the time to think any of this through. Had she, undoubtedly she would have talked herself out of coming to Teotihuacan at all.

She'd expected Teotihuacan to be a remote archeological site like the Igbo bobbies in Nigeria, not a tourist trap within a day's walk of one of the largest cities on the face of the planet. Once she was inside the complex and the tourists fanned out, though, she could almost envision this sprawling primitive metropolis as it must have been in its prime. Unfortunately, everywhere she looked were the ruins of ancient structures that reminded her of those submerged at the bottom of the lake in Antarctica, especially the massive pyramid in the far distance ahead of her. It rose from the horizon at the end of the wide gray path against the backdrop of a mountain that looked like another, even larger pyramid.

The active excavation wasn't hard to find. It was right in the middle of the main path, cordoned off with wooden posts strung with chicken wire, and partially shielded from view by two construction trailers. Despite being covered with dirt from head to toe, Evans was recognizable the moment he climbed from the enormous hole in the ground, where it appeared as though the Earth had collapsed in upon itself.

He set a large wooden crate onto a stack with several others, looked up into the cloudless sky, and wiped the sweat from his brow with the back of his gloved hand. After a moment, he shielded his eyes from the sun and turned in her direction. She offered a halfhearted wave, although she wasn't sure he saw her until he did an almost comical double take and headed straight for her.

Evans passed through the flimsy gate and stopped several feet from her. He cocked his head and appraised her for several seconds before smirking, pulling off his gloves, and proffering his hand.

"Dr. Jade Liang," he said. "I didn't think I'd see you again so soon. Or, you know, ever again."

"This isn't a social call."

"Knowing you, it never is."

She wanted to let him have it for even insinuating that he knew her, or anything about her, but bit her tongue because he was right.

"Is there someplace we can go to talk?"

He inclined his chin toward the trailer to his right, through the windows of which she saw several kids who barely looked out of their teens organizing stacks of bones on long wooden tables.

"Hard to believe we were ever that young, isn't it?" Evans said.

"Speak for yourself," Jade said, despite having been thinking the exact same thing.

He took the handle of her suitcase without asking and rolled it toward the trailer.

"You coming or what?"

She followed him up a set of weathered wooden steps and into what could only be described as a sauna.

"Jade?"

She turned to see Anya Fleming striding toward her from the office at the back of the trailer with a beaming smile on her face, and felt an uncomfortable—and surprising—pang of jealousy. Jade internally kicked herself and made a mental note to figure out where that emotion was rooted and weed it out.

"Oh, my God," Anya said. "I can't believe you're here! Wait until you see what we found. You are *not* going to believe it. I mean, *you* probably would, of course, but it's still . . ." Her words trailed off. Jade watched the younger girl's expression run the gamut from excitement to curiosity to suspicion. "I'm not going back to Antarctica. Don't even think about asking. It's all I can do to get through a single day without what happened down there consuming my every waking thought."

"That's not why I'm here."

"Good," Anya said, but there was no hiding the wariness in her voice. "Then why *are* you here?"

Jade glanced at Evans, who sensed her discomfort and rescued her.

"Show her the remains," he said.

This time it was Jade's turn to blanch.

"Not *that* kind of remains." Anya giggled and lit up once more. "Just regular old human remains, although I'm sure you'd be proud of the way I pieced together the cause of death for this one."

She whirled and headed for the opposite side of the trailer, where the graduate students were lost in their work.

"I didn't expect to find her here with you," Jade said, and cringed at the way the words sounded to her own ears.

Evans cocked an eyebrow, but proceeded as though he hadn't noticed.

"She and I have been here since leaving Antarctica. You'd be amazed at what all we've found in these underground tunnels, which we might never have found had we not activated that pyramid."

"Aren't you going to ask me why I'm here?"

"I'm not entirely sure I want to know."

Anya assumed the head of the examination table, which was essentially a sheet of warped plywood with improvised wooden legs, and waved her hands over the bones spread out across it. They'd been arranged anatomically as though the skeleton were lying on its back, only flattened into two dimensions since the ribs were disarticulated and the skull rested on its base.

"Comminuted fracture of the mentum," Jade said. "Complete absence of the odontoid process of the second cervical vertebra. The fracture line suggests anterior blunt-force trauma."

"He fell onto his chin and broke his own neck," Anya said.

"That's what I just said."

"Yeah, well—"

"What about the linear scratches in the cortices of the ribs here, here, here, and . . . here?" Jade asked.

Anya crinkled her brow and walked around to the side of the table so she could better see what Jade was pointing at.

"Those scratches are on the undersides of the ribs."

"The ventral surface, technically. As are those on the second through fifth lumbar vertebra and the iliac wings of the pelvis." Jade made eye contact with Anya. "Are they not ritualistic, postmortem injuries?"

"Not like any I've ever seen."

"What do you mean?" Evans asked. He leaned over Jade's shoulder to get a better look.

"There's no sign of remodeling," Anya said.

"You hadn't noticed them?" Jade said.

"Give me a break. We only recovered them this morning."

"They should have been readily apparent from the moment you first saw them."

Jade saw the hurt on Anya's face, took a deep breath, and forced herself to step back from the situation. As one of the world's leading forensic anthropologists, she could read the COD of this individual in her sleep, but there were historical and cultural variables for which she couldn't account.

"What do you think could have caused these injuries?"

"You're asking me?" Anya said.

"If I were to wager a guess, I would attribute the markings to the activity of scavengers."

"The only scavengers down there are insects."

"Based upon the preponderance of adipocere, there can't be very many to leave so much flesh on the corpses."

"Then what else could have caused the scratches?"

"I don't know." The words sounded foreign coming out of Jade's mouth. "It almost appears as though something was trying to claw its way out."

Evans took her gently by the shoulder and turned her to face him. His eyes locked onto hers.

"Maybe now would be a good time to tell us why you're here."

10
KELLY

4 miles north of Salisbury

What in the world was she doing here? Maybe there was a point in time when she could have convinced herself that Roche's work was somehow an extension of her own, but the similarities had always been superficial at best. Sure, there had been some amazing coincidences between her work with standing waves and his with crop circle designs, especially when it came to combining their research to activate the ancient machine inside the pyramid. When it came right down to it, though, she was a graduate student in seismology and he was a . . . what was he?

There really was no name for what he did, at least not one she'd be willing to say to his face. Before she'd been dragged out of her comfortable life back in Oregon and into this mess, she'd have thought he was positively out of his mind. And now? She didn't know what she thought about him. All she knew was that she thought about him a lot.

From where she sat on the rocky knoll overlooking the crop circle, she could clearly see him pacing the design through the withered leaves of the onion plants. He thought it looked like a map, although from where she sat, it reminded her more of a maze. And there he was, the man in the maze, a symbol memorialized throughout the American Southwest and attributed to the Tohono O'odham people, for whom it represented their creation, their rise to the surface from the underworld.

She'd compared the design against every known sound waveform and hadn't found anything remotely close to a match. The lack of symmetry basically precluded one from the start, but she'd at least needed to try to find one or she never would have been able to justify her presence here in England, let alone the need to withdraw from her classes and travel halfway around the world to work with a man eight years older than her and who reminded her of the most traumatic episode of her life.

Roche caught her looking and waved. Despite the smile on his face, she could tell that the situation was eating him alive. He was a man who needed to know everything—to *understand* everything—and yet the more they learned, the less they knew. Unfortunately, they'd now crossed the line from the marginally scientific into the speculative, which meant that she either needed to pack up and head back home or abandon any pretense of professional collaboration.

Her left hand was fretting—as her mother had called it—so badly she could barely manipulate her fingers well enough to close the file with the photographs of the primitive machine a hundred feet below her and then the laptop itself. The nervous tic made her look like she was jamming out on an air guitar, unless she invested an absurd amount of concentration into making it stop. It was only when she closed her hand into a fist and really thought about it that she realized she couldn't recall another incident since the first morning Roche had been waiting for her outside of customs with a greasy paper bag full of croissants and an unguarded smile that betrayed the fact that he hadn't been entirely certain she was going to come. Which made it that much harder knowing that she was going to have to walk down the hill and tell him that she was leaving.

Kelly tucked her laptop into her backpack and slid it onto her shoulders as she stood. Professionally speaking, the diversion hadn't been a complete waste of time. She'd recognized the potential for the primitive machine and gathered as much information about it as she could. While it had been constructed to utilize the flow of running water to produce a single burst of electrical current strong enough to essentially cook a design through the earth and into the field above it, the same principles could be applied to the generation of waves from subterranean seismic events to produce a constant stream of renewable energy, easily enough to power entire cities for the foreseeable future. She'd mentioned the idea to Dr. Davis Walters, her graduate advisor. With neither her knowledge nor her consent, he'd taken it to Dr. Edward Parsons, the Dean of Oregon State, who was already her biggest fan thanks to the funds Hollis Richards had funneled into the university to secure her services in Antarctica. Dean Parsons had personally contacted her this morning to let her know that the university would be more than happy to fully fund her research—at the cost of the patent, of course—and that he'd already arranged for a plane ticket to be waiting for her at Heathrow.

She had to shove her hand into the pocket of her jacket as there was nothing she could do to stop it from doing its thing. Roche would recognize its significance, and he would understand what it meant. She knew what leaving was going to do to him, largely because she knew what it was going to do to her.

Kelly was halfway down the hill when she heard what at first sounded like thunder in the distance. It quickly resolved into the frenetic techno beat of a helicopter streaking across the plains from the south.

Roche obviously heard it, too. He stared in its direction with an expression on his face that she hadn't seen since Antarctica, one that reminded her that there was still so much about him she didn't know.

The helicopter drew contrast from the slate-gray sky, a sleek black dragonfly coming in far too low. She didn't need to have Roche's military experience to recognize that this wasn't an ordinary chopper. It reminded her at first of the Coast Guard MH-60 Jayhawk that had rushed her from Corvallis to Seaside in advance of the tsunami she'd predicted, only this one was obviously manufactured for speed. It was upon them before she even reached the bottom of the hill. It buzzed the upper canopy of the beech grove as it banked around the field and started its final approach.

Roche attempted to discreetly wave her back uphill, but he must have forgotten who he was dealing with. She was at his side when the Sikorsky UH-60 Black Hawk settled into the onion field maybe two hundred feet from where they stood. It looked like the same model that had rescued them from the research station in the Drygalski Mountains and ferried them to the *Aurora Borealis*—the repurposed Coast Guard icebreaker that served as the mobile base for the organization known as Unit 51—where she had spent several days recuperating from her injuries and sheer exhaustion before being debriefed and sent to Argentina to begin the long journey back home.

Cameron Barnett, who claimed to have been the silent partner of Hollis Richards, the reclusive billionaire who'd initially gathered them all at AREA 51, had made professional overtures toward her at the time. She thought she'd made her feelings on the matter of serving as a consultant crystal clear, especially to a group whose purpose he wouldn't explain until after she signed a stack of nondisclosure agreements. Apparently she was going to have to try harder this time.

The motor whined and the rotors ramped down, from uprooting and hurling organic debris in every direction to merely flattening it to the ground. A man emerged from the copilot's door, clutched his cap to his head, and ducked as he ran toward them.

Roche took her by the hand and used it to draw her partially behind him. Her left hand. Not even her mother held her left hand. She was so surprised that she allowed him to do so without protest.

The man pulled up several feet from them and raised his head so that they could see his face. While Kelly recognized it, she couldn't put a name to it. Like all the others on the *Aurora Borealis,* he wore his dark hair closely cropped and had the angular features and sharp eyes of a bird of prey. She didn't need to see his black fatigues or the red triple-inverted-triangle insignia on his shoulder to know he served under Barnett in Unit 51.

"I apologize for dropping in unannounced," he said, "but I'm afraid time is of the essence."

"What can we do for you, Special Agent Morgan?" Roche asked. His voice was hard and firm, almost as though he'd become another person.

"Very good, Mr. Roche. Always maintain the advantage by keeping a potential adversary off-guard."

"Is that what we are? Potential adversaries?"

"I'd like to think that's the furthest thing from the truth, and yet judging by the expression on your face, and that of Ms. Nolan, I would say that has yet to be determined. At least from your perspective. Mine? I come bearing more than an olive branch; I bring you an opportunity I think you'll find more than a little intriguing."

"You can just climb back into that helicopter of yours and head back to wherever it is you came from," Kelly said.

"But you haven't even heard my offer."

"We don't need to."

"You're in that big of a rush to get back to Oregon?"

Roche's grip loosened ever so slightly, although he made no outward display of his surprise. Or his hurt.

"Don't worry," Morgan said. "We already made arrangements with Dean Parsons to secure your services."

"He doesn't own me," Kelly said. "And he definitely doesn't have the right to pimp me out."

"You should probably take that up with him. I don't think he shares your viewpoint."

"We're done here," Roche said.

"Let me show you what I have to offer, and if you still aren't interested, I'll get back in the chopper and you'll never see me again."

"I don't believe that for a second."

Morgan smiled. The expression was genuine, and yet didn't appear at home on his face.

"I wouldn't either." He reached into the breast pocket of his black jacket, removed a folded piece of paper, and handed it to Roche. "I'll be waiting in the chopper."

Without another word, he turned and struck off across the field.

Roche released Kelly's hand and unfolded the piece of paper. It was printed on thick stock, the kind used for photographs to retain the quality and resolution of the image. On it was what appeared to be a sheet of reinforced glass, only Kelly couldn't be entirely sure since there was nothing but darkness on the other side. A design had been painted onto it using an odd spectrum of colors, which she could tell represented a thermal gradient.

The design was exactly the same as the crop circle they stood in at that very moment.

"You know where this leads, don't you?" Kelly said.

The motor screamed as the rotors accelerated, buffeting Morgan as he fought to open the door and climb inside.

"Go back home," Roche said. "I'll let you know what I find."

He handed her the photograph and stared across the field toward the helicopter. He gave her an awkward hug, braced himself against the violent wind, and walked away from her.

Kelly looked at the picture. Her hand was fretting so badly she lost her grip and the printout blew away.

"Wait," she said in a voice so small that even she couldn't hear it.

She ran toward the helicopter and caught up with Roche before he reached the sliding door. This time she took his hand, and together they climbed into the chopper.

11
EVANS

Teotihuacan

Jade's appearance at the site had rattled Evans. It wasn't so much the fact that she was there as much as the timing of her arrival. He couldn't shake the feeling that her showing up on the same day they discovered the bodies wasn't entirely coincidental, but, for the life of him, he couldn't imagine how they could possibly be related. Worse, now he had to figure out what he was going to do with her. She wasn't the easiest person to get along with. He couldn't deny they shared chemistry, but half of the time it was the kind that made him want to strangle her.

They walked while she told them about what she'd seen in Nigeria. Evans had needed the air—he'd felt as though he were being cooked alive in that trailer—and Jade hadn't wanted to say anything in front of the graduate students. At first, she seemed reluctant to even talk with Anya around, but Evans was grateful the younger woman was there. With all of her talk and the many questions she asked, it bought him some time to think.

"You're certain it was a drone," Anya said.

"Were you not listening?" Jade said.

"I mean, versus whatever we want to call them. Originals. The F1 generation. Full-blooded aliens like Dale Rubley."

"Please don't say it like that."

"Why not?"

"It sounds absurd."

"More absurd than this thing wading into a river filled with crocodiles to get away from you?"

Evans opened his mouth, but Jade shut him down.

"Not a word out of you."

He smirked and looked out across the ruins. The dirt path cut a winding course through green fields positively crawling with black-and-white-striped iguanas that sprinted for their underground burrows as they approached. The walls of the *Cuidadela*—the Citadel—flirted in and out through the branches of the tree-yuccas and pepper trees.

"Tell me again what it said to you," Evans said.

"It said 'We know you.'"

"You're sure it said 'we'?"

"Are you questioning my memory or my integrity?" Jade asked.

"Neither. I'm just trying to make sense of it."

Jade sighed.

"Sorry."

"And after that?" Evans asked.

"'We still live.'"

"Jesus," Anya said. "That can't be right. I saw it get shot."

"We all did," Evans said. "And even if it didn't die, how in the world do you propose to find it? And for what possible reason?"

"To release it," Jade said.

"It can't still be alive, can it?" Anya said.

"Even if it is," Evans said. "I think we can all agree that none of us is in any hurry to see it again."

Evans led Jade and Anya through the trees. The walls of the Citadel rose above them. They were roughly thirty feet tall, a hundred feet thick, and a quarter mile to a side, enclosing a giant square large enough to accommodate the entire population of the ancient mecca. The fortifications were easily strong enough to withstand a siege of historical proportions, although who possessed an army ferocious enough to wage that manner of war was a matter of speculation.

The three of them ascended the lone set of stone stairs on the northern wall and stared down upon the massive courtyard. The Temple of the Feathered Serpent was offset to the far eastern side, opposite the main entrance from the Avenue of the Dead to the west, and surrounded to either side by the rubble of buildings believed to have housed administrative offices. The temple was actually a pyramid, although it had fallen to ruin, with the majority of the seven-tiered structure persevering as little more than a rounded mountain of stones. Only the very front of it had been preserved by the construction of the four-tiered Adosada platform, which shielded the ornate sculptures from time and the abrasive elements. The sculpted heads of Quetzalcoatl and Tlaloc, the fanged god of storms, protruded from bas-reliefs featuring the undulating bodies of plumed snakes. With the exception of a ceremonial stone platform set midway between the entrance and the Adosada, the remainder of the vast enclosure consisted of little more than flat, bare earth, where Villarreal stood in the shade of a hastily erected canopy tent, facing a row of laptop computers balanced on a padded gray storage case.

A handful of graduate students walked slowly back and forth through the field in a grid-like pattern. Some pushed ground-penetrating radar units that looked like lawnmowers with bicycle wheels, while others carried magnetometers reminiscent of football goalposts made of PVC pipes.

Villarreal shielded his eyes from the sun and watched Anya, Evans, and Jade descend the inner staircase from the wall before walking across the courtyard to meet them. Evans had worked with the archeologist off and on since his arrival six months ago, but had never really been able to get a good read on him. All of the researchers at Teotihuacan maintained a measure of autonomy, and yet Villarreal always seemed to have a hand in whatever he was doing. He could easily chalk it up to Villarreal taking an interest in Anya, for whom Evans felt an almost paternal attachment. Maybe that was the reason he couldn't seem to bring himself to embrace Villarreal's involvement in everything they did. Then again, it was also possible that he simply didn't like him, which was his instinctive reaction to those he perceived as his competition in the field.

"Come, come!" Villarreal said. "You must see this!"

The moment the archeologist recognized the dead man's carving as a feathered serpent from which the tree of life grew, he'd rushed off to gather the equipment and the personnel he needed to play a hunch he hadn't been willing to share with any of them. At least until he summoned them from the trailer, which undoubtedly meant he was seconds away from telling them just how right he'd been.

"What did you find?" Anya asked.

"The tree of life traditionally grows from the body of the Great Goddess, from whom all life is believed to have originated. The archetype of the tree of life, or the world tree, spans countless religions from around the world and serves as a bridge between the heavens in its branches and the underworld through its roots. I theorized that its usage in conjunction with the visage of Quetzalcoatl was less metaphorical than it was literal. And I was right."

Villarreal guided them beneath the canopy and gestured toward the computers, which had been turned in such a way that the sun didn't wash out the screens. He offered each of them a bottle of water from a portable cooler and introduced himself to Jade, really playing up that whole Antonio Banderas thing he had going for him, much to Anya's chagrin.

Evans looked from one monitor to the next, and then to the graduate students dripping with sweat as they marched the remote sensing devices through the courtyard. He took a long drink of the lukewarm water and rolled the bottle along the back of his neck, for all the good it did him.

"How did we not find this before now?" Evans asked.

"Because until recently it was not filled with water," Villarreal said.

Jade leaned in front of them and looked from one monitor to the next.

"What am I supposed to be seeing? This one over here looks kind of like an ultrasound."

"That's essentially what it is," Anya said. "In much the same way that an ultrasound shows a cross-section of anatomy in depth, like the different layers of skin and muscle, the ground-penetrating radar shows the layers of earth beneath your feet."

"It works by firing high-frequency radio waves straight down into the ground," Evans said. "The boundaries between the different layers of strata cause those waves to refract in any number of directions. Those that reflect back to the surface are collected and used to form an image like this one, which demonstrates the transition between the various layers of topsoil and the underlying limestone."

"So these peaks in the horizontal bands correspond to significant differences in density, like between top-soil and rocks," Jade said.

"Right," Anya said. "That's exactly what we look for when we're searching for ancient burials. Human remains and grave goods will cause the same kind of spikes in the data stream."

"The inherent flaw with the system is that it's limited by the nature of the strata," Evans said. "Radio waves are a form of electromagnetic radiation, and as such are subject to the same physical laws of conductivity. Most types of rock are naturally resistive, so the radio waves have to fight against them the entire time, which limits the maximum depth we can image to less than fifty feet, at the very most, but if you look at the label on the Y-axis, you can see that right here we're able to go all the way down to a hundred feet in places because—"

"Water naturally conducts electricity," Jade finished for him.

"The magnetometer is fairly similar," Anya said, "only rather than interpreting depth, it records spatial variations in the Earth's magnetic field caused by different types of materials."

"Like an MRI," Jade said.

"Exactly, but instead of creating pictures based upon the inherent differences between tissues, this allows us to see materials we wouldn't ordinarily think of as magnetic."

"You can use it to find buried archeological features," Evans said. "Like clay or brick. Decayed organic matter. Even burned topsoil from a campfire extinguished thousands of years ago. But because of the relatively small differences in magnetic properties, its effective resolution is generally limited to what we call near-surface phenomena, unless you have a distinct demarcation in the strata."

"Or, as in this case, the strata is moving," Anya said through an enormous smile.

Jade stood in front of the third monitor for several seconds before looking back at Evans.

"So when you combine them you're able to create a map of subterranean features."

"Kind of an oversimplification," Evans said, "but yeah. That's what you're looking at."

"That's not a natural formation," Jade said.

"No, it's not." Evans stared at the image on the screen and what had to be several thousand feet of narrow tunnels beneath their feet. "It's a maze."

12
TESS

The Cage, FOB Atlantis

Tess had been watching Subject Z for so long now that she felt as though she could intuit its mood from its behavior. Or at least she'd thought so until today. Something had changed in its demeanor since it reacted to Director Barnett's question by smearing the pig's blood on the window, something that made her believe that everything it had done up until this point was essentially a grand performance for their benefit. All of the notes she'd taken, the correlations she'd made, the research she'd done . . . it was all for naught. The more she thought about it, the more she realized that the creature had been in control of the situation since the very beginning and not, as she'd foolishly believed, the other way around.

Of course, she wasn't about to let it know that she'd caught on to its ruse. She'd gained a minuscule advantage, one she was certain wouldn't last very long and needed to be exploited, but she had to be careful. She had to proceed as though nothing had changed, although with the way its thermal representation stared at her through the monitor—as though it could not only see her, but inside of her—made her wonder if it couldn't do just that.

Ordinarily, it spent the better part of the day using the long bones scavenged from its meals to carve petroglyphs into the walls, seemingly lost in its work, between episodes of pacing like a caged tiger. She'd studied the pictures of the dens in Egypt and the cavern miles above her head and had simply assumed that it was in the process of creating the same thing down here. Perhaps that was what it wanted her to think. For the last eight hours, however, it had done little more than crouch with its knees drawn to its chest on the far side of the cavern, hidden behind the stacked remains of its meals. It had only risen twice, both times to defecate in the corner. The way it sat now, so silent and still and yet undeniably sentient, she realized that something fundamental had changed inside of it. If it had been toying with them before, what was it doing now?

Tess tucked her hair behind her ears, leaned forward, and pressed the button to activate the speaker. A clicking sound echoed from inside the chamber.

Subject Z inclined its head toward the sound. It waited expectantly for several seconds before lowering its head once more.

Tess wasn't sure exactly what she intended to say. It had demonstrated a willingness to communicate with them, if only on its own terms. She wasn't about to let it slam that door in her face, especially not when she thought she just might know a way in.

"You're not in there because he's afraid of you," she said. "You know that, right? You're in there because he's mad at you."

The creature cocked its head and a dark slash appeared on its face where its warm lips peeled away from its teeth and formed a hideous smile.

"You're in there because of what you did to his friend."

Uhr-uhr-uhr-uhr-uhr-uh.

She'd heard recordings of that sound from inside the demolished research station during the bloodbath six months ago, but until now had been unable to elicit the response through the course of her work.

"But you already knew that, didn't you?"

It cocked its head in a way that reminded her of Seldon, her childhood cat, and the way he would look at the balls of yarn in her mother's sewing basket before swatting one onto the floor to play with it.

"You even know where Hollis Richards is, don't you? That's the ace up your sleeve. I should tell you, though. Whatever leverage you think that gives you is worth somewhere between jack and squat. As far as the director's concerned, his friend is already dead and you *will* die and rot in there."

Uhr-uhr-uhr-uhr-uhr-uh.

Goosebumps raced up the backs of her arms. The intonation of the sound was different, almost as though it were attempting to communicate a different emotional response using the same basic phonemes.

It rose from its haunches and crossed the cavern in strangely coordinated, halting movements. It had broken the tips from a row of stalagmites and used the stumps like stepstools so it could better reach the wall where it was currently working on the masterpiece it refused to let them see. Whatever part of it had once been human was now long gone. Even the subtlest unconscious movements were alien, almost as though its body were somehow affected differently by the laws of gravity and inertia. Its elongated cranium appeared too bulbous and heavy for its slender frame, necessitating a hunched posture, sharper curvature of its neck, and a means of locomotion that reminded her of skating, as though it sat backward into its haunches and flexed its knees to keep its center of gravity aligned with its pelvis and ankles. It balanced on the balls of its feet as though wearing invisible heels and sharpened the broken tip of a pig's femur on a rough patch of rock, generating a faint bluish glow.

A bolt of inspiration struck Tess. She accessed the digital memory of the system, highlighted the pixels corresponding to the shade of blue produced by the friction of the bone against the stone, and reset the thermal gradient window to that value, plus or minus three degrees. The resulting image showed everything below 86.3 degrees as black and everything above it as white, essentially washing out all detail and leaving only the bright shape of the creature against a seamless black backdrop. She then programmed the system to gather all data within that thermal range since its inception and plot it simultaneously.

"Does it make you mad?" she asked. "Knowing that you're at the director's mercy?"

"As . . . you . . . are . . . at . . . ours?"

Its voice was deep and resonated from inside the chamber. The manner in which it spoke reminded her of trying to play a record backward.

Tess gasped and released the button. Her heart was beating so hard and fast that she could barely breathe, let alone think straight. She concentrated on staving off the onset of hyperventilation and focused on slowing her racing thoughts. Her hand still trembled when she pressed the button again, but her voice came out sounding a whole lot more confident than she felt.

"Is that what you believe? Don't think for a moment that I'm impressed by this whole caged-animal act. I have a hunch you genuinely think that you're only in there because you allow yourself to be, that you could get out of there any time you wanted."

It swiveled until it faced the window between them. The way it perched on the broken speleothem made it look like a gargoyle on a parapet.

"I see the way you attack your meals when you know we're watching, but I also see how you consume them when you think we're suitably impressed by your aggression."

It cocked its conical skull first one way, then the other. She'd gotten it to speak once. She had to figure out how to do so again. Perhaps her mistake from the start had been to appeal to its intellect, to attempt to draw it into conversation, rather than appealing to its base emotions.

"You want us to think of you as an animal because you believe that gives you the upper hand. You want us to underestimate you, to unconsciously concede any advantage that in reality you don't possess. You've overestimated your worth to this project. You're a curiosity at best, a cosmic parasite of no more importance in the grand design than a cockroach—"

It moved with such speed that its thermal signature was a blur.

Thud.

The steel door shuddered.

Tess threw herself backward from the console so quickly that she toppled her chair and nearly tripped over it.

The impact momentarily staggered the creature. The thermal camera directed at the interior door showed an animal at the mercy of its savagery, beating and slashing at the barrier with such ferocity that it opened fresh wounds from its knuckles and nails. The smears glowed orange against the black door.

Thuck.

It struck the door with its forehead so hard that it stumbled backward, lost its balance, and landed squarely on its rear end. Ribbons of blood unspooled from an ugly gash and dribbled over the prominent ridge of its brow, down its gaunt cheeks, and swelled from the tip of its peaked nose.

Uhr-uhr-uhr-uhr-uhr-uh.

Droplets of blood burst from its mouth as it issued the horrible sound.

After several long, silent moments, its chest deflated and it gingerly pushed itself back to its feet, stumbled forward, and pressed its forehead to the glass as though in an effort to see her. The blood on its face formed a ghostly orange image on the monitor. It reached up to the window and smeared the blood with its long fingers until it obscured the glass so she couldn't see inside.

An image appeared on the main monitor, signifying the completion of the task she'd programmed. It looked like thousands of blue lines drawn in every direction without any rhyme or reason. They cut through countless spectral white blobs, which overlapped one another like so many sunspots.

She righted her chair, took a seat, and instructed the

program to eliminate all points of data corresponding to thermal signatures greater than 89 degrees, which purged the white shapes from the screen. From there, all she had to do was digitally subtract the points of data generated in three-dimensional space that didn't coincide with the wall and strokes that weren't of overlapping nature and . . . voilà . . . she was left with a digital re-creation of what the creature had been carving into the limestone.

"Well, what do you know?" she whispered.

She removed the transceiver from the charger on her console and pressed the button to speak. A crackle of static from the open line echoed from the tunnel behind her.

"I need Barnett down here," she said. "Right away. Tell him I think I've found—"

Thud.

She flinched at the sound and dropped the transceiver. She could see the creature on the monitor, its hands to either side of the window and its face flattened to the glass.

"The . . . serpent . . . god . . . will . . . rise . . . from . . . the . . . dead . . . and . . . consume . . . you . . . all."

"Serpent god?" she said, but she knew it couldn't hear her.

It turned, walked to the rear of the cavern, and once more crouched in the same position as it had most of the day. Blood dripped from its forehead like the first drops of rain ahead of the coming storm.

"None . . . of . . . you . . . will . . . survive."

13
BARNETT

Uncharted, FOB Atlantis

"You're certain it's him," Barnett said.

"You tell me," Dr. Desmond Bly said. "I'm not entirely convinced it's even human."

The tunnel was barely wider than Barnett's shoulders. He wouldn't have ordinarily considered himself claustrophobic, but he'd never contemplated the idea of deliberately wedging himself into a crevice from which he wasn't certain he could be extricated. It wasn't what he thought of as a rational course of action. Of course, Bly wasn't necessarily known for being rational, which was what had drawn Barnett to him in the first place. He needed someone completely lacking in fear to explore some of these passages, where even the remote drones seemed hesitant to go.

"How much farther?" Moira asked from somewhere behind him.

"Another thirty meters," Bly called back.

Barnett was annoyed by the American's use of the metric measurement, but elected to say nothing since the distance sounded much shorter than a hundred feet, which he couldn't help converting to fifteen body lengths. With his arms pressed against the sides of his head and neck, he felt as though he were beginning to slowly asphyxiate. It took all of his concentration to focus on his movements.

Push with his toes; pull with his fingers.

Push with his toes; pull with his fingers.

The light mounted to the front of his helmet illuminated the limestone directly beneath his face. It was smooth and hard, yet looked almost like wax. The scratches were new and identical to those they'd seen in the ice cave. The trail of dried blood flaked with the slightest contact.

"How could anything drag someone my size through here without his active participation?" Barnett asked.

"You'd be amazed how pliable the human body becomes when even the unconscious control of skeletal muscles is suspended," Moira said. "I once worked a case where they found a teenager's remains wedged into a culvert barely larger than my thigh."

"Delightful," Barnett said, and again returned his concentration to the mere act of moving himself in maddeningly small increments while staving off the not-entirely-irrational fear that any single inhalation could broaden his thorax to the point of becoming stuck.

How Bly had even discovered this passage was beyond him. It wasn't on any of the sounding maps and they were nearly a half-mile diagonally into the mountain from where they'd found Jonas's body. He would have to see that more drones were dispatched into

these warrens or they might never find where Hollis
Richards had gone. As it was, with a six-month head
start, he could have found his way onto any number of
seafaring vessels that could have taken him to any port
around the globe. In many ways, Richards had been
like a father to him while his own had been traveling
the world investigating strange and troubling phenomena he hoped would one day help him solve the mystery of his own grandfather's death, mere miles away
inside the remote Nazi communications station. While
Barnett had agreed not to intervene in the events inside
AREA 51 that culminated in Richards's transformation, he owed it to him to put him out of his misery.

Barnett felt a sudden influx of cool, stale air against
his face when Bly crawled from the tunnel ahead of
him. With it came a stench that nearly relieved Barnett
of the breakfast he'd been eating when Bly tracked
him down in the command center. He did his best to
breathe through his mouth as he squeezed from the orifice, rolled onto his back, and used his arms to push off
against the bare stone. The return of the flow of blood
to his little fingers assailed him with pins and needles.

He crouched, covered his mouth and nose with his
hand, and took in his surroundings. The cavern was
maybe the size of a backyard shed and not quite tall
enough for him to stand fully erect. The stalactites
forced him to crawl and cast moving shadows from his
headlamp across the smooth walls.

The remains were suspended from the stalactites in
the middle of the chamber by a crisp brownish substance that reminded Barnett of the casing of a praying
mantis' egg sac. It deteriorated with the slightest touch

and fell to the mess on the ground like ashes. The puddle of blood was dry and congealed with chunks of flesh and bone that had leaked through the bottom of the cocoon-like casing, which was black and distended with more of the same.

Moira crawled from the egress behind him and nudged him out of her way. The flash from her camera strobed throughout the chamber, turning night to day and back again, as she captured the scene from all angles. She spoke into the recording device clipped to the collar of her jacket as she examined the body.

"The remains are completely bound and immobilized. Enclosed by some sort of fibrous, teardrop-shaped sling. Connected to the ceiling and the surrounding stalactites in a fashion reminiscent of—Jesus—a spider's web."

Barnett tilted his head and shined his light toward where she was looking. There was no other way to describe it. He revised his initial impression from a mantis's egg sac to a paper wasp's nest. Or maybe the nest of a cave swallow. There were distinct similarities to both.

"Fetal position, breech, head up and between its knees," Moira continued. "The skull is consistent in size and shape with *Homo sapiens sapiens*, which apparently needs to be specified down here. There is minimal residual soft tissue. Perhaps a swatch of desiccated scalp with either dark brown or black hair. An estimated ninety percent of the remains are concealed from view by unknown organic material, thus limiting structural evaluation."

"Is it Berkeley?" Barnett asked.

"Your eyes work as well as mine. You tell me."

Barnett had hoped she'd recognized something that he hadn't, because from where he stood, all he could see was a skull—red with dried blood and misshapen by tendons and connective tissue—that could have belonged to anyone. There were no identifying features, at least none that he could clearly see without doing what he dreaded doing next.

"Do you have all of the pictures you need?" he asked.

"I believe so. Why—?"

Before she could even finish her question, he had his knife in his hand and with a flick of his wrist slashed through the bottom of the sling. The remains sloshed to the ground in a rush of partially congealed blood and bodily dissolution.

Barnett scooted back, but not fast enough to keep it from flowing over his hands and covering the knees of his pants.

"That's my cue," Bly said from behind him. He was little more than a mole-like silhouette squirming into the Earth by the time Barnett turned around.

"You could have given me some warning," Moira said.

"Whatever did this to him is still down here. I kind of thought you might want to expedite the process to make sure you weren't still here if it decided to come back."

"When you put it like that . . ."

Barnett tugged at the torn sling and ripped off a piece with a sound like tearing carpet. The tensile strength was phenomenal in the direction parallel to the fibrous strands, and yet it peeled apart without much effort at all.

"What do you make of this?" he asked.

"They look like some sort of collagen bands, but without a microscope, all I can do is guess."

She knelt before the remains and traced them with her headlamp. The bones had remained articulated, largely because of the tendons and ligaments that had yet to decompose. Several had snapped upon impact, leaving the body partially splayed on its side, its appendages bent at unnatural angles. The victim's fatigues were tattered and sopping with blood, but there was enough left of the insignia on the left breast pocket to identify him as a member of the Exploration Division.

"It's Berkeley."

Not that there had ever really been any doubt, but confirming the body belonged to a man they knew was missing was vastly preferable to determining it belonged to someone they had yet to discover had vanished.

"Look at this," Moira said. "Right there. On his rib cage. Linear scratches. Here, here, and here."

"That's not the cause of death, though."

"No." She shined her light on the exposed cervical vertebrae beneath Berkeley's chin. "That is."

It looked like the bones had been repeatedly clamped in a vise until they shattered, leaving the tendons, connective tissue, and shriveled blood vessels to hold them together.

"Ouch," Barnett said.

"And then some."

"So what's the significance?"

"Of the scratches in the bone? They were inflicted

postmortem. Not even the slightest evidence of attempted healing. Same with these on his iliac crests down here, and even up here on his zygomatic arch and frontal bone."

"Apparently you're going to have to explain it to me," Barnett said.

"We found him balled up inside that . . . whatever that is. Picture him with his legs drawn to his chest and his head between his knees."

He stared at the carcass for several seconds.

"Oh, for heaven's sake," she said, and used her gloved hands to fold the remains back into fetal position. "Can you see it now?"

Barnett nodded. The scratches formed a straight line that connected its pelvis, chest, and the side of its face and forehead, almost as though something had crawled in there with him. Or, if the apparent direction of the scratches was to be believed, crawled out.

A buzzing sound materialized from the silence, followed momentarily by a faint red glow from the tunnel through which Bly had disappeared. Barnett recognized it as one of the drones they used to explore the tunnels. It had parallel treads like a tank, a circle of infrared LED lights mounted around a night-vision camera, and held a handwritten note in the clamp at the end of its remote-controlled armature.

Barnett read the note, crumpled it, and shoved it into his pocket.

"I assume you can handle this from here," he said.

"If you're asking if I'll be okay without someone jabbing the remains with a knife and ruining my work, I'll find a way to get by."

Barnett dove into the hole and followed the drone as fast as he possibly could. He'd known that he would likely be outside the range of their communications devices, but hadn't even considered the possibility that this would be the moment Dr. Clarke would choose to make the breakthrough he was beginning to think might never come.

BOOK II

*There are no beautiful surfaces without
a terrible depth.*
—FRIEDRICH NIETZSCHE

14
ROCHE

Surface Access Platform,
2 vertical miles above FOB Atlantis,
March 26

"**W**hat are we doing here?" Kelly whispered.

Roche could only shake his head. He'd been wondering the exact same thing.

Everything that had transpired since leaving the onion field in Wiltshire that morning was one big blur. Being hustled from the Black Hawk to the waiting Cessna Citation X private plane on the tarmac at Heathrow. Lifting off before they were even in their seats. Streaking through the sky without so much as a word of explanation from Morgan, whose only advice had been to get some sleep because they were going to need it. Landing on a dirt airstrip somewhere in Africa, as best as he could tell, and returning to the sky the moment the plane was refueled.

A Bell V-280 Valor tiltrotor aircraft had been waiting for them in Johannesburg and ferried them over the Southern Ocean, upon which they watched the ice-

bergs become increasingly prevalent with a growing
sense of dread, to the *Aurora Borealis*. The repurposed
Coast Guard icebreaker had been invisible through the
blowing snow and frozen in a solid sheet of ice. They'd
been rushed inside for a quick meal and an even quicker
bathroom break while the combination helicopter/air-
plane was refueled before heading inland through a
storm that made the one they remembered from six
months ago seem like nothing.

The winds had battered the aircraft, tossing it
around like a child's toy to the point that Roche's fingers hurt from gripping the arms of his seat so hard.
The front windshield had been opaque with ice and assaulted with snowflakes the size of moths, and yet
somehow the pilot had navigated them to an elevated
platform framed by flashing lights. He'd made reference to the ruins of AREA 51, high above them in the
jagged black mountains drifting in and out of the blowing snow, but when Kelly replied that she couldn't see
them he'd laughed and said that the only remnants they
were likely to find now were buried in the snow below
them.

The landing platform served as little more than a
raised foundation for a power station that looked large
enough to service an entire town. The racket from the
generators had been deafening and provided a constant
thrum that vibrated the ground beneath their feet.
They'd been rushed past men in full arctic gear without introduction, through mazes of pipes as thick as
tree trunks, and to an elevator suspended above a shaft
seemingly without bottom.

Kelly had clung to Roche's hand the entire time.
The physical contact had served to help him focus on

the situation and distract him from the sheer insanity of what they were doing. Never in a million years would he have thought he'd be anywhere near this godforsaken continent ever again, let alone riding an elevator into its depths with a man in black fatigues who seemed to draw immense pleasure from making him work to drag even the most trivial information out of him. Morgan seemed to think he knew everything there was to know about him, but he couldn't possibly have the slightest clue about the countless hours Roche had invested during the last six months into training himself to make sure he would never find himself in a position outside of his direct control ever again.

Despite the fact that they were traveling at a rate of speed just shy of free fall in a cage that would crumple like an aluminum can upon impact from any significant height, it was a welcome upgrade from the racket of machinery and the wicked elements.

Morgan piloted the elevator from inside the command console cutout, which offered a view of the entire shaft, obstructed only by the elevator to his right and the floor beneath his feet. The inset video monitor featured the view from a camera mounted to the bottom of the car. The perspective was disorienting.

"You look cold, Ms. Nolan," Morgan said. "We took the liberty of packing a balaclava with your supplies."

He nodded to the matching duffel bags his man Stevens had tossed into the elevator before watching them descend into the Earth.

Kelly shook her head and somehow managed a smile of gratitude.

"I'd just forgotten how cold it was here," she said. "Or maybe repressed is a better word."

The fur fringe of the arctic parka tickled her ear, judging by the way she rubbed at it with her shoulder, but she kept her left hand firmly in her pocket. Roche could only imagine how hard she had to work to keep her fingers balled into a fist.

"What's waiting for us down below?" Roche asked.

"The same thing as before," Morgan said. "With maybe a few minor alterations."

The faint smirk at the edges of the man's lips told Roche everything he needed to know.

"You still haven't told us why we're here," Kelly said. "I mean, really told us. I get that the picture you showed us is identical to the crop circle, but you could have just as easily handled all of this via Skype."

"Unit 51 is not known for half-measures, Ms. Nolan."

"Then what is it known for?" Roche asked. "It doesn't seem to me like anyone knows about it at all."

"You must be losing your touch, Mr. Roche, because I assure you that not only are people well aware of our existence, we've developed something of a reputation."

"For doing what?"

"I suppose you'll find out soon enough."

Roche saw a twinkle of amusement in the man's eye, but his face remained impassive. He was in no mood for games. He had thought that once they boarded the plane and passed the point of no return that information would be readily forthcoming, and yet here they were plummeting into a situation beyond his reckoning, and he had long since exhausted his patience. Granted, he had gathered far more information about Morgan and Unit 51 than he let on, but at the same time, it was staggering how little of any real substance he had learned.

Like Barnett had told them, the organization was funded by Hollis Richards—or, more accurately, his estate—but that only accounted for a portion of its budget. Even Roche hadn't been able to cut his way through the web of secrecy surrounding the organization, which, he supposed, was probably answer enough in itself. Why the government was funding a clandestine paramilitary unit whose primary mission seemed to be to investigate ancient alien phenomena was the real question, with the answer being of no small consequence.

Roche watched Morgan from the corner of his eye as the walls raced past behind him through the wire cage. Where the shaft beneath AREA 51 had been composed of solid ice, this one was reinforced with what almost looked like a seamless steel pipe, from which the overhead lights on the car reflected like so many shooting stars. They couldn't make the shaft solid enough for his tastes, not after he'd barely escaped the last one with his life.

He allowed his breathing rate to accelerate and made sure Morgan noticed. The other man needed to feel as though he were in complete command of the situation.

"The shaft isn't the only upgrade, as you'll see soon enough."

Maybe Roche was being overly paranoid, but he could no more ignore his training than he could his intuition. Something was extremely wrong here—he and

Kelly wouldn't be here if there wasn't—and the time had come to figure out what that was.

Roche discreetly reached behind him and transferred Kelly's hand to the rail.

"Did you send for any of the others?" Roche asked.

He looped his arm around Kelly's waist in a gesture he hoped appeared intimate and eased her left hand from her coat pocket. Closed it around the rail, too. Hoped she took the hint and held on tight.

"It's eating you alive, isn't it?" Morgan said.

"What is?" Roche asked. He fixed the control panel in his peripheral vision and transferred his weight to his left foot.

"The not knowing."

"I've made my peace with it."

"You're so full of crap. You and I are the same. Of course, if I were in your situation, I would have found a way to interrogate me before we were even halfway down."

"Are we halfway down?"

"More than. It only takes sixteen minutes and it's already been . . ." Morgan glanced at his watch. "Thirteen—"

Roche seized the opportunity and kicked the emergency stop button with his right foot.

The cage screeched as the brakes bit into the rails, showering them with sparks.

A klaxon blared.

Roche used the console for leverage and launched himself at Morgan, whose eyes widened in recognition a heartbeat before Roche hammered him into the wall.

Kelly screamed and sidestepped the fracas.

Roche pivoted his hips and came down on top of Morgan. Wrapped his legs around the other man's midsection. Maneuvered his head and arm into a sleeper hold.

"Now listen to me very closely," Roche said, and tightened his grip until Morgan stopped struggling. "You're going to tell us exactly what to expect when we reach the bottom or so help me—"

"S'o-lyve," Morgan grunted.

"What?"

"Iss o-lyve."

Roche loosened his grip, and Morgan bucked him off. Roche took an elbow to the chin and was on his rear end before he recognized his mistake.

"Goddammit!" Morgan gasped. His entire head was as red as a tomato, and he was panting hard.

Roche dabbed the blood from his lip, wiped it on his pants, and stood over Morgan. He'd caught the larger man by surprise the first time, but he was prepared to do it again if he had to.

Kelly gently placed her hand on his forearm and lowered his fist to his side.

When he looked at her, he saw something in her expression that he prayed never to see there again.

"He said 'It's alive,'" she whispered.

Her words hit him harder than any blow Morgan could have landed. He staggered backward and looked from Kelly to Morgan, who straightened his jacket and rose to his feet once more.

Roche felt a confusion of emotions play out on his face. He looked back and forth between them for several seconds before pressing the button to restart the elevator.

The alarm ceased and the whine of the motor resumed. The car accelerated to full speed and the walls once more raced past.

"It can't be," Roche said.

Morgan rubbed his throat. Rolled his head on his shoulders.

"I underestimated you," he said. "It won't happen again."

"Don't make me regret letting you breathe," Roche said.

"We saw it get shot," Kelly said.

"It survived," Morgan said.

"And you allowed it to get away?"

"Not exactly."

"What do you mean, 'not exactly'?"

The elevator slowed and a blinding light appeared from below them. The steel pipe opened and granted them their first glimpse of a world they thought they'd never see again.

"He means it's down here," Roche said.

He leaned against the cage, curled his fingers between the links, and rested his forehead against the wall. The lake that had been there before was gone, but the pyramid and the surrounding buildings remained, cleared of debris and out in the open, an entire ancient civilization laid bare before them.

"We need your help," Morgan said.

Something in his voice caused Roche to turn and look him directly in the eyes.

"What's going on?" he asked.

"That's just it. We don't know."

"And what makes you think we can help you?"

The elevator settled to the ground. Morgan unlatched the door, opened it onto a lighted concrete platform, and struck off toward the stairs leading down to a network of boardwalks. His voice carried back over his shoulder.

"Because it asked for you."

15
ANYA

Teotihuacan

If they were right about it being a maze, then it had to have both a beginning and an end, but that end didn't necessarily mean a way out. Perhaps that end was at the very middle. There was simply no way to tell for sure based on the sounding maps they were able to generate. The fact that the tunnels had been dry for so long before the sudden influx of water meant they were inherently unstable. Already they were undergoing unpredictable deterioration caused by erosion, and boring a hole straight down into them could potentially collapse the entire Citadel complex, which meant that if they wanted to find a way to explore the maze, they were going to have to find the entrance.

They could only assume that for there to be water inside, the source had to be distinct from the one that fed the San Juan River, or else they would have detected a corresponding change in its level six months ago. Hydrogeological maps proved to be of little use. Teotihuacan was located within what was known as the Valley of Mexico, a vast area of land contained by volcanic hills

and mountain ranges. The ground was composed of
layers of alluvial sediment and volcanic deposits inter-
stratified with basalt, which served to contain countless aquifers at various depths. So many, in fact, that it
was impossible to tell how many were beneath their
feet, let alone which one was responsible for the leak.

It was while studying the stratigraphy of the lower
portion of the main Mexico City aquifer that Anya had
made the connection that should have been staring
them in the face from the start. Regardless of their
depth, aquifers were still subject to the laws of gravity,
which meant that, like any pond or lake or even water
in a glass, the surface level remained constant. It had
taken the entire evening and well into the night to col-
lect the GPR and magnetometer readings of the sacrificial well they'd explored what felt like days ago now,
but the results had been conclusive.

The surface of the underground water was at the
exact same depth, which meant that the two bodies had
to be connected.

Her initial impression had been that the chamber had
always contained water, when she should have recognized that if that were the case, the bones would have
settled through the sediment thousands of years before
she had the opportunity to trip over them. They would
have eventually reached that conclusion, she knew, but
she prided herself on not making assumptions. Fortunately, she had the opportunity to make up for it.

There was no way they'd be able to drain that much
water, especially anytime soon, so they'd made an
early-morning run to Mexico City, where they'd rented
scuba gear for Dr. Evans and her. After her most recent
diving experience, this promised to be a walk in the

park by comparison, but she couldn't afford to take anything for granted. At least the water would be fifty degrees warmer and she wouldn't have to wear one of those cumbersome dry suits.

She had packed her swimsuit and after six months was happy to finally have the opportunity to put it to use. It appeared to have the desired effect upon Villarreal, who couldn't take his eyes off her while he helped her into the skintight wetsuit. She'd thought they were developing some chemistry, and it was nice to know that she was right. Maybe when they discovered the entrance to the maze, they could do a little celebrating of their own, assuming Evans left them alone for more than a few seconds. Why he didn't like Villarreal was beyond her. Evans didn't treat her like a father, per se; more like a big brother, whose expression betrayed how little he liked the way Don Juan, as he called him, was looking at his little sister.

Villarreal helped her zip up her wetsuit and gave her a twirl like they were dancing.

"Thank you, Juan Carlos," she said.

He smiled and stepped behind her. When he spoke, his lips were so close to her ear that she could feel the warmth of his breath.

"Your diving belt."

She felt him against her as he reached around her waist, clipped her belt, and cinched it tight. She placed her hand on his and—

"Come on, Anya," Evans said. He was already fully dressed and waiting impatiently, as usual.

She shrugged on the straps of her harness, seated the tank high between her shoulders, and clipped the buckle across her breasts.

"How do I look?" she asked.

Villarreal raised his eyebrows and appeared ready to say something when Evans cut him off.

"Like we won't be getting down there anytime soon if you don't hurry up."

She stuck her tongue out at him, then donned her diving mask.

"He is right," Villarreal said. "We are all dying to know what is inside the maze. Do not worry, though. I will be right here to help you out of your wetsuit when you return."

Anya was grateful that he could only see her eyes through the mask and not her cheeks, which must have been blushing something fierce. She connected the hose from the tank to the integrated regulator as she followed Evans down the ladder and to the mouth of the tunnel leading into the ceremonial well. By the time she caught up with him, she was fit to burst.

"I can take care of myself, you know."

Evans looked at her like he didn't have the slightest clue what she meant.

"Don't pretend you don't know what I'm talking about."

His tinny voice responded through the speaker mounted inside her mask, beside her right ear.

"Trust me, kiddo. I don't."

"There it is. Kiddo. You need to stop treating me like I'm a child."

"Okay," Evans said, and started crawling into the darkness.

"Wait a minute—"

"I said okay. That's what you wanted, right?"

"She thinks you're getting in the way of a romantic

liaison with Dr. Villarreal," Jade said through the speaker.

"Oh, my God," Anya gasped. "Who all can hear me?"

"There are four of us watching your feed now. They say there's no reason for you to feel embarrassed, though. Everyone already knows."

Anya resisted the urge to scream in frustration and quickly changed the topic to something—anything!—else.

"I'm not sure how much you guys are going to be able to see once we're in the water. It's pretty murky."

"We'll take whatever we can get," Jade said. *"The camera looks like it's pretty well aligned with your line of sight, so if you can see it, we should be able to see it, as well."*

Anya switched on the light mounted to the opposite side of her mask from the camera and squirmed through the tunnel behind Evans. It didn't look as though there were any way he was going to fit through there with the tank on his back, and yet somehow he made it all the way to the end and slid into the vile water, releasing a stench she could smell even through her mask. She groaned and dialed on the flow of compressed air.

"What's wrong?" Jade asked.

"Nothing. Just dreading the prospect of putting my head into this foul soup."

She maneuvered her body from the orifice and lowered herself into the cool water. Her light cast shifting shadows upon the faces of the feathered serpents leering at her from the walls, seemingly animating them in such a way that their eyes appeared to track her movements. Evans was already on the far side of the pool. From above the surface, the chamber was completely self-contained and gave no reason whatsoever for them to even suspect that there was potentially a passage beneath it.

"So we know the victims were sealed in here," Evans said. *"What we don't know is whether or not they were alive when that happened."*

"What difference does that make?" Jade asked.

"Maybe none, but I can't help wondering what would be the point of sacrificing so many people where no one could watch."

A clattering sound came through the speaker.

"The ritual of the sacrifice was of great importance to the Aztec and Maya," Villarreal said. Anya hoped he hadn't joined the others in the trailer, where they'd set up the makeshift monitoring station, until after her embarrassing gaffe. *"The same can be said of the other sacrifices we have discovered in Teotihuacan. It is my belief that whether or not they were alive at the time is of less consequence than the fact that they were sacrificed underground, where neither the citizens nor the gods could bear witness.*

"During the First Dynasty," Evans said, *"the ancient Egyptians utilized a practice called retainer sacrifice, in which servants were killed and buried alongside pharaohs to continue their service in the afterlife."*

"But they were killed," Anya said. "These people were left here to die."

A rumpling sound preceded Jade's voice. She and Villarreal must have been sharing the microphone and sliding it back and forth between them.

"For some unknown scavenger to consume."

Another clatter and a hum of feedback.

"What we can say with complete certainty," Villar-

real said, *"is that the victims were sacrificed to Quet-*
zalcoatl, beneath a city devoted to his worship, and po-
tentially at the entrance to a maze beneath his
pyramid. Whatever lies beyond is no doubt of extraor-
dinary value."

The excitement in his voice was palpable.

Anya nodded at Evans across the surface of the
water, from which their lights reflected and produced
sparkles that danced on the stalactites.

"Ladies first," he said.

Anya rolled her eyes for his benefit and lowered her
head beneath the water. Her headlamp turned the
brown water a vomitous shade of green that swirled
with organic matter and tiny air bubbles. She propelled
herself low across the bottom through the swirling
cloud of sediment that rose from her exertions. The
partially buried bones weren't all human, although she
could only speculate about which species they once
belonged to. The earth beneath the sludge was hard
and smooth, presumably the same limestone as the roof
of the cavern.

"Do you see anything?" Jade asked.

"I can barely see my hand in front of my face,"
Anya said. It felt weird talking underwater.

"I've got something over here," Evans said.

Anya swam toward the vague aura of his light until
his silhouette drew contrast from the murky water. He
crouched with his back to her, his headlamp focused
on the wall. He brushed a layer of phlegm-like sludge
from an outcropping, revealing a stone snout and a pair
of rectangular fangs.

"Are you seeing this?" he asked.

"It looks just like all of the others," Jade said.

Anya helped him smear the mess from its eyes and the fringe of feathers framing its ferocious reptilian visage. This feathered serpent was considerably larger than the others and lifelike in a way that they weren't. Its features were textured with either scales or a fine coat of feathers. Jewels had been fitted into its eyes and chiseled in such a way that the facets lent an aura of sentience. Its mouth opened all the way to the ground, creating a passageway easily large enough to accommodate someone her size, were it not for the sheer quantity of bones and debris wedged inside the orifice. A faint current trickled through the logjam and churned the debris floating in front of their faces.

"Looks like the flooding carried the bones in here from whatever's on the other side," Anya said.

"What do you say we find out what that is?" Evans said.

They pulled one bone after another from the mouth until they loosened them enough that the current cleared the rest. A rush of remains and slimy detritus tumbled toward them. Anya ducked to the side and completely lost sight of Evans through the dense cloud of sediment.

"We've lost visual," Jade said. *"Are you all right?"*

"We cleared the clog," Evans said.

His light materialized mere feet in front of Anya's face, and yet still she couldn't see him until she practically stuck her head into the hole beside his. He reached inside and scraped the sludge from the walls, revealing reddish murals that had nearly been scoured to the bare stone by the flooding.

A squeal of feedback.

"Can you get a better look at the Quetzalcoatl as a whole?" Villarreal asked.

Anya backed up and shined her headlamp onto the ornate orifice. Her light sparkled from the inset jewels.

"Stop right there," Villarreal said. *"Back up. Just a little more . . . there!"*

There were several petroglyphs above the crown of feathers, so faint they were nearly indistinguishable from the sludge. She cringed when she smeared it away with her bare hands. One design looked like a hand, or maybe the petals of a flower. It was hard to tell with the left half eroded to the bare stone. Beside it was a stylized face in a squared, yet flowing style with what almost looked like smoke coming from its mouth, and a third that could have been a face like that of the *moai* of Easter Island, only wearing a crown made of beads.

"These petroglyphs are not like any I have seen elsewhere in Teotihuacan," Villarreal said. *"They reflect a more primitive style, and yet one similar in many ways to both the Aztec and the Maya, who came much later."*

"Can you read them?" Anya asked.

"I cannot read the first one. The second? Perhaps a visual representation of the Nahuatl word cochcahua, *which means 'to sleep.' No, 'to let sleep.' The third is* teotl. *It means 'god.'"* Another voice mumbled something from out of the microphone's range. *"You are right, Emil. The first one is* ohuihcan. *It means 'dangerous place.'"* He gasped when it all came together for him. *"It is a warning. 'Do not wake the sleeping god.'"*

"What's the 'sleeping god'?" Evans asked.

He looked back at Anya, who met his stare through their masks. There was an element of doubt in Villarreal's voice that neither had heard there before.

"I do not know," he finally said.

"Well," Evans said. *"I guess there's only one way to find out."*

Anya lowered her head and shined her light into the tunnel, which extended beyond her beam's reach. A shiver traced the length of her spine. Suddenly she wasn't so sure she wanted to find out what was inside the maze after all.

16
TESS

The Cage, FOB Atlantis

"**N**one . . . of . . . you . . . will . . . survive."

Dr. Tess Clarke paused the playback and studied Director Barnett's face. She'd hoped his reaction would betray something, but she was beginning to think he didn't even blink without making a conscious decision to do so.

"Play it again," he said.

Tess tried to mask her expression of revulsion as she leaned in front of him to rewind the feed. He smelled like he'd just crawled out of his grave. She stopped at the point where she'd started antagonizing the creature and gratefully returned to her chair near the air vent.

If the director was angered by anything she had said about him, it didn't show. He merely watched the heat signature respond to her words by throwing a tantrum that escalated from guttural noises to verbal communication to hurling itself against the door like an animal.

"It initially responded to your challenge with the same arrogance as Mr. Rubley would have."

"You don't think there's a part of him that's some-how still alive in there, do you?"

"Unlikely, and probably entirely coincidental, but worth noting."

Tess wondered if his observation stemmed from a genuine desire to understand the creature or if he still held out hope that Hollis Richards—if they ever found him—could be saved.

"The . . . serpent . . . god . . . will . . . rise . . . from . . . the . . . dead . . . and . . . consume . . . you . . . all."

"Do you think it's speaking literally or metaphori-cally?" Barnett asked.

"Serpent god?" Her recorded voice sounded strange coming from the speaker.

"That's why I called you down here," Tess said. "I have a theory."

"None . . . of . . . you . . . will . . . survive."

She paused the playback at a point where the orangish creature crouched at the back of the cavern, its white eyes boring through the camera from beneath the ridged brow of its elongated cranium.

"It hasn't moved from that spot in"—she glanced at her watch—"just over three hours."

"So what's your theory?"

The tone of his voice suggested he was only humor-ing her and already had one foot out the door. He'd changed so much in just the few months since her ar-rival. While once he'd been outgoing and made an ef-fort to connect with everyone, he now came across as a man victimized by his own obsessions, one in dire need of sleep.

"Let me show you something," she said, and brought

up the image of the white blobs against the backdrop of
the blue streaks. "You know how Zeta has destroyed
every surveillance system you installed so we couldn't
see what it was carving into the walls? It hit me that
the pressure necessary to carve into the walls using the
bones of an animal had to be fairly significant, which
meant that the process had to produce a significant
amount of friction and, subsequently, generate a mea-
surable amount of heat. So I isolated that heat value
and programmed the system to run back through the
archives in order to generate a single image, kind of
like taking a picture of the stars with a really long exposure time. Once I subtracted all of the thermal signatures outside of the blue range and eliminated residual
heat not in direct physical contact with the walls of the
cavern, I was left with this."

She pulled up the final image, which she'd digitized
in such a way that it could be rotated 360 degrees on
any axis, essentially producing what looked like a
globe, only viewed from the inside.

"It's a star chart." Barnett was unable to hide the
disappointment in his voice. "Just like in all of the others."

There were thousands of blue dots of varying size.
Some were so small and so close together they almost
looked like clouds, while others were connected by
lines to form constellations whose shapes were open to
interpretation. It reminded her of lying beneath the sky,
far away from civilization and light pollution, and seeing the universe with the kind of clarity generally re-
served for telescopes.

"Yes and no," Tess said. "I loaded the data into a

program that compares it against the night sky from any geographical and historical point of reference, but the closest match was only ninety-one percent."

"Probably because it's not finished yet."

"Which is what I thought, too, until I studied the nature of the matches. You see, this particular chart was created to reflect a vantage point of this precise location, and the sky as it appeared on September twentieth of last year."

"Impossible. That was the same day Rubley activated the pyramid. I clearly remember that there was a blizzard outside. There's no way it could have seen the night sky."

"You're absolutely right, which then begs the question of how it could have re-created this star chart so perfectly."

"Do you have a theory?"

"I'm getting there."

"Get there faster."

"I believe it serves as a frame of reference."

"What do you mean?"

"Think of this star chart like one great big, ultra-detailed map. Now ask yourself what purpose it serves."

"That's why you're here, Dr. Clarke."

"Why would Zeta invest so much time and effort into creating a work of art so magnificent and detailed if it knew no one would ever see it?"

"You tell me."

"The answer is simple," Tess said. "It wouldn't."

"Despite what I can clearly see with my own two eyes?"

"Something it said got me thinking."

She rewound the thermal surveillance video to the point she'd bookmarked and let it play.

"Does it make you mad?" her voice asked from the speakers. *"Knowing that you're at the director's mercy?"*

"As . . . you . . . are . . . at . . . ours?"

"There," she said, and stopped the video. "Did you hear that?"

"I have other issues that require my attention, Dr. Clarke."

"Ours," she said. "Not mine. Ours. Take a step back and look at it from the most basic perspective. This is a sentient being composed of countless microscopic organisms that function like a hive mind of sorts. Our mistake has been in assuming that their ability to communicate is confined to those within a single physical vessel. What if this star chart wasn't designed to be viewed here, but to be viewed from any number of geographical locations simultaneously? What if the creature in there was able to re-create the night sky from this location using visual data shared from other vantage points?"

"You're suggesting there are more of these things out there. And that they share some sort of communal memory."

"That's exactly what I'm suggesting."

"So what are the implications?"

"If this individual can recognize an arrangement of stars corresponding to a certain location and date, then surely any other individual can, too."

"Then if you're right about there being others, then it's transmitting its location to them."

"More than that," Tess said. "I think it's sending them a message."

She pressed a series of buttons and the majority of the stars vanished, leaving only loosely gathered clusters.

"What's this?"

"This is six of the nine percent that doesn't match the historical star chart."

She rotated the image and focused on a jagged line of stars, which ascended the cavern wall from the floor all the way up to the ceiling.

"Now, imagine yourself standing in the very center of the room, at a point we know to be right here in Antarctica. What does this pattern look like?"

Barnett turned the display maybe ten degrees until it hit him with an unguarded moment of clarity.

"It's the western coastline of South America. All the way through Central America and up into Mexico."

"More accurately, it traces a series of deep sea trenches along the edges of several tectonic plates." She applied an overlay that outlined all the tectonic plates and active fault lines. "You can see right here where the route crosses Drake's Passage along the boundary of the Antarctic and Scotia Plates and heads north along the border of the Nazca Plate. It travels the length of the Peru-Chile Trench to the Middle America Trench, which branches inward into Mexico along what's known as the Mesoamerican Subduction Zone from Acapulco to Mexico City. And do you know which god primitive Mesoamerican cultures, from the Aztec to the Maya, worshiped?"

"Kukulcan, Quetzalcoatl, Tohil."

"Also known as?"

"The Feathered Serpent God." Barnett's expression clouded and Tess caught the most fleeting glimpse of what could have almost passed for fear. "If you'll excuse me . . ."

He rose from his chair and strode across the room, leaving the aroma of death in his wake.

"I'm not done yet," Tess called after him.

"Write it up and send it to me directly."

And with that he was gone. Tess heard the distant echo of his voice as he spoke into his transceiver, but couldn't make out his words. She wished she knew what connection he had made, but figured he wouldn't have told her even if she asked. The whole chain-of-command thing was new to her. She was used to the collaborative dynamics she'd taken for granted at the SETI Institute, which she vastly preferred to this need-to-know nonsense, especially considering there were still several other patterns besides the one mapping a route to central Mexico that she had yet to decipher.

The coastline of South America had jumped out at her from the start, but the other remaining stars—or points of data, as she chose to think of them, since they weren't really stars—had yet to coalesce into meaningful patterns. If the overall motif held true, then the points of data on the opposite side of the "globe" corresponded to points somewhere in Europe, the Middle East, and Central Africa, although if there was a relationship between them, it eluded her. Maybe if Barnett had shared his revelation it could have helped her make one of her own. Then again, perhaps if she rested her eyes for a while she'd be able to make sense of things on her own. As it stood now, she'd been staring at these monitors for so many hours that she'd lost count and her bladder felt as though it had swollen to the size of a bowling ball.

She stood and was halfway to the corridor leading back to the pyramid when she caught movement from the corner of her eye and stopped dead in her tracks.

The shadows were so deep that she could see nothing inside the darkness. She was prepared to dismiss the apparent motion as a figment of her imagination when she detected a subtle shift in the shadows. She took a step closer—

A small animal streaked out from beneath her console, across the floor, and disappeared into the dark corridor. She hadn't gotten a very good look at it, but she could have sworn it was a mouse, which couldn't possibly have been the case since there were no indigenous species of rodent on the entire continent and she could think of no good reason for anyone to have brought one.

17
KELLY

To say that everything had changed in the six months since they were last here was an understatement. Kelly couldn't fathom how in such a short span of time it had gone from a remote scientific installation to essentially what looked like a military base down here beneath the ice dome, where before there had been only darkness. She remembered how they'd initially arrived by mini submarine and the care they had taken to dim their lights so as not to damage the sensitive prehistoric ecosystem.

That felt like a different lifetime entirely.

The lake had been drained, and the ancient city, formerly hidden beneath the water and the accumulation of countless millennia of sediment, laid bare. The ruins looked real in a way they hadn't before, as though it were finally possible to see how real human beings had actually lived here, once upon a time. She was by no means an expert on architecture, but she'd traveled enough to recognize the similarities between these structures and the ruins of both early Mayan and Egyptian civilizations. The megalithic columns lording over the rubble were like a cross between those of the Celts and the Greeks. She could even see the Stonehenge-like ring, through which they'd ascended into the lake via a series of flooded tunnels from Snow Fell, in the far distance.

Morgan must have read her thoughts.

"We really haven't had much time to explore the ruins. After a while, you just start seeing them like any other rocks."

"I'm sure there are countless archeologists who would literally kill each other for the chance to study them."

"If anyone knew they existed."

They followed Morgan, who toted their assigned duffel bags over his shoulders as though they weighed nothing at all, away from the elevator platform. Their footsteps echoed from beneath the wooden planks of the boardwalk and reverberated all the way beyond the edge of sight, which really wasn't saying much. Despite the light posts erected seemingly every fifty feet, the entire base was swaddled in permanent twilight.

"What did you do with all of the water?" Roche asked.

"We estimate that approximately twenty percent of it was evacuated through the subterranean tunnels following the activation of the pyramid. We diverted the aquifers, dammed every inlet we could find, and pumped the remainder downhill to the ocean. From time to time, something thaws or springs a leak, but we haven't had any problems with flooding."

How two men who had been at each other's throats

mere minutes ago could act like nothing had transpired between them was beyond her. Theirs was a world separate from the one in which she was raised. They'd served their country in ways she could only speculate about and had undoubtedly seen things she didn't care to know. While her mother had been protesting the war in Afghanistan, these men had been living it, most likely in portable buildings like the ones they now approached.

Watching Roche interact with Morgan caused her to see him in a new light, one she was having a hard time reconciling. This was a man who would do anything for her, she knew, and yet, at the same time, he'd been trained to spy on his own people and to kill without conscience.

Kelly shoved her hands deeper into her pockets and shivered against the cold. She could tell that Roche saw through her ruse, though. Distancing herself from him had cut him worse than anything she could have said.

The ruins fell away behind them and were swallowed by the shadow cast by the pyramid. The futuristic-looking modular buildings formed a ring ahead of them on what was once a barren stretch of shoreline, upon which she remembered Roche running with that massive box speaker blaring the frequencies she'd deciphered from the petroglyphs towering over them like the Hollywood sign.

"Welcome to Forward Operating Base Atlantis," Morgan said, and gestured with a flourish toward the prefabricated buildings.

"Do you really believe these are the ruins of the lost city of Atlantis?" Kelly asked.

"Look behind you and tell me that's not exactly what this place is."

The deck outside the main entrance was big enough to accommodate a large gathering, only from where she stood the place looked deserted. There were several freestanding kiosks that housed flat-screen monitors, which cycled through a series of maps that resembled the kind posted at trailheads in national parks. Each of them was labeled by elevation and divided into color-coded sections, the notations inside of which meant nothing to her. Roche studied them with a concerned expression on his face. He caught her looking and smiled for her benefit.

"How many people are stationed here?" he asked.

"Fifty-four," Morgan said. "Fairly equally divided by rank and specialty."

"All of them Unit 51?"

"Most. The remainder are civilian consultants, like you guys."

"Is that what we are?" Kelly asked. "Civilian consultants?"

"Until you prove yourselves."

"What makes you think we want to be part of your unit?" Roche asked.

"You're here, aren't you?"

Morgan smiled and held open the front door for them to enter. The interior was sparse and barren, and yet had a lived-in feel at odds with the fact that they hadn't seen another soul. The center of the room was dominated by a long table, upon which dozens of computers sat, each of their monitors displaying a blank login screen. One wall was lined with enormous metal cabinets without labels, the other with various outer-wear from arctic gear to isolation suits, and the corresponding hoods, gloves, and boots.

"There are thirteen buildings in all," Morgan said. "They're arranged like the numbers on a clock with the mess hall in the center. Right now we're in Building Twelve, or Midnight as most call it, which seems fitting. Building One is to the left. You've been assigned to Building Three."

He led them through the doorway to the left and a windowless corridor that blew heat straight down upon them.

"Each building is twenty feet wide by forty-eight feet long, or nine hundred sixty square feet. That's a total of more than twelve thousand square feet of living space connected by another thousand feet of corridors. We like to think of it as our own Bel-Air mansion down here at the bottom of the world."

The majority of Building One was divided by a wall without windows and a door that sealed like a walk-in cooler.

"What's back there?" Kelly asked.

"That's the daylight room. We strongly encourage everyone to spend at least an hour a day in there. It's so bright it's like sitting on the surface of the sun, but the lamps provide the daily dose of UVA and UVB rays required for vitamin D synthesis and overall mental well-being."

They breezed through another heated corridor and into Building Two, which housed twelve bunk beds, six to either side. The lower bunk had been replaced with a bureau and writing desk that fit underneath it and created something of a private workspace. The "rooms" were separated by curtained partitions that qualified as little more than visual barriers. While all of them appeared to be in use, there were no effects of a personal nature.

Morgan preceded them through the hallway and into Building Three.

"You'll be staying in here," he said. "We try to populate the living quarters with people who share the same hours. While all of the barracks are co-ed, we don't necessarily offer joint accommodations."

"That's okay," Kelly said.

If her words had an impact on Roche, it didn't show. Not that they should have hurt him. It wasn't like they'd slept together yet. She reddened at the thought. The mere fact that she felt the need to qualify the sentiment granted her insight she wasn't sure she was ready to face.

Morgan walked to the rear of the structure and dropped one bag onto the floor at the base of a vacant bed to the left and the other to the right without announcing which one belonged to whom.

"I'd imagine you're both exhausted and more than a little overwhelmed. The director's budgeted four hours for you to catch up on some sleep, shower, or whatever you want—" His words abruptly ceased and he removed a handheld device from his breast pocket. He glanced at the screen and returned it to his pocket. The only hint of emotion was a subtle tightening of his lips. "I'm afraid that's going to have to wait."

"I guess that means you're not going to finish the tour," Roche said.

"There'll be plenty of time to explore later. Believe me. As for now, all I can say is that Director Barnett is dying to greet you in person and has requested that Special Agent Avila accompany you down as soon as possible."

"Down?" Kelly said.

Morgan smiled and left without another word.

18
DUTTON

Dry Storage, FOB Atlantis

People thought it was so easy being in charge of food service. They didn't ever stop to think that he had to have the day's meals prepared well in advance. He had to be in the kitchen by four in the morning to have breakfast served by five. Then he had to turn around and have lunch ready by 10:30, dinner by 16:30, and nutritious snacks for the graveyard crew by 22:00. Sometime in between he needed to be able to cook and prep, inventory and order, and somehow find time to sleep, which meant he had to take it where he could get it.

Les Dutton was lucky to be in bed by 22:30. While five hours might have been enough sleep for some of these younger kids, it was barely enough to touch his exhaustion, let alone take the edge off his constant headache. Fortunately, he had the rare talent of being able to sleep just about anywhere, which was how he got through his days. Before lunch, he took an hour-long power nap in dry storage on top of the sacks of rice and beans. After lunch, he had to be a little more creative, and utilized the pigpen, as he called it.

He'd volunteered specifically for the task of feeding whatever that thing in the cage was largely because no one else wanted anything to do with it—those who even knew about it, anyway—and because by doing so it secured him his own private space. He received the pigs on the same transport as the food supplies, and brought them down here, where he fed and watered them and stacked their cages against the wall by the feeding cart. He'd gotten used to their grunting and squealing and had almost come to enjoy his time with them. He no longer smelled the stink the guards who worked inside the room down the hall constantly complained about and had actually reached the point where he looked forward to seeing the pigs every day. Unlike the men, the pigs never complained about what he fed them or looked at him as though he were somehow a lesser species. They trusted and respected him clear up until the moment he loaded them on the cart and wheeled them down the hall, which was becoming harder and harder to do with each passing day.

As a child in Oklahoma, he'd grown up on a farm where he'd helped his father slaughter and butcher nearly every animal known to man. It had never really weighed on his conscience, either. It was simply something that needed to be done, like any other aspect of food preparation. As his old man used to say, "Supper ain't gon' climb up on the table on issown."

This was different, though. That thing in there? It took pleasure from ripping these pigs up first, and whether or not you believed what the Bible said about every living thing being food, there was something indescribably brutal about the way that creature hurt the animals before killing them. Most of the guards thought Subject Z was pure and unadulterated evil, but Dutton had been around long enough to know that the nature of the snake was to strike, inject its venom through its wicked fangs, and watch its prey die a miserable death before consuming it. There was nothing evil about it doing what God had designed it to do. It simply was what it was.

Dutton walked along the row of cages and rubbed the damp noses of the swine when they stuck them through the wire mesh. He dumped some pellets into their troughs, topped off their water, and headed to the back corner of the room, where he'd arranged three wire racks housing stacked sacks of pig feed into a U shape, leaving a gap in the middle that couldn't be seen from the door. He hauled down a couple of bags, laid them end-to-end, and stretched out on top of them. According to his watch, he still had a good ninety minutes before his alarm went off, which couldn't have worked out any better.

He closed his eyes and welcomed the darkness.

A pig squealed. Then another.

He opened his eyes and looked through the gap below the second shelf. Not a single swine was visible. They'd all shrunken back into the straw in the rear of their cages, where they squealed like they did when he led them down the hall.

"Knock it off already, would you?" he shouted, and closed his eyes once more.

If anything, the racket grew louder as they thrashed around in their pens, slamming into the walls and attacking the metal floors with their hooves. He did his best to ignore them, and was eventually rewarded with silence, although the whole place reeked of fresh urine and crap.

That weightless feeling settled into his legs and he was on the brink of sleep when he heard something that summoned him back to consciousness. He was disoriented at first and couldn't seem to recall what had caught his attention to begin with, until he heard a scratching sound off to his right.

Dutton turned to see nothing more exciting than bags upon bags of pig feed. Sometimes the pellets inside made noises when they settled, although generally not this long after delivery.

He closed his eyes and was again on the verge of sleep when he felt something on his leg, reflexively swatted it, and resumed his slumber. At least until he felt it again, moving up his thigh and across his belly. His eyes snapped open and he peered down at the folds in his shirt. He flattened them and found himself staring into the whiskered face of the ugliest mouse he'd ever seen. Its eyes were black, its head deformed, and its skin a sickly shade of gray.

"What do you know?" He picked it up by the tail so he could get a better look at it. "You hitch a ride in one of these sacks, little guy?"

It rounded on him and bit his finger.

"Son of a—!"

Dutton dropped it and thrust his finger into his mouth. Blasted thing broke the skin.

Pain in his tongue. Under his gumline.

He removed his finger and scrutinized the wound. The edges were already bright red and starting to pucker. It felt like there was a fiery hot barb embedded inside.

His bile rose and he felt the sudden need to vomit. He retched and leaned forward. Dry heaved. The pain in his stomach drove him to his back.

Tiny hook-like nails climbed the side of his neck, passed over his jaw, and embedded themselves in his cheek.

He smacked the mouse, which only made it dig its nails deeper into his skin. He opened his mouth to cry out and the freaking thing crawled inside. He choked and sputtered and tried to cough it out, but it scurried deeper, until it wedged itself in his throat.

What felt like needles knitted through the soft tissue in his throat and pierced his palate. Wormed their way inside his sinuses, behind his eyes, and into his brain.

The universe opened before him and for the briefest of moments he understood the creature in the cage down the hall and how wrong he'd been about it. It wasn't like a snake. It *was* evil, and it wouldn't rest until it killed every last one of them.

19
EVANS

Teotihuacan

The tunnel felt as though it grew smaller and darker as Evans swam over sediment bristling with bones. His light barely reached beyond his outstretched arms. Having spent considerable time exploring the ruins of ancient Egypt, he knew all about curses, which tended to be a whole lot more bark than bite, but this one was oddly specific. He had to believe that whatever god once slumbered down here had died long ago; however, it appeared to have taken an absurd number of men and animals with it. Surely there was an explanation for the sheer amount of skeletal remains ahead of them, although he was beginning to wonder if he really wanted to know.

Anya's light drifted hauntingly in and out of the curtain of silt behind him. He felt an irrational urge to tell her to return to the surface, but managed to suppress it. Whatever was going on inside his head was no reason to worry the others.

At least not yet.

The walls abruptly fell away to either side of him.

He paused at the junction and waited for Anya to catch up with him.

"What's going on down there?" Jade asked.

"I think we found the entrance to the maze."

"Then what are you waiting for?"

He couldn't quite describe the feeling, not even to himself. It was almost like the tingle he got in the pit of his stomach when he stepped to the very end of a high dive and knew that the slightest transfer of weight would send him plummeting to the water far below.

Anya must have sensed something, too. He didn't think she'd gone this long without talking in her entire life.

Evans made room for her to swim to the end of the tunnel beside him and tried to get a good look at her eyes, which stared straight ahead into the murk. She caught him looking and nodded ever so slightly.

He blew out a long breath and drifted out into the open. While earlier the walls had felt like they were slowly squeezing the life from him, he missed the security they provided. He couldn't see more than three feet in any direction, even with the addition of Anya's beam to his own.

"Do you see anything?" Villarreal asked.

"Nothing more than you do," Evans said.

He floated all the way out of the tunnel and fixed its location in his memory. He tried not to move any more than absolutely necessary. He couldn't see a blasted thing as it was. If they stirred up the sediment, they might not be able to find their way back to the surface until it settled again.

"What's that over there?" Anya asked.

He followed the beam from her headlamp toward

what almost looked like a fallen tree. They were nearly upon it before he realized what it was.

"Jesus," he whispered.

It was like swimming through the mouth of hell. The creation before him was unlike anything he'd ever seen. Its skeletal form was composed of the bones of any number of different species, bound together by copper windings, green with oxidation. The craftsmanship was astounding, which only served to make him that much more uncomfortable. It reflected the same style as the figures in the murals on the walls of the surviving structures, only somehow translated into three dimensions.

"That is Mictlantecuhtli," Villarreal said. *"God of the dead and king of Mictlan, the lowest level of the underworld."*

The hideous form sat on its haunches with its arms crossed and braced on its knees. It wore an elaborate headdress reminiscent of a samurai's helmet, carved from the same smooth obsidian as the eyes fitted into its sockets. The framework of wings rose from its back with long feathers made from the ribs of multiple species of varying size.

The figure beside it was somehow even more unsettling. It knelt with its hands raised in supplication, and wore a crown of what looked like monkey skulls around its human cranium, and another hanging from a necklace on its breast. The articulated spines of a dozen snakes dangled from its waist like a grass skirt. Its bony wings were partially folded around it like a bat.

"Mictlancihuatl," Villarreal said. *"Wife of Mictlantecuhtli. Goddess of the dead and queen of the underworld. They are gods of the Aztec pantheon. I cannot tell you*

why they are here or the significance of their presence."

"Seems like the whole hell theme speaks for itself," Evans said.

"The Aztec came after the Teotihuacano. Their gods do not pre-date the construction of the city above you, and yet here they are."

"They worshiped Quetzalcoatl, too," Anya said. *"Maybe the Aztecs built their pantheon upon the existing framework left behind by the Teotihuacano."*

"There's another one over here," Evans said.

He shined his light onto a sculpture lacking in all humanity. It had the head and body of a dog, but its legs had been mounted backward so that its feet faced the wrong direction. The way it was posed, with its head lowered and tilted back over its shoulder, reminded Evans of an animal accustomed to being beaten. Its outstretched front leg pointed deeper into the Earth.

"That is Xolotl," Villarreal said. *"Brother of Quetzalcoatl and god of sickness and disease. For as beautiful and revered as his brother was, he was equally ugly and reviled. There are many stories about him. Some say it was his lot in life to drag the sun through the underworld at night, while others claim he led the souls of the dead to Mictlan. There is one tale that stood apart from the others—at least as far as the context in which it was told—and now I am beginning to understand why."*

Evans floated closer to get a better look at the bone in the dog-thing's mouth, but still couldn't determine the species to which it belonged.

"Which story is that?" Anya asked.

"It is said that despite the efforts of his brother to

stop him, Xolotl traveled to the depths of Mictlan to unearth the rotting bones of an extinct race of beings. He tricked Mictlantecuhtli into allowing him to drag the vile carcass back to the world of light where the gods of the sky blessed it with a rain of their own blood. And thus life was born anew from the blood of the gods and the bones of the dead."

"And that, kids, is how your great-great grandfather became a zombie," Evans said.

"You joke, but you would be wise to remember that entire civilizations were built upon such stories. The people found in them meaning that translated in some way into every aspect of their lives. I am certain that the presence of these specific gods is not accidental and you should proceed with an added element of caution."

"Did these ancients happen to draw a map of hell? That would probably be a lot more helpful than stories now."

"Unfortunately, they did not. The early Mesoamericans were not as obsessed with every little detail of hell as your European ancestors, who brought it with them to Mexico many years later."

Evans inwardly chastised himself. Villarreal seemed like a decent enough guy whose life's work wasn't so different from his own, but there was just something about him that made Evans instinctively distrust him, something more than the way he flirted with his graduate students or the way he looked at Anya, something he couldn't quite pin down.

"Which way should we go?" Anya asked.

"Jade?" Evans said.

*"I can't tell. This map makes the maze look like a
bunch of squares of diminishing size."*

"Surely you have some input."

"Is that an insult?"

"For the love of God—"

*"Go right. Nearly ninety percent of the global pop-
ulation is right-handed. The odds dictate that the majority of turns will be to the right."*

"Thank you," he said. "Was that so hard?"

Jade said something in response, but he tuned her
out and carefully propelled himself past the disfigured
creations. It turned out that he could have gone in either direction, as both led to the same point on the
other side of the wall behind the statues and what had
to be the beginning of the maze, because there was
only one opening in the limestone wall. He glanced
back at Anya before swimming through the narrow
corridor.

Evans wasn't even to the end when he noticed a difference in the way the water acted around him. He
shined his light straight up, smiled, and swam upward
toward where his headlamp spotlighted the surface. His
head rose above the water and he swept his beam around
him. The smooth ceiling was barely high enough for him
to keep his chin above the surface. A closer examination
revealed it to be composed of sheets of sleek black obsidian fitted together like so many ornate tiles. They
were dotted with orange circles about the size of quarters. A single scrape from his thumb confirmed they
were composed of rust.

Evans felt Anya brush past his thigh and scooted to
his left. Even from this vantage point, he could barely

see far enough to tell that the passage terminated in a T-intersection ahead.

The walls were paneled with obsidian, too, although they lacked the regularly spaced patterns of rust. The way his light reflected from them seemed to create rainbows inside of the volcanic glass. He imagined entering the darkness carrying only a torch and how intimidating it would be.

"That much obsidian would have cost a fortune in their day," Villarreal said. *"To the Teotihuacano, it is the equivalent of covering every surface with solid gold."*

Anya breached the surface ahead of Evans. When she turned to face him, there was no mistaking the fear in her eyes.

"What's wrong?"

He swam toward her, heedless of the sediment rising beneath him.

"Go back down," Jade said. *"I didn't get a good look."*

"Don't move," Anya said.

"What is it?"

"I said don't move!"

Evans ceased his exertions and bobbed slowly toward her. The sediment rose past his legs and turned the surface of the water brown.

"This place is booby-trapped," Anya said.

The idea of setting traps for tomb robbers and scavengers was fairly common in primitive societies. The builders of some of the more elaborate tombs of ancient Egypt employed systems of portcullises and falling stone blocks to bar access to treasure troves, although they didn't inflict injury as much as they created immovable obstacles.

"Booby traps are more fiction than fact," Evans said.

"Try telling that to the guy down there."

Evans looked at her curiously for a moment before sinking straight down into the water. He shined his light past Anya, whose legs churned the swirling sediment, and toward the end of the passage.

"I don't see anything."

"To your right," Jade said.

Evans drifted to the end of the flooded corridor and peered cautiously to his right, and directly into the face of a dead man. The majority of his skeleton remained intact, if only because of the rusted iron spikes that had impaled him from above and staked him to the floor.

"Holy crap."

"He appears to be of Mayan ancestry," Anya said.

"That cannot be right," Villarreal said. *"The Mayans came long before either the Teotihuacano or the Aztecs."*

"You can tell by the breadth of the cheekbones, shallow orbital sockets, and sloped forehead."

"That spike was propelled from the ceiling at such a high rate of speed that he didn't have time to look up, let alone get out of the way," Jade said. *"Either someone triggered the mechanism that launched it remotely, or he did it himself."*

"I can see that," Evans said, although he wasn't entirely certain what it meant. This wasn't a simple trap meant to protect treasure or dissuade thieves; this was designed to kill. And while one victim could have been left as a warning to others, he couldn't afford to take the chance that this whole place wasn't similarly rigged.

"Whatever awaits us at the center of the maze must be of immense value," Villarreal said.

Evans ignored him. No amount of treasure or artifacts was worth spending the rest of eternity down here with a pike through his head.

"We should take our time mapping this place before we explore any deeper."

"Please," Villarreal said. *"Just a little farther."*

"You're more than welcome to come down here and explore to your heart's content, but we're—"

"I'll go," Anya said.

Evans caught her by the wrist before she could get past him.

"Oh, no you don't."

He removed one of the lead weights from his diving belt and held it in front of her mask. Before she could ask what he was doing, he tossed it ahead of him and dragged her back into the main tunnel with him. The weight fell in a diminishing arc until it disappeared into the cloud of sediment.

"You need to stop telling me what I can and can't—"

Thunk.

A greenish blur streaked straight past them. The spike embedded itself in the ground hard enough to shake the walls and cause the water to vibrate.

Anya reached out and touched it, as though confirming that it was indeed real and not a figment of her imagination.

"I think that's enough exploring for one day," Evans said, and swam—very carefully—back toward the surface.

20
BARNETT

Command Center, FOB Atlantis

By the time Barnett reached the command center, his
thoughts were racing so fast he could barely keep up
with them. He could positively feel the tumblers
falling into place. He should have known from the start
that nothing that had happened, since the very beginning, had been coincidental, least of all in the after-
math of the pyramid's activation.

He'd already confirmed the arrival of Mr. Roche
and Ms. Nolan and requested they be taken to Dr.
Clarke's lab, where he would meet them shortly. He
needed Morgan down here with him now and, if he
was right about the urgency of the situation, ready for
wheels up again in a matter of minutes.

He sat at his desk, logged into his computer, and
brought up the map showing the global ramifications
during the twenty-four hours following the events that
transpired inside AREA 51. Concentric circles marked
the epicenters of earthquakes reported all around the
world. None of them had registered higher than a six
on the Richter scale, and yet all of them had caused

considerable localized damage. Localized being the key word. The central courtyard of the ancient ruins at Teotihuacan had basically collapsed, while there were no reports of property damage in nearby Mexico City. The Pyramids of Giza and the Thornborough Henges had been similarly affected, although only passing mentions had crossed the newswires. Simultaneous earthquakes had been reported in the American Midwest and Central Africa, as well, but as far as he could tell, they didn't correspond to any sites of cultural or archeological significance.

Barnett had been closely monitoring the situation in Mexico, but apparently not closely enough. And now he was forced to admit that he was so far behind he wasn't sure he'd be able to catch up in time. While still ill-defined, his adversary, which until recently had been little more than a nuisance bird pecking at the edges of their investigations, was growing bolder with each passing day, and it was only a matter of time before it forced a confrontation. He had thought that securing the pyramid and what he believed to be the ruins of the Lost City of Atlantis would allow him to control that confrontation, but he'd been naïve. He should have realized that due to the interconnected nature of everything, his best efforts had accomplished little more than putting all his eggs in one basket.

He was having a hard time seeing the big picture. There was still too much he didn't know. It felt as though the dots were all there, yet he couldn't seem to connect them. All he knew with any kind of certainty was that—melodramatic as it might sound—the fate of the world potentially hung in the balance. He was convinced "the sleeping god" was a code name for some sort of covert operation. The first instance of its usage had been intercepted by Great Britain's national intelligence agency, MI6, which had shared the transcript throughout the counterterrorism community. It was while investigating the ruination of the Thornborough Henges in the days following the catastrophe in Antarctica that the report was called to his attention. Not forty-eight hours later his own team decrypted another message involving the sleeping god, captured at a remote listening station near Guadalajara, Mexico. And now here was another instance that pointed at something going down south of the border. Either this unknown faction was getting sloppy, or it was preparing to step from the shadows to make its move.

As much as he wanted to do so, Barnett was in no position to handle the situation personally, not with events here threatening to spin out of his control. He had operatives on the ground in Mexico, whether they knew it or not, and he had no choice but to activate them and pray they were able to figure things out before it was too late.

If it wasn't already.

Barnett switched to the live satellite feed and zoomed in on the ancient Mesoamerican complex. While the resolution wasn't what one would consider crystal clear by any stretch of the imagination, it was more than good enough to allow him to see the individual tourists strolling throughout the ruins, and the surprising lack of them inside the fortifications surrounding the Temple of the Feathered Serpent.

The . . . serpent . . . god . . . will . . . rise . . . from . . . the . . . dead . . . and . . . consume . . . you . . . all.

He shook off Subject Z's words and scanned the

ruins until he found what he was looking for. Unbe-
knownst to the scientists who survived the catastrophe
inside AREA 51, their treatment regimen upon their arrival on the *Aurora Borealis* had included the implan-
tation of a GPS beacon that allowed them to be located
anywhere on the surface of the Earth and at any given
moment in time, just like every other agent in his em-
ploy. Where he'd expected to find two tracers, he
found only one, and definitely not the one he expected
to find.

"Well, well, well. What do you know?"

Each global positioning implant broadcast a discrete
electromagnetic signature that appeared on the map in
small white numbers beneath the bright red beacon.
He'd memorized the last three digits of each and every
one, and he was more than a little surprised to find Dr.
Jade Liang halfway around the world from where he'd
last checked on her. A cursory glance at the saved GPS
data corresponding to her implant confirmed that she'd
only just arrived in Mexico after making what appeared to be a rather rushed journey from the hinter-
lands of Nigeria. He couldn't help but wonder why.

He manually typed in the implant numbers corresponding to Drs. Cade Evans and Anya Fleming and
initiated a search. Their last known GPS data corresponded to Dr. Liang's current location, as expected,
which suggested that their beacons were simply out of
range. A blip from Dr. Fleming's beacon roughly fifty
feet diagonally to the southeast from the fenced hole
beside the trailer proved as much. It popped up several
more times before the satellite latched onto the signal.
It captured Dr. Evans scant seconds later as he and Dr.
Fleming approached the hole from what Barnett as-

sumed to be a subterranean passage. He watched them emerge from the collapsed road on the satellite feed and head for the trailer.

Now was the time.

Barnett clicked on Dr. Liang's beacon, which opened her personal data file, and instructed the computer to connect him via the video calling feature on her cell phone. He imagined her pulling her ringing phone from her pocket, staring at the unknown name and number, and debating whether or not to answer—

"This is Dr. Liang."

The expression on her face morphed from curiosity to confusion to resignation when she saw his face. She closed her eyes and he could almost hear her debating whether she should just hang up. While this was amusing, he was running short on time and even shorter on patience.

"I have to admit I was more than a little surprised to find you in Mexico, Dr. Liang," he said. "And believe me when I say that's not something that happens very often."

She opened her eyes and looked back at him from half a world away. Her eyes were such a bright shade of green they appeared digitally enhanced and seemed to bore straight through him.

"How did you find me?"

"The GPS beacon in your cell phone." While it was a lie, he could have just as easily tracked her that way and she knew it. "It's funny to think that the American people rejected the idea of government registration, yet rushed right out and paid their hard-earned cash for the right to carry their own personal tracking devices."

Her footsteps echoed from what sounded like a plywood floor as she exited the trailer, presumably to distance herself from anyone who might overhear. The blazing Mexican sun created reddish highlights in her black hair.

She stared at him for several moments before speaking. It was her turn to catch him off guard.

"It's still alive, isn't it?"

While he prided himself on his ability to be prepared for any given situation, her question had come from so far afield that he hesitated before replying, giving her all the answer she needed. There was no point in denying it now.

"How did you know?"

Jade nodded and glanced off-screen, as though communicating with someone.

"You should have told us," she said.

"That information is available on a need-to-know basis, and you simply didn't need to know. So again I ask, how did you know?"

She shook her head.

"You didn't think that was something we needed to know?"

"Does this knowledge have anything to do with the reason you're currently in Mexico?"

This time it was her turn to hesitate.

"We're on the same side, Dr. Liang," he said. "Why don't we just lay all of our cards on the table so we can dispense with this maddening tête-à-tête?"

He caught a glimpse of Dr. Evans passing behind her in full scuba gear before she covered her camera with her palm. When she uncovered it again, she was in the shade of a wall composed of giant gray stones.

She sighed and seemed to deflate of her customary bluster.

"I encountered a drone in Nigeria."

Barnett sat straight up in his chair.

"You what?"

"Remember how I found that girl with the cranial deformation in Musari?"

Of course he did. He remembered every detail from her initial dossier to her debriefing aboard the *Aurora Borealis*.

"You went back in the hope of determining whether that little girl you found in the mass grave was an anomaly or part of a larger population."

She nodded. There was no need to explain. He understood how her mind worked. In many ways, they were the same—focused, driven, indomitable. There was no way he would have been able to let it go, either.

"And you found exactly what you were looking for."

"Yeah . . . A drone like Scott and Rayburn. Like Richards."

Armand Scott and Paul Rayburn were engineers who'd been stationed at AREA 51. They'd been infected by the alien organisms and transformed into drones that helped Subject Z hunt the men and women inside the station.

"And it told you that our subject was still alive?"

"It said to 'free us' and then waded into a river full of crocodiles."

Dr. Clarke had been right about their ability to communicate and about there being others out there, which meant that she was undoubtedly also right about it sending messages to them. It couldn't be coincidental that Dr. Liang had been the recipient of one that had caused her to head for Mexico, where two of the few people on the planet who would understand that message just happened to be excavating the site to which Subject Z had drawn a map inside the cavern beneath his very feet.

"What can you tell me about the feathered serpent god?" he asked.

"You're asking the wrong person. My work is clinical, not spiritual. There's no overlap whatsoever. I don't know the first thing about serpent gods, gods of the underworld, or sleeping gods. I'm out of my element—"

"What did you say?"

"If you want mythology, you'll have to talk to Cade or Juan Carlos. That's not my area of expertise."

"Where is Dr. Evans now?"

"Cade?" she called.

"What is it?" he answered from some distance away. The scuffing of his footsteps on gravel announced his approach. Dr. Liang tilted her phone and Dr. Evans appeared, his face flushed and his hair wet. The shock of seeing Barnett struck him like an uppercut. "I didn't think I'd ever see you again, Director Barnett. I suppose I should say I hoped I'd never see you again."

Barnett got right down to business.

"What do you know about the sleeping god?"

"I could ask you the same. I only just heard the name today and, honestly, I didn't think it was an accurate translation."

"Where did you hear about it?"

"There's an ancient inscription above the entrance to the maze."

"What maze?"

"How could you know about the sleeping god if you didn't know about the maze?"

There was obviously a connection they were missing, but it didn't appear as though Dr. Evans knew anything more about it than Barnett did.

"I want you to stay there until I can get a team to your position," Barnett said.

"Nuh-uh. I want nothing to do with anything even peripherally related to you or Unit 51."

"Listen to me very closely, Dr. Evans. You are a part of this, whether you like it or not, and I'm afraid that you and the others are in danger. I can have a team there in under twelve hours. I want you to stay where you are and call the number I'm sending to Dr. Liang's phone right now if you see anything remotely out of the ordinary. Anything at all. Do you hear me?"

"You obviously didn't hear me. I don't want—"

"Is there someplace nearby that's secure? Someplace where you can withstand a siege for any length of time?"

"What are you talking about? We're in the middle of a tourist attraction, for Christ's sake. We're surrounded by people from all over the world. What could possibly happen?"

That was the problem. Barnett simply didn't know.

"Twelve hours, Dr. Evans."

Barnett disconnected the call and grabbed his remote transceiver.

"I need someone from IT in here," he said. "Right now."

Special Agent Cheryl Love came through the door within a matter of seconds. She was wearing a tank top and cargo pants and carried with her the scent of the mess hall.

"I need access to any computers within the range of this satellite feed," he said. "Tell me you can do that."

"Without breaking a sweat." She shoved the last bite of cornbread into her mouth and talked around it. "What are you looking for?"

"Anything having to do with a maze. Preferably a file with any kind of imagery."

She knelt beside his chair, brushed off her palms on her thighs, and tucked her straight, shoulder-length blond hair behind her ears. Her fingers moved so quickly across the keyboard that his eyes couldn't keep up.

"There are fifteen active IP addresses that don't correspond to cellular devices."

An array of green dots appeared on the aerial image of the ruins.

"Get me into any one of them registered to the research center at Teotihuacan."

"Take your pick."

She gestured toward his monitor with a flourish. There were eight dots total, four of which were within a three-hundred-foot radius of the trailer where he'd found Dr. Liang.

"That one," he said, and tapped on one of the green dots inside the trailer itself.

"You want me to mirror it while we're in there?"

"Absolutely."

Within thirty seconds she'd hacked into the system and breezed through the directories faster than he could read them. It was no wonder the Department of Defense had put up such a fight to keep her.

Love pulled up an image and stepped back from the monitor.

"Is that what you want?"

Barnett stared at the gray-scale image of several concentric rectangles beneath the ground at the foot of the Temple of the Feathered Serpent. Suddenly everything made sense.

The pattern Subject Z had drawn in blood on the window of its cage.

The design of the crop circle in England.

The subterranean imaging of the maze beneath the temple.

All of the pieces fell into place and led him to an overwhelming realization.

They were already too late.

21
ROCHE

FOB Atlantis

Roche and Kelly had hardly found the restrooms and followed the scent of chili to the mess hall when Special Agent Maria Avila arrived. She was barely five feet tall and couldn't have weighed more than one-twenty with her boots on, but her black eyes were hard and flat and suggested that she wasn't one to be trifled with. She smiled when she introduced herself, although she wasn't quite able to pull it off. This assignment was beneath her, and she made no secret of it.

"Now, if you'll please follow me . . ."

Avila led them through the buildings at a much faster pace than Morgan had. Roche didn't even bother with the spoon and drank his chili from the bowl, which he hurriedly set on the table with the computers as they rushed through the main building and headed back outside.

She took a different boardwalk from the one that had led them to the base. They were nearly to their destination before Roche recognized where they were going. He glanced at Kelly from the corner of his eye.

She'd obviously figured it out, too. Her fingers were fretting so fast inside the pocket of her jacket that it looked like she was trying to smuggle a wild animal. He wanted to say something reassuring, but after the way she'd looked at him in the elevator, he wasn't sure that anything he could say would be interpreted as such.

Seeing the ruins lighted and drained had given him an almost clinical sense of detachment, but as the pyramid rose above him, the memories came flooding back. He remembered watching the monitors inside the research station while the men inside the pyramid brought the machine to life and nearly electrocuted themselves in the process. Rushing to the power station to help the wounded men from the elevator careening toward the surface, the impact from which had destroyed the shaft and tore the entire structure from the side of the mountain. Being hunted through the dark station and narrowly escaping a violent death at the hands of the alien creature that Morgan claimed was still alive. And presumably waiting for them somewhere down here in this horrible place.

They never should have come back.

Kelly gasped and appeared to be on the verge of hyperventilating.

"Are you all right?" Roche whispered.

She nodded and stared up at the pyramid, her feet seemingly rooted to the boardwalk. He placed his hand against the small of her back and guided her up the switchbacking stairs to the entrance to the pyramid. She closed her eyes when she reached the landing and took several deep breaths.

Kelly had told him once how she still dreamed about

this place and described floating outside this very doorway, fighting against the current with only one flipper, swallowing her fear, and swimming inside. The decision to enter today had to be a thousand times harder for her.

"Everything's going to be all right," he said, although he wasn't certain if he said it for her benefit or his own.

The main corridor was well lit and the walls were strung with so many power cords that he could barely see the petroglyphs behind them. A pair of workers in isolation suits brushed past them. The reflection of the lights from their visors concealed their faces.

"Don't worry about the suits," Avila said. "We don't need them where we're going."

"That's reassuring," Roche said.

He peered up the ascending corridor toward the chamber with the massive statues before ducking his head and following Avila down into the depths. It felt as though the walls were closing in on him, which they were to some extent, forcing him into a crouch before disgorging him into the room housing the primitive machine that had caused Dale Rubley's transformation.

The memory of the expression of sheer terror on Ron Dreger's face as this very room filled with steam assailed him.

The rungs of a ladder protruded from the well in the center of the floor. Avila descended first and stepped to the side. Roche followed and waited to help Kelly down.

"What happened to the Nazi sub?" Roche asked.

"What Nazi sub?" Avila said, but Roche could tell she knew exactly what he was talking about.

He hadn't been this far down before. When last he

was here, this tunnel had contained an underground river flowing fast enough to generate the power the pyramid required. It led them deeper into the Earth and to a point where the ceiling lights gave way to darkness, despite the sheer quantity of power cords lining the walls. A faint glow beckoned to them from the cavern at the end of the tunnel, most of which was walled off behind the kind of barrier that appeared to have been built to withstand a nuclear detonation.

Roche instantly realized what was on the other side of the wall. It took Kelly a few seconds longer.

"Oh, God," she whispered.

Roche didn't see the woman seated at the console to their right until she turned at the sound of Kelly's voice. In doing so, she revealed the bank of monitors in front of her.

There was no mistaking the shape of the thermal signature on the screens. It cocked its elongated head toward the camera and moved in a blur.

Thud.

The inset door shuddered.

Kelly screamed and stumbled backward.

"Jesus," Roche said. There was a part of him that thought—or maybe just hoped—that Morgan had been lying to them, despite the fact that he hadn't offered a single hint of doing so. "I saw that thing get shot."

"A ballistic hypodermic needle," a deep voice said from behind him.

Roche turned and watched a silhouette emerge from the dark corridor. He didn't have to see the man's face to know to whom the voice belonged.

"Cameron Barnett," he said.

"Surely you understand the kind of unprecedented

opportunity we had," Barnett said. "We couldn't afford to kill it. We might never have had another opportunity to study an actual living alien organism."

"You should have killed it when you had the chance."

Thud.

The door shuddered in its frame. Kelly backed even farther away from it and wrapped her arms around her chest. She couldn't seem to take her eyes off the monitor.

"I don't think it shares your sentiment," Barnett said.

"After it killed all of those people . . ."

"Unfortunately, Mr. Roche, there is more going on here than I could ever hope to explain."

"Not that you would."

Barnett smiled.

"Suffice it to say that the stakes are higher than you could ever imagine. Believe me when I say that I would never have reached out to you and Ms. Nolan had there been any other option."

"It can't get out of there, can it?" Kelly asked in a voice so small that Roche wasn't initially sure that she had spoken.

"That barrier literally makes an armored truck look like it's made of tissue paper," the woman at the console said. "Trust me. I wouldn't be anywhere near it if it didn't."

"Allow me to introduce Dr. Theresa Clarke," Barnett said. "Dr. Clarke, it is my honor to present Mr. Martin Roche, formerly of the United States Marine Corps and the National Security Agency, and Ms. Kelly Nolan, the brilliant graduate student in seismology at Oregon State whose work with standing waves helped unlock the secrets of the pyramid above us."

"Regretting that now, aren't you?" Dr. Clarke said, and proffered her hand to each of them in turn. "Call me Tess."

Kelly looked away from the monitor for the first time. Her face was a ghostly shade of pale.

"Have you been in there with it?" she asked. "I've seen it up close. I know exactly what it's capable of doing."

Tess opened her mouth, but no words came out.

"Before joining our team, Dr. Clarke was a senior research scientist at SETI," Barnett said, "where her work in xenoarcheology helped identify numerous manmade structures on planets throughout our solar system."

"*Theoretically* manmade," Tess said. "There's no way to either prove or disprove my findings without physically evaluating the structures, and I'm afraid we're a long way from having the ability to do so, which is why I no longer teach remote sensing and geospatial analysis at Penn State. After the way they destroyed my reputation, I was lucky SETI was even willing to look at my résumé."

Roche assessed her very quickly. There was nothing deceptive about her words or her mannerisms. Barnett, on the other hand, was wound so tightly that it looked as though the vein in his temple might burst at any second. His congenial manner belied the situation. There was something terribly wrong here and he was under an immense amount of pressure to fix it. Roche was in no mood for pleasantries and cut right to the chase.

"Morgan said it asked for us."

"In a way."

"You'll have to be a little more forthcoming if you want our help."

"It painted the same design as the crop circle you were investigating in England on that window right there in front of you."

"In pig's blood," Tess said.

"Thank you, Dr. Clarke."

"You were watching us?" Kelly said.

Barnett smiled patiently and placed his hand gently on her shoulder. She looked like she wanted to scream.

"I was hoping you might be able to connect the dots for me."

"If there's a connection," Roche said, "I don't see it."

Barnett scrutinized his face for any sign of duplicity before nodding.

"Then I hope you'll be willing to help me figure out what that connection is."

"You don't seriously want us to talk to it, do you?" Kelly said.

"It's Dr. Clarke's job to communicate with Subject Zeta—"

"You named it?" Roche interrupted.

"How would you propose we refer to it?"

"In the past tense."

"Be that as it may, I hope you will consider assisting her. I like to think that your specialty in particular, Mr. Roche, dovetails with hers. Speaking of which, I wonder if you could offer some insight into this printout, Dr. Clarke."

He removed a piece of paper from the breast pocket

of his jacket, unfolded it, and handed it to Tess. She held it up, but it was too dark in the cavern to see it, so she took it to her console, set it beneath a small reading light, and turned it on—

Thud.

The creature hurled itself against the door one last time before moving to the window, where the reading light limned its spectral features on the other side of the glass.

Roche was certain he caught a hint of recognition on its hideous face before it retreated into the shadows.

"It's a combination of ground-penetrating radar and magnetometer data," Tess said. "One overlaid on top of the other to give the impression of depth. What you're looking at here is a subterranean structure roughly a hundred feet underground. Manmade, by the look of it. And filled with water."

Roche discreetly studied it from the corner of his eye and did his very best to mask his surprise. Thanks to the Marines, who had taught him cryptanalysis, and the NSA, which had honed his considerable skills to a razor's edge, the recognition had been instantaneous.

He looked away from the printout to find Barnett appraising him with open suspicion.

"You see something, don't you?"

Roche glanced at Kelly. She looked so small and scared. He was accustomed to hoarding information and using it as currency to get what he wanted, but it was painfully apparent that he needed to get her as far away from this horrible place as possible. And the sooner, the better.

"Do you have a blank piece of paper?" he asked.

Tess eyed him strangely for a moment before tearing a page from one of her lined notebooks.

He placed it on top of the printout and carefully drew the design of the crop circle on top of it. He'd been right about it being a map.

It led right to the center of the maze.

22
DONOVAN

Drygalski Mountains,
2 vertical miles above FOB Atlantis

"**H**ow the hell did you find it out here?"

Special Agent Rick Donovan had to shout to be heard over the blizzard. The wind blew sideways with such ferocity that he had to stagger to maintain his balance and even then, with the way the storm reduced visibility to mere feet ahead of him, he couldn't be certain he was walking in anything resembling a straight line.

"Totally by accident!" Special Agent Nick Sokolov shouted. Only his eyes were visible through his full-face balaclava and beneath the fur fringe of his hood. There was ice in his lashes and on the neoprene over his mouth and nose. "I was on my way to perform routine maintenance and de-icing on the IMCS antenna array when the ground just kind of opened up underneath me!"

The Iridium Multi-Channel System array provided a data link during times when the main communications satellites were out of range, thus ensuring they never lost contact with the outside world in case of an emergency.

"How long ago?"

"Maybe two hours!"

The call from engineering had been routed to Donovan on the priority channel maybe ninety minutes ago. As both Director Barnett and Chief Morgan were indisposed, it fell to him to run down this lead. If this was indeed what they'd been searching for since their arrival six months ago, then he relished the opportunity to triumphantly pass the good news up the chain, but if Sokolov was wrong and this was just another wild goose chase, he would personally make sure that someone's head rolled.

Donovan stopped and shielded his eyes against the blowing snow. If the satellite tower was out there, he sure as hell couldn't see it, not that he would have been able to anyway with the permanent darkness. He needed a moment to catch his breath. His lungs burned, and his legs positively ached from trudging through the knee-deep accumulation. He had to be careful, though; the last thing he could afford was for any of his subordinates to smell weakness on him. Theirs was a cutthroat business where only the best of the best lasted for any length of time. The consequences of any single man being unable to pull his weight could be catastrophic, especially with the mounting threats they now faced. There were days when he wondered if he might not be happier selling his services to the highest bidder, and then he remembered that his team was the only thing standing between the world at large and the fate that had befallen the scientists at AREA 51.

"Not much farther!" Sokolov yelled.

The wind screamed from the sheer granite face of the mountain behind them and whistled from the exhaust vents jutting from its honeycombed interior. He glanced back and caught a glimpse of them before the storm swallowed them once more. Miles of winding ductwork connected them to the opposite side of the mountain, where the former research station once perched high above the ice cap. They should have expanded their search outside the network of caverns and tunnels months ago. Of course, even if they had, the extreme weather might have made it so they never found this lead anyway.

Sokolov led him up a slick, windswept slope, from the top of which he could see the array off to their right in the far distance and realized that the wind had driven them a full twenty degrees off course without him even noticing. They corrected course and followed the rocky topography along an S-shaped ridgeline that protruded from the snow like a black wave preparing to crash down upon the vast expanse of white. The wind tore straight through their clothing and the flesh underneath, reminding Donovan that regardless of how much of their will they imposed upon this continent, it would never be bent, let alone broken.

"Down there!"

Donovan followed Sokolov's outstretched arm downhill toward where the rocky crest vanished into the snow. He was halfway down the slope before he saw the crevice, the mouth of which was already nearly concealed by a massive drift. Loose talus skittered from beneath him and clattered into the accumulation. He lost his balance and slid a good twenty feet down the decline before righting himself and picking his way more cautiously toward the opening. The sound of the wind blowing across the orifice reminded him of someone back home in West Virginia playing a jug.

Sokolov skidded to his side and offered him his flashlight.

"Careful of that first step."

Donovan looked at him curiously for a moment before crawling to the edge of the crevice and shining the flashlight inside. The bottom was so far down that he couldn't initially see it, at least not with the way the ice reflected his beam. He slid his legs inside and braced his upper arms against the sides. He found the ridges Sokolov had chiseled into the ice to climb back out and used them to control his descent.

The fissure was maybe five feet wide in the center and tapered to a mere crack at either end. While not as deep as it had initially looked, it was more than deep enough to spare him from the elements. It had to be a good fifty degrees warmer, which, unfortunately, wasn't saying a whole lot. On the positive side, at least it was still cold enough to keep the carcasses strewn across the ground from thawing.

There were several different species of seals, penguins, and native birds, or at least what was left of them. The meat had been torn from their breasts and flanks, leaving behind masses of feathers and fur, and largely intact skeletons with beaks, tails, and flippers. The flesh that hadn't been scavenged was frozen. Most of it appeared to have undergone some amount of decomposition, which suggested it had been down here for some length of time before the eternal night fell and winter commenced in earnest.

He kicked at what was left of an emperor penguin. This had been another colossal waste of time. And now, not only did he have to trudge all the way back to the mountain and walk several miles in a crouch through the ductwork, he was going to have to write a report detailing how he'd wasted the better part of his day investigating what appeared to be nothing more than the den of some kind of animal—

His light fell upon the remains of a gray-feathered petrel. Its wings were broken and pinned beneath it, its head flopped backward and frozen to the bare rock. And right there, in the middle of its breast, were the perfectly preserved bite marks of the animal to which the den belonged.

"Christ Almighty," he whispered.

The ridges of the teeth were so undeniably human they might as well have been his own.

Donovan unholstered his transceiver, which produced little more than screeches of static as he dialed through the frequencies. He wanted to radio in his findings rather than deliver them in person. While the director would be grateful for the news and would likely reward him for finally ascertaining the fate of Hollis Richards, he knew the information would not be well received on a personal level.

They should have known that Richards would have fled the tunnels to avoid being captured, even if it meant braving the elements. He would have flushed like a pheasant from a cornfield and made a break for freedom. While he had obviously survived out here for some length of time, there was no way on this planet he could have survived the entire winter in this brutal environment.

Donovan killed the static, holstered his transceiver, and shined his light around him. There was a pile of pelts in one corner and a frozen mound of feces in the other. At a guess, Richards had lived down here for maybe a month, but it was obvious he hadn't been here in a long time. Wherever his body was now, it was undoubtedly frozen solid and buried under several feet of snow. Donovan doubted they'd ever find it, but at least they could call off the search parties and Barnett could devote all his attention to the task at hand. They could all feel it, a sensation that they were running out of time, and each day brought them closer to the inevitable confrontation with forces they had yet to identify and weren't prepared to engage.

Donovan used his cell phone to photograph the cavern and returned it to his jacket pocket. It was the newest and most advanced iPhone in the world, and yet down here it was little more than a paperweight with a handful of pictures from back home and a few games to play when he couldn't sleep.

There was nothing more he could do here.

He followed the howl of the wind and looked up the icy chute. He could barely see the night sky way up there with all the snow blowing past. The notches in the ice were his saving grace. There was no physical way he would have been able to climb out of there had Sokolov not chiseled the toeholds. Had their roles been reversed, Donovan had to admit he probably wouldn't have had the presence of mind to do so.

His left hand slipped and he nearly fell.

"Hey!" he shouted up to the surface. "Give me a hand, would you?"

Only the wind wailed in response.

Donovan braced his feet and pulled himself higher. He skipped the ledge that had betrayed him and pushed on until he was able to squeeze his arms through the narrow gap and pull his legs from the crevice.

There was no sign of Sokolov leading up the steep talus slope, nor were there any tracks in the snow heading toward the antenna array. He turned all the way around—

Donovan nearly lost his balance when he saw the red spatters across the snow and Sokolov lying facedown in the accumulation, surrounded by a riot of footprints. His survival instincts kicked in and he propelled himself from the orifice—

It was upon him before he could scream.

23
BARNETT

Surface Access Platform,
2 vertical miles above FOB Atlantis

Barnett burst from the door to the power station and braced himself against the elements. The wind hammered him sideways with such force that he could barely maintain his balance on the icy platform, which, despite being heated and continuously sprayed with de-icing agents, was like a skating rink. He shielded his eyes against the blowing snow, but still couldn't see the Bell V-280 Valor, even though the thunder of its props was all around him. They were short on time, and he needed this bird in the air.

He had debated calling in some favors and borrowing a special ops unit that could have gotten to Mexico sooner, but he didn't know what they were up against, which was precisely the nature of the threats his men had been trained to combat. There was no one on this planet he trusted more than Morgan to lead this mission, and not just because of his skill on the battlefield. He had the ability to think outside of traditional parameters and the confidence to make split-second decisions. Morgan and his men were loading the last of their supplies onto the tiltrotor when its silhouette emerged from the storm.

"How much longer?" Barnett shouted.

"We'll be in the air in under five minutes!"

There was nothing he could do to expedite that timeframe now. The Valor would get them across the Southern Ocean at 300 miles an hour and to a remote airfield in southern Argentina, where a Cessna Citation X would be fueled and waiting. At more than 700 miles per hour, it would make the remainder of the journey in just under nine hours, which was still longer than he would have liked. He was just going to have to hope that his assets on the ground had enough sense to keep their heads down. Then again, it was always possible he was overreacting, but he had to believe that if he knew about the maze and the sleeping god, then so did his unknown adversary. And it was high time he drew this secretive opposition out into the open.

"What are the rules of engagement?" Morgan shouted. His arctic gear was already white with snow, and his stubble was frozen on his cheeks.

"We need to know what we're up against. Do whatever you need to do to get me that information."

"What about civilian casualties?"

"Our adversary has been too careful to attract attention. Its operatives will wait until the site is deserted before making their move."

"And our assets?"

"They need the scientists even more than we do right now. They'll use any means necessary to beat us to the center of the maze. Assuming they've yet to make the same connection as Mr. Roche, they're going to need those scientists alive to get them through it."

"Did you share the route with our assets?"

Barnett hesitated.

"No."

The last of Morgan's men jogged past them on the platform, climbed into the Valor, and slid the door closed behind him. They were only going in with four men, including Morgan, since they had to sacrifice weight for fuel efficiency and speed, and could only hope that the enemy didn't arrive with vastly superior numbers. Knowing what was at stake, however, Barnett found it hard to believe they would take any chances, which meant that the element of surprise was by far the most powerful weapon in his arsenal.

He hoped it would be enough.

"You're not going to tell them, are you?" Morgan asked. "You're counting on that to buy us some time."

"The maze is flooded," Barnett said. "It'll slow them down."

"What about our assets themselves?"

"We're just going to have to hope our scientists are as smart as they think they are."

"And if they're not?"

Barnett watched the propellers tilt into the vertical position. The motor screamed, and the rotor wash assaulted him with a cloud of snowflakes that felt like needles piercing the bare skin of his face.

"The mission comes first!" he shouted. "You understand the consequences of failure?"

Morgan nodded solemnly. He knew better than most what they were up against and the fate that would befall them all should any of the secrets even peripherally related to Subject Z fall into the wrong hands.

He turned, lowered his head against the brutal wind, and jogged toward the Valor.

"I want to know the moment you're on the ground!" Barnett shouted.

Morgan climbed up into the copilot's seat. The tiltrotor lifted off before he even closed his door. It was barely fifty feet into the air when Barnett lost sight of it in the storm. He whirled and rushed back toward the power station. Even the few minutes he had spent in the elements had chilled him to the marrow, and his legs hurt with the impact from every footfall. There were still preparations to be made on their end and one glaring question for which he needed an answer.

What was the sleeping god?

The answer was of no small consequence. They had to figure out exactly what they were up against. And there was only one person who knew for sure, and he was going to get it out of him—or, rather, it—one way or another.

24
JADE

Teotihuacan

"I don't like this," Anya said.

"Neither do I," Jade said. She sat on a cot that doubled as a couch beside Evans and leaned closer to the fan perched on the counter beside her. It was so humid that it felt like she could wring a bucket of sweat from her clothes.

While the first mobile home served as a field lab, the second functioned as a combination break room and living quarters. There were framed photographs of various archeological digs and newspaper clippings on the walls. Sand art and crafts made of yarn. The furniture was on its last legs and some of it looked like it wouldn't hold even Jade's diminutive form. Emil was asleep in the back half of the trailer, behind the curtain, his arm flopped over his face, snoring softly. They spoke in whispers not just to keep from waking him, but to make sure that no one else heard.

"You're telling me that Barnett never once contacted you prior to today," Evans said. He took a sip of warm iced tea from a glass beaded with condensation.

"I don't know how else to say it so you'll believe me."

"Look at it from my perspective. You show up here—out of the blue—and mere hours later we're talking to the same guy who rescued us from the Antarctic research station the last time we were all together. Doesn't that sound like more than just coincidence to you?"

He was seriously grating on Jade's nerves, but she had to admit that he had a point. The way events were coming together made her feel like she didn't have the slightest control over what was transpiring, as though she were merely an actor in a play for which she'd never read the script. What *were* the odds that Barnett would call her here in Mexico, where she'd gone on a whim because she needed to talk to someone who would understand what she'd experienced in Nigeria and not question her sanity?

Anya slurped the last of her lunch from her fingertips, leaned back in her chair, and drew her legs to her chest. The light passing through the gap between the drawn curtains behind her, which fluttered on the breeze from the open window, bisected the table and a stack of foil-wrapped tamales delivered by a local woman, close to three hours ago now, from the back of a dirt-brown Ford Aerostar.

"He didn't even try to deny that it was still alive?" Anya said. "What possible reason could they have for keeping it that way?"

"Look around you," Evans said. "What would a living, breathing Teotihuacano be worth to any of the researchers here?"

"They'd all be out of jobs," Jade said.

"I don't buy that they just want to keep it alive so they can study it," Anya said. "When has mankind ever been content to merely observe? You know what my colleagues would do if they encountered a species of hominin they thought was extinct? They'd take it apart, piece by piece, just to put it back together again."

"You're talking about cloning," Evans said.

"Cloning. Breeding. Hybridizing. You name it. The only reason no one's done so yet is because all of our samples of DNA are too old and degraded."

"They don't need to clone this species," Jade said. "It's fully capable of cloning itself."

"In a sense," Evans said. "There's something different about the drones, though. They lack a certain quality that only the original possesses."

"Is that your professional opinion based on your extensive experience with them?"

"I got way closer to them than I would have liked. I looked into their eyes. They were different and you know it."

Evans abruptly stood from the cot and paced the front half of the trailer. Despite having showered, he still reeked of the water from the underground tunnels.

"The distinction is of no practical relevance to us now," Anya said. She picked up a tamale, opened the foil, and closed it again, as though she were still hungry but couldn't bring herself to eat. "Whether an original or a drone, its main biological imperative seemed to be killing everyone and everything around it. There's no precedent for that kind of behavior in the natural world. Predators hunt and kill for food. This is not a predatory species as we've come to understand it. It's more like a virus in how it can infect other hosts without caring about the damage it does to the larger host population.

If left untreated, a virus will continue to replicate itself until it eradicates an entire species."

"While I don't disagree with your analogy," Jade said, "you have to be careful ascribing human traits to lower orders of life. There is nothing malicious about a virus. Its sole function is to reproduce. It neither knows nor cares how it affects the host organism. It will continue to replicate until it's no longer able to do so and then it will die. It is incapable of what we consider communication. This thing, this species, is different. It is malicious. It can deliberately infect any host it chooses and it can communicate over great distances. How else could a drone in Nigeria have known that the creature we thought had died in Antarctica was still alive?"

"Assuming it was a drone," Evans said.

"Tell me you're just doing that to get a reaction. If we were ten years old, would you pull my pigtails?"

"You think I . . . ? I've been all around the world, and nowhere have I encountered anyone as maddening as—"

"Shh!" Anya hissed.

Emil groaned and flopped onto his side. The entire trailer shook.

Evans ran his fingers through his damp hair and plopped down on an overturned bucket that functioned as a chair. Jade caught herself staring at the way his shirt clung to the sweat on his broad chest and forced herself to look away.

"Like I said, the distinction is unimportant right now," Anya said. "What is important is what Barnett said."

Evans nodded and opened the cooler beside him. He

tossed each of them a bottle of water and drained half of his in one drink.

"What exactly did he say?" Anya asked.

"He said we were in grave danger," Evans said.

"From what?"

"He didn't say, but he wanted to know if there was a secure location nearby where we could withstand a siege."

"Jesus," Anya said. "Do you think he was referring to more drones?"

"I don't think so," Jade said. "He admitted that the creature was still alive. I think he would have told me if the threat was drones."

"Did he seem genuinely concerned about our safety?"

"We wouldn't be having the conversation if he didn't."

"I agree with Jade," Evans said.

"That's a first."

Evans opened his mouth to say something, but obviously thought better of it. He closed his eyes momentarily, composed himself, and spoke in a level tone.

"I believe that if Barnett suspected we were in danger from drones, he would have said so, if only to secure our cooperation. What worries me is that he didn't tell us the nature of the threat. I'm not convinced he knows what it is."

"Doesn't know?" Anya said. "Then why call in the first place?"

"He was fishing for information," Jade said. "That was the impression I got from the start. I surprised him with the knowledge that—what did he call it?—the *subject* was still alive, but he seemed to just be playing a hunch. It wasn't until I mentioned the sleeping god that his entire demeanor changed."

"That was the first thing he asked me about," Evans said, "and yet he knew nothing about the maze. Even if he somehow hacked into our computers or our communications, he couldn't have known about one without the other, which means that he had heard of the sleeping god before he called us. Maybe even before we saw the warning in the sacrificial chamber."

"Do you think that our having any knowledge at all of this sleeping god was enough to confirm whatever suspicion led him to call in the first place?" Anya asked.

"Stands to reason, don't you think?"

"But he doesn't know any more about it than we do," Jade said.

"That's how it sounds to me," Evans said.

"And yet what little you told him was enough to convince him that we were in so much danger we needed to barricade ourselves in here."

"You don't think this sleeping god is like Dale Rubley, you know, only . . . different, do you?" Anya asked.

Jade cringed at the thought. For all the time she had spent thinking about the creature and the physiological mechanisms by which it could have symbiotically—or, perhaps, parasitically—subsumed the body of the engineer Rubley, she'd never once entertained the notion that there was another predatory species like it out there. She looked at Evans, who appeared to have turned his eyes inward, as well. The prospect alone was overwhelming.

"No," Evans finally said. "Barnett said to find someplace safe, not 'get the hell out of there,' which implies that we aren't the direct target of this threat. Whatever he thinks is about to happen has more to do with the sleeping god than it does with us."

"If that's the case, then there's something in that maze that someone really wants," Jade said.

She rose from the cot and repeatedly tugged at the hem of her shirt to fan her chest. The scent reminded her that it had been far too long since her last shower. She sat at the table opposite Anya and forced herself to eat, if only because she couldn't remember the last time she'd done so.

"You said he didn't know about the maze," Anya said.

"But he knew about the sleeping god," Jade said. "Mentioning it in conjunction with the maze could have been just what he needed to put whatever pieces he had together."

"This site is connected with the one in Antarctica, right?" Evans said. "That's the whole reason we're here. What if the sleeping god is connected to both, too? And what if this god—who not even Dr. Villarreal has heard of—isn't necessarily a mythical creation, but rather a literal one? What if the sleeping god is what's at the center of the maze?"

Jade set down her food. It felt like she was swallowing stones just to fill her gut. She could see where he was going with that line of thought, but wasn't entirely certain of the implications.

"We need to figure out what we're going to do," Anya said. "Do we believe that this threat is credible?"

"I believe that Barnett does," Evans said, and looked at Jade. "Do you agree?"

She nodded and ordered her thoughts before speaking.

"Then if we all agree that we're dealing with a legitimate threat, the first thing we need to do is clear this place out."

"The site closes to the public at five," Anya said. "That's just over an hour from now."

"Good," Jade said. "So the way I see it we have three options. We can do nothing and leave with everyone else. That's one. We can barricade ourselves in here and wait another ten-plus hours for Barnett's team to arrive, which is what he wants. Or we can go back down there and see if we can find out anything about this sleeping god."

"You're out of your mind," Evans said. "You saw the booby traps down there."

"Nothing's going to happen up here as long as there are witnesses everywhere, right?"

"You're assuming the threat is human in nature."

"If it weren't, Barnett would have been here already. He would have told us to evacuate this place and get out of here ourselves."

"He nearly let us all die in Antarctica," Anya said. "He waited until the very last minute to send help."

"I don't think he would have called us at all if that was his intention. He could have just watched us via satellite and waited to see what happened."

"I agree," Evans said.

"So what about this?" Jade said. "We take a shot at discovering what's at the center of the maze. If we don't find it before this place closes, we get out of here before anything can happen."

"You keep saying 'we' like you're going to be down there."

"You're right, Cade. This is your call."

He hesitated. It wasn't Jade's favorite option either, but she hadn't traveled halfway around the world to lock herself inside a trailer that smelled of body odor and bad Mexican food, one that likely wouldn't hold up to a stiff breeze, let alone anything resembling a siege.

Evans finally nodded, rose without a word, and headed for the back of the trailer, where his wetsuit hung in the shower stall.

Jade pulled back the curtains over the window with the intention of staring out across the ruins. Instead, she found herself looking right at the archeologist, Villarreal, who smiled awkwardly and strode toward the door like that had been his intention all along. She couldn't help but wonder how long he'd been standing there.

Or what he might have heard.

25
TESS

The Cage, FOB Atlantis

Tess had seen Subject Z agitated before, but never to this extent. It didn't just pace its cage; it stalked it, as though aggressively scrutinizing it for any weakness it somehow hadn't seen before. Testing and probing the walls. Digging its fingers into the seams around the barricade. Perhaps because of its physical form, or maybe because of its capacity for higher orders of communication, she'd begun to think of it in human terms, and yet what she watched on the monitor now lacked anything resembling humanity. It was an animal, one seemingly worked into a frenzy by the presence of the prey that had eluded it in the past.

Until Kelly and Roche arrived, she'd been able to distance herself from the events that had transpired here before her arrival. No, not events . . . the slaughter of nearly everyone inside AREA 51, the station preceding this one. The creature in front of her had ripped apart human beings just like her with its claws and teeth and infected others with whatever evil sentience animated it so they could join in the bloodletting. This was not a curiosity. It was a monster, and if it were to ever escape its cage, it would no doubt run her down and do the same thing to her.

Not since her first day had she felt this way, and even then she'd been more intrigued than afraid. She couldn't help but notice that there was an element of escalation to its pattern of behavior. In a matter of days, it had gone from playing the perfect lab rat to hurling itself against the door in an effort to break out. Where before it had been content to humor her with its guttural clicking sounds, it was now talking directly to her and smearing the blood of its meals into messages on the window. It terrified her to think what might come next, although not nearly as much as it did Kelly, who sat several feet behind her, within visual range of the monitors and yet simultaneously with one foot out the door, as well. The girl with the red and green streaks in her hair had seen things that Tess didn't want to imagine. She wondered if, had their roles been reversed, she would have been strong enough to survive, let alone come back here and share the same room with it.

Roche stood at the window, staring into the dark cage while the creature skulked invisibly in front of him. It was almost as though the being on the other side could smell him, for every few minutes it stopped, raised its face, and sniffed until it was again overtaken by bloodlust.

Barnett had instructed them to wait to begin until he got back, but he'd been gone for so long now that she was beginning to wonder if he'd forgotten about them. She didn't know what was in Mexico, only that Special Agent Morgan and his team were on their way there in a big hurry. Whatever the reason, it had something to

do with the underground maze he had shown her and
the route Roche had drawn to the center. A part of her
wished Barnett had sent her, too. Seeing the sun for the
first time in months would have been amazing. More
important, however, she couldn't shake the feeling that
something bad was happening here in Antarctica. It
was a sensation she couldn't quite put into words, and
yet one that grew more insistent with each passing
minute.

"Do you really believe that aliens built structures on
other planets?" Kelly asked.

Tess rounded on her, prepared to launch into her
standard diatribe, but hesitated when she saw the expression on the younger woman's face. She wasn't
used to people genuinely wanting to hear her answer.

"I can tell you with complete certainty that there are
non-naturally occurring structures on any number of
planets, including our own moon, although any theory
about who or what built them would be pure conjec-
ture."

"How can you be so sure?"

"Nature abhors perfection. At its most basic level,
it's essentially an agent of chaos. There are no right
angles in the natural world, no perfect squares or circles. Pyramids like the one above us don't accidentally
come into being. Not here, and certainly not on other
planets with varying gravitational forces and, in some
cases, complete lack of geothermal and hydrogeological activity."

"So if sentient beings either lived on or visited these
planets, then do you believe they've been on this planet?
That they could still be here?"

That was the real question, and the one that destroyed

her credibility in the world of academia. When it came to omnipotent beings living in gated communities in the clouds, people were willing to believe almost anything, but when it came to otherworldly species, they demanded a level of proof that couldn't be demonstrated without producing a body. That was what Kelly was asking her, she knew. Was this creature in front of them a product of organisms that had arrived from another planet? Or worse, were there more of them out there?

"You're asking a question for which there is no answer. Belief is the kissing cousin of faith. There are people who believe in the ancient astronaut theory, that life-forms from across the galaxy were responsible for building the pyramids or using slave labor to mine the Earth's resources or even for the evolution of mankind itself. My own feelings are mixed. What I can say with complete certainty is that we are not alone in the universe and it's only a matter of time before we make first contact, if we haven't already, but if whoever's out there is anything like this monstrosity, I have no desire to be around when we do."

"Whatever it is," Roche said, "they should have killed it six months ago. Nothing good can come from keeping it alive."

The echo of footsteps announced Barnett's arrival.

"You'll have to forgive me for taking so long." He emerged from the dark corridor into the now dimly lit room. The chiaroscuro on his face exaggerated his exhaustion. "I regret that my time is at a premium right now."

Tess didn't know what to say, so she said nothing.

Roche retreated from the window, but appeared physically unable to turn his back on it.

"What fail-safes do you have in place?" he asked.

"The electromagnet on the door is so strong that you couldn't pull it open with a tank," Barnett said.

"And the power to it?"

"Redundant features on different grids."

"What would happen if they all lost power at once?"

"That can't happen. We have enough reserve power to outlast any storm—"

"Unless something happens to those generators. You forget I've been here before."

"What happened here before was a tragedy, Mr. Roche. I like to think we've learned well the lessons—"

"Where's the kill switch?"

"Rest assured, Mr. Roche, there is no way the subject will ever leave that cage unless it does so in a body bag."

"We don't even know for sure that it can be killed."

"That's absurd."

"Is it? We're dealing with a single organism composed of many. In my experience, it's survived electrocution, scalding steam, a fall from considerable height, and being tranquilized. You'll have to forgive me for not taking your word for it."

"Be that as it may, you're just going to have to. I'm not about to give someone with your particular skill set enough information to figure out how to destroy it."

"It's only in there because, for whatever reason, it's chosen to allow it," Roche said. "It's only a matter of time before it finds a way out of there."

"Then perhaps we should get right down to business."

26
ANYA

Teotihuacan

Small groups remained scattered throughout the park. Soon they would converge upon the exit, where the other tourists were already haggling over the prices of souvenirs and piling back into their vehicles and lining up to board one of the waiting buses. It was only a matter of time before the remaining researchers joined them. If Barnett was right and they were in some kind of danger, then they were running out of time to figure out what was in the maze.

Evans had gone down half an hour ago, but had made precious little progress. He'd insisted that Anya remain in the trailer, and while she made a grand show of resenting being treated like a child, she was happy enough to watch his feed on the computer monitor with Jade, who'd brewed a pot of overly strong coffee while she was helping Evans into his gear. Assuming that whatever threat was heading their way wouldn't reveal itself in front of so many witnesses, their plan was to reach the center of the maze before the site cleared out. Failing that, they would join the last wave of the exodus and avoid Barnett's danger entirely. While they were all more than a little curious, they remembered what happened the last time they let their curiosity get the better of them. If Barnett wanted whatever was down there so badly, he could come and get it himself.

"How much longer do we have?" Jade asked.

"Twenty minutes," Anya said. "Half an hour at the most."

"I do not understand why you must do this today," Villarreal said. "Surely there is no rush."

The archeologist had insisted upon joining them when he found out what they were planning to do. At first, Anya thought that maybe he was sticking around for her. Unfortunately, he appeared far more interested in Evans's progress than anything she was doing.

"If you have someplace else you need to be . . ." Jade said.

Villarreal shook his head and scooted his stool closer to Anya's so he could better see the monitor.

Evans had already taken several wrong turns, each of which led into a cul-de-sac from which he had to carefully retreat toward the last fork. He'd encountered several other human skeletons either similarly skewered from above or crushed beneath massive stones that had once been fitted into the ceiling.

"We're just about out of time, Cade," Jade said.

"This is hopeless," Evans said. *"I could be down here another ten hours and still not find my way through."*

"My best guess is that you've covered roughly a quarter of it."

"And accomplished nothing."

"Give yourself some credit. At least now you know where not to go."

"Very funny."

"And you haven't gotten yourself killed yet."

"Yet?"

Anya heard a crackle of static from outside the trailer. One of the security guards walked past the window of the trailer on his way to rounding up the stragglers. Once they were done, the guards would insist upon escorting the remaining researchers to their cars, as well. While it felt like they were way out in the middle of nowhere, they were close enough to Mexico City that they needed to remain vigilant, especially considering the cartels had expanded from drugs to extortion and kidnapping, and Americans were some of their favorite targets.

"We're down to fifteen minutes." She let the curtains close. "If that. We should just call it and get out of here."

"Anya says we only have fifteen minutes," Jade said. "How does it look down there?"

The image on the screen was grayish-green. The bubbles from Evans's regulator occasionally burbled through the swirling sediment. His light barely limned the walls. A corridor opened to his right. He turned to get a better look and came face-to-face with a skull that had been speared through the back of the head and out between its eye sockets. The rest of the body lay in a disarticulated heap below it.

"I think that about wraps it up," Evans said. *"Whatever's down here is someone else's problem now."*

"What do you think this 'sleeping god' is?" Villarreal asked.

"It's starting to look like we might never know," Anya said. "I'm not entirely sure that's such a bad thing, either."

A knock on the door startled her.

Emil opened the door just far enough to stick his head inside.

"Catch you guys tomorrow," he said. "Peace out."

Anya caught a glimpse of Alexandra and several others with him before he closed the door. Their scuffing footsteps trailed them toward the exit.

"Can you find your way back out?" Jade asked.

"I think I can manage," Evans said.

"Okay." Jade set the headset down on the table, stretched her arms over her head, and yawned.

Anya couldn't understand how Evans could possibly be attracted to someone like Jade. Not that she wasn't beautiful, which she totally was. It was just the way she talked to people. She was blunt to the point of bitchiness seemingly every single moment of the day.

There had been a part of Anya that had really hoped to find something down there, and yet the relief of having not done so overwhelmed her. She wanted nothing more to do with Cameron Barnett or anything even tangentially related to—

A dull thudding sound from outside. Barely audible. She would have dismissed it as a figment of her imagination had Jade not turned toward the window at the exact same time.

The curtains fluttered gently on the faint breeze blowing through the open window.

Anya climbed down from her stool and drew back the drapes.

The shadows from the surrounding granite temples and black pepper trees stretched across the Avenue of the Dead. There was no sign of whatever had made the sound.

She let the curtains fall closed again, shrugged for Jade's benefit, and crossed the room to the examination table where she'd set her backpack. The sooner she was out of there, the sooner she'd be able to relax. She'd allowed Barnett to get inside her head, and the paranoia was eating her alive.

"You can stay at my place, Jade," she said. "If you want. It's certainly not the nicest apartment you'll find, but it serves its purpose."

"Thank you," Jade said. "I appreciate the offer—"

Thu-thump.

All three of them turned toward the window as one.

The faint hiss of static droned lazily in the distance.

"What is it?" Villarreal asked.

"I don't know," Anya said.

She set down her bag, opened the door, and stepped out—

Emil lay facedown in the dirt maybe a hundred feet to her left, his floral-patterned shirt flaring on the wind. Alexandra was crumpled on her side next to him, her face hidden by her long hair. There were two more bodies near the edge of the road, obscured by the weeds where they'd fallen. A uniformed security guard was sprawled at the base of a stone wall twenty feet past them, his walkie-talkie buzzing from beside his outstretched hand.

Anya slammed the door and grabbed the edge of the nearest table.

"Help me!"

"Anya, what's—?"

Thump-thump-thump.

The bullets tore straight through the siding and embedded themselves in the opposite wall.

Anya screamed and jerked on the table.

She could still feel the heat of the bullets' passage on her right ear.

"What is happening?" Villarreal shouted. He clasped his hands on top of his head and turned first one way, and then the other, as though unable to figure out what to do.

Jade shoved him aside and helped Anya scoot the table in front of the door, for all the good it would do them. If whoever was out there wanted to get inside badly enough, there was absolutely nothing they could do to stop them.

Anya caught motion from the corner of her eye. Through the gap beside the blinds. A black figure, moving stealthily toward the door.

She turned in a circle. There was no other exit. They were trap—

The front window shattered. Glass skittered across the table and cascaded to the floor.

Anya screamed and ran to the back of the trailer. Threw open the window. Punched out the screen. Pulled herself up onto the ledge and looked down.

The sinkhole was maybe four feet down and five feet away.

A silhouette moved through the shade on the far

side of the road. More motion from the left corner of her eye.

There was no time for debate.

She jumped down and sprinted for the hole.

A figure seemingly clothed in the shadows stepped out from the ruins and sighted an assault rifle—

The ground gave way beneath her and she tumbled into the pit. Landed squarely on her shoulder. Pushed herself to all fours and crawled toward the tunnel.

Thump-thump-thump.

Splinters flew from the siding of the trailer.

She heard screaming as though from a great distance, and then felt someone push her from behind. She glanced back and saw the terror in Jade's eyes and, behind her, a blur as Villarreal threw himself down into the collapsed street.

Anya squeezed into the tunnel and scurried as fast as she could. Fell from the narrow opening. Lunged to her feet. Ran squarely into something solid and screamed.

"What's wrong?" Evans asked.

He gripped her by the shoulders and attempted to steady her, but she swatted his arms away and shouted right into his face.

"Run!"

27
BLY

r. Desmond Bly was roughly a mile away from the base camp, as he thought of it, and currently in no position to turn around, no matter the reason why. The tunnel through which he squirmed felt like a birthing canal. He'd been in tighter places, though. Some of the labyrinthine fissures in Hang Sơn Đoòng had been so narrow he'd been forced to dislocate his own shoulder while barely managing to keep his nose and lips above the water level. Whatever gene caused claustrophobia was simply not present in his DNA. He understood that this lack of fear would ultimately lead him to a horrible end, but he'd long ago come to terms with it. Everyone had to die sometime; better down here doing what he loved than in a hospice somewhere, rotting from the inside out.

He needed some time away from people so he could think. Finding Berkeley's body had really gotten to him. It wasn't just the fact that the guy was dead—after all, he'd seen plenty of corpses through the course of his work, most of them drowned, asphyxiated, or shattered from a fall—it was the condition of his remains. Something had eaten him. There was no other way to describe it. Something had cocooned him inside what looked like a cave swallow's nest and proceeded to crawl in there with him and consume him.

He shuddered at the memory and forced himself to think about anything else.

A cave was like any other living thing. If you paid close enough attention, you could feel it breathe and hear it speak. Bly had always had something of a preternatural connection with the Earth itself, one that helped him sense things that others couldn't. He didn't need to be able to see the tunnel ahead of him to know that it would slope gracefully upward for a short time before branching vertically into a chimney. That was just the natural consequence of a steady trickle of water and its erosive properties on calcium carbonate. If he closed his eyes, he could feel the almost imperceptible movement of air and the smooth stone guiding him inexorably toward it.

The bend was right where he expected it to be and the chimney roughly the height he predicted. He placed one of the mousetraps from the stuff sack tied to his ankle at the base and contorted his body to squeeze his torso inside. It was a matter of minutes to squirm upward through the narrow chute and out into the bottom of a broad well, where once the water dripping from the stalactites overhead had accumulated in a small pool before eating through a weak spot in the limestone, a process that had undoubtedly taken hundreds of thousands of years.

Only there were no stalactites.

Bly shined the beam of his headlamp across the bare

ceiling. The dagger-like speleothems must have been broken off at their bases and filed down to nothing. They would have eventually re-formed, were it not for the flooding that helped preserve this amazing system, if not the petroglyphs carved into the walls.

The designs had been scoured nearly smooth by running water and yet, to his trained eye, they might as well have been painted with neon colors. He retrieved a piece of blue chalk from his harness pocket, flattened it against the wall, and rubbed it up and down until the faint impressions became clear. He scooted around the curvature of the cavern, scribbling as he went, until all that was left was a sliver of chalk he needed to hold in reserve in case of an emergency. He returned it to the tiny waterproof pouch and checked to make sure the GoPro live-action sports camera mounted to the bracket on the side of his helmet was actively recording. He slowly turned his head to make sure the camera captured every inch of the design.

He'd never seen anything quite like it. The majority of cave art, at least from his extensive experience, was rudimentary and stemmed from the Paleolithic Period, when man first developed stone tools. It told simple stories of the hunt or memorialized sacred iconography with little artistic flair. These, however, were extraordinary and elaborate. They were like the petroglyphs throughout the ruins surrounding the pyramid, so intricate in their sculpting that he could almost imagine the three-dimensional characters as they'd once been. He'd heard them described as a cross between the styles of ancient Egypt and Sumer, which seemed fairly accurate to him. There were men in robes with stylized beards and conical hats. Others had bare chests and legs and the heads of animals. Some were giant and others small. Most wielded weapons, while others merely sat or looked to the sky. The designs surrounding the figures were largely unrecognizable, although they reminded him of the religious iconography he'd seen in the Himalayas.

If the panels told a story, it was lost on him.

Bly came to rest on the final image, which featured two bearded men, one standing to either side of a rectangle, inside of which was a third, taller man with his arms crossed over his chest. He wished he had more chalk to bring out the other, largely invisible petroglyphs, but the researchers were just going to have to make do with what he could give them. He swept the camera across the remaining walls for the sake of documentation. Maybe they'd be able to glean the designs from the LiDar scan.

He removed the laser scanner from his stuff sack and set it up in the middle of the chamber. The pinwheel laser started to spin as he moved deeper into the cavern, where a series of flowstone steps ascended to an opening in the wall, through which he could see a space of indeterminate size. He climbed up and perched on the highest ledge. A tunnel stretched away from him into the distance. Unlike the others, the walls had been artificially smoothed, although the petroglyphs adorning them were no better preserved. He traced them with his fingertips as he walked down the manmade corridor.

If he was correct, he was approximately thirteen meters above the ice caves. It seemed strange that anyone would invest so much time and effort into creating such an elaborate sanctuary that no one, outside of skilled spelunkers like him, would ever see.

The passage veered sharply to the left and terminated at a keyhole crevice. His light revealed an igloo-like space on the other side, the walls of which were similarly covered with weathered petroglyphs, but it was the massive granite box in the center that drew his eye.

He'd easily explored ten miles of tunnels and caverns inside this mountain, but never once found anything remotely like this. It was easily eight feet long, wider than the entrance, and shaped like a coffin. He couldn't even figure out how they'd gotten it into the small cavern in the first place. The only other ingresses were a slender fissure on the opposite side and a chimney in the domed roof.

He approached it at a crouch so as not to hit his head and smoothed his palms over the rectangular box. A four-inch-thick slab of granite served as the lid. The characters carved into it were similarly smoothed. Using the last of his chalk went against everything he knew about spelunking, but his curiosity got the better of him. He removed the remaining nub and rubbed it gently over the lid, barely pressing down so as to make what little he had left last. When it was gone, he used his fingertips to spread the blue dust to the edges.

The design was in the same style as the others, and yet unlike all of them. In the center was a figure with the face and antlers of a deer. Its arms were folded across its chest and what looked like wings were pinned underneath it. To either side of its supine form were serpentine shapes that reminded Bly of dragons, their legs raised to display their fanned claws and their faces turned to showcase their sharp teeth.

They'd encountered countless burials at the bottom

of what had once been a lake, but this was the first tomb. And if he was right, they'd finally found where this lost civilization buried its royalty.

He removed his communications device from his stuff sack and turned it on. A crackle of static burst from the speaker.

"Hello?" He smacked the side of the transceiver and tried again. "Hel-hello? Can anybody hear me?"

A garbled voice replied, but he couldn't decipher what it said. He was at the very farthest extent of its range and he knew it, but he had to try, if only to minimize his guilt over what he intended to do next.

He set the transceiver on the lid, braced his feet, and shoved the lid.

A deafening screech echoed through the cavern, but the lid only moved a quarter of an inch. If that. The blasted thing had to weigh five hundred pounds. He pushed back the sleeves of his cave suit, put his shoulder into the stone slab, and drove—

Click-click-click-click-click.

He turned at the sound, but there was no sign of anything behind him. He swept his light across the orifice and the surrounding walls. There wasn't so much as a hint of movement. He returned his attention to the lid, braced himself once more, and pushed with everything he had.

The granite made a grinding noise and slid maybe six inches, just far enough for him to be able to see over the edge. The stench that gusted from within left no doubt as to what the box contained.

Bly tilted his head in such a way that he could shine his light inside. The remains were brown and mummified, the parchment skin shrunken to the contours of the bones. He saw a pair of knobby, bare legs. Cloth, black with the fluids of decomposition. A cavernous abdomen and chest rippled with ribs. And the bony snout and antlered skull of a deer.

Click-click-click-click-click.

This time he could tell exactly where the sound originated.

He slowly raised his light toward the ceiling—

Eyeshine.

He caught a glimpse of scaled lips peeling back from teeth glistening with saliva. He raised his arms to shield his head. A blur of feathers and it was upon him.

His hand vanished with a crunch of bone. Claws pierced his upper back. Searing pain in his shoulder and neck. A sensation of weightlessness as it lifted him, kicking and screaming, toward the hole in the ceiling from which it hung.

The sound of his blood spattering the granite lid followed him into the darkness.

28
KELLY

The Cage, FOB Atlantis

Kelly drew her knees to her chest and practically disappeared into the chair. She'd never been so cold in her life and couldn't seem to make herself stop shivering. It was this place, she knew. This awful, awful place where so many horrible things had happened. She wanted to go home. More than anything, she just wanted to go home.

"This serpent god you mentioned," Barnett said. "Is it like you? Do you see yourself as a god?"

His voice echoed from the speakers inside the cavern. On the monitor, the creature made no appreciable indication that it had even heard him. Its thermal representation just sat there, surrounded by bones, staring at them through two feet of solid steel and concrete.

Roche pulled up a chair beside hers and took her by the hand. She leaned into him and allowed him to wrap his arm around her.

"We know about the maze in Teotihuacan. We know the pattern you drew on the window is the path through it."

The being cocked its elongated head. Its multicolored silhouette looked like something from a science fiction movie.

"What's at the center of the maze? What do you want us to find?"

It rose and stalked across the cavern in its halting, disjointed way. It was just on the other side of the glass, and yet Kelly couldn't see it without the aid of the thermal imaging.

"Tell me about the sleeping god."

An orange smile slashed its face.

"Free . . . us."

Kelly flinched at the sound of the voice straight out of her nightmares. She clutched Roche's hand so tightly that her fingernails bit into his flesh.

"Tell me what I want to know and I'll consider it."

The smile mutated into a snarl.

"You . . . lie."

"As long as you inhabit that form, you will never leave this cage," Barnett said. "Is that what you wanted to hear? No matter how smart you think you are, you will die in there."

"As you will . . . die . . . out there."

Kelly shivered. This time it had nothing to do with the cold.

"This isn't accomplishing anything," Tess said, and gently rested her hand on Barnett's.

The director looked at her as though seeing her for the first time, and leaned away from the microphone. He abruptly stood and walked away from the console. Kelly could feel him pacing behind her as she stared at the hideous face on the computer screen. The smile returned, only somehow even worse.

Tess pressed the button and spoke into the microphone.

"You're referring to the feathered serpent god, correct?"

Uhr-uhr-uhr-uhr-uhr-uh.

"What is the sleeping god?"

"Let him . . . ask."

"Let who ask?"

"Martin . . . Roche."

Kelly felt him stiffen next to her. Tess glanced back, but said nothing. It took her a moment to compose herself. There was no way it could have seen him through the blood-smeared glass.

"Tell it he's in England," Barnett said.

"The director says he's in England."

"He is . . . here. I can . . . smell . . . him."

The way it emphasized the word "smell" made Kelly's skin crawl.

Tess looked at Barnett, who stopped his incessant pacing only long enough to spear Roche with his stare.

"You up for this?"

Roche stared at the dark window for several seconds before releasing Kelly's hand. He stood and approached the console.

The creature's smile grew impossibly wide.

Roche licked his lips and pressed the button on the microphone.

"What is the sleeping god?"

"Have you . . . broken . . . the code?"

The tone of its voice was cruel, taunting.

"What code?"

"You are . . . running out . . . of time."

"I should have killed you when I had the chance."

"Events already . . . in motion."

"Ask it what it means," Barnett said.

"Screw this. I say we end this monster right here and now."

"Just ask it. Please."

Roche stared at Barnett for several seconds before looking away and pressing the button.

"What events?"

The creature's smile faded. It rocked back like a wolf preparing to howl and drew a long inhalation through its nose. When it lowered its head, Kelly was certain it looked straight at her through the monitor. It held up its left hand and tapped its abnormally long fingers against its thumb, just like Kelly was doing at the exact same time. She closed her eyes as tightly as she could and felt the warmth of tears on her cheeks.

"Kelly Nolan . . . knows."

She sobbed at the sound of her name coming from its mouth.

"Leave her out of this."

It smiled and retreated into the cavernous depths of its cage.

"Don't let it get under your skin," Barnett said. "Focus on the task at hand. Ask it again about the sleeping god. We need to know what we're up against."

"You ask it. We're done here."

Roche extended his hand to Kelly, who took it and allowed him to pull her to her feet.

Barnett's transceiver crackled. He stepped out into the tunnel and lowered his voice so they couldn't overhear what he said.

"How does it know our names?" Kelly whispered.

"I assume the same way it learned our language,"

Tess said. "I believe it assimilates the memories of its host."

"We barely met Rubley," Roche said.

"But you knew Hollis Richards, who, from what I understand, learned everything he could about each of you."

The thought made Kelly sick to her stomach. If that was true, it knew where she lived, where she worked. None of them would ever be safe as long as it was alive.

The creature turned to face the camera. The expression on its face was not that of a higher order of life, but rather that of a predatory species.

"Kill it," Kelly said. "Kill it now."

An alarm klaxon blared.

Kelly screamed and nearly came out of her skin.

"What's going on?" Tess asked.

Barnett holstered his transceiver as he entered the room.

"Everyone to the surface," he said. "We're on temporary lockdown."

The creature settled once more into its nest of bones and stared at them through the monitor, seemingly unperturbed by the siren.

"What's happening?" Kelly screamed.

The creature's voice was barely audible over the shrill sound, but there was no mistaking its words.

"The . . . sleeping god . . . awakens."

29
CARSON

"Everyone needs to get to the base," Special Agent Drew Carson said. He had to raise his voice to be heard over the alarm. "That means you, too, Dr. Clarke."

He was getting more than a little tired of babysitting civilians, especially those who couldn't seem to follow the simplest of orders. It almost made him nostalgic for his days guarding the oilfields of Iraq for men who didn't give a rat's ass about the war and were only in it for the money. Men like that were easy to deal with because their motivations were transparent. And predictable. They were going to make a fortune regardless of how many lives were lost or whose side they were on.

Dr. Clarke, on the other hand, was exasperating. The creature on the other side of the wall was an abomination that had viciously murdered people just like them and here she was trying to make sure that everything was in order when they should have just triggered the failsafe and incinerated the freaking thing, or at least left it to rot in there while they followed their orders.

"Come with me," he said in the most level tone he could muster and took her gently by the arm. "Please."

"Okay, okay," she said. "I just need to make sure that all of my data is saved and backed up—"

"You've already done that multiple times."

"I can't leave anything to chance," Tess said. "Not with something this important."

"There's no way it can get out of there, can it?" Kelly asked.

"No, ma'am," Carson said. "As long as we're on lock-down, there's no way that door can be opened without a manual override."

"Who all knows the code?" Roche asked.

"No one who has any desire to let that monster ever set foot outside that cage again, if that's what you're asking." Carson positioned himself behind them so he could herd them toward the corridors leading to the base. "Now, if you wouldn't mind . . ."

"We're going," Dr. Clarke said, and led them at a jog down the hallway toward the underground entrance to the pyramid.

They were nearly there when the pigs started screaming. It was like the sound they made when Dutton rolled that cart of his down the hall, only every single one of them seemed to be making it at once.

"Keep going," he said. "You know the drill. Gather in the central hub and wait for further instructions."

"I'm sure we can handle it on our own from here," Dr. Clarke said.

"I'll be right behind you."

Carson watched them until they reached the ladder before heading back and opening the door to the infernal pigsty. The smell smacked him upside the head the moment he crossed the threshold. The single emer-

gency light was in the far back corner and hidden behind the racks of pig feed Dutton had arranged so he
could hide while he took his little naps. Everyone
knew about it, but no one cared. As long as he continued to serve the bacon crispy and the eggs fluffy, the
cook had a blank check to do whatever he wanted as
far as any of them were concerned.

The squealing was so loud he feared it might rup-
ture his eardrums. If it were up to him, he'd let these
infernal swine hurl themselves against the walls of
their cages until they battered themselves to death, but
Barnett would have a coronary if he let that happen. It
would take more than a week to arrange for replace-
ments and if anything happened to that beast in the
other room in the meantime, Barnett would make sure
someone's head rolled, and there was no way on this
planet it was going to be his.

"Dutton?"

Carson approached the wall of cages. There were
fourteen of them in all: seven columns stacked two
high. All of the wire doors stood open, and yet he
could still see the dark shapes of the animals cowering
in the back of most of them, just squealing and pissing
themselves like it was the end of the world.

He closed the doors one at a time. It wasn't like
Dutton to leave them open. He must have been in the
middle of feeding them when the alarm sounded and
just ran for the barracks. Not like the squealing wouldn't
have been enough to drive him out of his mind anyway.
Maybe if someone silenced the blasted klaxon they'd
shut their bleating snouts for two seconds.

Crack.

The sound came from somewhere behind him. He closed the last cage door and turned toward Dutton's little hidey-hole.

There was something back there.

Carson drew his sidearm and sighted down the shadow, which blended in with the darkness so well that all he could see was the outline of a head and hunched shoulders.

"Come out of there," he said. "Slowly."

Crack.

Without taking his eyes from the sightline, he removed the mini LED Maglite from his utility belt and shined it backhanded into the corner—

The beam reflected from a pair of eyes that were simultaneously human and bestial. The mask of blood on Dutton's face nearly concealed his features. Most of it dribbled from the torn skin along his hairline, which had retracted to reveal the bare bone of his elongated forehead. The rest belonged to the dead pig clutched in his grasp.

"The hell is wrong with you?"

Dutton dropped the carcass, revealing the gaping hole in the pig's neck and the broken vertebrae inside. The edges of the wound appeared to have been inflicted by teeth.

The cook looked up at Carson and tensed, like a spring compressing. He'd stripped off all his clothing and crouched naked on a sack of feed. His skin had a grayish cast, mottled black and purple with bruising.

"Don't move a muscle, Les, or so help me I'll—"

Dutton lunged at him.

Carson dropped his flashlight and pulled the trigger in rapid succession. The flash of discharge created a strobe effect, making Dutton appear to fly toward him in lurching movements.

The cook struck him squarely in the chest. Got inside his arms, forcing his shots high and wide. Drove him to the ground.

Carson grabbed Dutton by the hair and attempted to yank his head back, but only succeeded in ripping the scalp from the cook's deformed skull. Before he could press the muzzle against the other man's temple, Dutton buried his face in the side of Carson's neck.

He bellowed in agony and prayed that Dr. Clarke hadn't followed orders for the first time in her life.

His cries reverberated through the empty corridors until they dissolved into the shrill alarm and the squealing of pigs.

30
EVANS

Teotihuacan

Anya blew past Evans and sprinted into the darkness. He caught a fleeting glimpse of Jade's face before she did the same. He didn't know what the hell had them so scared, but he had no desire to find out.

Villarreal nearly barreled into him. Evans stepped to the side and caught him by the arm.

"What in the name of God is—?"

Bullets sang past his ear and pounded the mound of dirt and debris behind him. He hit the ground a heartbeat before Villarreal and scrambled deeper into the warrens. He wasn't about to stick around long enough to figure out who was shooting at them.

Evans's light illuminated Jade and Anya, casting their long shadows onto the ground ahead of them as they ran. They ducked in and out through the four chambers and ran into the straightway. If they continued on their course, they'd careen headlong into a dead end.

He pushed himself harder. Grabbed Jade by the wrist. Slowed her momentum.

"Anya!" he shouted.

She dashed ahead as though she hadn't heard and was nearly past the lone remaining branch when he finally got her attention.

"Anya!" She slid on the damp ground and spun to face him, her eyes wide and wild. "There's only one way—"

A light materialized behind them, silhouetting Villarreal ever so briefly. Muzzle flare preceded the *thack-thack-thack* of bullets hammering the limestone.

Evans ducked from the path and descended the ladder as fast as he could. He hopped off the moment he sensed the ground below him and shined his light upward for the others.

The ladder was slowing them down while their pursuit was only gaining on them.

Jade landed first. Stumbled. He pushed her unceremoniously through the mouth of the tunnel.

"Go!"

He pulled Anya from the ladder by her hips and ushered her into the hole behind Jade.

Swinging lights appeared above them, crossing the mouth of the pit before settling on the uppermost rungs of the ladder. They were coming too fast.

Villarreal leaped down and scurried into the tunnel. Evans dove like he was sliding into second base as a beam of light struck the dirt behind him. Bullets impacted the soft earth mere inches from his feet.

Thump-thump-thump.

"Hurry!" he shouted and shoved Villarreal's heels.

Evans kicked and clawed for anything resembling traction. Banged his head and elbows repeatedly. Spilled out through the opening and splashed into the water.

A beam of light burst from the tunnel behind him, followed by a barrage of bullets that sizzled from the surface and ricocheted from the face of one of the feathered serpent statues.

Anya screamed and dove out of the way.

Evans coughed out a lungful of the wretched water and slogged away from the tunnel before another fusillade screamed through the chamber. He hurriedly donned the diving mask once more and switched on the light.

Took Jade by the hand and pulled her to him.

"The entrance to the maze is about three feet down and five feet that way. Right under that head there."

"What are you talking about?"

"There's nowhere else to go. We're sitting ducks here!"

"We can block the entrance—"

"Would you just listen to me for once!"

An oblong aura of light focused on the ruined face of the feathered serpent god, growing brighter by the second.

"Take the biggest breath you can hold and go!"

Jade looked past him and her eyes widened. She whirled and dove in one motion. Kicked off against his shins. He had to hope she was a good swimmer because that tunnel had to be at least twenty feet long.

The lens of a flashlight appeared from the corner of his eye. They were out of time.

Anya vanished beneath the water a split second before the beam settled upon her ripples.

"Go!" Evans shouted, but Villarreal was already gone. His kicking feet broke the surface mere seconds before Evans dove where they'd been.

Between the four of them, they'd churned up so

much sediment that he wasn't even sure he'd be able to find the tunnel until his shoulder grazed the side and he realized he was already inside. He swam for everything he was worth and ran into Villarreal from behind before he even saw him. They propelled themselves out the opposite end and straight toward the surface. Breached and gasped for air in the eight inches between the surface of the water and the ceiling of the cavern.

"It won't take them long to figure out where we've gone," Jade said.

"Our only advantage is that we've explored the maze before."

"Twenty-five percent of it."

"You can stay here if you'd rather."

"You have the only light," Anya said. "We'll follow you."

"On my count."

"Just go!" Jade said.

Evans finally had the chance to dial on the flow of air as he dove back into the cloudy water. His light flashed across the hideous sculptures of Mictlantecuhtli and Mictlancihuatl, the god and goddess of the dead, and followed the outstretched forelimb of dog-faced Xolotl toward the mouth of the maze. Rounded the stone wall and swam until he reached the first fork before making a beeline for the surface. The others emerged seconds later, panting in the cool, stale air.

"We need to find—" Villarreal started, but the sloshing water rose over his mouth and cut him off. "We need to find someplace to hide."

"We have to distance ourselves from them first," Evans said.

"We do not even know for sure that they are following us. Surely they will leave once they have what they have come here to find."

"Do you want to wait here long enough to find out for sure?" Jade asked.

"So which way do we go?"

"Left," Anya said. "Then right. That's as far as I know for sure."

"Keep going straight after that until you hit the wall," Evans said. "We'll regroup there."

"We should stay above the water," Villarreal said.

"That will make too much noise and lead them straight to us."

"What about the booby traps?"

"That's where the flooding works in our favor."

"Almost like it was planned that way," Anya said.

"Just don't touch the floor or any of the walls and we should be fine."

"Should?" Villarreal said.

"You expect us to tread water indefinitely?" Jade said.

"Let me know if you come up with a better plan," Evans said.

"We're wasting time," Anya said.

"If you encounter resistance of any kind, stop right where you are. Don't try to push through anything that doesn't belong there."

"Like what?" Jade asked.

"Like a rope that could be supporting a counterweight or any sort of mechanism. Anything that gives or moves when you touch it."

"How are we supposed to avoid them if we can't see anything?"

"Stay right behind me and try not to stray from my path."

"And what if something happens to you?"

Evans stared at her for several moments. Something in her voice caught him by surprise. She was one of the toughest and most confident people that he'd ever met. The idea of being completely reliant upon someone else terrified her.

"Just stay close," he said, and dove once more.

He swam until his headlamp focused on the mortared stones of the wall. Veered left. Dodged the skeleton staked to the ground. Kicked toward the far wall. Breached and waited for the others.

Any second now whoever was out there would discover the tunnel leading to the maze.

They were running out of time.

Jade came up first and sputtered a mouthful of water.

"I don't know how much longer I can tread."

"You can and you will tread for as long as you have to."

Villarreal splashed to the surface several feet away and swam toward them. He nearly smacked Anya in the head when she rose.

"Which way now?" he asked.

"Right," Evans said. "Then another immediate right. If we keep going straight we'll eventually run into a dead end."

"And after that?"

"Right. No, left."

"Are you sure?" Anya asked.

"We'll find out, won't we?"

A splashing sound echoed from the distance, followed by the sound of heavy breathing.

Anya clapped her hands over her mouth to stifle a startled cry.

Evans pressed his index finger to his regulator. He prayed the others understood and remained silent. He closed his eyes and strained to hear. There were at least two people behind them, he was certain, but couldn't tell if there were more of them or not. He had to assume there were at least three and hope for the best.

"Are you ready?" he whispered.

He looked at each of them in turn, nodded to himself, and switched off his headlamp.

The resultant darkness was complete.

31

BARNETT

FOB Atlantis

"They last checked in at the south gate more than two hours ago," Special Agent Avila said.

"The exhaust ducts?"

"Yes, sir." Avila had to jog to keep up with Barnett as he strode through the base. The emergency lights cast a red pall over the entire station, including the men and women rushing to assume their positions. "Donovan responded to Sokolov's call for support."

"Why wasn't I informed?"

"The call was routed to both you and Agent Morgan before it even reached Donovan. He was next in the chain of command."

The events leading up to this catastrophe didn't matter now. There would be plenty of time for analysis down the road. Right now he needed to assume authority over the situation before it spiraled out of his control. With Berkeley and Jonas confirmed dead and Donovan and Sokolov missing, presumed dead themselves, there was no way in hell he was going to be able to keep a lid on this. He should have activated

Protocol Delta and initiated a lockdown when they first found Jonas's remains. He'd made a command decision based on the information available to him at the time and it had returned to bite him in the ass.

"Would someone kill that infernal siren?" he shouted.

He was passing through the corridor to the command center when the racket finally ceased. As per protocol, the majority of the power had been shunted to storage, and what little still flowed diverted to critical functions in an effort to conserve enough to last for several months. Which meant they were going to have to deal with the emergency lights for the foreseeable future.

Agent Love was behind Barnett's desk when he entered the command center.

"Tell me you have eyes," he said.

She toggled some keys on his computer and stepped back so he could take his seat.

"We've got a drone sweeping the area around the ICMS, but with the storm—"

"Give me a visual."

She reached across him and brought up the live-feed window. He maximized it and leaned closer. Everything was white, from the ground to the air to the frost forming on the edges of the lens. A gray crescent appeared in the corner of the screen, where a jagged ridge cut through the windswept accumulation.

"What was the nature of the emergency?" he asked.

"Sokolov called in a possible finding related to Subject Alpha," Avila said.

"And you didn't think that was worth interrupting whatever I was doing at the time?"

"We get several reports every day. Should we drag you out into the tunnels every time someone finds a scrap of fabric or something that 'kind of looks like a footprint'?"

Barnett ignored her and focused on the monitor.

"Walk me through it. From the start."

"Best we can tell, Agent Donovan met Agent Sokolov inside Exhaust Port C and proceeded to follow him to a point or points unknown."

"There are no cameras past the south gate, correct?"

"No, sir. We reappropriated them when we installed the airlocks."

"So it would have taken them half an hour to reach the exhaust ports. They would have stepped outside and wouldn't have been able to see much more than we can through the storm."

"Reported visibility is fifteen feet."

"Take the drone down. I want to see what they would have seen from the ground."

Love used a joystick to bring the drone closer to the ground, which tilted wildly as the propellers fought against the tempestuous wind.

"Sokolov would have basically had to trip over whatever he found. Take me back to the exhaust port."

The drone rose and headed due north, toward where the sheer black granite of the Drygalski Mountains appeared from the storm, far closer than he expected. The drone streaked through the mouth of the exhaust port and hovered beside the open grate, momentarily shielded from the blowing snow.

"The IMCS is due south from there, correct?"

"Approximately."

"And the wind's blowing which direction?"

"East, sir, at forty miles per hour."

"It would have driven them off course if they lost

sight of the antenna. Alter your course ten degrees and follow that ridgeline down there." He tapped the screen. "And take me down to ten feet."

"We risk crashing at that altitude with the way the wind—" Love started.

"Then zoom in, for Christ's sake."

The snow drifted from the top of the rugged ridge, sparing the loose talus along the western slope. If Barnett were out there on foot, that's exactly the route he would have chosen to shield himself from the brunt of the elements.

"What's out there?" he asked.

"As far as we know," Avila said, "there are no natural formations of any kind."

"How about manmade? A power box. A shed. A vehicle. Anything."

"The ICMS is the only piece of equipment in that valley and we have someone out there twice a day to service it. If there was anything, we would have found it by now."

"We obviously didn't, though, did we?"

She bristled at his words. Her lips writhed, but she held her tongue.

"What's that right there?" Barnett tapped the edge of the screen, where he thought for a second he'd seen something stand apart from the snow. "No. Right there. Now, zoom in."

The image tightened on the ground at the edge of the loose rock. The wind blew sideways across the accumulation, bringing with it new snowflakes and whipping up the accumulation. There was an irregular shape that at first looked like a shadow until he detected the faint pinkish hue.

"It must have followed them outside," he whispered, and then louder: "Are the airlocks sealed?"

"We sealed them on both sides of the mountain the moment we sent the drone through," Love said.

"I want every vent not physically contained within this complex sealed. Every shaft. Every tunnel."

"All of our fail-safes are activated."

"But if it got back inside first . . ."

He didn't need to finish the sentence, nor did he need to point out the crevice between the rocks uphill from the bloodstained snow.

Love piloted the drone into position and hovered right over it. It was going to be a tight fit, if she was able to squeeze it through there at all. She maneuvered the drone diagonally and then straight down between walls rimed with ice. The image darkened and she switched on the drone's light. The focus blurred until the aperture adjusted and revealed the animal carcasses littering the ground. Barnett took it all in at once. The pelts in the corner, the condition of the animal remains, the fecal material. He knew exactly what it was.

Hollis Richards had passed through their net before they even cast it.

"Dammit," he said, and abruptly stood.

"What do you want me to do?" Love asked.

"Document every inch of that cave. Find me a clue as to where he might have gone."

"What about Sokolov and Donovan?" Avila asked.

Barnett turned and stared directly into her dark eyes.

"If they're not already dead, I have no doubt they wish they were."

He hustled from the command center and made his way to the main building with Avila trailing in his wake.

"Get me a head count. I want everyone not physically inside this base here within the hour, regardless of their location, and I want them reporting in every fifteen minutes until they arrive."

"Should we raise the readiness level?"

"Initiate Emergency Protocol Delta."

"Yes, sir."

She hesitated and fell a step behind. He whirled to face her.

"You have your orders, Agent Avila."

The cracks in her ordinarily impervious façade betrayed her fear.

"What do you think is out there?" she asked.

"I don't know," he said, "but I have a feeling it's only a matter of time before we find out."

He left her to her task and made his way through the chaos. The entire station had practiced for this eventuality, while hoping to never have to do it for real. In a matter of minutes, he would have all non-combat personnel inside the mess hall, which could be isolated from the rest of the buildings by closing off the connecting corridors. Below it was a heated recess large enough to accommodate all personnel alongside reserve generators, fuel, and enough food to last a month. He prayed they wouldn't have to put that to the test.

Barnett had already lost four men and he still didn't have the slightest idea what they were up against. He understood what Avila was asking, but he could tell that the animal carcasses had been down there in that den for a long time. If Richards had survived the elements, he was long gone, unlike whatever had killed

Jonas and Berkeley. That thing was still somewhere
out there, and, if he was right, growing more brazen by
the minute. Sokolov and Donovan were by no means
pushovers, nor were they small by anyone's definition
of the word. They hadn't surprised their killer and triggered its survival instincts, like Dr. Murphy theorized
had happened to Jonas and Berekely; they'd been
hunted, overwhelmed, and their bodies removed from
the scene with frightening speed and efficiency. So
much, in fact, that he had to wonder if there wasn't
more than one—

Roche appeared from his peripheral vision, caught
him by the arm, and pinned him to the insulated wall,
their faces mere inches apart.

"Tell me what's going on right now or so help me—"

Barnett shoved Roche away from him.

"You should be in the mess hall with the others."

"Not until you tell me what's happening."

"We have a situation, and I have neither the time nor
the inclination to discuss it with you."

"It can't get out of there, can it?"

"Zeta? It's the least of our worries right now."

"So there's another one. You found Richards."

"You'll have to excuse me," Barnett said.

He brushed past Roche and hurried to the front entrance, where members of his team converged on the
main deck from all directions. He stared across the ruins
in the crimson light. The shadows between the ancient
structures were as fathomless as tar. Men in black fatigues with assault rifles slung over their shoulders
climbed the rungs on the sides of the buildings and
took up their posts on the rooftops. They wore dual-

sensor night vision goggles, which fused thermal and infrared technology in such a way that body heat stood apart from the green-scale background like a bright orange beacon.

Barnett stepped back inside, armed the electromagnetic lock, and ran to the command center.

32
ROCHE

While Roche didn't care for the way Barnett had dismissed him, he'd learned what he needed to know. Barnett no longer had everything under control. Worse, he had no more idea what was going on than Roche did.

Thumping sounds overhead. Footsteps.

They'd posted sentries.

Roche glanced at the doors leading into the mess hall. They were different from all the others in the outer buildings. The panels next to them controlled what looked like heavy hydraulic barriers that would slide into position with the push of a button. Something big was going down. He didn't like the idea of being sealed inside here, but, at the same time, vastly preferred it to being outside.

Kelly's face was devoid of expression. It was as though she'd retreated somewhere inside of herself, a reaction common in people suffering from post-traumatic stress disorder when exposed to repeated trauma. He didn't blame her, and it certainly wasn't a reaction that was within her control, but now was not the time for her to shut down. He needed her sharp if they were going to figure out what was happening around them.

He tipped up her chin and looked directly into her eyes.

"Stay with me, okay?"

She barely seemed to recognize him at first, but managed to nod her head. He saw Tess from the corner of his eye and grabbed her before he lost her in the crowd again.

"What's going on?"

"Your guess is as good as mine. All I know is they've raised the alert level, which means we're all stuck in here until further notice."

"Does this have anything to do with the search assignments on the boards outside?"

"I don't know. Scientific doesn't participate in the searches."

"What are they looking for?"

"Hollis Richards, or so I'm told. They recently doubled the assignments, though. I heard someone say they were searching for something else, and no one's seen Greg Jonas or Bryan Berkeley in a while."

"What happened to them?"

"No one tells us anything. There's a distinct line drawn between scientific and military personnel."

"Is that what all of these people are? Scientists?"

"Most. Those guys over there are mechanical and mainly work on the rig up top, so we don't see them very often. Those two at the table? They're archeology. They work in the ruins. Anna Messerschmidt and Mats Karlsson. One's a paleoarcheologist; the other's a lexicologist, but I don't remember which is which."

"Who's that?"

Roche inclined his chin toward the woman sitting at the end of the adjacent table. Her hands shook when she brought her coffee mug to her lips. Her face was stark white.

"Moira Murphy. Her bunk's across from mine."

"Would you mind introducing me?"

Tess looked at him, then at Kelly, as though inwardly judging him, but led him across the room anyway.

"Moira, this is—"

"Martin Roche. I know. I've studied the footage from the research station."

Roche took the seat across from her and looked directly into her eyes. His initial assessment had been right. She knew exactly what was going on, and it scared the hell out of her.

"What's out there, Moira?"

"Nothing that can get in here." She took a sip of her coffee. "I hope."

"Tell us, Moira. We need to know. Cameron Barnett is not the kind of man prone to overreacting. In fact, quite the opposite. So if something out there has him taking these kinds of precautions, I guarantee you, we're all in serious danger."

She glanced up at him and he read the truth in her expression.

"What is it?" he asked.

"If anyone else finds out, it will cause mass panic, which will only make things worse."

"Christ," Tess said. She sat down at the end of the table and buried her face in her hands.

"That's how people end up getting killed," Roche said.

"Trust us," Kelly said, and slid into the seat beside him. "When everything happened here before, Barnett knew, and still he waited to evacuate us until the very last second. People died because of that decision. If something like that is happening here now, we need to know so we can protect ourselves."

Moira's gaze lingered on each of them before she apparently reached a decision.

"We don't know what's out there," she finally said.

"So it's not Richards," Roche said.

"Not as far as I know."

"Then what is it?"

"We had two men working in the ice caves down below. Whatever they found, it killed them and dragged one of their bodies into the tunnels. I originally thought they must have startled it and it attacked them, but after I saw what it did to Agent Berkeley . . ."

"Is it like Dale Rubley?" Kelly asked. "Like what he became?"

"As far as I can tell, it's some sort of animal."

"No animal could frighten Barnett like this," Roche said.

"The problem is we don't know for sure what it is. No one's seen it. All we know is that it has a carapace like an armadillo, the jaws of a crocodile, and can climb straight up walls."

"You're telling me something has been alive down there all this time?" Tess said.

"No. I believe it was in a state of cryobiosis and they somehow awakened it."

"So this thing killed two men and no one thought to evacuate us?"

"It's only an animal, Tess. It can't be much larger than a dog. We didn't see a reason to panic."

"But here we are now," Roche said, "which means that something else has happened."

"Oh, God," Moira said, and looked straight up at the ceiling. If it were possible, she was even paler when she lowered her head and let her tears drain down her cheeks.

"I want both of you to look around this room and tell me if anyone who should be here is missing."

Tess stood and surveyed the mess hall. There had to be at least twenty people sitting at the tables, milling around the snack table, or talking in groups.

"The little guy," Tess said. "The one who looks like Steve Buscemi."

"Desmond Bly," Moira said. She turned around and searched the room for him. "I don't see him, either."

"Where does he work?" Roche asked.

"That's the thing. He's a speleologist. It's his job to map all of these tunnels. He could be anywhere."

"Beyond the range of the siren?"

"You don't understand. He literally disappears for days at a time. This is nothing out of the ordinary for him." She paused and furrowed her brow. "Of course, he was the one who found the nest. I can't see him straying too far off on his own. Not after that."

"What nest?"

"Where it took Berkeley after it killed him. We found him cocooned and his remains partially consumed."

"What are we still doing here?" Tess said. "We should be halfway to the surface by now."

"Is there a way to reach this Bly?" Kelly asked.

"We all carry transceivers when we leave the base, but their range is limited."

"It's worth a try," Roche said. "Can you get ahold of a transceiver?"

There was a charging station in every building, where anyone could exchange a dying unit for one that was fully charged. Moira grabbed one from the rack and waited until she returned to the table before turning it on. Between the various specialties and work groups, they utilized more than a dozen different frequencies. The main channel broadcast an emergency signal.

"Which frequency would Bly use?"

"Channel seven, I think," Moira said, and dialed in the number.

"*. . . I repeat,*" a woman's voice said from the speaker. "*Dr. Bly, if you can hear this, please acknowledge. Protocol Delta is in effect. Return to Forward Operating Base Atlantis immediately.*"

"May I?"

Roche took the transceiver from her hand before she could respond and clicked through channel after channel of static before he found what he wanted.

"*. . . stay sharp.*"

"*What are we supposed to be looking for?*"

"*Apparently that's on a need-to-know basis.*"

"*And no one thinks we need to know? We're the ones out here in the open.*"

"*Just keep your eyes open. You see anything that shouldn't be here, you put a bullet in it. You hear me?*"

"His beacon," Moira said. "Bly has an RFID beacon

implanted in his hand and a range extender built into his cave suit, which allows the system to track him through the tunnels and create a virtual map of the passages."

"Can anyone access it?" Kelly asked.

"All of the data is available to the entire research staff. I don't see why not."

"So we should be able to find him, right?"

"If he's out of the transceiver's range, I can't imagine the system will be able to find him, either."

"At least we'll know where he was last," Roche said.

"It's worth a try."

Moira rose from the table and led them through the corridor into the main building with the long table covered with computers. A uniformed agent sat at a console at the opposite end of the room with his back to them, silhouetted by a half-dozen monitors displaying surveillance footage from both the cameras on the helmets of the men outside and static units positioned so that they faced the buildings.

"Nothing from any of the motion detectors," he said into his headset. "I don't see anything in the ruins, either."

Moira sat at the closest terminal, turned the monitor away from the agent, and pressed the power button. The agent heard the click and whirled to face them.

"You can't be out here," he said. "Get back to the mess."

"I just need to check one thing, Agent Young. It'll only take a second."

"It's for your own protection, Dr. Murphy."

"Two seconds. I promise."

Young pressed his hand to the speaker on his ear as though to better hear whoever was talking. He grimaced, waved her on, and returned his attention to the screens.

Within a matter of seconds Moira brought up Dr. Bly's ever-expanding map. It reminded Roche of the inside of an anthill. There were easily ten times as many tunnels as he expected and seemingly all of them were connected like capillaries. Bly's beacon was in one of the larger branches, just outside of the main cavern. It funneled into what remained of the old elevator shaft, which Roche tried his best not to think about.

"He's almost here," Moira said. The relief in her voice was palpable.

"Then why isn't he responding?" Roche asked.

"Probably just to be difficult. I'll introduce you when he gets here. He's what one might consider an acquired taste."

"He's an arrogant prick," Tess said.

The beacon moved slowly toward their location on the map until it looked like it was right outside of the main entrance.

"This is Midnight," Young said. "Still nothing on my end."

Roche furrowed his brow and watched the beacon until it was right on top of the very building inside of which he now stood. The door never opened, nor did Young appear to acknowledge Bly's arrival.

Something wasn't right.

"According to the map, he should be here already,"

Moira said, and then louder. "Do you see anyone outside, Agent Young?"

"Negative," he said without turning. "There's no one out there."

"Are you sure?"

"I can see everything within a hundred feet of the door. I'm telling you, nobody's out there."

"Then why is Dr. Bly's RFID beacon right on top of us?"

"What?"

Young slid back from his station and hurried down the aisle to join them.

"See?" Moira said.

He leaned over her shoulder and studied the monitor.

"That can't be right."

Roche had a sinking feeling in the pit of his stomach. Something Moira had said suddenly returned unbidden.

All we know is that it has a carapace like an armadillo, the jaws of a crocodile, and can climb straight up walls.

"Get your men off the roof," Roche said.

"Why the hell would I do that?" Young asked.

"Get them inside. Now!"

Young stared at him for a split second before recognition dawned.

"Hurry!" Roche shouted.

Young yelled into his microphone as he ran back to his console.

"Harrison! Do you copy?"

"This is Harr—"

"Look up! At the roof of the cavern!"

The image on the monitor to the left followed the pyramid to its apex and then continued up the slope of the ice dome—

A bright orange shape eclipsed the view.

Thud.

The roof buckled overhead.

Tess screamed.

Shouts erupted all around them.

33
JADE

Teotihuacan

Condensation dripped from the stone roof with a soft plinking sound. They moved in minuscule increments, keeping their shoulders beneath the water, but even then the sloshing sounds were far too loud. It was all Jade could do to keep her mouth and nose above the surface with as badly as her legs and buttocks were starting to burn. From the increasingly haggard sounds of the others' breathing, they weren't in any better shape than she was. It was only a matter of time before her body betrayed her, but the mere thought of grabbing onto anything to help support her weight scared her to death.

She clung to what little residual sense of determination remained. If she was right, they were heading north, toward the entrance to the maze, only from the opposite side. At least the movement of the water helped define her surroundings. She could hear it slapping against the walls to either side, which made it possible to navigate between them, although any second now they were going to be faced with their first

critical decision, and if they chose wrong, they could
only hope that whatever mechanism activated the trap
had rusted.

She grazed her fingers across Evans's back, just to
make sure he was still there. He reached behind him
beneath the water and touched her hip. She drew reas-
surance from the contact, for as long as it lasted.

Evans stopped in front of her. She could feel the dis-
turbance under the water as he felt around him with his
arms. The sloshing sounds were louder to her right, but
she couldn't feel a proportional increase in the movement of the water. She realized with a start that the
men hunting them were mere feet away, on the other
side of the wall.

A faint tapping sound. Then another. An elbow
bumping the wall as someone swam, maybe. A beam of
light shot through a pin-size hole between the mortared
stones before darkening once more.

Once their pursuers reached the end of that straightaway and turned right, they would be able to clearly
see Jade and her friends.

"Keep going," Jade whispered.

"Left," Evans whispered.

The current of his passage guided her around a
ninety-degree bend. Anya laid her trembling hand on
Jade's shoulder before returning it to the water.

They moved as fast as they dared. If they could get
a couple more turns between them and their hunters,
they could risk turning on the light again, but unless the
men following them made a wrong turn, they would
continue to gain on them with every passing second.
Fortunately, their pursuers must have recognized the

danger surrounding them or they would have already overtaken them.

Jade's fingers brushed the obsidian paneling beside her and she nearly cried out.

Evans slowed once more. The water sloshed against the walls ahead of them and to their right, which meant there was only one way to go.

"Left," Evans whispered. He led them around the turn, but suddenly stopped.

Jade heard the susurration of water all around them now. They had swum into a dead end.

She gasped at the realization. Her heart rate accelerated as panic took root.

"It bends back upon itself," Evans whispered.

A faint light materialized behind them.

Jade could see he was right. The route bent parallel to the last corridor, at the end of which was the origin of the light. The men were still distant, but they were gaining.

She followed Evans around the bend and the light once more vanished. The sloshing sounds became chaotic. There were walls to all sides of her, and yet she could sense several openings as well. Evans hesitated before advancing in maddeningly small increments.

"Careful to your right," he whispered.

Jade eased left, but not far enough to avoid the sharp object that raked her ribs. She reached for it and felt a sharp metal tip protruding from an object she recognized immediately. The spike was horizontal and had passed through one side of the victim's skull and out the other, shattering the temporal bone above the spigot-shaped external auditory meatus.

She worked her way around it and focused on slowing her heartbeat for fear the throbbing in her ears would mask the more subtle noises that could make the difference between life and death.

Anya whimpered behind her.

"I can't do this," Villarreal whispered.

"Shh!" Jade rounded on him. He was going to get them all killed. "You can and you will. Do you understand?"

She turned around again and bumped into Evans.

"There are two left turns," he whispered. "Or we can keep going straight."

Jade closed her eyes, for all the difference it made, and listened.

Either left turn could lead them into a dead end. Odds were that at least one of them did. Maybe even both.

"Straight," she whispered.

"Are you sure?" Evans whispered.

"No."

"As long as we're clear on that."

Evans started forward once more. Jade wasn't going to make it much farther. Not without resting her legs. They hurt from the accumulation of lactic acid, which was rapidly decreasing the efficiency of her muscles.

"Stop right there," Evans whispered. "There's something—"

A loud crack and a groaning sound overhead.

Evans shoved her squarely in the chest without warning. Her head went under. She cried out and inhaled a mouthful of fluid.

Something large passed through the water, generat-

ing a wave that knocked her backward again. She
reached for the surface and found nothing. Splashed
and flailed. Someone grabbed her by the wrist and
pulled her up. She emerged coughing and there was no
way of stopping it.

Shouting in the distance. The echoes of the voices
made it hard to divine their location.

"Go back!" Evans whispered. "We can't get through
that way. The whole ceiling came down."

A flicker of light.

Villarreal ducked through the nearest orifice.

"Keep going!" Evans whispered.

They were barely around the corner when the light
brightened, granting them just enough illumination to
see that the passage turned to the right. There was a
wall fifteen feet ahead. Jade saw what looked like an
opening to the right before the light faded once more.

"This way," someone said. Jade didn't recognize the
voice. While still distant, it was far too close for her
liking.

"Careful," another said. "Do not touch—"

An agonized shout erupted from somewhere behind
them and to their left.

"Go!" Evans whispered, and pushed her from behind.

They needed to take advantage of the momentary
confusion to expand their lead. Whatever happened, it
couldn't have been pleasant.

What looked like one branch to the right was actually two running side-by-side and separated by a single
wall. The sloshing of water to the left was louder, at

least what she could hear over the shouting, suggesting an enclosed space.

"Go right," she whispered, and swam past Anya and Villarreal.

"Wait," Evans whispered.

The shouting degenerated into coughing. Deep and wet. Jade recognized the sound right away. The man had punctured a lung. His pleural cavity was rapidly filling with blood, no matter how hard his body tried to cough it out.

"Do not shoot—!"

Thoom!

The gunshot was deafening. Its echo rolled through the maze like thunder. When it faded, only silence remained. Their hunters had executed one of their own.

They were going to die in here.

The thought cut through the exhaustion and triggered her primitive fight-or-flight instincts. Adrenaline surged through her, and she swam as fast as she could, heedless of anything in her way. She both felt and heard an opening pass to her left.

Something caught her by the leg and jerked her backward. She turned and lashed out with both arms like a wild animal.

Evans managed to catch one of her wrists and wrapped his other around her lower back. Drew her to him.

"It's okay," he whispered. "It's okay."

She grabbed the strap of his oxygen tank and sobbed silently into his shoulder.

What little strength remained in her legs abandoned her and she started to sink.

"Don't you dare," Evans whispered. "Keep fighting it."

Jade released him and stroked with both arms, but she couldn't seem to keep her mouth above the surface. She managed to take a deep breath through her nose before she went under, knowing full well what might happen if her feet hit the ground.

34
BARNETT

Command Center, FOB Atlantis

Barnett watched helplessly as the chaos unfolded around him. The bank of monitors on the wall of the command center displayed images from the cameras on his men's helmets and from strategic points around the complex. He watched through their eyes as Harrison was driven to his back and assailed by a flurry of claws, felt their terror when they looked up to find the ice dome overhead crawling with what had to be at least a dozen indistinct orange shapes. Their shouts crackled through the speakers alongside gunfire he could simultaneously hear through the walls of the building.

Footsteps overhead. Running.

Thump-thump-thump-thump-thud.

"We need to fall back to the central hub," Avila said.

Clack-clack-clack-clack-clack.

Wet tearing sounds emerged from the speakers as, one by one, the screams were cut short and the gunfire ceased. His men's cameras recorded images of the polyfiber-coated steel rooftops and the rocky lake bed. One showed an ice dome entirely bereft of the heat signatures.

Twelve highly trained operatives gone in a matter of seconds, leaving the outer defenses of the base exposed and vulnerable.

The external monitors showed orange shapes stalking the rooftops, scurrying up and down the arched sides of the buildings, moving so fast that the fusion cameras couldn't get a clear picture of them.

"There's nothing more we can do for them," Avila said.

Barnett felt as though he were rooted to his chair. Never in his worst nightmares had he imagined that something like this could happen. There were so many of them. Where in the name of God had they come from?

Clack-clack-clack-clack-clack.

He looked up at the ceiling and could tell exactly where it was. It went straight down the wall beside him without losing traction.

"Director!" Avila shouted.

Barnett stood so fast he sent his chair clattering to the floor.

"Everyone fall back to the mess hall!" he shouted.

"You heard the man!" Avila shouted. "Everyone assume fallback positions!"

He walked around the front of his desk and stared at the wall of monitors.

One of his men rolled over and for a second Barnett thought he was still alive, until the ground rushed past beneath him, his camera clattering from the rocks until it broke and the screen went black.

Barnett shook off his stupor and ran for the central hub. He caught a glimpse of orange from the corner of his eye and stopped halfway out the door. Turned to face the monitor and saw what looked like a palsied hand lower into the screen, blurred by proximity. It splayed when it hit the ground. One of the fingers remained erect, like the tail of a scorpion, although rather than a stinger, it was crowned with a massive hooked claw.

"Jesus."

He sprinted through the corridor into the adjacent building and veered right toward the tunnel leading to the mess hall. He could feel the panic radiating from inside. Men and women shouted to be heard and practically trampled one another as the remaining agents began sealing off the doors on the far side.

"Start moving people into the vault!" Barnett shouted, but even he couldn't hear himself over the bedlam. He pushed his way into the hub and grabbed the nearest agent. Shouted into his face. "Is everyone accounted for?"

"How the hell should I know?"

Barnett shoved him aside and climbed up onto the table in the center of the room so he could see over everyone's heads. Eight of the twelve doors were already barricaded, and it would only be a matter of seconds before the last four followed suit. It would take nothing shy of an act of God to open them from the outside once they were sealed.

Avila had overturned the serving station to access the floor hatch, which stood wide open as men and women commenced with the arduous process of funneling down the narrow staircase into the vault. The walls were composed of the same concrete-reinforced steel as Subject Z's cage and were even stronger and more secure than the President's Emergency Operations Center under the East Wing of the White House.

"I've got things under control up here!" he shouted to Avila. "Make sure everyone gets down there and fire up the generators!"

She nodded, fought her way to the head of the line, and ducked down the stairs.

"Director Barnett!"

Barnett turned at the sound of his name to see Special Agent Young hailing him from the mouth of the lone unsealed doorway. He jumped down from the table and hustled to meet his agent. If the door was jammed—

"I have to show you something!" Young shouted.

Barnett read the direness of the situation on the man's face.

"Make it fast."

Young turned without another word and ran straight through the corridor into Midnight, past the row of computers, and to a monitoring station glowing with lights. The screens displayed the same images as those in the command center, only from the limited perspective of this individual building.

"What's so important—?"

Barnett saw it before he could even finish his sentence. The external view of the main deck from the vantage point of the light post showed an orange shape on the ground, approximately fifty feet from the front door. There was no doubt it was human.

"He's still alive," Young said.

The man on the screen reached out with one arm and dragged himself forward, leaving behind a diffuse orange trail that faded before their eyes. Several seconds later, he did the same thing again.

"Christ Almighty," Barnett said.

"We can't leave him out there."

"Who is it?"

"Does it matter? We need to get whoever it is inside before they come back for him."

"We don't even know that they're gone."

Barnett looked from one monitor to the next, but could see no other heat signatures. At a guess, the cameras covered a radius of maybe three hundred feet, which wasn't nearly as much as he would have liked.

"It'll take less than thirty seconds if the two of us do it."

"We open that door and we risk the lives of everyone in this station."

"We don't and he'll die."

Barnett bellowed in frustration.

"Get the door, goddammit!"

Young raced past him and drew his Glock 17 from the holster on his hip. He waited for Barnett to do the same and held his hand over the control panel for the electromagnetic lock.

"On my mark," Barnett said. He watched the monitors from across the room for the first hint of orange. "Three. Two. One."

Young hit the button and the lock disengaged with a thud. Barnett shouldered through the door and ran straight out across the deck, the echo of his footsteps like a drumroll. The man lay facedown right where he expected, only he seemed so much farther away. Young caught up with him by the time he reached the fallen agent, who no longer made any effort to move.

Each of them grabbed a wrist and backed as quickly as they could toward the open door. The trail of blood rushing from the unconscious man glistened in the red glare. Barnett recognized Special Agent David Harrison by the profile of his face, which bobbed limply against his chest as they dragged him. He was one of the best sharpshooters in the world. His skill with a rifle had even earned him the nickname Talibang, because he'd picked off countless Al-Qaeda operatives before becoming disillusioned with the military-industrial complex. He'd jumped at the opportunity for a fresh start, and this was his reward.

They were nearly to the door when Barnett detected movement in his peripheral vision.

"Hurry!" he shouted.

More movement from the other side. And from behind him, the clacking sound of nails on top of the prefabricated building.

They weren't going to make it.

"Run!" Barnett shouted and shoved Young toward the door. He fired blindly in the direction of the movement, holstered his weapon, and dropped to his knees. Lifted Harrison onto his shoulders and shouted as he struggled to his feet. Turned and pushed his body harder than he ever had before. Watched Young pass through the open doorway and take position at the electromagnetic lock.

"They're right behind you!" he shouted.

Barnett didn't dare look back. He focused on the doorway.

Fifteen feet.

Ten.

A shadow fell upon him from above.

Five feet.

He was nearly to the door when something clipped his heel and sent him sprawling. He hit the ground hard and lost his grip on Harrison, who slid under the table. Computer monitors crashed to the floor. Chairs toppled.

"Get the door!" Barnett shouted.

Young grabbed the handle and yanked it—

Something stopped it.

He tried again.

A shrill cry.

Both men looked up at the sound to see the creature trying to jerk its head back out. It snapped its jaws. The elongated scales on its jawline and the ridge of its skull bristled like quills.

Barnett flipped over, grabbed Harrison by the arms, and dragged him across the room.

"I can't hold this much longer!" Young shouted.

"Give me as much time as you can!"

Barnett backed through the tunnel and into the mess hall, where Avila met him and helped him pull Harrison toward the hatch.

Thump. Thump. Thump.

The sound echoed from the main building, where the creatures outside hurled themselves against the door.

Young shouted and stumbled back from the entryway. Barnett could see him through the corridor, a dark silhouette in the red glow. He shot several times behind him and ran toward them.

The door flew open behind him and shadows streaked across the ground at his heels.

Young blew through the tunnel, but they were upon him before he took a single stride into the mess hall.

He hit the ground on his face. When he looked up, his features were covered with blood, which dribbled from his mouth when he spoke.

"Go!"

Young rolled onto his back, raised his weapon, and fired back into the corridor. He screamed and pulled the trigger as fast as he could, his spent casings pinging from the wall. An errant shot hit the control panel for the door, which dropped from the ceiling and slammed down onto his midsection.

His head rocked back and he brayed in agony. Blood sputtered from his mouth and flooded out from beneath him.

Barnett unholstered his Glock, sighted down the top of Young's head, and ended his suffering.

His ears were still ringing when he closed the hatch, sealed it from the inside, and descended into the vault.

35
MOIRA

The Vault, FOB Atlantis

"**S**omebody help me!" Avila shouted.

She lost her balance and slid down the final three stairs, dropping Special Agent Harrison's legs. Barnett stumbled, but managed to hold on to the man's torso.

Moira rushed to his aid and helped him lower the injured soldier to the floor. She could tell at first glance that there was nothing she could do. While field medicine was one of her many skills, this surpassed even what a classically trained surgeon could handle under the best of conditions.

"Get me some light so I can see what I'm doing!"

She gripped either side of Harrison's shirt and ripped it open, sending buttons skittering into the room. She was about to call for the emergency medical kit when Barnett set it down beside her.

"Do everything you possibly can," he said, and backed away.

She unzipped the soft case and threw open the top. Found a pair of scissors and cut straight up the front of his T-shirt. His chest was pale and covered with so much blood that at first she couldn't see where he was injured, until she tugged on the waistband of his pants and his abdominal contents nearly spilled out.

"I need water to irrigate this!"

She carefully unbuttoned his pants and pulled them down past the wound. A ragged laceration had been drawn diagonally from his right hip to just beside his navel. The skin and superficial fascia had pulled away from the underlying muscle.

"Here."

Someone thrust a cup of water into her hand. She took it without looking and splashed it onto the wound, causing a fresh layer of blood to rise to the surface.

"Is he still breathing?" Moira shouted.

Avila assumed position near Harrison's head. She leaned over him and brought her ear to within millimeters of his lips.

"I can't tell."

"Can you feel a pulse?"

Avila pressed her index and middle fingers into the side of his neck.

"I think . . . I think so."

Moira dumped the contents of the emergency kit onto the ground. Tore open a package of four-by-fours and tried to sop up the blood inside the wound so she could see what was going on. If any of the bowels had been nicked, she was better off letting him die now and sparing him a grueling and ultimately fatal bout of sepsis.

"Tell me you can save him," Barnett said.

"Where's that light?" One of the engineers—Russo,

if she remembered correctly—crouched beside her and shined a handheld flashlight onto the wound. "Keep it pointed right there until I tell you otherwise."

The subcutaneous tissue and rectus sheath were both cleanly parted. She retracted them with a pair of forceps. All four layers of the abdominal muscles underneath were lacerated, but even that wasn't enough to justify the sheer volume of blood. The wound had to be deeper than she'd initially suspected.

She parted the rectus abdominus muscle and blood flooded to the surface. The incision had passed straight through the muscle and punctured the peritoneum. She grabbed more gauze and blotted it as fast as it rose.

Harrison arched his back and made a violent gasping sound.

"Hold him down!" Moira shouted. She'd lost traction and had to dig back through the muscles to find the opening into the abdomen. The rich black blood that welled from inside overwhelmed the gauze. "More water!"

She doused the wound again, but there was nothing she could do. A loop of intestine bloomed through the hole. She pushed it back inside and felt something solid and roughly the size of a cantaloupe underneath. Compartment syndrome, she feared. It was a consequence of severe internal bleeding that caused the exponential increase in abdominal pressure, essentially creating a giant blood balloon within an enclosed space. If she was right and inadvertently breached it, he would bleed out and there wasn't a blasted thing she could do to stop it. At the same time, if she didn't relieve the pressure, it was only a matter of time—

Harrison shuddered and released a quivering sigh.

Moira looked up from the wound and read the truth on Avila's face.

"Dammit," Barnett said. He stormed off into the underground command center and slammed the door behind him.

Avila placed her palm over Harrison's forehead and gently closed his eyelids.

Moira stared down at her red hands. Already she could feel the blood tightening on her skin as it dried. No amount of water would get it all off.

"You did your best," Tess said from behind her, and placed what she'd surely meant to be a comforting hand on Moira's shoulder, but she shrugged it off.

"The wound was too deep. It went nearly all the way through."

All around her: the sounds of panicked whispering, crying, and desperation.

"What are we going to do with him now?" someone asked.

"He just died, for Christ's sake," Avila said. "So did Agent Young, who gave his life so that all of us might have a chance to live. Show some respect."

Moira hung her head and released the tears she'd been fighting to contain.

"He can't stay in here with us," Love said. She reached out for Avila and momentarily hesitated before resting her hand on the smaller woman's arm. "We should move him outside before . . . you know . . ."

"We open that hatch and those things will be down here in a heartbeat."

"Blankets," Moira said. She continued to stare at her hands as though they belonged to someone else. "Grab some of those silver space blankets."

The first-aid blankets were made from polyethylene terephthalate foil and designed to prevent hypothermia and stave off the early effects of shock. The airtight foil served to reduce heat loss caused by the evaporation of perspiration or massive bleeding, but in this case, would hopefully at least slow the process of decomposition until they could find a better solution.

Russo dropped several blankets beside her. She looked down at them for several seconds before somehow making her hands reach for them.

"Let me help you," Roche said.

He unfolded one of the blankets and draped it over Harrison's body.

It had been at Moira's insistence that Barnett stocked the space blankets down here. She figured that if they ever had to use the vault, a large number of them would be suffering from shock. Now she had to wonder if it wasn't just a matter of time before they were all laid to rest beneath them.

36
KELLY

The vault was roughly the same size as the building above it. The back third was walled off to house the standby generators, which produced a constant vibration Kelly could feel through the floor. The scent of the liquid propane that powered them permeated the entire subterranean complex, despite the vents that shunted the exhaust to the surface. The bulk of the space served as communal living quarters and was filled with folding cots, where the injured rested alongside those working through the various stages of shock. Shelves filled with emergency rations, blankets, and myriad supplies lined the walls beside drums of potable water. There was a constant grating din of whimpering and crying, beneath which lurked the droning buzz of the emergency lights. The majority of what she had come to think of as the military personnel were gathered in the adjacent room, hopefully figuring out how to get them out of there before she started to lose her mind.

There were thirty-three of them in the vault, thirty-four if you counted the agent who had bled out on the stairs, although they'd moved his body into the generator room. Moira had tried valiantly to save him and yet nothing she did stemmed the flow of blood. Roche sat on a cot near the door of the command center in hopes of overhearing something. Kelly and Moira sat across from him. From time to time, they heard shouting through the wall, but not clearly enough to make out the words.

"What happens from here?" Roche asked.

"We await emergency retrieval." Tess clenched and unclenched her hands as though she were losing feeling in them. She breathed slowly, in through her nose and out through her mouth. "That's all I know."

"No one's coming for us." Moira didn't look at any of them when she spoke. She just continued to rub water onto her hands and scrape at her cuticles, seemingly unable to scour away the last of the dead agent's blood. "Not with those things out there. It would be a suicide mission."

"Then we need to get to the elevator," Roche said. "We can barricade ourselves in the power station on the surface and they can airlift us from the roof."

"You think they can't get up there? They were hanging upside down from the ice dome, for Christ's sake."

"We can't just stay down here," Kelly said. "Eventually we're going to have to do something."

"Someone will come," Tess said.

"Are you willing to stake your life on it?" Roche asked.

"At least whatever those things are can't get to us down here."

Kelly hoped Tess was right. They thought they'd been safe in the research station six months ago, too, but the creatures had used the air ducts as a conduit to reach them wherever they went. At least it looked as though Barnett had learned his lesson in that regard, though. The vents were mounted high on the concrete walls, near the ceiling, and couldn't have been much larger than the ones in her house back home. There was no way anything large enough to hurt them was getting through there.

The hatch appeared solid, too. It latched with a wheel like the airlock of a submarine and utilized an electromagnetic locking mechanism that couldn't be opened from the outside as long as the power still flowed. If what they said was true and the generators would last several months, they would likely run out of food and water long before that happened.

"I'm going to find out what's going on," Roche said.

He stood and headed for the door to the command center. Kelly was at his side when he opened it.

She took in the room at a glance. A table ran the length of the rear wall. Rows of monitors displaying rolling views of the base, both inside and out, were mounted above it. A row of automatic rifles like the ones the men aboard the *Aurora Borealis* had carried lined a rack to her left. A half-dozen individual computer stations led to a radio transceiver. There were only nine men in the room, all of them too distracted to even notice that the door had opened.

Barnett sat at the desk with his back to Kelly, his fingertips pressed to his temples.

"So how many are we talking about, Agent Avila?" he asked.

"Our best estimates are anywhere between eight and twelve," she said.

"There's a big difference between eight and twelve. See if you can narrow that down. Do we at least know what we're dealing with yet?"

"I managed to get a screen-grab of one of them inside Building Four," a woman with shoulder-length blond hair said. "The resolution's distorted by the zoom and it's too dark to get a clear look, but it gives us a good idea of scale."

She pressed a button on her remote control and the center image changed. The legs of the animal on the screen were blurred by motion, but enough of it remained in focus that they could see its outline. It was roughly the same length as the toppled chair behind it. Its back was a horizontal line from its snout to the tip of its tail. Quill-like protuberances jutted from its head and neck and bristled from its tail.

"It looks like a freaking dragon," Barnett said.

"Only a fraction of the size," the woman said.

"Don't let its size deceive you, Agent Love. Those things took out some of our best men."

"Speaking of whom . . ."

She switched to a different camera. Kelly recognized the main building—the one they called Midnight—by the isolation suits hanging on the wall and the long table in the center of the room, which had been tipped onto its side. The computer monitors lay shattered on the ground amid a riot of toppled chairs and electronic components. The front door stood wide open. Several enormous teardrop-shaped sacs hung from the ceiling, obstructing the view of the remainder of the room. Kelly didn't have the slightest idea what they were until she watched the silhouette of a creature emerge from the top of one and caught a glimpse of a man's face inside.

She gasped and everyone in the room turned to look at her.

"You can't be in here," Avila said, and strode directly toward them.

"We know how to track them," Kelly said. Avila looked at Barnett, who gestured for Kelly to proceed. "At least one of them, anyway."

"Close the door," Barnett said.

Avila stepped behind Kelly and did as he asked.

"One of them swallowed someone named Bly's RFID beacon. We saw it on the computer."

Barnett nodded to Love, who crossed the room to one of the computer stations and brought up the map. The beacon still glowed from somewhere right above their heads.

"You're certain that's not Bly?" Love said.

"If it is, he's undoubtedly inside one of those cocoons," Roche said. "They're just like the nest you found with your missing man, aren't they?"

"You've been talking to Dr. Murphy," Barnett said.

"She seemed to think there was only one of those creatures. There's definitely a whole lot more than that now."

"You have a talent for stating the obvious."

"As you do for overlooking it. She described those sacs as nests, and what are nests if not vessels for rearing offspring? You want to know how there got to be so many of them? The answer's staring you right in the face."

Barnett turned and faced the monitors. There were

several other nests hanging in any number of the other rooms.

"If we wait down here much longer," Roche said, "this entire place is going to be crawling with them."

"How fast can they possibly breed?"

"You tell me. You went from one to at least eight in a matter of days."

"Call for evacuation," Barnett said without turning around.

"You mean you haven't already done so?" Kelly nearly screamed. "Are you trying to get us all killed?"

"We're safe in here. These walls are more than two feet thick and you couldn't open that hatch from the outside without bringing down the entire ice dome." He finally turned to face them. "Trust me. Nothing's getting in here."

37
ANYA

Teotihuacan

Anya heard a wet gasp and felt something grab at her leg. She caught Jade by the sleeve and went under with her. Pulled and kicked toward the surface again. There'd been no time to take a breath, and what little air she had in her chest was already growing stale. She didn't have enough strength left for both of them, but there was no way she was letting go.

Evans's hand brushed against her arm. Wrapped around Jade's back and against Anya's thigh. With his help, they struggled back to the surface, both of them coughing until Jade vomited the aspirated fluid.

If the men hunting them hadn't known where they were, they sure as hell did now.

"We have to risk it," Evans said, and clicked on his light.

Jade was a shade of pale just this side of the grave. Her hair hung in clumps and even her brilliant green eyes had taken on a grayish cast.

"They just want what is at the end of the maze," Villarreal said. "If we give them what they want, they will let us go."

"You didn't see what they did to the people outside the trailer," Anya said.

"We have to move fast before they see our light," Evans whispered.

He wrapped Jade's arms around his neck and transferred her weight to his back. His face went under and the light on his helmet diffused into the greenish-brown water. If he said anything more, Anya couldn't hear it.

He kicked and propelled himself forward, leaving Jade to keep her mouth above the surface. They turned right, then right again. Anya had to stroke to keep up. A quick left revealed a dead end in the distance. They turned around and swam toward another wall. Veered left and rounded the bend into a straightaway that terminated in a T-intersection. There was no difference in the intonation of the sloshing waves, at least not that she could hear over their splashing and heavy breathing.

Evans ducked right and accelerated toward a dead end in the distance. There was a single opening to the right, which, if she hadn't completely lost her bearings, should take them toward the center of the maze. He turned and pulled up suddenly.

Jade went under, but quickly raised her head. Evans appeared to be struggling with her added weight. Anya could barely see the silhouette of his body through the murky water. It looked like he was only kicking with one leg. She felt warmth on her bare arm and realized exactly what had happened.

"Oh, my God," she gasped and swam to Evans's side.

She grabbed him by the upper arm and pulled him higher. The aura of his headlamp took on a faint pinkish hue.

"Help me!" she whispered to Villarreal, who took Evans by the other arm. Jade rolled from his back and did her best to tread on her own.

"Where are you injured?" Anya asked.

Evans spoke through bared teeth.

"Right leg."

Anya dove and swam toward where his right leg appeared to be stuck—

And nearly impaled herself on a foot-long spike. Dozens of them protruded from a planed tree trunk, which leaned diagonally across the passage. A trail of blood drifted from his calf, where a spike had entered through his shin and exited through the meat of his muscle.

She swam back to the surface. Looked Villarreal dead in the eyes.

"Get a good grip on him."

"What happened?" Villarreal asked.

Anya ignored him and took Evans by either side of his diving mask.

"This is going to hurt." His lips tightened over his teeth. He mustered a nod. "I mean a lot."

"Get it over with."

She took a breath and dove again. Grabbed his leg. One hand on his knee, the other on his ankle. Pulled straight back.

His left foot kicked wildly next to her.

At first, she didn't think his leg was going to come off the spike, like maybe there was a barb hooked in his flesh, but then it slid backward and released a cloud of blood into the water. She pulled off her shirt from over her bikini top and tied it around the wound. Pulled it tight. Barely caught his other leg before he impaled it, too. Swam for the surface and gasped for air.

"We need to get him out of here," she said.

"Could you tell if it nicked an artery?" Jade asked.

"No. I mean, I don't think so."

"They're still coming," Evans said. "We have to keep moving."

"We cannot go on like this," Villarreal said.

"We don't have a choice," Anya said. She carefully swam around the spiked log, grabbed Evans by his harness, pulled him away from the booby trap, and swam deeper into the maze.

There was no way they could outrun their pursuit. Not now. Their only option was to find a place to hide and pray they weren't found.

Evans grew heavier by the second, although to his credit, he gave it everything he had. Another left, then a right. Right again. She didn't like having her course dictated to her. She needed to make a decision or they were merely prolonging the inevitable. And they needed to get out of the water. Jade was trying her best, but she wouldn't make it much farther and there was no way Anya was going to be able to drag Evans indefinitely, not with as quickly as his strength was fading. If they didn't get out of there soon, someone was going to—

Anya's heart stopped. She'd led them into a dead end.

She closed her eyes and felt her own strength wane.

If they turned around now, they'd be swimming right into the teeth of their pursuit, but they couldn't stay here and tread water for any length of time, either. She opened her eyes and looked for anything they could hold onto. A crack in the wall. The edges of a brick. Anything at all.

The wall against which the corridor terminated was unlike the others. It was made of a single block of chiseled granite, which didn't fit perfectly against the walls. It was smaller and, now that she really looked at it, seemed completely out of place. She followed its smooth face up toward the roof—

"Up there." There was a slim gap above the stone block. And a dark recess in the ceiling into which it had once fit. It was a booby trap meant to fall on someone's head, or maybe just block the passage. Perhaps even the same one Evans had tripped earlier. "Hurry!"

She boosted Evans as high as she could, driving herself underwater in the process.

He grabbed the upper lip and pulled. She pushed against his rear end until he was able to slide through the opening and drag his injured leg up onto the stone block.

Villarreal pushed past Jade and climbed up beside Evans, who reached down to help Jade up. With the last of her energy, Anya reached as high as she could, secured a grip on the ledge, and pulled. The others grabbed her by the arms and helped her squeeze through the narrow gap and into the tight recess.

Evans killed his light and the darkness swallowed them.

"We cannot stay here," Villarreal whispered.

"Shh!" Jade whispered.

"Cade is injured and the rest of us are exhausted."

Anya found Villarreal's hand and squeezed it. She hoped he got the message.

A faint glow spread across the water below them. Anya could see the outlines of their feet and ankles. If their pursuers shined their light directly at them and looked up, they would be impossible to miss.

Water shushed against the block. The light brightened by degree.

Anya held her breath.

The light grew brighter and brighter until she could see the makeshift bandage on Evans's calf. Blood overflowed from the saturated cloth and dribbled to the stone, where it pooled before trickling over the edge and down the front of the massive block. It was going to give them away, but there was nothing they could do about it now.

The sloshing sounds became louder. The light brightened to such an extent that she could see the fear on the faces of the others, mere inches from her own.

"Dead end," a voice said from maybe ten feet away.

Anya bit her lip to keep from crying out. If the men looked up, it was all over.

The light dimmed.

The men were turning around.

"I cannot do this anymore," Villarreal said.

Anya squeezed his hand again, but he jerked it away.

The light was nearly out of range again. She could barely see the faint red stain of Evans's blood beside the outline of her feet.

"Come back!" Villarreal shouted. "We are up here!"

"What are you doing?" Anya whispered.

Evans grabbed him and Jade covered his mouth, but he fought free.

"Up here!"

"Juan Carlos . . ." Anya whispered.

Splashing sounds rapidly approached. The light brightened by the second until it was directly beneath them.

"Slide through to the other side," Evans said. "I'll hold them off."

Jade dropped to her knees and reached through the gap on the other side. Before she could get her head through the opening, there were hands on her ankles and she was jerked backward into the water.

Anya knelt and grabbed her hand, but couldn't slow her momentum. One of the men grabbed Anya by the upper arm and wrenched her through the hole. She barely caught her breath before she went headfirst into the water. The man jerked her back to the surface.

"Come out, Dr. Evans," the man gripping Anya's arm said. He wore a black tactical mask molded to look like a skull, with a series of breathing holes where the teeth should have been. A fine mesh partially concealed his eyes. She thrashed in an effort to break his grasp. "We have no desire to kill any of you. However, make no mistake, we have no qualms about doing so, either. Just do exactly as we say."

"You promised no one would get hurt," Villarreal said.

His words hit Anya hard enough to knock the wind out of her.

He lowered himself to his hands and knees and stuck his head through the gap.

"We will help you find it. I swear."

His eyes met Anya's. She couldn't bear to look at him. Never in her life had she felt so betrayed. She'd practically thrown herself at him and he, in turn, had served her up to these men on a silver platter.

The man holding Jade had a similar tactical mask, only his had an iridescent silver cast and looked like an alien. He pressed the barrel of a semiautomatic pistol to the side of her head.

"My colleague is holding a gun to the head of Dr. Liang," the first man said. "If you do not come out of there by the time I count—"

"I'm coming," Evans said. He fell to his knees, reached his arm through the gap, and tumbled out behind it.

The man shoved Anya aside and grabbed Evans by the harness. He ripped off the diving mask and nuzzled the barrel of his weapon against the base of Evans's skull.

"You are not going to give us any trouble if we let you swim on your own, are you, Dr. Fleming?"

Anya shook her head, but couldn't seem to find the voice to respond. There was no reason for these men to keep all four of them alive. They'd be outnumbered in an environment where anything could happen, despite being armed. Her only option was to do what they asked and pray she survived.

"Very good. Now, if you please, I would like you to take the lead."

Suddenly, Anya understood exactly why they'd let her live. They needed someone to swim ahead of them and set off whatever traps lay in their way.

BOOK III

*Long is the way and hard, that out of Hell leads
up to light.*
—JOHN MILTON

38
RUSSO

The Vault, FOB Atlantis,
March 27

The generator room was barely wide enough for the generators themselves, let alone the men responsible for monitoring them. Undoubtedly, whoever designed this place did everything he possibly could with the space he'd been allotted, but he obviously hadn't spared a thought for the poor saps tasked with maintaining the equipment. Theirs was the most critical job of all. Without power, they would only last a matter of hours down here. It wasn't just about getting electricity to the computers. If the generators failed, they wouldn't be able to force outside air into the vault, which meant that their finite supply of oxygen would rapidly diminish. The electromagnetic lock, which took an absurd amount of energy to maintain, would fail. Everything else would fall like dominos. The lights would go first, followed by the heat, as it slowly dissipated into the cold earth. There was a reason that Paulo Russo and the other engineers had been recruited for Unit 51. It was for times just like this one, when lives hung in the balance, whether anyone knew it or not.

Each of the liquid propane generators featured an 18.3-liter CAC—charge-air cooled—engine with a power output of 300 kilowatts. They produced a considerable amount of heat and required a chiller unit to blow a constant stream of cool air across them. The temperature needed to be carefully monitored. The fuel lines needed to be checked for leaks. The vibration isolators had to be monitored for cracks, as did the exhaust lines and the mufflers. Any number of things could go wrong at any given moment. And while he didn't believe in cutting corners, especially not with whatever the hell awaited them up there on the surface, he couldn't get out of that suffocating little room soon enough.

"It's already starting to stink," Reuben Sands said.

"That's just your imagination."

"Is it even possible to imagine a smell?"

"Just finish taking your readings so we can get out of here."

Russo wiped the sweat from his brow with the sleeve of his shirt. The thermostat on the chiller read 74 degrees, but it felt even warmer than that. He decreased the temperature by a single degree. He'd check it again in an hour. They couldn't risk dialing down the thermostat on the chiller too much or the entire unit could freeze and lock up.

He caught a whiff of the smell and tried to breathe through his mouth.

"What did I tell you?" Sands said.

When Russo was a child, a rat had crawled under his mother's clothes dryer and died. Who knows how long it had been under there, but after running some number of loads, the smell that came out from beneath there was bad enough to cause his mother to retch. It had fallen to him, as the oldest of four, to take care of the problem. The stench that had come from that little body as he carried it out to the dumpster had been enough to scar him for life. And while Harrison's body wasn't nearly to that point yet, he had no doubt it would get there soon, especially in this heat.

He glanced into the corner of the room, where the body lay beneath a mound of blankets. They'd wrapped it in several of those insulated silver numbers first, for all the good they did. He hadn't really known Harrison all that well. They'd eaten together and shared the light room from time to time, but he'd never really gotten to know the guy. That wasn't to say he wished him ill or anything. In fact, quite the opposite. He just didn't want to spend any more time with him now that he was dead. Someone needed to figure out what they were going to do with his body before the smell forced them all to evacuate the vault. And weren't there diseases that bred inside corpses?

"I don't mean to sound insensitive or anything," Sands said, "but we should really do something about it now before it gets worse. Even moving it out into the other room where it's cooler would help slow down the process, don't you think?"

"I'll let you pitch that idea to Director Barnett."

"Someone's going to have to."

"Be my guest."

Russo noted the airflow and the back pressure from the exhaust line in cubic meters. Checked the digital control panel for alarms. He was about to check the fuel consumption when something moved in his peripheral vision. When he looked in that direction, there was nothing there. Only the mummy-shaped bundle of blankets.

The system coolant and engine jacket water levels were within range, the speed regulation within half a percent.

Again, movement. This time, he turned to see the blanket bulge, then settle once more.

"Did you see that?" he asked.

"See what?"

Russo shook his head. The flow of air from the chiller must have caused the top blanket to billow. He'd watched Harrison die before his very eyes. He'd seen the sheer volume of blood he'd lost. There was no way he could possibly be—

The blanket rose from Harrison's belly. Slowly, as though gentle pressure were being applied from underneath.

"Did you see it that time?" Russo turned to see Sands staring straight at the corpse, his mouth hanging open. He didn't need to answer. "Go tell Barnett."

"And just what do you propose I tell him? That the guy we thought was dead has somehow come back to life?"

"Give me that pipe wrench, would you?"

Sands did as he was asked. Russo turned it around and used the long, slender end to lift the edge of the top blanket and pull it back. He did the same with the blanket underneath and watched for any sign of movement as he pried back the first of the silver space blankets.

"Jesus," he gasped, and covered his mouth and nose with his free hand. The smell was enough to make his eyes water. It couldn't have been more than two hours. How much worse would it be after ten more?

"There's no way he's still alive," Sands said.

"You think?"

Russo peeled away the final blanket, cast it aside, and stepped back.

Harrison's face and neck were swollen and misshapen. One arm was draped across his chest, the other sprawled at his side. His bare chest was pale and marbled with bruises so dark they stood out even through the dried blood. The edges of the wound on his abdomen had retreated to expose the lacerated layers of tissue—

The muscles shifted sideways and swelled outward.

"There's something in there," Russo said, and pressed the bulge with the wrench. A sharp implement tented the muscles, then parted them cleanly. "What the hell?"

The creature unfurled from Harrison's abdominal cavity in one fluid motion, reared up like a snake, and struck at Russo.

He stumbled backward. Lost his balance. Hit the ground on his back.

It was on his chest before he could even raise his arms. When he screamed, no sound came out. A heartbeat later he felt the pain and the warmth of the blood pulsing from his neck.

He grasped the wound in a desperate attempt to hold it closed and rolled over. Panicked at the sight of the crimson pool forming beneath him and the deluge sluicing from between his fingers. Watched Sands run for the door. It leaped onto his back and slashed through his jacket and the flesh underneath, driving him to his knees.

It gripped Sands's throat in its jaws and shook its head until he dropped.

The creature rounded on Russo, who caught the reflection from its eyes before it released a shrill cry and lunged for his face.

39
TESS

Tess heard what sounded like a whistle of steam and turned toward the back of the room. The door to the generator room was closed. The people sitting closest to it were huddled beneath blankets and didn't appear to have noticed.

"What was that?" she asked.

Moira looked up at her through blank eyes before she resumed scraping the nonexistent blood from her tattered cuticles.

Tess stood and paced the aisle between the cots for several minutes until she couldn't take it anymore. There was no way she was going to be able to stay down here for another hour, let alone an unknown number of days. She needed something to occupy her mind. Surely Barnett had access to the camera from her workstation, and, if so, she could continue her research from the vault. If he was going to let Kelly and Roche stay in there, then there was no reason he wouldn't allow her to do the same, especially now that she finally had Subject Z communicating with them.

She opened the door to the command center, stepped confidently inside, and instantly regretted it.

The tension in there was electric. Everyone was gathered around the wall of monitors at the far end of the room, where the images showed scenes stolen from a nightmare. It looked like a war had been fought inside the base. Tables and beds were overturned. Computers and televisions were broken. The red glare reflected from puddles on the floor that might well have been blood. Sparks spat from overhead lights shattered by the process of hanging massive nests from the ceiling.

"We can't afford to wait any longer," Roche said. "We don't know anything about them, let alone their gestation period. By the time we finally make a decision, there could be twice as many of them. Maybe more."

"That doesn't change the fact that there are still at least eight of them up there," Barnett said. "You think they're just going to let us walk right out the front door?"

"We have weapons." Roche nodded toward the rack of assault rifles on the wall. "And we have the advantage of knowing where they are."

"And then what, hmm? The elevator is more than five hundred feet away and you saw how fast they can run."

"We'll need a distraction."

"Are you volunteering?"

"How many people can the elevator hold?" Kelly asked.

"Eight," Avila said. "We could probably push it to nine if no one's opposed to being crammed in there like sardines."

"It'll take five trips to get everyone out of here," Love said.

"And they're not just going to let us wait around on the pad," Barnett said.

"How much longer until the extraction team arrives?" Roche asked.

"Just over an hour."

"And how many passengers can the Valor hold?"

"Fourteen."

"That's still three trips."

"If you have a better idea, now would be a good time to share it."

"We attack them," Roche said. "Right now. Before they can multiply anymore."

"I lost twelve of my best men, none of whom were able to take a single one of those things with them. You think any number of us in here will fare better?"

"The creatures had the element of surprise before. This time it'll be ours."

"You think so?"

Barnett abruptly stood and tapped the monitor displaying the mess hall, directly above their heads. A dark shape darted from behind an overturned table and vanished underneath one of the serving centers. Another slithered through the six-inch gap below the door propped on Young's body and took a bite from the meat of his shoulder. The other raced across the room, snapped at it, and drove it back into the corridor.

"We can't just wait for your men to rescue us," Roche said. "What if they're no more effective than the men you already lost? By then there could be ten times as many of them and we won't stand a chance. We need to make our move now. While we still can."

Tess found the monitor she was looking for in the bottom right corner. The thermal image of Subject Z crouched at the door of its enclosure, its legs bent and its clawed hands flat on the bare ground. It was a posture she hadn't seen before, one that made her instinctively uneasy.

"How do you propose we do that?" Barnett asked. "The moment we open the hatch we'll be swimming in them. And even if by some miracle we're able to get out of the vault, how in the name of God do you propose we eliminate all of them?"

"We have to freeze them," Moira said from directly beside Tess, who jumped at the sound of her voice. "Acute exposure to cold should trigger a state of cryobiosis, which is how the first one survived in the ice caverns. It took a flamethrower to revive it, and that's why they need the bodies to hatch their offspring. They thrive in the heat."

"How are we supposed to do that?" Avila said. "I left my freeze ray at home."

It struck Tess that Subject Z was probably hungry. It had come to rely upon them to deliver its meals through the hole in the door. With no one left out there to do so, it was only a matter of time before it starved to death. Regardless of its nature or the atrocities it had perpetrated, it didn't deserve to die like that.

"That can't be entirely true," Barnett said. "They got to two of my men outside the complex in the snow."

"Then there must be some sort of time threshold."

"We flood the place," Roche said. "The water from the lake is below freezing, isn't it?"

"Even if we could," Barnett said, "there's no guarantee it would work."

Tess detected movement on the screen beside the one displaying the creature's cage. Little more than a shifting of shadows. She recognized her office and her console in the dim red light, but not the man who emerged from the dark corridor and approached the outer wall of the cage. A silhouette, his features indistinct. With the exception of his elongated cranium.

"No," she whispered.

The man approached the control panel beside the door and started to type.

"What's wrong?" Kelly asked.

"Override access to the door lock!" Tess screamed.

"Jesus," Love said, and raced to the nearest terminal.

She was too late.

The man stepped back from the control panel and turned toward the door as it slid into the recess in the reinforced wall. Despite the bruising and deformities, she recognized his face. She saw it every day. Les Dutton, the chef who brought the creature its meals.

On the adjacent monitor, Subject Z's multicolored form rose to its full height, cast one final glance at the camera, and walked right out through the open door.

There was nothing they could do to stop it.

"Don't lose sight of it," Barnett shouted. "I want a visual on it at all times. And isolate that image. We need to know who in God's name released it and how we let this happen!"

A scream from the room behind her.

Tess glanced back and saw the people who'd been

dozing near the back wall jump up from their cots and back away from the generator room. She walked toward them as though in a trance. The entire world felt like it was unraveling around her.

Another scream.

She recognized Anna Messerschmidt when the lexicologist turned and toppled over an unused cot. Mats Karlsson nearly tripped over her in his hurry to distance himself from the generator room. Dark fluid seeped out from beneath the door. Tess kept telling herself it was oil clear up until the point when she could no longer deny what it truly was.

Thud.

She looked up from the puddle and to the door.

"Director Barnett?" she said.

She could hear him barking orders from inside the command center. He seemed oblivious to the screaming, which grew louder and more frantic by the second.

Thud!

The door shook in its frame. The knob rattled.

She backed slowly away. Stumbled over a cot. Regained her balance.

Thud!

Tess turned and sprinted for the command center.

Behind her, the frame splintered with a loud *crack* and the door burst open.

40
EVANS

Teotihuacan

"**Y**ou've got me," Evans said. "Let the others go. I won't cause any trouble."

Black Skull pressed the barrel of his pistol harder into the back of Evans's head in response.

While they moved much faster with the lights on, they still made several wrong turns. Anya floated in the lead. She'd managed to keep from tripping several booby traps and avoided some that had already been sprung. Lord only knew how much longer her luck would hold out, though. Not that Evans was going to make it very much farther, either. He was growing colder by the second and a bone-deep exhaustion threatened to overwhelm him.

Their captors had replaced Anya's saturated shirt with a field dressing of their own, and while it was considerably more effective, Evans was still losing blood at an alarming rate. If he wasn't able to hold his own swimming, they would have no further use for him. He needed to do whatever he could to get Anya and Jade out of harm's way before that happened.

"I can help you find what you're looking for," he said. "Just let them go. They're of no use to you."

Black Skull nudged him with the pistol hard enough to drive his mouth and nose underwater. The two men did their best to keep their talking to an absolute minimum, which suggested there was something about either their speech patterns or their voices they feared might give away their identities. Like Villarreal, they didn't use contractions, a common trait among people for whom English was a second language, although neither had any trace of an accent. They were both over six feet tall and in exceptional physical shape, as defined by the musculature beneath their wet fatigues. Their tactical masks covered the entirety of their faces, save for the mesh eye sockets that revealed the occasional glimpse of their stark white skin, light eyebrows, and piercing blue eyes, and yet still they did their best to minimize their frontal exposure. They stayed behind their captives and dictated their route with monosyllabic instructions.

"Right," Silver Alien said. He clenched his fist in the neckband of Jade's shirt and used it like a choke collar to control her.

Evans could tell she wasn't going to last much longer, either. While the momentary respite had helped, she was fading fast.

"Left."

"I have done everything you asked," Villarreal said. "Please. Take what you have come for and let us all go."

Evans wanted nothing more than to break his nose. He'd betrayed all of them to these men, who, he had no doubt, intended to kill them all once they had what they wanted, assuming it was even down here at all.

"Right."

Anya glanced back. The sharp bend prevented the lights from illuminating the passage ahead of her.

"Right," Silver Alien said again, and tightened his grip on Jade's collar until she gasped for air.

"Don't hurt her," Anya said.

She took a deep breath and swam cautiously around the corner.

"How much are they paying you, Villarreal?" Evans asked.

Villarreal answered from somewhere behind him.

"It is not about money."

"Then what is it about?"

"Quiet," Black Skull said and jabbed him in the base of the cranium.

"Answers," Villarreal said.

The short corridor terminated in front of Anya, leaving her only one direction to go. She waited for the command to be given.

"Right."

She swam slowly away from the light and into the darkness once more.

"You do realize they're going to kill all of us, don't you?" Evans said.

"They will not. We have a deal and I have upheld my end."

"And what was that?"

"I would notify them the moment we discovered what I believed to be the royal burial."

"All of this to loot a tomb?"

"I care nothing for treasure, although I am certain a fortune in jade and obsidian awaits. I am interested only in the remains themselves. Do you not see? For all of the surviving murals, there is only record of one king. The largest and most advanced civilization of its kind in all of the New World, one that thrived for more than five hundred years, and we have record of only one ruler?"

"None of the surviving murals are complete. You said so yourself."

"They represent the first example of statist propaganda. Their rulers would have been memorialized alongside their gods, and with even greater frequency."

"Turn right," Silver Alien said.

"You are a scholar of ancient Egypt," Villarreal said. "Consider how detailed the surviving records are. Every dynasty and every pharaoh are recorded in perfect detail, while there are no such records here, despite how similar the two societies are in nearly every other way, from the arrangement of the pyramids to the designs of the cities themselves. Have you not asked yourself how two civilizations so similar could develop simultaneously on opposite sides of the planet?"

Anya gasped. The sound echoed from around the corner.

They rounded the bend and the lights swept across the water, revealing her shoulders and the back of her head. She turned to face them and held up her forearm, revealing deep diagonal lacerations from her wrist to her elbow.

"Jesus," Jade whispered, and swam toward her. Silver Alien jerked on her neck to stop her. She rounded on him with fire in her eyes. "I'm going to help her, whether you like it or not."

She tried to remove her own shirt, but her captor wasn't about to relinquish his leverage.

"Cut off my sleeve," Evans said. "The neoprene should provide enough compression to help stop the bleeding."

Something sharp pressed into the back of his arm. He glanced over his shoulder in time to see the blade pass through the neoprene and enter his arm.

The pain was instantaneous.

Evans gritted his teeth as Black Skull used the knife to draw a circle around his biceps until the sleeve separated. Evans tugged it from his wrist and cringed at the amount of blood diffusing into the water. Granted, the cuts were superficial, but he was running out of blood to give.

He held out the sleeve for Jade. He saw the sympathy on her face. The fear. The understanding of what was to come. His hand lingered on hers when she took it from him.

She pulled the sleeve as tightly as she could over Anya's forearm.

"This will only slow the bleeding," Jade said.

"She needs a hospital," Villarreal said. "Please. Let me take her. She has nothing that you want. She has not seen your faces."

"Keep going," Black Skull said.

"There's a log with spikes." Anya's voice trembled when she spoke. "Right below the surface. We're going to have to swim underneath it."

"Then do it."

"I need the light."

Black Skull shoved Evans forward and shined his light down at the water. The beam hardly penetrated the murk.

"Well?"

Evans could barely discern the outlines of the spikes right in front of Anya.

Tears dripped from her chin when she looked down at the water. She was positively terrified.

"I'll go," Evans said.

"If you try anything—anything at all—she will die slowly," Black Skull said. "While you watch."

Evans shrugged out of the man's grasp, pulled on his diving mask, and switched on the light. He dove without a word and swam cautiously past Anya's treading legs. His own legs were rapidly losing strength. Numbness had settled like a lead weight into his right foot, while a white-hot pain radiated from his calf.

The log was mounted to the walls roughly three feet above another one just like it. The razor-sharp spikes were splintered from obsidian and easily a foot long, leaving the narrowest of gaps between them through which to swim. There was no way he was getting through there with his air tank, so he unclipped his harness and let it sink into the cloud of sediment. He turned his head sideways and watched the spikes pass, mere millimeters away, from the corner of his eye as he swam. One sliced through his wetsuit and the skin on his shoulder, forcing him to alter his course ever so slightly. By the time he drew his legs through the other side, he was out of air and swam toward the surface. It took several moments to catch his breath.

"The gap is maybe a foot wide," he said. "I'll go back down with my light so you can see. Watch out for those spikes."

He dove again and shined his light through the obsidian gamut.

Anya passed through first, followed by Black Skull. Despite Villarreal's protests, he made it to the other side without incident. Jade came next, with Silver Alien right on her heels. While Evans could have easily pushed him down onto the spikes, he had no doubt Black Skull would kill the others without hesitation. He waited just long enough for the second man to pass through before streaking toward the surface, where his captor was ready and waiting to press the gun to the back of his head once more.

They swam through a long straightway toward the distant wall, which drew contrast as they neared. The ceiling rose at an angle above them until it leveled off, maybe five feet over their heads. There were no branching passages, at least that Evans could see.

"What do you expect to find with the remains?" he asked.

"There is a reason the Aztec named this place Teotihuacan," Villarreal said. "This is the birthplace of gods. The signs are all around us."

Evans laughed. He couldn't help himself. What Villarreal proposed was insane.

"You honestly believe you're going to find the remains of a god?"

"When the Spanish conquistadores arrived in the sixteenth century, the Inca genuinely believed they were gods. Viracochas, they called them, because their white skin resembled that of their creator god. The motif of light-skinned outsiders figures prominently in the legends of every indigenous culture throughout the Americas. The Aztec, the Maya, the Inca. They all have stories of white gods arriving from the sky, bringing with them knowledge beyond the understanding of the natives and instructing them in how to build advanced civilizations and pyramids. Like the one above us. Like those in Giza. Or the one in Antarctica. You of all people should understand. You have seen the proof with your own eyes."

"A superior race of white beings," Evans said. "Where have I heard that before?"

"Quiet," Black Skull said.

"You mock me, but it is true. In our field, we make the mistake of viewing history through modern eyes. Instead, it must be evaluated with an open mind. We must take into account the fears and superstitions of the times, for they are critical to understanding the people and their motivations. The Mayan and Mixtec codices, the bas-reliefs of Tiahuanaco and Palenque, the Ica stones and Nazca lines . . . all of them speak to the arrival of white gods from the sky, gods from whom all men descended. Even the story of Quetzalcoatl that led us here tells us as much. We are on the verge of solving one of the oldest riddles in the history of mankind."

Anya stopped at the end of the corridor. There was nowhere else to go. She looked back at them with sheer terror in her eyes. Unless they'd made a wrong turn some time ago, they'd reached the center of the maze.

And nothing was there.

"You're just as guilty of imposing your own interpretations upon these so-called findings," Evans said.

"You are wrong," Villarreal said. "I seek only the

truth, whatever it may be. I care nothing for the ideology of these men or their Aryan—"

The gunshot was deafening.

Evans shouted in surprise and whirled to see Villarreal sink beneath the water, his blood running down the obsidian wall.

41
ROCHE

The Vault, FOB Atlantis

Roche lunged for the rack of assault rifles, grabbed a SCAR 17, and pulled back the charging handle to load a round into the firing chamber. Shoved past Avila and Love. Pulled Kelly to the side of the open door.

"Stay right here."

He fought his way out of the command center while all the others were trying to get into it. People were tripping over each other. Trampling each other. Screaming. Crying. Toppling cots and racks of supplies. Scattering their contents across the floor.

The door to the generator room stood open, the trim surrounding it broken. The inside of the door was gouged with scratches. The pool of blood continued to expand outward from inside the small room, following the course of the trident-shaped footprints that led into the main room before vanishing amid the chaos.

He grabbed the nearest person, a man he didn't recognize.

"What's going on?"

The man shouted something unintelligible and struggled free of his grasp.

"It's over there!" Tess screamed.

Roche followed her line of sight to the left side of the room as a rack stuffed with boxes of dried rations crashed to the floor.

Barnett appeared at his side, a rifle seated against his shoulder.

"How did it get in here?" he shouted.

"I don't know," Roche said, "but we'd better figure it out in a hurry before any more of them get in. If they haven't already."

Avila emerged from the command center with one of the bullpup assault rifles at her shoulder.

"Get everyone inside and lock the door!" Barnett shouted.

She took up post beside the door and sighted the vault down her short barrel as she hustled people past her and into the command center.

A scream.

Roche swiveled toward the sound. A flash of movement from his left and the screaming stopped. A woman collapsed to the ground in a wash of blood.

He advanced in a shooter's stance. Waved Barnett farther to his left so they could hopefully corner it—

A blur of movement behind a shelving unit.

Roche lunged backward before it fell and it still nearly took off his toes.

"Do you see it?" Roche asked.

"Negative," Barnett said.

Roche watched the director from the corner of his eye as he stepped around the fallen shelving unit. Barnett crouched over the fallen woman and without taking his eye from the rifle, felt for a pulse in the side of her neck. He removed his hand dripping with blood.

"Everyone's inside!" Avila shouted.

"Lock the door behind you!" Barnett shouted.

The command center door slammed shut. Avila sealed the others inside with the thud of a deadbolt. And locked Barnett and Roche outside with a creature they couldn't see.

"Are the walls of the command center bulletproof?" Roche asked.

"All of the interior walls are reinforced with galvanized steel."

"Will they withstand a direct shot from one of these?"

"Probably."

"That's not very reassuring."

"Then let's not put it to the test."

The walls behind the fallen shelves were bare concrete. The units that remained upright granted glimpses of spaces behind them that couldn't have been more than a few inches deep, at the very most.

"It can't have gotten very far," Barnett said.

Roche turned slowly to his right, scrutinizing the dim room down the bullpup rifle's short sightline.

There was nothing moving through the overturned cots or behind the drums of water. It was as though whatever it was had simply vanished into thin—

Something streaked through his peripheral vision and struck the ground with a soft *plat*.

Roche raised his rifle and threw himself backward in one motion. Hit the ground on his shoulders. Pulled the trigger.

A dark shape raced across the ceiling.

He fired over and over again.

Bullets ricocheted and concrete shrapnel flew.

Skree!

Blood spattered the ceiling and the creature plummeted from above him.

Roche flipped over, propelled himself to his feet, and ran toward where it hit the ground. Kicked over cots until he saw something move—

It reared up from the ground and struck at him.

He dodged to the side and rounded on it.

"Coming your way!" he shouted.

Discharge spat from Barnett's rifle. Sparks flew from the floor and bullets sang through the air before embedding themselves in the outer wall of the generator room.

The serpentine shadow veered back toward Roche, who was ready for it this time and put a bullet through the side of its throat.

Its momentum carried it to the middle of the room, where it collapsed and slid through its own blood.

"Is it dead?" Barnett asked.

Roche could barely hear him over the ringing in his ears. He shoved the cots away from where the creature lay and approached with his finger on the trigger.

It was like nothing he'd ever seen before. His first instinct was to call it a bird, but its legs and quill-like feathers were the only parts of it that were remotely avian. They bristled from its sharp jawline and neck, grew in a fan from its reptilian tail.

"It's a goddamn dinosaur," Barnett said, although even that term insufficiently captured its ferocity.

Its snout was like a crocodile's, only shorter and thinner, its facial architecture that of an adder, much like the rest of its body, which was serpentine, and yet simultaneously plated, like an armadillo. Its hind legs reminded him of those of a raptor, especially the way the middle digit—with its long, hooked talon—stood erect.

Roche stepped on its head, kicked its body over, and put one final shot through its heart for good measure. Its belly lacked the protection of its back, especially near its gut, which bulged unevenly as though it had swallowed a bunch of rocks. He nudged them with the toe of his boot and felt them slide over each other. He pressed harder and what looked like the abdomen of a yellow jacket unfurled from the underside of its tail. One of the rocks squeezed down the length of it and dropped to the ground in a pile of sludge.

"It's an ovipositor," Barnett said. "Parasitic wasps use them to lay their eggs inside of host species."

He turned on his flashlight and shined it onto the egg sac, the walls of which were so thin that they could see the outline of the creature inside, curled tightly into a ball, its tail wrapped all the way over its head, shoulders, and back. It started squirming the moment the light hit it.

"It cuts its prey with those long claws," Barnett said, "and uses its ovipositor to lay its eggs inside of it."

Everything fell into place for Roche, who sprinted to the generator room.

A pair of giant sacs hung from the ceiling, the bottoms of which were black and saturated with blood. Past them, in the far back corner, was what was left of Harrison, his entire midsection torn open.

"How long was it between when you found Harrison and when those egg sacs appeared upstairs?" he shouted.

"I don't know."

"Think!"

"An hour, maybe?"

Roche backed from the generator room and closed the door.

"Get everyone out of here," he said.

"We've been over this—"

"Those things up there are all about to hatch. If we don't get out of here now, we won't be getting out of here at all."

Barnett looked from the dead creature to the generator room.

"Jesus," he whispered. "Their gestation time is a matter of hours."

"Get that hatch open!" Roche shouted as he ran past him to the command center. He banged on the door until Avila opened it and searched for Kelly. Took her by the hand and pulled her to his side. "Everyone out!"

"Where are we going?" Kelly asked.

"To the surface."

"I'm not going back up there," Anna cried.

"If you stay here, you will die."

Roche pulled Kelly to the base of the stairs. Brought his face to within inches of hers.

"Stay right behind me," he said. "Hold on to the waistband of my pants and don't let go."

The electromagnetic locking mechanism above them disengaged with a loud *thunk*. Barnett gripped the wheel in both hands and looked down at him.

"What's the plan?"

"Is there someplace we can take all of these people where they'll be safe?"

"If we can get them all to the power station—"

"We can't all use the elevator at once."

"Then we split up."

"We have a better chance if we stay together."

"Zeta's cage," Tess said from somewhere behind him. "It's easily large enough to hold all of us."

Roche looked up at Barnett in the red glare.

"It could work," Barnett said.

"There's no time to debate it."

"Then we have no choice." Barnett spun the wheel until the secondary lock disengaged. "Tell me if there's anything above me."

Avila stood in the doorway to the command center. She glanced at the wall of monitors.

"Not that I see."

"We go up fast. Mr. Roche and I will take the lead. Avila, Love, Tolliver. You bring up the rear. Don't let anything get the jump on you."

Love yanked the charging handle, seated the assault rifle against her shoulder, and glanced at the man beside her.

"Nothing's getting past us," Tolliver said.

"Everyone else. Stay close to us and keep your eyes open. If anything happens to us . . . if we have to split up for any reason . . . get to the northern end of the first sublevel. Are we clear?"

Kelly curled her trembling fingers under Roche's waistband. Her hand felt so small and cold against his back.

He turned without thinking, leaned his face closer to hers, and kissed her. She gripped him by the neck and kissed him back with an almost desperate urgency.

"On my mark," Barnett said.

Roche pulled away and met Kelly's stare.

"Nothing will happen to you. I promise."

"Three. Two. One."

Roche bounded up the stairs as Barnett climbed through the open hatch.

42
JADE

Teotihuacan

Jade's ears echoed with a high-pitched ringing sound, beneath which she could hear Anya screaming as though from far away.

Black Skull held his pistol in his outstretched hand, across from which the wall was decorated with bone, brain matter, and high-velocity spatter. The dark shape of Villarreal's body sunk out of sight beneath him.

Before Evans could react, the man pressed the barrel of the gun against the base of his skull, producing the smell of singed hair.

"Unless you are eager to learn how many bullets I have left, I recommend you find a way forward."

Anya continued to scream.

Jade pulled her closer and got right into her face.

"Calm down, Anya. Right now."

"They just killed Juan Carlos!"

"And they'll kill us all if we give them a reason, so you need to settle down and use your head."

Anya's wild eyes searched hers for any sign of

hope. Her panic fled her on a rush of tears as she started to cry.

"We have to go back the way we came," Evans said. "We must have taken a wrong turn."

"No," Jade said. "This is the right way. We've exhausted all other options."

She knew it and the men with the guns knew it, too. Either she and her friends found what their captors had come here to find, or this was where they would die. Even if they did find it, at best they were only buying themselves some time. Once these men had what they wanted, there would be nothing to prevent them from eliminating any potential witnesses. Jade had worked enough crime scenes and understood that even forensic evidence often wasn't enough. Without eyewitnesses, criminals nearly always went free, even in the face of a preponderance of evidence. These men were professionals. Whether anyone had seen their faces or not, they would leave no one who could possibly identify them behind.

"I'll look down below," Evans said.

"If you are not back up here within fifteen seconds, I will kill one of your friends."

Evans stared at Black Skull with hatred in his eyes, but dove without saying a word.

Jade watched the aura of his light grow smaller below her feet until it was barely visible. It made a circuit around the dead end before rising to the surface. He breached, took a deep breath, and dove back under again.

"We have to be missing something," Jade said. "Shine your lights on the walls."

The man who held her by the collar did as she asked. His beam explored the wall to her right, starting at the level of the water and working higher and higher until it reached the ceiling. He moved on to the wall that blocked their way and did the same thing. It was covered with the same kind of strange characters and primitive writing she'd seen throughout the ruins, only these were carved directly into the stone, rather than painted onto it.

"What do they say?" Black Skull asked without looking up from where he watched the light below him through the churning sediment.

"You just killed the only person who could have told us."

The man had no response.

Jade studied the petroglyphs as the light passed over them. The lower ones were crusted with accumulated sediment from the flooding. Above them was a giant circular design, at the center of which was a skull with an open mouth and extended tongue. Immediately surrounding it were the alternating heads of Quetzalcoatl and Tlaloc, just like on the face of the pyramid above them. The rings radiating outward were symmetrical and filled with animals: jaguars and coyotes, rabbits and snakes. The outermost rings featured random, unrecognizable designs. If there was some significance to them, she couldn't decipher it.

Other characters framed the circle. She recognized the skull-faced god of the dead, Mictlantecuhtli, and his wife, Mictlancihuatl, on their thrones in the underworld. Quetzalcoatl, his serpentine visage fringed with feathers, appeared to be aligned against Xolotl, with the face of a dog and the body of a man, in an attempt to prevent him from reaching what looked like a gate or threshold, inside of which was a figure with a circular face, from which pointed rays radiated.

She recalled the story Villarreal had told them, about how Xolotl had traveled to the depths of Mictlan to unearth the rotting bones of an extinct race of beings, and experienced a sudden moment of clarity. Villarreal had said these men had come here in search of remains he'd inferred they believed were of extraterrestrial origin, an extinct race of beings. Was it possible the legend had somehow grown from a seed of truth?

The light followed the course of the drawing all the way up to the ceiling, where there were three rectangular holes, almost as though whoever built the wall had forgotten the last three bricks. They were maybe eighteen inches wide and eight inches high, not nearly large enough for them to squirm through, even if they were able to climb that high.

"There has to be a way to get to the other side," Silver Alien said.

If these petroglyphs represented the story Villarreal had told them, then she had to believe that the way through was hidden somewhere within it.

Xolotl had tricked Mictlantecuhtli into allowing him to take the carcass. How did one trick death?

Evans burst from the water behind her and gasped for air.

"Can you see any more carvings on the wall down there?" she asked.

"There aren't any below the waterline."

"Like they were designed only to be viewed with the tunnels flooded?"

"The same way we were able to navigate the booby traps."

Jade studied the designs. Had they been carved there as instructions or as a warning?

The man behind her shined his light onto the wall to her left.

"Go back to the carvings," she said.

"What do you see?" he asked.

"The story. There's something about it . . ."

How *did* someone trick death? Maybe Xolotl hadn't tricked Mictlantecuhtli, but had made a deal with him instead. A deal with death. A deal he then reneged upon. He hadn't tricked Mictlantecuhtli, he'd cheated him.

He'd cheated death.

The phrase had an alternate meaning. They'd circumvented numerous booby traps throughout the maze, cheating death every step of the way. Perhaps the ancient Teotihuacano had set one final trap for them. And if that were the case, she needed to figure it out in a hurry because she wasn't going to be able to tread water much longer. As it was, she could barely keep her mouth above the surface.

And then she saw it.

The skull at the center of the circular design was meant to be Mictlantecuhtli, who was often depicted with his tongue hanging out. His mouth was perfectly circular as well, although the edges of the disk fitted into his jaws weren't perfectly aligned.

"There's a hole in his mouth," Jade said.

Silver Alien shined his light onto the center of the design.

"Where? I do not see . . ." His words trailed off when he recognized the deception. "Very clever."

He swam closer to it and appraised it from several angles before nudging it with the barrel of his gun. The disk turned sideways in the hole, making it easy to grab and wiggle out. He shined his light through the hole and peered inside.

"There is something back there."

"What do you see?" Black Skull asked.

"There is a room behind the wall, but it is too dark to estimate its size."

"We need to find the way in."

"You have to cheat death," Jade said. She stared at the hideous visage of Mictlantecuhtli. He held out his arms: one raised to the sky, the other extended and gripping a spear shaft. "You have to reach through the hole."

"You mean *you* have to reach through the hole," Black Skull said, and turned his weapon on her.

Jade didn't have enough strength left to argue. Her legs were done and no amount of willpower would save her from drowning. Her only hope was to get out of the water.

She looked at the hole for several seconds, took a deep breath, and stuck her hand inside. Slowly. Feeling every inch of the cold stone until she found the inner edge.

Her legs gave out, transferring the strain to her arm. She grabbed the protruding tongue with her other hand and did her best to hang on.

Evans took her around the waist, squeezed his fingertips into a crevice, and attempted to keep her from sinking.

"Get on with it," Silver Alien said.

She reached carefully into the open air until her fingers grazed what she knew would be there. The spear shaft was nearly petrified and as thick as a shovel handle. It was a lever, she knew, but what she didn't know was what the depiction of Mictlantecuhtli hinted was above her.

"I need a belt," she said,

"Why?" Black Skull asked.

"Just give me your belt!"

He hesitated, but ultimately slid it from the waistband of his pants and handed it to her. She removed her hand from the hole, fed the end of the belt through the buckle to form a loop, and thrust it through the hole. It took several tries to slip the loop over the wooden lever. She pulled it tight, extricated her arm from the hole, and handed the end of the belt to the man with the gun pointed at her. It was all she could do to wedge her fingertips into the edge of the circle and hold on.

"Pull it," she said. "Hard and fast."

"You do it," Black Skull said and held the belt out for Evans.

He looked at Jade, who nodded that it was going to be all right.

Evans wrapped the end of the belt around his fist and gave it a solid jerk.

Nothing happened.

He pulled it again, harder this time.

Still nothing.

He tugged again and again.

"Stop," Silver Alien said. "Something must be—"

The lever abruptly moved. Evans toppled backward into the water. The severed end of the belt whipped past Jade's cheek. The obsidian guillotine passed through the darkness on the other side of the wall and embedded itself into what sounded like wood with a resounding *thuck*.

"The mechanism must have been stuck," Evans said.

He'd barely finished the sentence when the wall in front of him dropped several feet straight down with a *thud* that shook the entire maze.

There was a three-foot gap above the level of the water. Jade threw both arms onto the top of the sunken door and clung to it for dear life.

Silver Alien pulled himself out of the water and onto the top of the wall, where he crouched and shined his light down into a square chamber roughly ten feet to a side.

Water fired through the hole in Mictlantecuhtli's open mouth and spattered the dry ground with the force of a fire hose. At the center of the room was a broad, tiered stone plinth. On top of it rested a granite sarcophagus, inside of which was presumably what the Teotihuacano had gone to such extreme lengths to hide.

And what these men had come to find.

43
KELLY

The Mess Hall, FOB Atlantis

They emerged from the vault into a world that had changed dramatically since they'd last been there. The mess hall looked like a tornado had blown through. Tables and chairs were toppled and scattered throughout the room. The door to the walk-in cooler stood wide open, a grating buzzing sound echoing from within.

Kelly held on to the back of Roche's pants as though her life depended upon it, while the fingers on her left hand went crazy at her side.

Barnett led them to the nearest door and started typing on the control panel. She didn't at first see the dead man at her feet, his abdomen smashed beneath the door. His face and shoulders were skeletal where the meat had been torn from the bones.

She cringed when the panel issued a loud beeping sound. The door retracted into the ceiling with the whirring of hydraulic gears.

The adjoining corridor was narrow and dark. She could barely see the red light inside Midnight over Roche's shoulder and past Barnett's head. They entered in single file. Slowly. Barnett slid to the left and Roche took point on the right. They sighted their assault rifles from one side to the other as they advanced.

The main table lay on its side, surrounded by broken computers. The security monitors at the front of the room flickered with rotating live feeds from elsewhere in the building. One of them had fallen and shattered on the floor.

She passed an enormous egg sac on her right. The almost flaky outer layers glistened with the fresh application of some viscous fluid, almost like papier-mâché. Blood dripped from the bottom and pattered the floor in a puddle that positively reeked of death. She could see the side of a man's face through a gap between the fibrous strands that bound the nest to the ceiling. His cheeks were pale and the skin around his eyes dark. She'd never seen him before, and yet felt a pang of guilt. This entire mountain should have been destroyed and the ice dome collapsed onto this horrible place.

A crackling sound from inside the nest.

Her first thought was that the man might still be alive, but the half-lidded expression on his face convinced her otherwise. There was something else in there with him. Something alive.

She felt Roche tense. He turned toward the sound and stared at the nest for several seconds before hastening his pace toward the door.

Someone whimpered behind her.

Kelly closed her eyes and prayed that the creatures hadn't heard. As it was, the sound of their tread was too loud. The soles of their shoes were sticky with blood and peeled from the floor like masking tape.

She glanced back over her shoulder.

Avila brought up the rear with the other flashlight, silhouetting the men and women in front of her. She was only now entering the corridor between buildings. The survivors in between shied away from the nest as strips of the casing fell away. A dark shape slithered from one of the gaps, ascended the side, and disappeared through the gap by the man's face. A crunching sound, followed by ripping. The creature scurried back out and dropped to the floor. It was already a good two feet long. Roche stomped on its head before it could test its legs.

The second nest passed to Kelly's right, even more active than the last. She could hear them in there. Hear them moving, chewing. They made crackling sounds, like maggots inside roadkill. A drowsy reptilian head, its eyes still closed and its feathers slicked back, protruded from the nest beneath a man's chin. It opened its bloody snout wide and made a screeching noise.

Barnett stepped over the fallen monitor and paused long enough to stare at the remaining screens. He cast a sideways glance at Roche, who raised his rifle and turned toward the tunnel to his right. Both men started firing before Kelly even saw the hideous beast scurry out from the roof of the corridor and climb up the arched wall.

A spray of blood patterned the ceiling and the creature dropped to the ground. It landed on the other side of the table and scrabbled for cover.

"Go!" Barnett shouted.

He whirled to his left and fired into the other dark passageway.

Roche ran toward the front door, which revealed little more than a swatch of the deck. He shouldered it wide open and dragged Kelly out under the ice dome. She suddenly felt exposed and vulnerable. Tess bumped into her from behind. Roche turned back toward the building and sighted down the roofline before making a break for the boardwalk to the left.

Barnett's footsteps echoed all around them as he ran to catch up.

"Where are they?" he shouted.

Screams erupted from inside the building, followed by the prattle of gunfire.

Kelly looked back. Detected movement from the corner of her eye.

The creature emerged from beneath the walkway and scampered over the railing. Opened its jaws wide and struck—

Roche stepped between it and her. Jammed his rifle into its open mouth. Pulled the trigger. The back of its head dissolved into a red cloud and its body flopped backward over the rail.

More screaming from behind them.

They weren't going to make it.

"Close ranks!" Barnett shouted.

He ran toward the middle of the pack as a shadow appeared above the roofline. He stopped and aimed. By the time his bullets ricocheted from the building, it was already airborne. It hit the paleoarcheologist, Karlsson, squarely on the shoulders. He cried out and tumbled to the ground. The creature's momentum carried them over the edge. The moment they clattered to the rocks, it dragged him underneath the boardwalk and his screams suddenly ceased.

Barnett stood over them and shouted as he fired straight down through the wooden planks. Ejected the spent magazine. Slammed another into the breech.

He looked directly at Kelly.

"Run!"

Another creature appeared from the ruins to their right and jumped up onto the boardwalk in front of them. Roche shot at it. The bullets chewed up the wood, but merely served to chase it off the other side.

Roche grabbed her by the hand and together they ran around the side of the pyramid. The darkened ruins stretched out beside them, toward the dry lake bed and a ring of stones reminiscent of Stonehenge. She could feel the creatures out there, moving through the shadows. Closing in on them.

They rounded the front of the pyramid and hurdled the switchbacking stairs two at a time. The entryway loomed over them, dark and forbidding. Roche pulled up short and aimed his rifle into the main corridor.

With power diverted to emergency functions, the inside of the pyramid was completely dark. They couldn't see a thing.

He fired three times to clear their path. The resultant strobe of discharge limned the walls of the empty passageway as the bullets ricocheted deeper into the darkness. He advanced all the way to the end of the main branch and released a triple burst down into the descending corridor. Again, the momentary flashes illuminated the vacant tunnel.

Barnett caught up with them and shined his light up toward the statuary and into the ascending corridor—

Eyeshine.

He instinctively retreated and knocked Kelly into

the wall. The creature streaked past her face, so close she could feel the wind of its passage and smell the carrion on its breath. Tess ducked and it struck the woman behind her in the face. Bounced her from the wall and pinned her to the ground. Opened her throat before she could even scream.

Barnett shoved past Kelly, planted his foot on the creature's back, and fired down at its head until there was nothing left of it, leaving those still funneling into the pyramid to step over its mangled remains.

He assumed the lead again and guided them down the descending corridor in a crouch. He paused when he reached the bottom. Shined his light across the cavernous chamber and the ancient machinery. Ran for the well in the center, from which the top rungs of the ladder stood.

"Do you remember your way?" he asked.

"Yeah," Roche said.

Another light materialized from the tunnel behind them. It brightened by the second until Avila appeared, holding her flashlight beneath the stock of her rifle.

There were far fewer of them than when they set out from the vault.

"Avila and I will cover you," Barnett said. "Just get everyone to the end of the hall. And pray that Zeta isn't still down there."

Roche nodded.

The terror struck Kelly so hard that she couldn't breathe. It was down there. The monster that had once been Dale Rubley. In the darkness beneath their feet. The demon that stalked her nightmares. And it was no longer contained by the cage.

They were all going to die.

"We should just stay here," Kelly said. "We can hold them off—"

"For how long?" Roche asked.

"For as long as we have to!"

"We don't have a choice." He took her by the hand and led her toward the ladder. Barnett shined his light down into the hole. Avila slipped past him and clattered down the ladder. "You can do this, Kelly. I'll be right here with you the whole time."

"You know what's down there, don't you?"

"I also know what's up here. If we can reach the cage, you'll be safe inside."

"Until it opens the door. You saw how it got out of there. How long before it comes for us?"

"You'll be safe. I promise."

Avila jumped as soon as she was close enough to the ground. Dropped to one knee. Swung her light and her rifle first to the left, then to the right.

"All clear!" she shouted.

"You can't know that," Kelly said.

Roche placed his hand on her cheek and turned her face to meet his.

"Do you trust me?"

Her eyes searched his in the dim light.

"Hurry!" Barnett shouted.

Tess stepped around them and started down the ladder.

"Yes," Kelly whispered.

"Then go," he said, and urged her toward the hole.

She grabbed the ladder and looked down. Tess descended ahead of her, toward where Avila had taken post, her light shining—

A dark shape appeared from nowhere and knocked

Avila onto her back. She shouted and pulled the trigger. Bullets sparked as they ricocheted from the ceiling.

Tess screamed and started climbing back up.

Avila got her forearm under the creature's neck. Pushed its snapping jaws away from her face. Worked the barrel of the rifle under its chin.

It shrieked like a hawk.

Skree—!

A burst of red exploded from its feathered head.

Tess tumbled over the edge of the well and crawled away from the hole.

Avila tossed the creature off her and stood. She staggered to the base of the ladder and looked up at them, her face a mask of blood.

"Hurry! Before more—"

Shadows struck her simultaneously from both sides.

"The elevator!" Roche shouted.

He dragged Kelly away from the ladder, through the people in his way, and straight into the descending corridor.

Avila's screams echoed from behind them.

Roche fired as he ran to at least make whatever might be up there think twice about stepping into their path. They blew through the main corridor and out of the pyramid. Nearly fell down the stairs before catching their balance and jumping to the landing.

Kelly heard the others hit the stairs behind her, but couldn't bring herself to look back. The boardwalk ahead of them led straight across the rocks and toward the distant escarpments. She couldn't remember exactly where the elevator was, only that it was near the face of the mountains, where they rose up into the ice.

Stone dwellings passed to either side, discolored by the accumulation of sediment and algae through the millenia. The overrun base appeared through a gap to her right and vanished every bit as quickly.

The elevator shaft materialized from the darkness ahead of them. The emergency light on the roof of the car glowed red. As did the lights leading upward into the shaft.

They ran to the platform and ascended the stairs. Roche guided her through the open door and into the car. Took up post beside it and covered the others as they ran toward them.

"Get inside!" Roche shouted.

Kelly stumbled backward as Tess entered, followed by more and more people who shoved her deeper inside. She met resistance behind her and had to fight for what little space she had. In the process, she lost sight of Roche.

"Martin!" she shouted.

The elevator door closed with a loud clang.

She couldn't see anything over the heads of the others packed inside with her.

"Martin!"

"Kelly!"

She turned to her left. He stood on the opposite side of the cage, his fingers curled into the wire mesh.

"What are you doing?" she screamed.

"Barricade yourselves inside the power station until help arrives."

"Don't leave me!"

"Someone has to end this."

She thrust her fingers through the mesh on top of his.

The elevator shuddered and the motor hummed.

"I'll catch up," he said. "I promise."

He kissed her knuckles and pried his fingers out from beneath hers.

Kelly screamed and beat her fists against the siding of the elevator as it rose from the platform.

He watched her ascend until she was nearly to the ice dome, then turned and followed Barnett and a handful of others back toward the ruins.

Tess placed her hand on Kelly's shoulder.

She brushed it off and turned to face the others.

There were only nine survivors in the elevator. The creatures had slaughtered more than half of those who'd sought shelter in the vault during their desperate attempt to escape.

The elevator entered the narrow ice shaft. The walls closed in upon them in the suffocating darkness, metered by the occasional red emergency light that flashed past on the rails.

Kelly buried her face in her hands and slid down the wall to her rear end. Her shoulders shook as she cried.

44
ANYA

Teotihuacan

Anya dragged herself up onto the lowered wall as the last of her energy fled her. Exhaustion overwhelmed her and she nearly collapsed forward into the dark room. It was all she could do to hang on as the emotions she'd held at bay assailed her. She sobbed. For herself. For Villarreal. For all of them. Her body wanted nothing more than to just shut down, but she understood the consequences of allowing that to happen and willed herself to stop crying. There would be time for that later.

If she survived.

"Go," one of the men said and shoved Evans from on top of the wall.

He landed on his injured leg, which crumpled underneath him. He pushed himself up onto all fours as the water rose around him. It fired from the hole in the wall and struck the spear-like lever, splitting into two streams, both of which bored into the granite plinth and filled the air with spray. Already several inches had accumulated around the outermost ring of the tiered platform. Jade jumped down on her own before either man could push her. Anya followed her lead, although far less gracefully. Her trembling legs deposited her onto her rear end the moment her feet hit the ground. She crawled to the base of the plinth and up onto the bottom level.

The men climbed down at the same time and shined their lights around the chamber. Walls adorned with elaborate murals whipped past. The gears and counterweights that raised and lowered the door were mounted to either side. The flashlight beams produced rainbow reflections from deep inside the obsidian columns in the four corners of the tomb before settling upon the sarcophagus. The men ascended the massive platform to the top and ran their palms over the smooth lid.

Anya searched the room for another way out. The walls appeared seamless, at least as far as she could tell through the deep shadows. The area surrounding the plinth functioned as a trough and was already filled nearly to the first step. Animal carcasses stood from the rising water, partially articulated and held together by desiccated skin and fur. There were pumas and jaguars, monkeys and wolves, all mummified where they lay. Sacrifices to whoever was buried inside.

She heard what sounded like voices in the distance. She looked back in the direction from which they'd come, but all she could see was darkness.

Movement from the corner of her eye.

The remains of a jaguar, its pelt faded to a dirty brown, moved ever so slightly. The water must have broken up the adipocere that adhered it to the floor.

"Drive with your legs," Black Skull said.

Anya glanced over her shoulder and watched the

two men shove the lid several inches. If she was going to die, she at least wanted to know the reason why.

She climbed to the top and pulled herself up at the foot of the coffin, which had to weigh several tons by itself. How any number of men could have lifted it all the way up there was beyond her.

The masked men groaned and pushed again, creating a slim gap from which the intermingling scents of dust and decay gusted. Silver Alien shined his light inside and revealed the tattered pelts covering the body.

A faint aura of light blossomed at the far end of the flooded corridor.

Anya knew exactly what that meant.

Reinforcements.

She and the others had to get out of there before they arrived. There had to be another way out. She spun in a circle, but couldn't see anything resembling a means of escape. There were no doors, no holes in the ceiling, no missing bricks like there were in the outer door.

The water was rising too fast. It was nearly to the top of the first step and getting deeper by the second. The body of a black howler monkey floated to the top and appeared to roll before vanishing back into the water. For a second, it almost looked like it moved on its own.

The lid of the coffin screeched as the men pushed again, widening the view enough to see the shape of the body underneath the pelts. Its arms were crossed over its narrow chest. They shined their lights onto its head and Anya stumbled backward. It had the face of a crocodile and a headdress made of parrot feathers.

"This is it," Silver Alien said. "We found it."

The excitement in his voice only served to rob Anya of the last vestiges of hope. If these men had what they had come for, they no longer had any use for her or her friends.

She turned away and slumped to the ground. The light at the end of the flooded corridor brightened and took the form of a flashlight, behind which several shadows swam.

Again, something moved in her peripheral vision.

By the time she turned, all she could see was the arched back of a dead puma breaching the surface. She was already looking away when something tore through its brittle skin and fur from the inside.

Anya glanced at Evans, who drew Jade behind him as the reinforcements approached. He could barely put any weight on his right leg, and yet appeared ready to make his stand.

She looked into the flooding tomb and saw a dark shape cut through the water, its long tail flagellating behind it.

More movement, from the far side of the plinth.

A jaguar's stiff leg rose from the depths. Its flank bulged, then deflated. Something erupted from the carcass and cut a V across the choppy surface.

The light couldn't have been more than ten feet away now, close enough to partially illuminate the blurry shapes beneath the water rising toward the second tier of the plinth.

Whatever these creatures were, they'd been hiding inside the bodies of the dead animals, although how anything could have survived entombed in here for thousands of years—

Anya thought of the human remains walled inside

the Sacrificial Well. The linear scratches on their bones. The *undersides* of their bones. As though inflicted from the inside. Men willingly sacrificed at the mouth of the tunnel that led to the maze, at the center of which was a door with holes near the ceiling, and living animals entombed with the sarcophagus.

A shadow slithered up the wall in her peripheral vision and vanished into the darkness clinging to the ceiling.

"We have to get out of here," she whispered.

"Don't make any sudden moves," Evans whispered.

"Listen to me. There's something in here with us. We have to get out of here right now!"

The men in the outer corridor reached the sunken wall and shined their lights inside.

Anya raised her hands over her head and prayed they didn't shoot.

Something grazed her ankle. She stepped up out of the water, which had risen over the top of the second step.

Black Skull and Silver Alien pushed back the lid of the sarcophagus. It teetered momentarily before toppling down the opposite side of the plinth with a series of deafening crashes. The final impact shook the ground.

She peered into the coffin and saw little more than a skeletal shape underneath rotted fur and that awful face. The eyes of the crocodile had been carved out, leaving dark holes through which she saw the sunken orbits of a man who had to be nearly seven feet tall.

"Come out of there," a woman's voice said.

Anya turned toward the source and was momentarily blinded by the light shining in her eyes.

"We have what we came for," Black Skull said. "We no longer need them."

"Until the remains are safely aboard the plane, we need them alive," the woman said.

"You are being paranoid."

"And you are being careless."

The man narrowed his eyes and appeared ready to argue with her, but turned away without another word. The balance of power had shifted. Maybe there was still hope after all.

Anya waded toward the wall, careful to avoid the stream of water that bifurcated from the wooden lever. She stumbled over a submerged carcass and nearly screamed. She could positively feel whatever manner of creatures survived in there all around her now.

"Slowly," the woman said, her voice muffled by a golden tactical mask with an ornate Celtic cross, the arms of which curled around her eye mesh. The vertical post split her face to her chin. The man beside her, whose face was concealed behind that of a Kabuki devil, thrust his gun into Anya's face for emphasis. "You two, as well. Do not make me repeat myself."

Anya braced her elbows on the wall and pulled herself up. She dangled her legs over the opposite side and waited for Evans and Jade before lowering herself into the water.

The woman shined her light upon the men on top of the plinth. The shadows retreated from the aura of her beam, along with the serpentine silhouettes inside of them.

"Wrap the body in this," the woman said, and tossed a backpack into the chamber.

Black Skull descended into the water and grabbed it before it sank. He removed a folded plastic sheet and a silver bundle. Tossed the plastic to his partner and unfolded the bundle, which ended up being a body bag.

"Let the others go," Evans said. "Please. They won't tell anyone. I'll do whatever you say."

"My dear, Dr. Evans," the woman in the golden mask said, "a single hostage is worth less than none. Without demonstrating a willingness to kill at least one of your hostages, you cannot expect anyone to take you seriously."

The men carefully wrapped the remains, pelts and all, in the plastic sheet and lifted the bundle out of the sarcophagus. It was long and skinny and seemed somehow unimpressive for all the death it had caused. They stretched out the body bag, slid the remains inside, and zipped it closed.

A shadow slithered up the wall behind them.

This time Anya saw it clearly, but so did the woman.

"Pass the body bag out to us," she said.

The men descended the plinth and splashed through the water, which was nearly to their thighs now. They fed the bag, feetfirst, over the wall.

A scuttling sound from above them.

Anya looked up as a dark shape plummeted from the ceiling. It landed on Silver Alien's back and drove him into the water. He emerged coughing and sputtering.

"What the hell was—?"

His back arched and blood burst from his lips.

"Close the door!" the woman shouted. "Hurry!"

Another creature hopped up onto the top of the sarcophagus, extended its long neck, and opened its reptilian snout to release a shrill cry.

Skree!

Others appeared as if from nowhere and converged upon Black Skull, who shoved the body over the wall and turned to face them. They washed over him in a wave of slashing claws and snapping teeth.

The woman took Evans by the shoulder, spun him around, and shouted into his face.

"Close that door or we are all dead!"

Somehow Black Skull managed to break away. He looked back at them, his fiberglass mask jaggedly broken and his face lacerated to the bone.

"*Für die arische Rasse,*" he said and pushed the lever.

The primitive gears on the walls clanked and thumped. The counterweights lowered from the ceiling.

Feathered reptilian creatures sprinted across the ceiling. They vanished behind the rising door, which struck the roof with a reverberating thud.

Black Skull's screams diminished in volume before being cut short.

Snapping jaws protruded from the holes in the top of the door. The creatures shrieked and flailed as they tried to squeeze through. Clawed appendages scratched at the stone in an attempt to widen the gaps enough to release them from the sealed chamber.

"Come," the woman said. "We must not let the sacrifice of our brother be in vain."

45
BARNETT

FOB Atlantis

It would take sixteen minutes for the elevator to reach the surface and another sixteen for it to come back down. While half an hour wasn't an overly long period of time, it felt like an eternity down there in the darkness. Barnett just prayed they were able to do what needed to be done and make their way back in time. There were only five of them left in the ruins, and the furthest thing from what one might consider an elite fighting force. While Barnett could hold his own in a pinch, the idea of being the best among them mortified him. He'd gathered nearly twenty of the best men available for just this contingency, only those who hadn't been massacred in a matter of seconds during the initial siege were in a completely different hemisphere, preparing to take on an unknown threat in Mexico. What chance did he and four other nominally trained agents have against Lord only knew how many of these infernal creatures?

Roche had demonstrated his usefulness, and Tolliver had served in the Marines prior to joining Unit

51, but he'd been recruited for his other skills. The same was true of Louis Delaney and Rudy Monroe, who'd spent time with the U.S. Army Corps of Engineers. Their expertise had been integral in draining the lake and the tunnels underneath. He only hoped they were every bit as good at undoing what they had done.

Assuming they survived that long.

The control room for the dams was at the opposite side of the base from Barnett's command center. The mere thought of heading back there made him sick to his stomach, but it was their only play. If they didn't take these monsters out, it was only a matter of time before they found their way up the elevator shaft or through the seemingly endless tunnels and escaped from this mountain. He couldn't afford to loose any of these monsters upon the outside world.

"How long are you going to need?" Barnett asked.

"Five minutes," Delaney said. "Ten at the most."

"You'll be lucky to get three."

"This isn't just a matter of flipping a switch," Monroe said. "These dams were designed to stay closed. We have to shunt the pressure and lower the barriers, and even then we still have to disable the water gates and self-closing flood barriers. Think of all of the redundancies and fail-safes we built into the system. Every single one of them has to be manually overridden."

"How long will we have after that to make it to the elevator?" Roche asked.

"You don't want to know."

They advanced in a pentagon formation, with Barnett at the point. Roche and Tolliver brought up the rear, walking backward to make sure that nothing outflanked them. With the way their footsteps echoed from beneath the boardwalks, they couldn't risk going any faster or they'd bring the whole population down on them.

Just because they couldn't see the creatures didn't mean they weren't out there in the ruins at that very moment, hunting them from the anonymity of the shadows. Their direct attack had been hugely successful. They'd taken out more than half of Barnett's team during its aborted attempt to reach Subject Z's cage and the subsequent flight to the elevator. Perhaps they recognized the danger posed by the weapons the men carried and were patiently waiting for their opportunity to strike. More likely, however, they had as many victims as they could handle and were right now suspending the bodies in those horrible nests and laying their eggs inside of them. He and his men couldn't afford to take that chance, though. Not if they had any hope of living through this nightmare.

The base materialized from the pale red glow, a dark shape squatting at the foot of the stone escarpments that encircled the lake. There was no way they were going in through the front door again, which meant their only choice was to circumnavigate the outer perimeter and enter through the machine room at the rear of the complex, the approach to which was a narrow corridor between the back of Building Five and the stone cliff. The machine room had been built into the mountain itself to prevent the noise and vibrations from adversely impacting the fragile ice dome overhead. It was connected to the main structure by a short corridor with an external door.

If their plan succeeded, however, they wouldn't have enough time to take the circuitous route back to the elevator. They had no choice but to head straight through the base, regardless of anything standing in their way.

Barnett climbed over the rail and covered the others while they did the same. The smooth rocks clattered underfoot. There was absolutely nothing they could do about the noise. He watched the rooftops as they neared and worked his way deeper into the shadows clinging to the stone escarpments. There was no sign of movement from either the base or the ice dome.

They rounded the side of the complex and passed out of the range of the emergency lights. The darkness was cold and smothering. The walls closed in from either side until they were inside a passage maybe five feet wide. It was the perfect place for an ambush. They kept their weapons trained on the roofline above them as they approached the dead end, from which the sounds of their footfalls echoed.

The door at the top of the staircase was locked. Barnett typed the override code into the control panel and it opened with a hiss of pressurized air.

He stepped back, rifle at his shoulder, and waited for something to lunge out at him. When nothing did, he went in low. Swung his weapon to the left, then to the right in the wan red glare. The reinforced door to the machine room remained closed. He could barely feel the thrum of running water and forced air on the other side. The door to the right remained closed, as well. It opened with the same code and granted access to the hydrological control room.

A desk ran the length of the rear wall. The chairs had been overturned from the stations, each of which featured a pair of computer monitors and was positioned beneath an array of screens mounted to the wall. The images on them reminded Barnett of electrical schematics and represented the various pipes and tunnels through which the lake had been diverted. Each was individually labeled, and the water pressure and temperature were monitored at discrete intervals.

"You're on," Barnett whispered.

Delaney and Monroe assumed their stations and set to work, their trembling fingers flying across the keys.

Barnett turned his back to them. The corridors to either side of the room offered glimpses into the adjacent buildings. The end of the passageway to the central hub remained sealed.

There was no sign of movement.

Roche and Tolliver took up position in the mouths of the outer passageways. Neither of them took their eyes from the sights of their rifles for a second. The only sound was the typing of keys, which was far too loud in the silent base.

The lights radiating from the monitors behind Barnett changed from green to red. He glanced over his shoulder to find alarms flashing from every screen and console.

A klaxon blared.

The warning lights on the panels to either side of the room lit up. Pressure gauges spiked. Individual components issued beeping sounds.

"I've got movement over here," Tolliver said.

"How much longer?" Barnett asked.

"Two minutes," Delaney said.

Tolliver shouted and fired into the corridor to the left.

Barnett approached the control panel that would

open the door to the mess hall and prepared to type in the override code.

He saw something move from the corner of his eye, followed by the flash of discharge and the crack of gunfire. Roche backed away from the corridor to his right.

"Don't give up ground," Barnett said.

"There are at least two of them over here!"

Barnett hoped that by allowing them to converge from the sides, it would clear a path straight up the middle.

Tolliver fired several times in rapid succession.

"I can't hold them off!" he shouted.

"How much longer?" Barnett asked.

"We're going as fast as we can!" Monroe shouted.

The ground shivered.

"What was that?"

"Millions of gallons of water preparing to come flooding back in here," Delaney said.

Roche fired again. Bullets ricocheted from the ceiling of the outer corridor.

"We're out of time!" he shouted.

More lights flashed and countless alarms joined the chorus.

The earth shuddered.

Barnett leaned against the wall to keep his balance.

"Come on, boys."

Tolliver yelled and shot into the darkness. A silhouette knifed through the strobe of discharge. Scurried from the corridor. Scaled the wall.

Barnett whirled and fired in one motion.

The creature lunged from the ceiling and caught Monroe by surprise. He tumbled from his chair and tried to push it away, but it was too fast. His scream became a hiss when it opened his throat.

Delaney jumped up and backed away from the console. Raised his rifle.

A spray of blood spattered his chest and face as Roche shot the monster from behind before it could attack.

Delaney lunged back to his station, typed one final command, and clicked the mouse.

"Go!" he shouted.

A deafening *crack*.

The ground dropped out from beneath them.

Barnett typed the override code for the door and sprinted through the corridor before the inner door even opened. He watched it rise and through the gap saw the toppled tables—

A reptilian form streaked straight at him. He pulled the trigger again and again until its head bucked and it slid across the ground toward him.

He jumped over it. Veered left. Skirted Agent Young's half-consumed remains. Sprinted straight through the main corridor toward Midnight and the open front door.

A rumbling sound in the distance grew louder by the second.

The floor shook.

He fired into the main building and burst into a room crawling with creatures. They scrambled up the walls and across the ceiling. Leaped from the swinging nests.

Barnett shot in a fan pattern in the hope of clearing a path to the door.

Something struck his back. He reached over his shoulder, grabbed a handful of feathers, and flung it aside. The hatchlings were nowhere near as large and ferocious as the adults, but considering how much they'd grown since he'd first seen them peek from the nests, it wouldn't be long before they were.

He blew through the door and hit the deck at a sprint, certain there would be dozens of them waiting to converge upon him.

The rumble became a roar.

Jagged chunks of ice plummeted from above and shattered on the deck, destroying the wooden slats in the process. Megalithic stones tumbled from the ruins and pounded the ground.

There were several creatures to his left, although they didn't appear interested in him. They all stared off to the north, past the pyramid and across the ruins.

Barnett followed their lines of sight to where a massive wave reared up against the ice dome. It appeared to hover momentarily before crashing down upon the dry lake bed.

"Holy shit," he whispered.

The churning wall of destruction raced outward toward the ancient city.

46
EVANS

Teotihuacan

Several men, similarly dressed in black fatigues and tactical masks, met them inside the maze and helped carry the body bag with a disconcerting amount of reverence. Evans tried to figure out a way to overcome their captors while they retraced their route, but by the time they swam through the narrow tunnel and reentered the Sacrificial Well, he'd burned through every last ounce of energy and couldn't have so much as raised his hand to swat a fly. For as scared as he was, he felt worse that there was nothing he could do to save Anya and Jade, who looked every bit as defeated as he felt. They'd barely been able to crawl from the water and had been shaking so badly he wasn't sure if they'd be able to climb the ladder behind him.

He did his best to remain physically between them and the man in the Kabuki mask, who more than once had offered to shoot one of them to lighten their burden, although the man who brought up the rear in a white mask with a crimson handprint over his left eye wasn't a whole lot better. They were eager to get as far from Teotihuacan as possible, especially after witnessing what had happened to their comrades inside the tomb.

The woman, on the other hand, remained icily composed, as though completely unsurprised by anything that had transpired. Almost as though she'd expected it.

The earthen tunnels were dark and cool. The tools the researchers had used only the day prior to sift through the dirt and sort relics were neatly stacked to the side. Evans imagined the graduate students carefully putting them away with the intention of returning to them the following morning, not knowing that for them tomorrow would never come.

The mere thought made his blood boil.

"Just tell me why," Evans said. "What's so important about these remains that so many innocent people had to die?"

Kabuki Mask continued silently through the tunnel.

"They were just kids. They wouldn't have even tried to stop you. What kind of monsters—?"

The man moved in a blur.

Evans was on his hands and knees before he even sensed the blow coming. He grimaced and blood dribbled from his mouth.

"That is enough," the woman in the gold mask said. She set her hand gently on the man's arm. "We will be done here soon."

Kabuki Mask stared down at him for several seconds through eerie blue eyes before turning and following her toward the surface.

Jade reached beneath Evans's arm and helped him to his feet. He wiped the blood from his chin with the back of his hand.

"I'm starting to think you might be bad luck," he said.

"I don't believe in luck."

"Then maybe you can explain how this kind of thing happens whenever you're around."

"Have you considered it might be you?"

"You're not the first to have suggested as much."

"I'm sure."

They passed through the four chambers and paused at the mouth of the tunnel to the surface. The men in the lead dragged the body bag through the orifice. The woman followed. The man who'd clocked Evans held a gun on him while he crawled inside.

The fresh air on his face felt amazing. He took several deep breaths before emerging into the crater in the middle of the Avenue of the Dead. He was surprised to see the faint outline of the mountains to the east. It wouldn't be long before dawn commenced in earnest.

He heard the grumble of tires on gravel in the distance. Headlights appeared seconds later from the far side of the visitors' center and rocketed toward them.

Evans climbed out of the hole and shielded his eyes against the high beams, which silhouetted the woman and the two men carrying the ancient remains. He tried not to look at the bodies scattered around the trailers, at the men and women with whom he'd spent the last six months and the tourists unfortunate enough to have chosen yesterday of all days to linger in the ruins.

Three black Chevrolet Suburbans sped straight toward them and split up at the last possible second. The two on the outside parked sideways to serve as a barrier for the third, which swung around and presented its rear.

The woman strode to the bumper, lifted the tailgate, and climbed up into the trunk of the SUV. She looked directly at Evans through inhumanly blue eyes nearly identical to those of the others.

"We will radio when we are in the air," she said. "Try not to kill them before then."

"Or at all," Evans said.

Crimson Handprint kicked him in the backs of the knees and he went down hard. There was a gun pressed to the back of his head before he could even look up from the ground.

Anya shrieked and hit the dirt beside him. He reached out and took her trembling hand in his.

"It's going to be all right," he whispered, but he knew he wasn't fooling anyone.

Jade collapsed on the other side of him and, with sheer hatred in her eyes, looked back at Kabuki Mask, who'd knocked her down. He pressed his gun to her brow between them.

"Just do it if you're going to," she said.

"Turn around," he said, and swatted her with the barrel.

She closed her eyes and hung her head. Blood dribbled from the laceration across her hairline.

Evans struggled to rise, but was driven back to his knees.

"Do not worry," Kabuki Mask said. "Your turn will come soon enough."

The two men carrying the ancient remains loaded the body bag into the trunk beside the woman, who traced the contours of the animalian face through the vinyl almost lovingly.

"At long last," she whispered.

A crash of shattering glass.

Evans looked up in time to see a silhouette on the hood of the Suburban reach through the broken windshield and haul the driver out over the steering wheel. It buried its face into his neck before he could cry out. Blood spattered the dirt road.

The men behind Evans fired at the silhouette. The report so close to his ears was deafening.

Bullets sang from the hubcap, punched through the front quarter panel, and made the body of the driver jump.

The attacker dove into the SUV and bounded into the backseat. The side window shattered and glass cascaded all around it.

The woman scurried from the back of the truck and grabbed the end of the body bag.

"Help me!" she screamed.

The two men rushed to her aid and lifted the silver bag out of the trunk.

The dark form of their assailant scrambled over the backseat and paused for the most fleeting of moments, its hands braced between its feet, its shoulders hunched, and its elongated head lowered between its knees. Evans caught a flash of eyeshine when it looked at him, and recognized it for what it truly was.

"Hollis?" he whispered.

Richards would have been unidentifiable were it not for his facial features, grossly distorted though they were. His body had been completely transformed into that of an alien being. His skin was gray and marbled with the black vessels underneath. Like Dr. Dale Rubley, he'd mutated into something completely lacking in humanity.

He'd transformed into the alien species colloquially known as Grays.

The creature opened a mouth full of razor-sharp teeth and issued an undulating sound that chilled Evans to the core.

Uhr-uhr-uhr-uhr-uhr-uh.

It sprang from the tailgate, hit the ground on all fours, and pounced onto the back of one of the men carrying the remains. His wet jacket and the flesh underneath opened beneath a flurry of claws. He stumbled. Lost his grip. Collapsed onto his chest with the weight of the creature upon him.

"Go!" he shouted.

The creature reached around his neck and underneath his chin and, with a flick of its wrist, released a spray of blood onto the ground.

Evans grabbed Jade by the hand and pulled her toward him.

"This is our chance!"

The men behind them fired. Their bullets kicked up dirt at the creature's heels, but it was too fast. It took down the other man, who lost his grip on the body bag on his way to the ground. He clawed at the earth in a desperate attempt to distance himself from the monster, which was upon him before he could even scream.

A bullet took a bite from the creature's shoulder and knocked it from on top of the man, who seized the opportunity to make a break for it, only to be struck in the leg by friendly fire.

Evans shoved Anya out from beneath Crimson Handprint's pistol as it bucked in his grasp and rained smoldering brass casings all around them. She scrambled to her feet and sprinted toward the side of the road.

"Run!" Evans shouted, and pulled Jade up behind him. "Don't stop until you find someplace to hide!"

The woman in the golden mask screamed and dragged the body bag toward the nearest SUV, which reversed between her and the creature. The driver rolled down his window and started shooting straight back at the others in the hope of cutting the creature to ribbons in the crossfire.

Evans hobbled as fast as he could. Every inch of his body ached, and he was certain it would give out on him long before he reached anything resembling freedom, but they wouldn't get a second chance to escape.

The taillights of the third SUV lit up and the wheels spun. Gravel pinged from the undercarriage until the tires gained traction and the Suburban launched straight backward at the creature.

It jumped up onto the fender, cleared the roof, and came down on the hood with the hollow *thump* of buckling metal. The driver raised his weapon and shot at it through the windshield. It rolled over the side and bounced back up the moment it hit the road. Hurled itself at Kabuki Mask, who'd been prepared to put a bullet through the back of Evans's head only seconds prior. Opened him right up the gut as it drove him to his back.

Anya blew past the trailers and the fenced-off hole and headed for a gap between stone temples.

Evans's leg gave out and sent him sprawling. He released Jade's hand before he took her down, too.

"Keep going!" he yelled.

She grabbed him by the arm and dragged him through the dirt.

"Damn it, Jade! Just go! I'll catch up!"

She looked up from his face and froze. Her eyes widened.

Evans followed her gaze to where the creature lunged from the top of the screaming man before the Suburban could back over it. The tires bounced from Kabuki Mask's body, and mercifully silenced his screaming.

The woman in the golden mask dragged the remains around to the far side of the distant SUV. The interior light came on when she opened the rear door. The driver reached between the front seats and helped her pull the body bag into the backseat. She climbed in behind it and slammed the door.

The creature turned at the sound.

Uhr-uhr-uhr-uhr-uhr-uh.

It sprinted after her vehicle, dodging the SUV swerving around for another pass at it and ducking behind the idling SUV with the shattered windshield. Its hideous visage turned blood red in the glare of the taillights as the Suburban accelerated away from it.

The man with the crimson handprint on his mask, who'd struck Jade across the face, climbed into the other SUV. It took off before he even had both legs inside and raced down the Avenue of the Dead. It caught up with the other vehicle as it rounded the visitors' center and sped off into the night.

When the creature realized the race was lost, it stopped and screamed in frustration. The sound was like the hiss of steam through a ruptured pipe. It dropped to all fours in the wash of the abandoned Suburban's headlights, rounded on Evans, and bared its horrible teeth.

"Run!" he shouted, and propelled himself to his feet behind Jade.

47
ROCHE

The roar of the incoming water echoed from the ice dome like a coliseum full of spectators shouting for their deaths. The ground bucked underfoot. Chunks of ice the size of meteorites struck all around them.

They weren't going to make it.

Roche sprinted straight down the boardwalk, his sole focus on the darkness ahead, where the elevator shaft hid in the deep recess. He prayed not only that they'd make it that far, but that the elevator would be there when they arrived.

A reptilian shape streaked past him through the shadows to his left. He caught movement from the corner of his eye to his right. Recognized what was about to happen and slid as though trying to beat the tag at home plate.

The creatures attacked from either side and converged at a point directly above his face. They screeched and scrapped as he glided out from beneath them, flipped over onto his stomach, and fired repeatedly into the tangle of talons and feathers.

A block of ice slammed to the boardwalk beside them and they flopped, bleeding, down into the darkness.

Roche lunged back to his feet and ran. Two silhouettes stood apart from the shadows ahead of him. Barnett was way out ahead of everyone else, while Tolliver tried his best to catch up. He never saw the creature slither out from beneath the lower rail and lash out at his legs. He screamed and landed squarely on his face. Rolled onto his back and started shooting.

A flash of discharge and a bullet screamed past Roche's ear.

He dodged left and collided with Delaney, who managed to rebound from the railing without losing his balance. A block of ice streaked past the back of his head and destroyed the wooden planks at his heels.

Tolliver yelled and shoved the creature's snapping jaws away from his face. He was unable to ward off the second, which appeared from beneath the boardwalk and clamped down on the side of his neck.

Roche pushed himself to get there, although by the time he was within range, there was nothing he could do. The feathered serpents dragged Tolliver's body over the side, leaving behind deep scratches in the wood and a pool of blood that drained through the cracks.

The advancing wave hit the ruins with a thunderous explosion, filling the air with spray and hurling rubble ahead of it.

Roche glanced to his left. All he could see was a churning black mass of destruction bearing down on him.

They weren't going to make it.

Massive granite blocks bounded across their path, de-molishing entire sections of the boardwalk at a time. Roche leaped over a gap as the leading edge of the water rushed across the stones below him.

The elevator shaft separated from the shadows. Still maybe two hundred feet ahead of him. His heart nearly stopped at the realization that the car wasn't there.

Dark waves hammered the side of the boardwalk, rising as a wall of spray beside him before crashing down upon the planks. He splashed through the freez-ing water as it attempted to sweep his feet out from un-derneath him.

A creature scrambled up onto the railing ahead of him, lowered its shoulders, and extended its long neck. Its eyes reflected the red glare. The comb of feathers along its neck stood up. Its wicked teeth parted and it issued a high-pitched screech.

Skree—!

A megalith erupted from one side of the boardwalk and crashed through the other, pounding the creature's breast and sending it careening off into the darkness.

Roche jumped over the rubble, lost his footing on the slick wood, and barely caught the railing before being carried over the side. He climbed up on top of it, raised his arms for balance, and ran as fast as he dared.

Barnett pulled up short of the elevator platform. The car still wasn't there. Something must have happened to the others. It should have been there by now.

He glanced back, shouted something Roche couldn't hear over the deafening advance of the water, and sprinted for the shaft.

The boardwalk vanished beneath the waves, which

propelled all kinds of debris ahead of them, forcing Delaney to climb up onto the railing behind him.

Barnett reached the empty chute, slung his rifle over his shoulder, and started to scale the ladder-like support girder. He was barely five feet up when Roche reached the end of the railing and jumped down into the water, which pulled him under the moment his feet hit the slick boards. It was so cold it made his skin hurt. He fought to the surface and slogged toward the platform.

The water rose up the steps and raced across the concrete pad into the shaft. It struck the back wall and fired a flume twenty feet into the air.

They weren't going to make it.

Roche stumbled up the stairs. The rising water was above his knees by the time he slung the SCAR over his back, grabbed the girder, and started to climb.

Delaney grabbed for the rail as a wave bludgeoned him from the side, hurling him against the back wall.

Roche reached down and caught him by the wrist before he vanished beneath the violent waves. Bellowed with the strain of dragging Delaney against the current. The moment the other man had a grip on the girder and his head above water, Roche started to climb, but the freezing lake was rising faster than he was.

Shouting.

He looked up to see Barnett scurrying back down toward him as the elevator sped down the shaft toward them.

"Stop!" he shouted. "For the love of God—!"

The brakes bit down on the rails and showered them with sparks.

Barnett jumped and caught the girder several rungs

farther down. He chest struck and he nearly bounced right off.

The elevator screamed to a halt mere inches above his head.

For the elevator to stop, that meant there had to be someone—

"Hurry!" Kelly screamed.

She pressed her face against the side grate in the driver's cutout and looked down at them only briefly before ramping the motor up once more. The car lurched and the brakes disengaged. Slowly, the car started back up toward the surface.

"Jesus," Roche whispered.

Barnett lunged for the support rails on the bottom of the elevator and swung across them toward the far end, where he would be able to crawl through the door and into the car.

Roche climbed as fast as he could and followed Barnett's lead. He barely managed to secure his grip before the water flooded up over his feet. He swung from one rail to the next, toward where Barnett was already pulling himself up into the elevator.

Delaney climbed the girder until he was within range and jumped. Caught the support post right behind Roche. Lost his grip. Grabbed Roche's right leg and nearly dislodged them both.

"Hold on!" Roche shouted.

He wrapped his right arm around the rail and reached down.

The water eclipsed the mouth of the shaft and raced upward in a solid column.

It was all Roche could do to hold on as the freezing lake rose over his head and into the elevator.

The cold was such a shock that he nearly let go. His entire body clenched. There'd been no time to take a breath and what little air he had was already heavy in his chest.

The water suddenly retreated and took Delaney with it.

Roche gasped for air and watched the water level fall below him.

Delaney burst from the surface twenty feet down, flailing his arms in an effort to stay above the water, even as the current sucked him under. Roche saw the sheer terror on his face a heartbeat before a dark shape erupted from behind him and scurried up his back in an effort to use him as a life raft. It buried its claws into the muscles beside his neck.

Delaney screamed and both of them went under.

The lake washed back out of the shaft, taking Delaney's body with it. The ground grew farther and farther away as the elevator ascended, until it was lost to the darkness beyond the reach of the red glow of the emergency lights.

"Give me your hand!" Barnett shouted. He hung upside down from the open door of the elevator and reached toward Roche.

"We have to go back for him!" Roche yelled.

"There's nothing we can do for him now!"

"We can't just leave him!"

"He's already dead and you know it!" Barnett shouted, his expression not without sympathy.

Roche tried for Barnett's outstretched hand, but quickly grabbed the rail again. He was shivering so badly he couldn't trust his grip.

Kelly pressed her face against the wire mesh and looked down at him from the control cutout.

"Don't you dare leave me now."

He reached out with a trembling hand and Barnett clasped him by the wrist.

"It's now or never!" Barnett shouted.

Roche let go of the rail and swung toward the girder, the horizontal posts of which blew past in a blur. He grabbed Barnett's other hand and nearly sent them both plummeting to their deaths.

Barnett shouted with the exertion and pulled him up through the open door. Roche braced his elbows on the floor and searched for anything he could use to drag himself the rest of the way into the car.

Kelly threw herself to the floor beside him and tugged on the back of his coat.

His heels clipped the girder as he tucked his legs inside and squirmed away from the door. Barnett closed it the second his feet were inside.

Kelly pulled him to her breast and squeezed him so tightly he could barely breathe.

"You're supposed to be barricaded inside the power station with the others," he said.

"And you're supposed to be grateful that I came back for you."

She kissed him. He wrapped his arms around her and reciprocated with everything he had left as the elevator rocketed away from the dark, flooded ruins.

48
JADE

Teotihuacan

Jade sprinted between two of the multi-tiered temples lining the Avenue of the Dead and immediately recognized their mistake. A vast expanse of grassland stretched out before her, the tall, wavering blades shimmering silver in the moonlight. There were spotty groves of trees in the distance, maybe even dense enough to find someplace to hide . . . if they were able to reach them. There were undoubtedly countless hiding places in the ancient city, but they didn't dare turn back now, not with the creature that had once been Hollis Richards on the warpath. How in the name of God had it traveled all the way to Mexico, and, more important, why? It appeared to have been attempting to get at the remains they'd just liberated from the maze, but for what possible reason?

The waist-high weeds threatened to snare her feet as she raced into the field. Anya was maybe twenty feet ahead of her and nowhere near anything resembling cover. Evans fell farther behind by the second. With the way he was favoring his injured leg, there was no way he was going to be able to keep up.

A silhouette appeared on top of the temple above Evans. A flash of eyeshine and it was moving again, leaping down the terraced ruins through the shadows.

If Jade really pushed herself, she might be able to catch up with Anya before she reached the thicket. They could hide within the thorny branches and pray it didn't see them. Unfortunately, that would mean sacrificing Evans to buy them some time, which she wasn't prepared to do.

Before she even realized she'd made a conscious decision to do so, Jade turned around and ran back toward Evans. Took him by the hand and practically dragged him behind her.

"Go on without me," he said. "I'm slowing you down."

"Then run faster!"

The tall weeds rippled off to her right.

It was coming.

She veered left and set her sights on a sparse grove of black pepper trees, maybe a hundred feet away. It offered little in the way of cover, but they had no other option. They'd be lucky to even make it that far, anyway.

A high-pitched whine in the distance. A light appeared against the horizon to her left.

Crashing sounds to her right. The creature tore through the weeds, barely above the ground, moving to intercept them.

Anya tripped and vanished before Jade's eyes. The younger woman pushed herself back to her feet and altered her course when she saw the creature's wake knifing through the field.

The light divided into two smaller sources that streaked straight toward them. It was an airplane. A small, private model, coming in far too low, as though it were planning to land right on top of them.

A tug on her arm and Evans went down.

Jade managed to remain upright, whirled, and tried to pull him back to his feet. Even in the dim light she could see that the field bandage on his leg had come open, exposing deep puncture wounds from which a seemingly endless supply of blood flowed. She knew that wasn't the case, though. His face was stark white and his eyes appeared to have sunken into bruises. He was losing blood far too quickly and if they didn't find a way to stop it soon, he wasn't going to make it, even if they somehow survived the creature's impending attack.

"Leave me," he said. "I'll be fine. I've made it through worse."

"You're joking, right?"

She reached beneath his arm and tried to lift him. Despite his best efforts, his legs betrayed him and dropped him to the ground, taking her with him.

His eyes sought hers and held them.

"You have to go, Jade."

"Not without you!"

She grabbed his wrists and pulled—

The creature emerged from the weeds maybe ten feet away. It remained in a crouch to minimize its exposure, but the moonlight reflecting from its eyes behind the swaying grasses gave it away.

"Over here!" Anya shouted, and hurled a rock at it.

Uhr-uhr-uhr-uhr-uhr-uh.

"Don't move," Jade whispered.

It ducked its head once more and advanced slowly, with only the crunching of the weeds to betray its approach.

The whine of the airplane became a scream.

Lights struck the field and momentarily turned night to day. She glanced back in time to be buffeted by a violent breeze, which shook the weeds all around her. The plane passed no more than a hundred feet over their heads as it descended toward the field on the far side of the Pyramid of the Sun.

The creature reappeared from the overgrowth, far closer than she expected.

It watched them from beneath its ridged brow and elongated head.

"What are you waiting for?" Jade screamed.

Evans struggled to his feet, transferred all his weight to his good leg, and attempted to pull Jade behind him.

"We are . . . not . . . done with you . . . yet."

The voice coming from between those wicked teeth was not that of Hollis Richards. It was deep and resonant and belonged to the monster they had narrowly escaped in Antarctica last year. This being was a drone, like the one she'd encountered in the Nigerian jungle before it waded to its death.

"Go," Evans said. "I'll hold it off."

Jade stepped around him and stared down the creature.

"Why were you so interested in those remains?" she asked.

"It is . . . the body of . . . God."

Anya shouted and waved her arms over her head in an attempt to distract it.

When it looked in her direction, Evans nudged Jade backward and retreated a step to match.

The creature advanced and lowered itself to all fours, well within striking distance.

"What god?" Jade asked.

Were it possible, the creature smiled, its teeth knitting together like needles.

"Death."

A spotlight struck the creature from above. It raised its spindly arm to block the beam and looked up.

Bullets rained down upon it. Tore up the dirt at its feet. Punched straight through its shoulder girdle. Spattered the weeds with blood. Knocked it to the ground.

The overlapping reports echoed across the plains.

Four spotlights shined down at them from beneath black parachutes nearly indistinguishable from the night sky. The men wore black, too, and for an instant Jade feared they were part of the same masked group that had stalked them through the maze, until she saw the red Unit 51 insignias on their shoulders and nearly sobbed in relief.

The creature sputtered, rolled over, and let the blood drain from its mouth. It tried to crawl away through the grass.

"Stay back," Evans said.

The lights zeroed in on the creature. It darted forward through the weeds. Scurried one way, then the other, but it was unable to escape the circles of light, which constricted as they neared the ground.

The creature rounded on Evans and Jade, who read its intention in its eyes.

It crouched, issued a gurgling scream, and lunged straight at Evans.

The men opened fire.

Bullets tore the creature apart before it reached them. It slid to a halt at their feet, bleeding from innumerable gunshot wounds on its gray back.

Jade stepped around Evans and crouched over it. Like the drone in the jungle, this one had been given ample opportunity to kill her and yet, for whatever reason, hadn't done so. It attacked the other faction in Teotihuacan with unbridled ferocity and butchered them without mercy. It could have easily done the same thing to them, but had instead chosen to communicate with them.

"Why?" she whispered.

Its words replayed in her mind.

We are . . . not . . . done with you . . . yet.

The creature made a gagging sound and blood dribbled from the corner of its mouth. She could hear the air whistling from its punctured lungs.

"Doctor . . . Liang . . ."

Jade leaned even closer. The voice was not just weaker; it was somehow . . . different.

"Get away from it!" one of the men shouted from above her.

"You must . . . stop . . ."

The voice . . . Dear God . . . it belonged to Hollis Richards.

Some part of him had survived inside his mutated form.

"Stop what?"

"The end . . ." The creature contorted with spasms and bared its teeth. Looked up at her through eyes that for the briefest of moments appeared almost human. *". . . of the . . . world."*

And just like that, Hollis Richards was gone.

The creature narrowed its eyes, snarled, and lunged—

A fusillade of bullets destroyed its elongated head and hammered it to the ground. This time, it made no effort to rise.

The men alighted around them and quickly folded up their parachutes.

Jade looked up at Evans.

"You heard him, didn't you?"

Evans stared at her mutely for several seconds before nodding.

"That was Hollis, wasn't it?" she said. "He was still alive in there."

"We have to get you out of here," one of the men said, and pulled her to her feet. She caught a glimpse of the nameplate on his breast: Morgan.

She stared at Richards's disfigured body as she was manhandled back toward the ruins. Two of the men blocked her view as they bundled the carcass into one of their chutes.

"I want to examine the remains!" she shouted.

"All in due course," Morgan said, "but now's not the time."

She ducked beneath Evans's arm and helped him limp back toward the ruins. They passed between the megalithic temples and headed north on the Avenue of the Dead, toward the massive pyramid and the waiting Cessna. Anya caught up with them and slid underneath Evans's other arm.

Jade glanced back at the ruins one final time. The men with Richards's corpse hurried to keep up with them, while the fourth man photographed the crime scene surrounding the Suburban abandoned by the masked group that had been willing to kill all of them in order to secure the remains, which, if the creature were to be believed, belonged to the God of Death.

49
TESS

The Valor materialized from the blizzarding snow and hovered above the icy landing platform. Its vertical rotors blasted the accumulation toward the power station as it settled to the ground.

"It's here!" Tess shouted, and ran from the window to where the others were donning the heavy arctic gear hanging from the racks.

"The elevator isn't back yet!" Love said from the control console.

"How much longer?"

"Three minutes."

"Then we load everyone else now and make sure we're ready to lift off the moment they arrive."

Tess ran back to the frosted window. The side hatch of the tiltrotor slid open and a man in winter fatigues hopped out, raised his rifle, and advanced toward the building through the blowing snow. The copilot climbed from his door and covered him, the rotor wash buffeting him from behind.

"We have to go!" Tess shouted.

She waited until the first man from the Valor was nearly to the door before shoving aside the tool cabinets and chairs they'd used to barricade the entrance and disengaging the locks. The wind pushed the door back at her as she opened it and admitted the storm.

"How many of you are there?" the man shouted.

"Eight in here, with an unknown number on their way up from below."

"Where's the director?"

"Hopefully about to arrive on the elevator."

The man brushed past her into the room.

"Everyone!" he shouted. "Form a single-file line. Hold on to the person ahead of you. Head straight for the Valor and start filling the seats from back to front."

"Two more minutes!" Love yelled.

"Go!" the man shouted, and herded the survivors out into the darkness, where the copilot covered their approach from the platform fifty feet away.

Tess glanced at the elevator console. The inset monitor showed a red beacon rising rapidly toward the surface beside numbers counting down the vertical feet and time until arrival.

"I've got this," Love said. "Get out of here."

The shaft was little more than a deep black maw in the middle of the floor. The cage surrounding it allowed the cables to pass through the roof to the crane-like mechanisms that added additional power to the traditional counterweights. The surrounding machinery chugged and clanged, and the pipes provided a constant rushing sound.

Love stepped away from the console and faced the

cage. She seated her rifle against her shoulder and aimed down the shaft.

"Come on!" The man pulled Tess toward the door. "I need you on that plane!"

She glanced at the console one last time and rushed down the aisle between the steaming pipes to catch up with the others. They were already halfway to the Valor, six silhouettes in fur-fringed hoods, hunched against the brutal storm. The copilot hurried to meet them and guided them to the open side door of the tiltrotor. He suddenly stopped and pointed his rifle straight at them.

Not at them, Tess realized with a start.

Above them.

She turned around and looked up at the roof of the building behind her as two reptilian shapes, their feathers ruffling on the wind, arched their backs, lowered their heads, and screamed down at them.

Skree!

The copilot opened fire.

Tess instinctively ducked, cradled her head in her arms, and ran toward the waiting aircraft.

Bullets whanged from the power station. She couldn't risk looking back to see if any of them had found their targets.

More gunfire, only this time from behind her.

Tess blew past the copilot, whose attention remained focused solely on the sightline of his rifle. His barrel flashed with discharged gasses as he continued to shoot at the roofline behind her.

She saw the expressions on the faces of the men and women piling through the sliding door and recognized the severity of their predicament. Someone had to take charge before the situation spiraled out of their control.

"Get inside!" she shouted.

She urged the stragglers into the Valor and toward the closest empty seats. Climbed in behind them. Looked back out across the windswept tarmac toward the power station.

The emergency lights diffused into the storm, through which she could see more and more dark shapes pouring over the building. The copilot and the man standing directly beneath them in the open doorway of the power station could only fire up at them in the hope of stalling their advance.

"Everyone sit down and buckle up!" the pilot shouted back over his shoulder.

Love screamed from inside the building.

"There are still more people coming!" Tess yelled.

"If they're not on board by the time those things reach us, we're taking off without them!"

Tess leaned out the door and shielded her eyes from the blowing snow.

"Come on . . ."

50
KELLY

A shadow sliced through her peripheral vision. Kelly spun, but could only see the steel-reinforced walls blurring past. She furrowed her brow and glanced at Roche.

"Did you see someth—?"

Clang!

She looked up at the roof of the elevator and screamed.

The creature scurried over the side and struck at them from the outside of the cage, banging its snout into the wire mesh over and over in a futile attempt to reach them.

"Stand back!" Barnett shouted.

He jammed the barrel of his rifle through one of the holes and pulled the trigger. The report was deafening in such close quarters.

The creature contorted its serpentine body and slithered back up onto the roof. The clattering of its nails cut through the ringing in her ears.

More movement.

"They're coming up the walls!" she screamed.

Roche pulled her to the center of the car, away from the sides.

Something bumped against the floor from underneath.

"How much longer?" Roche shouted.

"We're almost there," Barnett said.

"We have to radio ahead. They need to seal off the shaft before these things get out."

"There's no way to seal the shaft."

"Then we're all dead."

The creature scurried out from under their feet and raced up the back wall.

Roche shot at its exposed belly, but it was already past him. Its feathered tail whipped the elevator as it climbed onto the roof with the other one. The impact caused the entire car to wobble.

"We could take the elevator back down," Kelly said. "It would at least buy the people up top some more time."

"It's too late for that," Barnett said.

The elevator slowed as it approached the surface. The whine of the motor was eclipsed by the sound of gunfire.

Another creature scaled the wall of the shaft beside them.

The temperature dropped by the second and she felt the first stirrings of the frigid wind. The shaft brightened, if only by degree. Claws scratched at the edges of the emergency hatch above them in a frantic attempt to get inside.

"I really hope that evacuation team of yours is here," Roche said.

"Don't worry. They'll be here."

Gunfire from directly above their heads. A loud screech and a feathered form flopped past them, bounced from the wall, and plummeted into the depths.

"Get down!" Roche shouted. He tackled Kelly and shielded her body with his.

Bullets ricocheted from the roof and the side of the elevator.

Barnett hit the ground in front of Kelly, his face only inches from hers. A sliver of metal shrapnel protruded from his forehead. The blood was already running through his eyebrow. He groaned when he pulled out the sliver.

The elevator rose through the floor of the power station and they ascended into chaos.

Love shot wildly around them, her bullets striking the machinery and the creatures alike. Her eyes were feral, her blond bangs stuck to her face by a crimson spatter.

Barnett threw open the door and burst from the elevator. He started shooting the moment he passed Love.

The creatures were everywhere. Scurrying up the walls and across the ceiling. Ducking through the maze of pipes.

A ferocious gust of wind blew straight down the central walkway from the open front door, through which she could see only blowing snow. Kelly nearly sobbed in futility until the Valor momentarily emerged from the storm. It vanished every bit as quickly.

"Get to the plane!" Barnett shouted.

Kelly grabbed Roche's hand and sprinted for the door. He held the bullpup SCAR by the pistol grip and fired behind him toward the ceiling.

An agent in winter fatigues backed slowly away

from the front door and onto the slick platform, shooting at the roof above him as he went.

The moment Barnett passed him, the man turned and ran for the tiltrotor.

Kelly dashed out into the blizzard behind them and zeroed in on the open side door of the tiltrotor. Tess leaned out and shouted something Kelly couldn't hear over the roar of the rotors ramping up for liftoff.

Shadows passed through her peripheral vision and struck the ground to either side of her. Bounced up and raced to cut her off.

Roche shot to either side, which only served to drive the creatures wider in their approach.

Love screamed from right behind her.

Kelly glanced over her shoulder in time to see Love hit the ground. Her rifle clattered away from her outstretched hand. Her eyes locked onto Kelly's and she reached for her, a scream on her lips—

The creatures were upon her before she could release the sound. They tore at her with their hooked claws and ripped chunks of flesh from any part of her they could sink their teeth into.

"No!" Kelly screamed.

They looked up at her as one, their scaled snouts dripping with blood, and moved with blinding speed. They halved the distance between them before Kelly regained her momentum.

Barnett climbed up into the Valor and fired back over their heads.

Kelly ducked and focused on diving through the open door the moment she was within range.

The rotor wash battered her in the face. The plane rose a good foot before settling to the ground again.

"Hurry!" the copilot shouted from the cockpit as he closed his door.

The camouflaged agent stopped when he reached Barnett, shot several times behind them, and tossed his weapon inside. He gripped the rail inside the door and reached for her.

"Come on!"

Kelly grabbed his hand and he pulled her up into the plane. Roche scrambled in behind her.

The moment they were all onboard, Barnett pulled the sliding door closed.

Thump-thump!

The creatures struck the side of the plane as it lifted off, knocking it sideways. One leaped up onto the door, clung to the metal, and repeatedly struck at the window.

The plane rose into the storm, leaving Forward Operating Base Atlantis behind. The rotors tilted and the creature's feathers blew wildly. It shrieked and tried to hold on, but the force of the impelled air was far too great.

Kelly pressed her face against the glass and watched the creature fall to the landing platform, where a dozen others attacked its bloody carcass the second it hit the ground.

Roche gently pulled her into the seat beside him. She buried her face in his shoulder and started to cry.

51
BARNETT

The Hanger, Unit 51 Base of Operations,
Joint Base Langley-Eustis, Hampton, Virginia,
March 29

Barnett felt like he hadn't slept in a week. His eyes burned, his head ached, and every inch of his body hurt, but he wouldn't allow himself to rest until he made sense of the events that transpired simultaneously at Teotihuacan and FOB Atlantis. There was no doubt in his mind that the two were intrinsically related. He just didn't know how. Not yet, anyway.

Debriefing the various parties involved had helped gather a wealth of information, although correlating it was like trying to put together a puzzle without having any idea how the finished product was supposed to look. There were pieces scattered everywhere, and yet he was only able to make a few of them fit together, which did little more than hint at the overall picture. Worse, he could sense that time was no longer on his side. His adversary had stepped out of the shadows in what he considered a declaration of war, although he had yet to figure out where the battles would be fought, or even who they were fighting, only that one of them had spoken in what sounded like German, Villarreal's last word had been "Aryan," and all the masked assailants appeared to have the same blue eyes. The only thing he knew with complete certainty was that the consequences of losing would be dire, especially if what Dr. Liang said about Hollis Richards's message during his final moment of lucidity was true.

Unit 51's base of operations was known as The Hanger, a name owed to Hollis Richards, who wanted to name it Hanger 18 after the building purported to contain UFO technology at Wright-Patterson Air Force Base in Ohio, but the Department of Defense hadn't shared his sense of humor. It had, however, very much liked the idea of sharing his money, so a compromise had been reached.

While on the surface it looked like an ordinary abandoned airfield in a remote corner of Joint Base Langley-Eustis, beneath the surface it was something else entirely. The facility was originally built in the early 1950s at the fringe of what was then known as Langley Air Force Base as an emergency relocation center for the National Military Establishment in the event of a nuclear holocaust, to ensure the continuity of the national security apparatus and command of the armed forces. After the fall of the Soviet Union and the momentary end of the Cold War, the three-hundred-thousand-square-foot bunker was largely forgotten and the aboveground structures converted into storage, at least until Hollis Richards caught wind of its existence and made the DoD an offer it couldn't refuse.

The subterranean complex had since been given a complete renovation. There were three sublevels, each of which required increasing levels of security clearance. Few ever saw the offices, computer labs, and temporary residential suites on the first sublevel, let alone the state-of-the-art scientific and medical laboratories on the second. Maybe a dozen or so people even knew of the existence of the third sublevel, and of them, only a handful had been granted access to view the unique artifacts stored in the climate-controlled vaults, the majority of which the world at large could never be allowed to know existed.

Barnett strode down the main corridor on Level 1, away from his office, where he'd been poring over his notes from the debriefings. He was in a vile mood, as evidenced by the fact that everyone went out of their way to be anywhere he wasn't, so for him to be summoned so unceremoniously to the computer lab suggested they'd finally found something useful. He didn't so much care that he had the Pentagon breathing down his neck or even that the President himself was demanding an explanation he couldn't give; the deaths of forty-five men and women who'd devoted their lives to the cause—his cause—weighed heavily upon him.

Morgan was waiting outside the lab when he arrived. There were cracks in his ordinarily impassive façade.

"That good?" Barnett said.

"You wouldn't believe me if I told you."

The name "computer lab" didn't really do it justice. The suite had been converted into a computer forensic laboratory rivaling that of the FBI, including advanced forensic workstations, rapid-action imaging and duplicating devices, and even a wireless interceptor. The room was clean to the point of sterility and illuminated by pale blue lights.

Avery Price was sitting at the main terminal beneath the display screen on the wall. He was a little guy with thick glasses, a clubfoot, and tattoos covering every inch of his body, and he could work the kind of magic with computers that had made him a legend at the NSA, where digital wizardry was a minimum qualification.

He turned, jutted out his lower jaw, and blew his bangs from his eyes.

"Did you prepare him?"

Barnett glanced at Morgan, who shook his head.

"So here's the deal," Price said. "I had the system running through all of your ancillary digital video files from Atlantis like you asked. Surveillance, logs, chats, blah blah blah. Anyway, I came across a series of auto uploads from a guy named Bly, right?"

Barnett sat beside Price and stared almost reluctantly at the screen. He had no desire to relive yet another death.

"He was our speleology consultant."

"The guy who mapped all of the caves. I know. That's some *sick* stuff he was doing down there. You ever see any of his footage? Just watching it made me claustrophobic." Price read the impatience on Barnett's face and got right down to it. "So, as you know, while he was actively spelunking—that's the formal term, you know—he was recording with a camera that automatically downloaded the footage into archives from which the main computer generated three-dimensional re-creations of the caverns using the actual physical measurements. Just like a virtual colonoscopy, in a way. Anyway, the raw footage was never really meant to be watched. I suppose Bly might have done so eventually. You never know. But with there being a final recording and all . . ."

"You watched it?"

Price bit his lower lip and nodded.

"You found something in the video."

Again, Price nodded.

Barnett had officially listed Dr. Desmond Bly's status as Missing-In-Action, Presumed Deceased. He was still in the process of piecing together the events surrounding the initiation of Protocol Delta and the subsequent attack on FOB Atlantis, but as best he could tell, Bly had never made it back to the base. Until now, he'd been reasonably comfortable in the assumption that the speleologist, like so many others, had been killed by the creatures during the siege. His remains were among those that hadn't been recovered, and likely never would be.

"Let's get this over with," Barnett said.

Price used a handheld remote to start the recording. The time display in the corner showed that they were 0:28:32 into a 4:19:16 recording. There was no audio to accompany the video, yet Barnett found himself straining to hear.

A flashlight played across intricate petroglyphs visualized with the aid of what looked like chalk. Those surrounding the colored section were worn nearly smooth.

"Where is this?" Barnett asked.

Price gestured at the monitor to his right, which showed the entirety of the warrens in 3-D. Barnett was well acquainted not only with the map, but with the location, which was roughly forty feet straight up from the ice cavern where Berkeley and Jonas had been attacked.

On the screen, Bly walked through a narrow corridor that almost looked manmade. The walls were smooth and even, the corners sharp. He ran his fingers along them as he walked.

"Can you get me detailed imagery of his immediate vicinity?"

Price framed that area of the map inside a box. With a click of the mouse, it expanded to show Barnett exactly what he expected. There were large gaps of missing data above the ice cavern where the tunnels had been too small to properly map, but he could easily see how they led to the cavernous space Bly approached in the recording.

"Jesus," he said.

On the monitor, Bly's flashlight focused upon a stone sarcophagus nearly identical to the one underneath the Temple of the Feathered Serpent in Teotihuacan. He watched helplessly as Bly shoved back the lid far enough to reveal a mummified corpse with the head of a stag.

Both Price and Morgan turned away, leaving Barnett to watch alone as the view swung upward to show the ferocious jaws of the creature that struck at him from where it hung upside down through a hole in the ceiling. He witnessed Bly's death from his perspective and felt the speleologist's terror as he looked down and watched his legs flail and his blood spatter the granite slab. Until the twitching ceased and the creature released his body. Bly landed on the sarcophagus, where he lay still, his blood pooling beneath him and dripping over the edge of the lid. The angle of the camera revealed just a hint of the desiccated cadaver inside.

The blood dribbling onto its bony forearm almost made it appear to move.

Price clicked the remote and fast-forwarded nearly three hours. He stopped when the point of view abruptly shifted and rewound just far enough for Barnett to witness the speleologist's body rolling off the sarcophagus and flopping to the ground.

Bly lay flat on his chest, his head turned to his right. The majority of the screen was filled with the limestone directly underneath him, but the right corner revealed the side and a portion of the head of the sarcophagus. Human legs passed through the field of view and stopped at the very edge of the image, where the man to whom they belonged fell to his knees and leaned over the open coffin.

Barnett caught a glimpse of a face covered with blood and bruises. The man's features were deformed, but not to the point of being completely unrecognizable.

"Les Dutton," Barnett said.

Another pair of legs crossed the screen. There was no mistaking to whom they belonged. The bare skin was pale and gray, the heels elevated so that the creature walked on the balls of its feet, its long nails striking the floor.

Subject Z stood behind the kneeling cook and reached around the front of his neck.

Dutton closed his eyes.

In one violent motion, the creature tore out his throat and he collapsed forward in a wash of blood.

"What the hell is it doing?" Barnett asked.

"Best we can tell?" Morgan said. "Bleeding the victim onto the remains."

"For what purpose?"

"Your guess is as good as mine."

Subject Z held Dutton there for several minutes before casting his body aside. The creature walked around the side of the sarcophagus and stopped right in front of Bly's camera, so close that the entire screen became fuzzy and gray. The image resolved when it stepped back, and for a split second revealed the withered legs dangling over Subject Z's arm.

"It took the remains," Barnett said.

He snatched the remote from Price's hand and fast-forwarded. Minutes passed and the view didn't change. An hour.

"There's nothing else," Price said.

When he reached the end of the recording, there was a rush of black water. Bly's body slid toward the wall, his headlamp constricting against the limestone. Then only darkness when the flooding destroyed the camera.

Barnett looked from Price to Morgan and back again.

"Why in the name of God would it take the remains?"

52
EVANS

Evans stood between two rolling dry-erase boards. He'd enlarged photographs of the massive statues inside the pyramid and taped them up in the same order as they appeared in the Grand Gallery outside of the chamber that had transformed Dr. Dale Rubley into the creature—now classified as Subject Z—that had nearly killed them all six months ago. When they first entered the pyramid, what felt like years ago now, his first impression had been that the gallery had been designed to hold a large number of people, to impress upon them the might and majesty of the gods who were responsible for the transformative powers of the ancient machine contained within. Here were these same gods, only now he had seen two of them in the flesh.

There were fourteen statues total, seven to either side of the central walkway. Some were considerably taller than the others. All of them wore animal masks and stood bare-chested in all their glory. He stared at the fifth statue on his right. The man had the wings of an angel and a sun disk mounted above his head, which was concealed beneath a mask with the face of a crocodile and the plumage of a tropical bird. It wasn't just that he had seen the same mask on the corpse in Teotihuacan that bothered him; it was that he had seen the creatures represented by the mask both inside the flooded tomb and on the videos recorded at Forward Operating Base Atlantis.

While he was no expert on extinct life-forms, he felt fairly confident that they represented a species of dinosaur that had somehow survived into the dawn of the era of man. It not only made sense that the creatures should be revered by primitive societies, but that they would use them to protect their most valuable treasures, in this case, the bodies of what they believed were the corporeal forms of their creator gods.

Although Dr. Murphy, who'd miraculously escaped Antarctica physically, if not psychologically, unscathed, was still formulating her theory, she believed the feathered serpents were capable of entering into extended periods of cryptobiosis, a state triggered by hostile environmental conditions in which all metabolic processes simply ceased until more favorable climates prevailed and they returned to metabolic life as though waking from a deep sleep. It wasn't unheard of in the natural world. There were numerous species of shrimp, insects, and nematodes that could exist indefinitely in a state of suspended animation and countless mammals and reptiles capable of extended periods of hibernation and brumation. It stood to reason that the extreme cold shift in Antarctica following the crustal displacement had triggered cryobiosis, or perhaps merely the sudden disappearance of prey species had caused the creatures to effectively shut down, like they speculated was the case in Mexico. If their theory was correct, the dinosaurs had been hatched inside the human remains in the sealed Ceremonial Well and found their way through the maze to where the animals were entombed with the body of the Feathered Serpent God. They'd slithered through holes only large enough to accommodate them in their juvenile form and entered a state of cryptobiosis when there was no longer any available food. Or perhaps it was the lack of water. Or heat. Or a combination of factors.

Regardless of the mechanism, it was the nature of the booby trap that concerned Evans. Why had the bodies of these supposed gods been entombed where no one was likely to ever find them and why had they been left guarded by a species that would no doubt slaughter whoever came in search of the remains? Was it because they didn't want grave robbers to disturb the eternal rest of their gods, or was it because they feared what might happen if their gods ever got out? The Teotihuacano had called theirs the "sleeping god," which, by the mere definition of the term, suggested there was also a waking state. As absurd as it sounded, it was that notion that had brought him down here from his accommodations on Level 1.

Evans turned toward the opposite dry-erase board and leaned on his crutch, which he absolutely despised. It chafed his armpit and made him feel like an invalid, but it was far better than the alternative. His entire right leg was immobilized in a soft cast while his injuries healed. The surgeon had done a remarkable job of repairing the muscle and closing the wounds, or so he had told Evans multiple times, although they still itched like nobody's business.

He stared at the statue of the woman with the snout and antlers of a deer. While they had assumed the corpse in the sarcophagus Dr. Bly discovered was male, it could just as easily have been female, and the once-living embodiment of this stone goddess. Two deities from this pantheon, both similarly entombed and guarded by creatures capable of overcoming any of the weapons of the time, linked by the discovery of their tombs thousands of miles apart and mysteriously connected by the activation of a pyramid beneath the Antarctic ice. Both gods were immortalized in the Grand Gallery outside the chamber responsible for the physical metamorphosis of Subject Z, the very creature that had dispatched one of its drones to the burial site of the Feathered Serpent God in Mexico and somehow infected Les Dutton to effect its own escape from FOB Atlantis, along with the body of this very stag-faced woman. But not without first slitting the throat of its drone and spilling its blood onto her remains.

While Evans had been beating his head against the wall trying to figure out why, Jade had made the connection. The legs in Bly's video had provided the answer. When Subject Z had lifted the ancient remains from the sarcophagus, the legs had dangled from its arm, while those of a mummified corpse would have been brittle and incapable of bending at the knees without someone physically breaking them.

Again, he thought of the inscription above the maze. If the creatures left to defend the sarcophagus had merely been in an extended period of suspended animation, was it so hard to believe that the gods themselves weren't, as well? And if that were the case, then were these sleeping gods even human at all?

Evans feared that the answer, as insane as it sounded, was of great consequence.

Prior to the events in Antarctica, he would have laughed at the mere suggestion that an alien race had ever visited the Earth. But now that he'd seen the proof of it with his own eyes, he could feel the threat it posed at the very heart of his being, and he was forced to contemplate the reason these beings had come in the first place, which—if the drone that spoke in the voice of Hollis Richards were to be believed—was nothing shy of enacting the end of the world.

"Are you hungry?"

Jade's voice startled him. He turned to find her standing in the doorway with an apple in either hand. He shook his head, but gratefully accepted her gesture anyway.

Jade joined him in his re-creation of the Grand Gallery and looked over the photographs of the sculptures.

"Do you think they're real?" she asked.

"Of course. I saw them with my own eyes. Probably even took these pictures."

"That's not what I'm asking." She looked him in the eyes when she spoke, as though searching inside of him for an answer beyond that conveyed by his words. "Do you think they're really gods?"

"Gods?"

"You know what I mean."

"Do I think they're real and not products of fiction? Yeah, probably. But do I think they are omnipotent beings descended from the sky . . . ?"

He didn't know how to finish his thought, so he let his words dissipate into the silence.

Jade nodded.

"I'm not sure what I think, either."

She gazed around the rest of the largely empty room. It wasn't until that very moment that Evans realized he'd already made plans for what to do with the rest of what he inwardly thought of as his office.

"Barnett offered to fly me back to Nigeria," she said.

"Are you going to take him up on it?"

"As much as I want to help the UN and the people of Africa, I don't know if I can just step back into that life, you know?"

"Yeah," Evans said. "It seems almost unreal now, doesn't it?"

She smiled wistfully and disappeared inside of herself for a moment. It was a rare unguarded moment for a woman who was the living embodiment of a fortification.

"So what comes next?" he asked.

"The remains of Hollis Richards are scheduled for autopsy tonight. I've already gotten authorization to participate."

"That's not what I meant."

Evans held her hand. It took her several moments to meet his stare.

"I thought you were leaving," she said.

"So did I."

"It's what Hollis said, isn't it? You believe him, don't you?"

"I don't know what I believe anymore."

She smirked.

"That makes two of us. If someone had told me a year ago that I'd be in a secret underground bunker waiting to do an alien autopsy, I'd have probably laughed myself to tears. And yet"—she gestured with open arms to the room around her—"here I am."

"Here you are," he said, and pulled her closer.

"Everything changes if we go down this road," she said.

"I'm counting on it."

Evans slid his fingers through her hair, cupped the base of her skull, and brought her lips to meet his. Her hand slid around his waist and drew his hips against hers. Her lips parted and—

"I can't leave you guys alone for two seconds, can I?"

Evans withdrew and leaned his forehead against Jade's. He didn't need to look back to know who it was.

"You really need to work on your timing, Anya," he said.

"And you need to find a better hiding place."

"We weren't hiding," Jade said.

"Oh, I could see exactly what you were doing."

"What can we do for you, Anya?" Evans asked.

"I thought you'd want to see this."

She strode into the room and held out a piece of paper. It was a computer printout of a photograph. Evans glanced at it and started to return it to her, but pulled it back when his brain caught up with his eyes.

"Where was this taken?"

"Mosul."

"Iraq?"

"Unless you know of a different one."

"I mean, you're certain it was taken in Iraq?"

"Director Barnett said the picture was taken by a Kurdish soldier fighting to liberate Mosul from the Islamic State."

Evans's heart rate accelerated as he studied the photograph.

"When do we leave?"

53

ROCHE

"You're telling me the drone used some sort of internal homing mechanism to follow the changes in the Earth's magnetic field," Barnett said.

"Is that somehow less plausible than following a star chart drawn on a cavern wall thousands of miles away?" Kelly asked. "Think about it. How else could it have navigated by that map if it spent the majority of its time hiding in the hold of a ship?"

They sat at one of the long tables in the conference room outside of Barnett's office. The walls were positively covered with photographs from both Teotihuacan and Atlantis. There were pages upon pages of eyewitness accounts, maps, drawings, and anything else that could possibly be of use.

"We don't know for certain that's how it traveled," Roche said.

"How else could the drone have gotten off Antarctica?" Barnett asked.

"Subject Zeta got a drone to release it from its cage."

"You think it walked a drone through the rental agreement for an airplane and taught it how to fly?"

"Maybe Richards—"

"The drone."

"Maybe *the drone* swam."

"That far? And in water that cold?"

"It survived outside of the base for several months," Kelly said. "We have proof of that. Maybe its skin provides a superior amount of insulation."

Barnett sighed and pushed back from the table. Roche understood his frustration. They'd been talking in circles for days now and had yet to get down to the real issue, which was why Subject Z had gone straight for the entombed remains upon its release, and why it had dispatched a drone to Mexico in an attempt to do the same.

"At this point," Barnett said, "I care less about how the drone got all the way to Teotihuacan than I do about figuring out where Subject Zeta is going. I'll be damned if I'm letting it get off the continent."

"We know for sure that the drone didn't just flag down a passing ship," Roche said. "There are only so many vessels willing to brave the sheet ice, even fewer shipping lanes through the Southern Ocean, and the nearest port is a thousand miles away from Atlantis."

"Unless it took a plane."

"That's a stretch."

"You're missing my point," Kelly said. "If it can sense gradations in the Earth's magnetic field, it could easily find its way to the South Pole and the research station—"

"Amundsen-Scott," Roche said.

"There are planes flying in and out of there all the time in the summer," Barnett said, "but they're few and far between in the winter."

"They still send trucks on the South Pole Traverse."

"The ice road from McMurdo? If Subject Zeta reached the station, it could very well get to anywhere in the world."

"Assuming that's its goal," Kelly said.

"And also assuming it survived the flooding," Roche said. "All of this speculation is predicated upon it making it to the surface before we undammed the lake. It would have basically had to head straight for either the elevator or the ventilation shafts the moment it secured the remains. It could very well have drowned down there and we'll never know."

A uniformed agent entered without knocking, walked directly to Barnett, and whispered into his ear.

Roche scrutinized the director's expression, then glanced at Kelly. She'd seen the same micromomentary flash of concern, too.

"Bring it up on the monitor," Barnett said.

The agent placed an iPad on the table in front of the director and stepped back.

When Barnett woke the screen, a video file was already primed and loaded.

"Who sent it?" he asked.

"The DoD via the NSA, who plucked the transmission from the NSF."

The mere mention of the National Science Foundation told Roche everything he needed to know. The NSF was in charge of the United States Antarctic Program, which operated McMurdo Station, the largest settlement on Antarctica and the hub through which all personnel and cargo either going to or coming from Amundsen-Scott South Pole Station had to pass.

Kelly was right.

Barnett pressed the "play" icon and the screen filled with an image of what looked like a warehouse. Crates were stacked against the far wall beside a rack of wooden pallets. A forklift sat unmanned in the foreground. The field of view panned to the right and revealed an open garage stall and the inside of the semi-trailer backed up to it. The audio quality was poor, but it sounded like the man holding the camera said something about a bear, although it was common knowledge that there wasn't a single species endemic to the continent. A second later, Roche understood what he meant. The bearded man sprawled at the foot of the mound of cargo looked like he'd been attacked by a wild animal. His face had been cut clear to the bone and his neck lacerated so deeply that Roche couldn't be sure if the man's head was still connected to his trunk.

"How long ago was this?" Barnett asked.

"Maybe eight hours," the agent said.

"That's a long time. How many ships have departed since then?"

"Just two."

"I want eyes on them right now."

"Way ahead of you. Morgan sent the pilots to the Arcade the moment we received the video."

Barnett leaped from his chair and hurried down the hallway. Roche and Kelly didn't wait around for an invitation. By the time they caught up with Barnett, he was already entering the room they called the Arcade, which, in a way, almost reminded Roche of a Dave & Buster's. The four consoles at the back of the room looked like video games with their pilot's chairs, joy-sticks, and multiple monitors. There was a refresh-ments table with a cappuccino maker, boxes of protein bars and hard candy, and a mini-fridge full of energy drinks. There was even a seating gallery for spectators.

Barnett walked straight up to the men manning the stations, while Roche and Kelly hung back in the gallery, where they had a clear view of all the video screens. The men worked in two-man teams, one con-trolling the movements of the drone, the other its re-mote sensing devices. A large central screen was positioned between the two units and alternated feeds from the smaller, dedicated monitors. Those in front of the pilots each showed a different ship. Both were shrouded in mist and sailing through black waters spotted with ice floes. The vessel on the left had the telltale red and white markings of a Coast Guard ice-breaker. The one on the right was heavily laden with multicolored shipping containers and the enormous cranes used to unload them. Roche could see no sign of panic on either ship.

"What am I looking at?" Barnett asked.

The agent manning the sensors to the left responded.

"USCG polar-class icebreaker *Northwind*. Departed McMurdo Sound six hours ago. Currently one hundred twelve miles north-northwest of Ross Island. We've been in contact with the CO, who's ordered an all-hands search of the vessel, but has yet to find anything. He insists they'd progress at a much faster rate if we told him what we were looking for."

"I'm sure he does," Barnett said. "What about the other one?"

"Behemoth," the other scanner said. "General cargo

vessel registered in the United States. Commercial and project fleet. The captain says they unloaded seventy-six shipping containers at McMurdo and still have nearly as many onboard."

"What's their destination?"

"South Georgia Island."

"I want every inch of that ship searched before it reaches port."

"The captain says it would take days to search all of the containers."

"Tell him we don't have days," Barnett said. "How far apart are the ships?"

The pilot on the left zoomed out, and the screen showed the cargo vessel trailing in the wake of the ice-breaker, maybe a quarter mile back.

"No one gets off either of those boats until—"

A drumroll of footsteps from the hallway. Morgan burst into the room.

"Switch to the closed-circuit channel," he said.

The central monitor abruptly cut away from the Southern Ocean and to what appeared to be a live news broadcast. The voiceover and the words scrolling past on the bottom of the screen were in Spanish. The images were obviously taken from a helicopter and showed a dense pine forest at the base of a bald, snow-covered mountain. Black smoke gushed from the trees, several of which were actively burning.

"Where is this?" Roche asked.

"East of Rio Grande, Argentina," Morgan said.

The helicopter banked around the churning smoke to get a better view of the orange and white airplane that had crashed into the forest, tearing up entire trees and leaving a deep furrow in the hard earth. The tail had broken off and only a single wing remained attached to the fuselage. The camera zoomed in on the wreckage. It was the same model of plane upon which Roche and the others had been initially flown to Richards's Antarctic research station, the same kind likely to ferry passengers to the mainland from McMurdo.

"No," Roche whispered.

Barnett glanced back at him as understanding dawned on his face.

The roiling smoke and the dense branches nearly obscured the ground, but Roche was certain he saw a silhouette with a spindly body and an elongated head moving quickly away from the wreckage through the pine trees.

54
JADE

"I can't tell you that what I'm asking of you won't be dangerous," Barnett said. "Nor will you receive the thanks of your grateful nation. No one will ever know what you do here. What I can say is that we are in desperate need of your skills and expertise, now more than ever before."

The director had gathered them in the conference room in the wake of the announcement that Subject Z had reached the mainland. Jade perched on top of the back table beside Evans, while Anya and Tess occupied the chairs beside their legs. Roche and Kelly sat at the table in front of them.

"I don't need to explain to you what we're up against," Barnett continued. "Between trying to track down both Subject Zeta and the adversary that we drew out in Mexico, we're stretched beyond thin and to the point of breaking. I'm asking for your help."

"You're asking for more than our help," Evans said. "You're asking for a commitment."

"There are things you will see in this facility and through the course of your work that must never leave this building, things you can't be allowed to see unless I can trust you explicitly."

"What if we say no?" Kelly asked.

"Then I will do everything in my power to convince you otherwise."

"And what if you can't?" Evans asked.

"I don't think any of you are prepared to walk away," Barnett said. "Tell me I'm wrong."

He looked at each of them in turn. None of them could hold his stare.

"I'm in," Jade said. The words were out of her mouth before she realized she'd reached a decision.

Barnett nodded and looked at Evans.

"There are obviously things you aren't telling us," Evans said.

"Obviously."

"If I sign on, I not only want to know everything you know, I want carte blanche to come and go as I please."

"I can offer a reasonable amount of autonomy, but make no mistake, Dr. Evans, this is my unit."

"What about our research?" Anya asked.

"I'm confident you'll be able to continue your research through the course of your work here. After all, that's what attracted us to you in the first place."

"It's not like we'd be able to publish any of our findings, though," Tess said.

"Are you searching for answers or acclaim, Dr. Clarke?" Barnett asked.

"If what Hollis said is true," Jade said, "then we have an obligation to try to do something about it."

"Do you believe him?" Kelly asked. "I mean, really? Do you believe strongly enough that you're willing to risk your life? Because that's precisely what he's asking us to do."

"I'll be the first to admit how crazy it all sounds, but considering everything we've seen, can any of you just return to your old lives, knowing what's out there?"

"What the hell," Evans said. "Count me in."

"Me, too," Anya said.

"I'm not wearing black fatigues," Kelly said. "And I'm not stripping the color from my hair, either."

"I want access to all of NASA's databases," Tess said. "And the Hubble Telescope. Oh, and the Allen Telescope Array."

"Does that mean you're all on board?" Barnett asked.

"What do you say, Martin?" Evans asked.

All eyes fell upon Roche, who deflected to Barnett.

"Mr. Roche has generously agreed to serve as team lead and liaison."

"Team?" Jade said.

"As one of his conditions, Mr. Roche has requested that you be granted a degree of separation from the larger unit, while retaining access to its considerable resources."

Roche shrugged.

"So are we doing this or what?" he asked.

There was a chorus of assent.

"Then allow me to formally welcome you all into the ranks of Unit 51," Barnett said. "Now get to work. We're wasting time we don't have."

EPILOGUE

*What now is proved was once only
imagined.*
—WILLIAM BLAKE

*Location: Unknown,
March 30*

The vaulted chamber was round and built from bricks quarried from the surrounding mountains. The only illumination came from the recessed windows, which admitted slanted columns of moonlight that struck the broad pit in the center of the room. It was ten feet in diameter and built from the same polished granite as the rest of the floor. In the middle was a blue marble inset of the black sun: a ring from which lightning bolts struck at the circle in the center.

A procession of six figures in black cloaks entered through the heavy oak door, their breath trailing them in clouds from their drawn cowls. They carried a coffin between them. It was made of solid gold and inlaid with esoteric symbols. They set it on the floor, opened the lid, and carefully removed the body from inside. It was absurdly tall and wrapped in layers of gauze through which they could see only the hint of its emaciated form. They stepped down into the ceremonial pit and placed the remains gently onto the marble design.

The figures took their seats on the raised sides of the circle and awaited the arrival of their final member, who entered wearing a white cloak and carrying a lantern inside of which burned a copper flame. The green glow flickered on the walls as their leader used it to light the circle of ancient bronze torches. The flames burned high and hot and issued twirls of black smoke toward the ceiling.

The white-cloaked figure descended into the pit and knelt over the head of the bundled corpse.

"Come," the figure said in an undeniably female voice.

There was an awful bleating sound from the outer corridor. All of the hoods turned toward the open door and the cloaked figure that carried the lamb into the chamber, its legs bound together at the hooves. The woman raised her arms and waited for the animal to be brought to her. She accepted the offering and cradled it to her breast.

The others converged upon the corpse, unwrapped the layers of gauze they'd used to swaddle it after meticulously cleansing its mummified flesh, and laid bare the remains. The woman leaned over the crocodilian face and removed a ceremonial dagger from beneath her robe. The hilt was a golden Irminsul, the blade forged of steel and sharpened to a deadly point.

The lamb struggled and bleated.

"Shhh," the woman whispered, and thrust the blade into the side of its neck.

Rich arterial blood pulsed from the wound, spattering the woman's white cloak and pouring onto the animalian mask. It ran in rivulets down the scaled snout and beaded on the aged feathers.

The bleating degenerated into gurgling, and finally to silence marred by the patter of the lamb's lifeblood dripping through the ragged holes where the reptile's eyes had once been and onto the concealed face of the deceased. It pooled in the sunken sockets, which slowly appeared to bulge—

The eyes snapped open and the dead man gasped.

"Soon . . ." the woman whispered.

PROLOGUE

Man is not what he thinks he is; he is what he hides.

—ANDRÉ MALRAUX

Queen Maud Land, Antarctica
December 30, 1946

Their compasses couldn't be trusted this close to the pole. All they had were aerial photographs taken six days ago, which were useless in this storm. The wind propelled the snow with such ferocity that they could only raise their eyes from the ground for seconds at a time. They couldn't see more than five feet in any direction and had tethered themselves to each other for fear of becoming separated. Their only hope was to maintain their course and pray they didn't overshoot their target, if it was even there at all.

Sergeant Jack Barnett clawed the ice from his eyelashes and nostrils. He'd survived Guadalcanal and Saipan, two of the bloodiest battles in the Pacific campaign, with no more than a few scars to show for it, but no amount of experience could have prepared him for what he'd found down here at the bottom of the world. When his commanding officer assigned him to an elite expeditionary squad, he'd assumed he was being sent back to the South Pacific with the rest of the 2nd Marines.

It wasn't until his briefing aboard the USS *Mount Olympus* that he learned he'd been drafted for Operation Highjump, whose stated mission was to establish a research base in Antarctica.

His mission, however, was something else entirely.

Jagged black peaks materialized from the storm. He'd studied the aerial reconnaissance and committed the configuration of the Drygalski Mountains to memory. They had to be nearly right on top of the anomaly they'd been dispatched to find.

The Nazis had made no secret of their interest in the South Pole, but it wasn't until eighteen months ago, when two German U-boats unexpectedly appeared off the shores of Mar del Plata and surrendered to Argentinian authorities that the intelligence community sat up and took notice. All charts, books, and identification papers aboard had been destroyed, and the captains had refused to divulge the nature of their mission to Antarctica, the whereabouts of a jettisoned dinghy, or the reason their passengers were covered with bandages.

The Counterintelligence Corps had been tracking various networks used to smuggle SS officers out of Europe and into South America, but none of those so-called ratlines passed through the Antarctic Circle. During their investigations, however, they'd encountered rumors of a mysterious Base 211 in Queen Maud Land, a veritable fortress commissioned by Hitler in the face of inevitable defeat. They couldn't dismiss the stories out of hand and potentially allow the Nazis to regroup and lick their wounds, so nearly 5,000 men had boarded a squadron of aircraft carriers, destroyers, and icebreakers under the auspices of scientific research and embarked upon a perilous four-month journey through a gauntlet of icebergs and sheet ice. Sorties were launched in every direction in an attempt to reconnoiter the entire continent, upon which, in addition to vast stretches of snow and ice, the cameramen aboard the planes photographed surprising amounts of dry land, open water, and what appeared to be a bunker of German design nestled in the valley ahead of them, which was why Barnett's squad had parachuted into this frozen wasteland.

The wind screamed and nearly drove Barnett to his knees. The rope connecting him to the others tightened and he caught a fleeting glimpse of several of his men, silhouetted against coal-black cliffs rimed with ice. Barnett shielded his field glasses from the blizzard and strained to follow the course of the ridgeline eastward toward a peak shaped like a shark's tooth. He followed the sheer escarpment down to where it vanished behind the drifted snow. The ruins of a rectangular radar tower protruded from the accumulation.

Barnett lowered his binoculars, unclipped his line, and unslung his M3 carbine. The semiautomatic assault rifle had been equipped with an infrared spotlight and a special scope that allowed him to see in complete darkness. The Nazis had called the soldiers who wielded them *Nachtjaegers*, or night-hunters, which struck him as the perfect name as he struck off across the windswept snow, which broke like Styrofoam underfoot.

The twin barrels of a FlaK anti-aircraft turret stood up from the drifted snow, beneath which a convex slab of concrete protruded. Icicles hung from the roof of the horizontal embrasure like fangs, between which Barnett could see only darkness.

He crouched in the lee of the bunker and waited for the others, who were nearly upon him before they separated from the storm. Their white arctic suits would have made it impossible to tell them apart were it not for their armaments. Corporal Buck Jefferson, who'd served with him since the Solomon Islands, wore the triple tanks of his customary M2 flamethrower on his back. They'd rehearsed this scenario so many times that he didn't need to be told what to do. He stepped out into the open and raised the nozzle.

"Fire in the hole."

Jefferson switched the igniter, pulled the trigger, and sprayed molten flames through the embrasure. The icicles vaporized and liquid fire spread across the inner concrete floor. Gouts of black smoke churned from the opening.

Barnett nodded to the automatic riflemen, who stood, sighted their M1918 Browning automatic rifles through the gap, and laid down suppressing fire. The moment their magazines were empty they hit the ground in anticipation of blind return fire.

The thunderous report rolled through the valley. Smoke dissipated into the storm. The rifleman cautiously raised their heads.

Barnett waited several seconds longer before sending in the infantrymen, who climbed through the embrasure and vanished into the smoke. He rose and approached the gun slit. The flames had already nearly burned out. The intonation of their footsteps hinted at a space much larger than the unimpressive façade suggested.

He crawled into the fortification, cranked his battery pack, and seated his rifle against his shoulder. The infrared spotlight created a cone of what could only loosely be considered light. Everything within its range and the limitations of the scope appeared in shades of gray, while the periphery remained cloaked in darkness, through which his men moved like specters.

The bunker itself was little more than a storage corridor. Winter gear and camouflage fatigues hung from hooks fashioned from exposed rebar. A rack of Sturmgewehr 44 assault rifles stood beside smoldering wooden crates filled with everything from rations to ammunition. Residual puddles of burning gasoline blinded his optics, forcing him to direct his sightline toward walls spattered with what looked like oil.

"Sergeant," one of his men called.

A haze of smoke collected near the ceiling amid ductwork and pipes that led him into a cavernous space that reflected both natural and manmade architecture. To his left, concrete gave way to bare stone adorned with Nazi flags, golden swastikas and eagles, and all kinds of ornate paraphernalia. Banks of radio equipment crowded the wall to his right. He recognized radar screens, oscilloscopes, and the wheel that controlled the antenna.

"It's a listening station," Jefferson said.

There was no power to any of the relay boards. Chairs lay toppled behind desks littered with Morse keys, handsets, and crumpled notes, both handwritten and typed.

"Give me some light," Barnett said.

He lowered his weapon and snatched the nearest man's flashlight from him. He didn't read much German, but he recognized the headings *Nur für den Dienstgebrauch* and *Befehl für das Instellunggehen*. These were top-secret documents, and they weren't even encrypted.

Barnett turned and shined the light deeper into the cavern. The rear wall was plastered with maps, the majority of which were detailed topographical representations of South America and Antarctica, all of them riddled with pins and notes. His beam cast the shadows of his men across bare rock etched with all sorts of bizarre and esoteric symbols before settling upon an orifice framed with wooden cribbing, like a mineshaft. Automatic shell casings sparkled from the ground, which was positively covered with what could only have been dried blood.

"Radioman," he said.

A baby-faced infantryman rushed to his side, the antenna from the SCR-300 transceiver on his back whipping over his shoulder.

"Open a direct line to Rear Admiral Warren. Ears-only."

A shout and the prattle of gunfire.

Discharge momentarily limned the bend in the tunnel.

Barnett killed his light and again looked through the scope. The others followed his lead and a silent darkness descended.

A scream reverberated from inside the mountain ahead of them.

Barnett advanced in a shooter's stance. The tunnel wound to his right before opening into another cavern, where his infrared light reflected in shimmering silver from standing fluid. Indistinct shapes stood from it like islands. He placed each footfall gently, silently, and quieted his breathing. He recognized the spotted fur of leopard seals, the distinctive patterns of king penguins, and the ruffled feathers of petrels. All of them gutted and scavenged. The stench struck him a heartbeat before buzzing flies erupted from the carcasses.

He turned away and saw a rifle just like his on the ground. One of his men was sprawled beside it, his boots pointing to the ceiling, his winter gear shredded and covered with blood. Several hunched silhouettes were crouched over his torso and head. They turned as one toward Barnett, who caught a flash of eyeshine and a blur of motion.

His screams echoed into the frozen earth.

1
RICHARDS

*Two possibilities exist: either we are
alone in the Universe or we are not.
Both are equally terrifying.*

—ARTHUR C. CLARKE

Queen Maud Land, Antarctica
Modern day: January 13—8 months ago

The wind howled and assaulted the command trailer with
snow that sounded more like sleet against the steel siding. What little Hollis Richards could see through the
frost fractals on the window roiled with flakes that
shifted direction with each violent gust. The Cessna ski
plane that brought him here from McMurdo Station
was somewhere out there beyond the veritable armada
of red Kress transport vehicles and Delta heavy haulers,
each of them the size of a Winnebago with wheels as
tall as a full-grown man. The single-prop plane had
barely reached the camp before being overtaken by the
storm, which the pilot had tried to use as an excuse not
to fly. At least until Richards made him an offer he
couldn't refuse. There was no way that he was going to
wait so much as a single minute longer.

It had taken four days, operating around the clock,
for the hot-water drill to bore through two miles of
solid ice to reach a lake roughly the size of the Puget

Sound, which had been sealed off from the outside world for an estimated quarter of a million years. They only had another twelve hours before the hole closed on them again, so they didn't have a second to waste. They needed to evaluate all of the water samples and sediment cores before they lost the ability to replenish them. It wasn't the cost that made the logistics of the operation so prohibitive. The problem was transporting tens of thousands of gallons of purified water across an entire continent during what passed for summer in Antarctica. They couldn't just fire antifreeze into the ice cap and risk contaminating the entire site, like the Russians did with Lake Vostok.

Richards pulled up a chair beside Dr. Max Friden, who worked his magic on the scanning electron microscope and made a blurry image appear on the monitor between them. The microbiologist tweaked the focus until the magnified sample of the sediment became clear. The contrast appeared in shades of gray and at first reminded Richards of the surface of the moon.

"Tell me you see something," Richards said. His voice positively trembled with excitement.

"If there's anything here, I'll find it."

The microscope crept slowly across the slide.

"Well, well, well. What do we have here?" Friden said.

Richards leaned closer to the monitor, but nothing jumped out at him.

"Right there." Friden tapped the screen with his index finger. "Give me a second. Let me see if I can . . . zoom . . . in . . ." The image momentarily blurred before resolving once more. "There."

Richards leaned onto his elbows and stared at what

looked like a gob of spit stuck to the bark of a birch
tree.

"Pretty freaking amazing, right?" Friden said.

"What is it?"

"That, my friend, is the execution of the bonus clause
in my contract." The microbiologist leaned back and
laced his fingers behind his head. "What you're looking
at is a bacterium. A living, breathing microscopic creature. Well, it really isn't, either. We killed it when we
prepared the slide and it's a single-celled organism, so
it can't really breathe, but you get the gist."

"What kind?"

"No one knows exactly how many species of bacteria there are, but our best estimate suggests a minimum
of 36,000 . . ."

Richards smiled patiently. He might have been the
spitting image of his father, from his piercing blue eyes
to his thick white hair and goatee, but fortunately that
was all he'd inherited from his old man. He could
thank his mother—God rest her soul—for his tempera-
ment.

Friden pushed his glasses higher on his slender
nose. The thick lenses magnified his brown eyes.

"I don't know," the microbiologist said. "I haven't
seen anything quite like it before."

Richards beamed and clapped him on the shoulder.

"That's exactly what I wanted to hear. Now find me
something I can work with."

Richards's handheld transceiver crackled. He snatched
it from the edge of the desk and already had one arm in
his jacket when he spoke into it.

"Talk to me."

"We have eyes," the man on the other end of the connection said.

Richards's heart leapt into his throat, rendering him momentarily speechless.

"Don't go any farther until I get there."

He popped the seal on the door and clattered down the steps into the accumulation. The raging wind battered him sideways. He pulled up his fur-fringed hood, lowered his head, and staggered blindly toward the adjacent big red trailer, which didn't appear from the blowing snow until it was within arm's reach. The door opened as he ascended the icy stairs.

"You've got to see this," Will Connor said, and practically dragged him into the cabin. The former Navy SEAL was more than his personal assistant. He was his right-hand man, his bodyguard, and, most important, the only person in the world he trusted implicitly. The truth was he was also the closest thing Richards had to a friend.

The entire trailer was filled with monitors and electronic components fed by an external gas generator, which made the floor vibrate and provided a constant background thrum. The interior smelled of stale coffee, body odor, and an earthy dampness that brought to mind memories of the root cellar at his childhood home in Kansas, even the most fleeting memories of which required swift and forceful repression.

Connor pulled back a chair at the console for Richards, who sat beside a man he'd met only briefly two years ago, when his team of geologists first identified the topographical features suggesting the presence of a large body of water beneath the polar ice cap and he'd only just opened negotiations with the government of Norway for the land lease. Ron Dreger was the lead driller for the team from Advanced Mining Solutions, the company responsible for the feats of engineering that had brought Richards to the bottom of the Earth and the brink of realizing his lifelong dream.

The monitor above him featured a circular image of a white tube that darkened to blue at the very end.

"What you're looking at is the view from the fiber-optic camera two miles beneath our feet," Dreger said. He toggled some keys on his laptop, using only three fingers as he was missing the tips of his ring and pinkie fingers, and the camera advanced toward the bottom. The shaft was already considerably narrower than when the hot-water drill broke through, accelerated by a surprise flume of water that fired upward as a result of the sudden change in pressure, which had inhaled fluid from the surrounding network of subsurface rivers and lakes they were only now discovering.

The lead driller turned to face Richards with an enormous grin on his heavily bearded face, like a Viking preparing to pillage.

"Are you ready?"

Richards stared at the monitor and released a long, slow exhalation.

"I've been waiting for this my whole life."

The camera passed through the orifice and into a vast cavernous space, the ring of lights around the lens creating little more than a halo of illumination. The water had receded, leaving behind icicles hanging like stalactites from the vaulted ice dome. There was no way of estimating size or depth. There was only up, down, and the unfathomable darkness in between.

"Should I keep going?" Dreger asked.

Richards nodded, and the camera slowly approached the surface of the lake, which remained in a liquid state due to a combination of geothermal heat rising from beneath the mantle, insulation from the polar extremes by two vertical miles of ice, and the pressure formed by the marriage of the two. The image became fluid. When the aperture rectified, it revealed cloudy brownish water through which whitish blebs and air bubbles shivered toward the surface. A greenish shape took form from the depths, gaining focus as the camera neared. The rocky bed was covered with a layer of slimy sediment, from which tendrils of sludge wavered. It looked like the surface of some distant planet, which was exactly what Richards hoped it was.

There were countless theories regarding the origin of life on earth, but the one that truly resonated with him was called *lithopanspermia* and involved the seeding of the planet by microbes hitchhiking through space on comets and asteroids, whether having survived on debris ejected from a collapsing planet or by the deliberate usage of a meteorite to plant life on a suitable world by some higher intelligence. Fossilized bacteria of extraterrestrial origin were found on a meteorite recovered from this very continent less than twenty years ago, but it wasn't until living samples were collected from Lake Vostok that Richards realized what he needed to do.

Ever since that fateful night sixty years ago, when he'd run into the wheat fields to escape the sound of his father raining blows upon his sobbing mother, he'd known mankind wasn't alone in the universe. He remembered every detail with complete clarity, for it was that single moment in time that altered the course of his life. He recalled staring up into the sky and begging for God to answer his prayers, to take his mother and him from that horrible place. Only rather than a vision of the Almighty, he saw a triangle formed by three pinpricks of light hovering overhead. He'd initially thought they were part of a constellation he hadn't seen before until they sped off without a sound and vanished against the distant horizon.

He'd been looking for them ever since.

"What's that over there?" Connor asked.

"Where?" Dreger said.

Connor leaned over Richards's shoulder and tapped the left side of the screen. The driller typed commands into his laptop, and the camera turned in that direction.

"A little higher."

The change in angle was disorienting at first, at least until Richards saw what had caught Connor's eye.

"What in the name of God is that?"